I WORKED MY WAY TO THE TOP OF THE SLOPE AND LOOKED DOWN AT THE MEN BELOW.

"Is Zachary Frost in these wagons?" Kingston was demanding in his bull voice.

"Ain't nobody named Frost with us," came the answer. "Now you and your men git."

I knew some good people were going to get hurt, and did the only thing I could do. I stood up in full view and emptied my Dragoon in the general direction of Kingston and his men.

It was though my shots set off a chainfire. The air around me was suddenly alive with whining lead. Something stung my leg and I found myself face down in the grass. Running hooves drummed hard ground and became a roar. I raised my head. Horsemen were coming toward me at a gallop and Frank Kingston was in the lead.

"Its Frost!" he roared waving his gun. "I want him! *Get him!*"

WESTERN STORYTELLER
ROBERT KAMMEN
ALWAYS DEALS ACES WITH HIS TALES
OF AMERICA'S ROUGH-AND-READY FRONTIER!

DEATH RIDES THE ROCKIES   (2509, $2.95)

DEVIL'S FORD   (3163, $2.95)

GUNSMOKE AT HANGING
WOMAN CREEK   (2658, $2.95)

LONG HENRY   (2155, $2.50)

MONTANA SHOWDOWN   (2333, $2.95)

WIND RIVER KILL   (3164, $2.95)

WINTER OF THE BLUE SNOW   (2432, $3.50)

WYOMING GUNSMOKE   (2284, $2.50)

*Available wherever paperbacks are sold, or order direct from the
Publisher. Send cover price plus 50¢ per copy for mailing and handling to
Zebra Books, Dept. 2559, 475 Park Avenue South, New York, N.Y. 10016.
Residents of New York, New Jersey and Pennsylvania must include sales
tax. DO NOT SEND CASH.*

DAN PARKINSON

THE
WESTERING

ZEBRA BOOKS
KENSINGTON PUBLISHING CORP.

ZEBRA BOOKS

are published by

Kensington Publishing Corp.
475 Park Avenue South
New York, NY 10016

Second printing: April, 1990

Printed in the United States of America

PART ONE

BLOOD BOUNTY

I

I knew he was close when I neared the ridgecap. He hadn't been more than a mile behind when I left the pilot trace, back yonder where it topped out of the valley, and the way I'd come he had plenty of time to catch up.

I didn't know his name. I didn't know anything about him at all, except that he carried a gun and before this day was over one of us could be dead. He wasn't the first to come looking for me, nor the first to find my trail. The bounty Frank Kingston had put on me had been a petty thing at first—an act of spite, a final insult to send me on my way. But there had been those who tried to collect, and things had gotten out of hand.

The first ones had been careless. I guess they knew I was unarmed and alone, and saw easy pickings. I was unarmed because I didn't own a gun then. I didn't own much of anything except the clothes on my back, the tools in my satchel and Frank Kingston's horse. I wouldn't even have known there was a bounty on me, except that Uncle Earl got a message to Hobbstown and it was waiting for me there.

A man who knows he's hunted has that to arm him.

So I watched for them, and after the first one came I wasn't unarmed any more. What I had was just an old

7

short-barrel musket and a little powder and ball, but it was enough. The second one to find me had a good Colt revolver and a pouch full of loads. I set aside enough to carry and practiced with the rest.

I don't know whether Frank Kingston had ever figured that anybody might try to collect a paltry bounty like he put on me. It wasn't even for my life, not at first. It was for my ears. Ten dollars for Zack Frost's ears, was what those first ones came after, and it cost one man a busted nose and an old musket, and the next one a broken arm and a revolving handgun. The third one came gunning and it cost him his life.

And I guess by then the word had gone back to Frank Kingston that his joke had gone sour. Maybe the first bounty had been bluster—just words to impress his cronies, to make him a big man again after I'd made him crawl. But the bounty now was real, and the men who would collect it were hard men who knew their business.

I knew from my first glimpse of the one following me from the pilot trace that the ante had been raised. The rider back there was tough and canny, and it wasn't my ears he was after.

Climbing toward the ridgecap, I held to the thickets as much as I could, stopping often to listen, not knowing where he was but certain that he was close by. Riding in cover I kept low in the saddle and watched the roan's ears. The horse could hear sounds that I might not, and his sensitive ears would twitch and turn when he did.

Even so, I was as taut as a fiddle string, expecting ambush at every bend and feeling gunsights on my back at every clearing.

I wondered whether Frank Kingston knew what he had started. Pushing folks around is one thing—bulling around,

8

showing off, threatening and blustering and in general having to have your own way. But when you put a bounty on a man it changes things. Other folks get involved then, and about the only thing that's certain is that somebody is going to get killed.

I guessed he'd just never thought it through. I'm not saying that Frank Kingston was ever dumb. He could be smart as a barn rat when he needed to. But generally a man who throws his weight around is a man who doesn't cotton to careful thinking.

Maybe I could have avoided it, too. Maybe I could have just turned the other way and forgot about Lady Blue, and then stayed out of his way after that. But I wasn't raised that way. When the Lord had it put in the Good Book that a man should turn the other cheek, I guess He didn't know about the folks that would settle the Knob Hills. A man who turns the other cheek in that country gets his head realigned.

On the other hand, I might have put a stop to it before it got out of hand. When I got Uncle Earl's message at Hobbstown, I could have turned right around and headed back to New Albany and done a mite of hill gospel on Frank Kingston's skull. But I didn't. It just didn't seem worth the trouble at the time.

So things plain got out of hand.

When I saw the rider behind me on the pilot road there wasn't much doubt what he was about. I had angled off the track a mile back to look at a black gum stand, thinking that if I passed this way again some time I could cut some hubs to cure. Then I went on, and when I looked back from a rise there he was, where I had been, leaning to look at my sign. I watched him for a time, trying to make him out. It was too far to see features, but he rode a good horse well equipped, and he rode like a tracer. This wasn't some hooraw out for sport. This was a bounty man. They came up through the hills sometimes, up to the river, tracking runaways from the south. They'd come as far as Louisville or Hardinsburg openly, and sometimes they'd cross the river if they were on a hot lead, though over on the Indiana side they couldn't do much about runaways unless they could fetch up to them alone with no witnesses.

But a bountyman will take bounty on anybody, and if it's a white man he's after then both sides of the river are the same.

I could have enjoyed skinning Frank Kingston then. But at the moment, all I had to worry about was staying alive. That was why I had taken to the ridge. A man doesn't just ride away from a good tracer. You might outrun him for a bit, but he keeps coming. And there's no use arguing with a bountyman. He only has one thing on his mind. I was hoping, though, that this was one of those that make their livings running down poor darkies that have got loose and making for the north. Seemed to me, a man like that might have got used to easy prey.

And though I was a long way from my usual trails, maybe this was still more my ground than his. I'd cut my teeth on country like this. Maybe he hadn't.

Had these been the hills I grew up in—around Hardinsburg and those parts—or even those higher hills above New Albany where I had roamed the old Shawnee trails during the time I worked for Carl Froehner, learning the wheelwright's trade, I would have known every nook and cranny, every game trail and hidey-hole. A man that feels toward the land as I do, and as my pa did before me, he just naturally learns it as he passes through. It talks to him and whispers secrets and sometimes it even sings.

10

But this was new country to me, and all I could hope was that it was even newer to the man back there who would kill me if he could.

Where there is law, killing a man for a bounty is murder. But it is done anyway. Who, after all, is going to bear witness? Not the one who does the killing, and not the one who pays for it. Generally the only other participant is dead. Such commerce has never been uncommon.

The roan racer under me now was a fine horse. He took the rises with easy power and was sure-footed and quick on the precarious slopes. I could understand how Frank Kingston was upset about losing him. My old mare, Lady Blue, alive, wouldn't have swapped out for the shoes on this roan. But when old Frank decided to have himself some sport there on the street in New Albany, we traded horse for horse.

I guess he just wanted to see if he could spook the poor old thing. But the shot he fired went wild and took her in the neck. She was dead when she hit the ground. And Frank Kingston had just bought himself a dead horse.

I set the price. His horse for mine. And even though there were a plenty of witnesses to attest to the fairness of that, I still had to collect the hard way. Frank wasn't in very good shape when he signed that bill of sale.

That's the kind of thing that will fester in a man like Frank Kingston. Maybe it was the losing of a fine horse, and maybe it was the beating he took there in front of all those people. I don't know how it went after that. I had been fixing to leave New Albany. I had my river passage and I had my tools packed. Mr. Froehner was two weeks dead and there was nothing to keep me there, so I was headed yonder. The only thing that had kept me was to find a pasture for Lady Blue, where she'd be cared for when I was gone.

So I cashed my river passage, loaded my gear on my new roan horse and set out.

I had thought Uncle Earl might go along. There was nothing there to keep him that I could see. But just about that time he had got busy on some new thing he was into. He didn't say what it was and there was no use asking, the way Uncle Earl is. But whatever it was he seemed downright excited about it.

So I just shook his hand and said I was headed yonder.

He tipped back his hat, looked up at me in that slantwise way of his and said, "Mind your manners out there, Zack. Wouldn't surprise me if we saw each other again soon enough."

He thought I ought to take my passage money and buy me a revolving pistol like the one he carried, but I needed a new pair of boots so I bought them instead.

Riding out of New Albany that last time I looked back once, and Uncle Earl was standing there in the street watching me go. He didn't have any more notion where I was going than I did, except that it would be west. Ever since we were a pair of shirt-tail tads, Uncle Earl and me, I'd had an itch to see what was out there, and he knew it.

His message about the bounty had been waiting for me at Hobbstown. He would have figured I'd stop there. There was a smith in Hobbstown who could sweat an iron tire onto the felloes of a wagon wheel so snug that it would roll a thousand miles and never shiver. Uncle Earl would have figured that I'd like to see how that man did that.

I was a day out of Hobbstown when that first one came at me, and I'd been busy since then. Among other things, I had killed a man. I'd never done that before, and it didn't set well at all. But now, there were two of us on this ridge

12

and it looked like one of us was sure enough going to die.

The ridge was one of those that angle out toward the river valley in the country below Marston's meadows on the Kentucky side. Wild lands, not much settled yet because of old title disputes and better land to be had in other places. Plum thickets and gullies, a dozen kinds of hardwood trees and up above a ridgecap that would have sheers on its west face . . . I hoped. I'd run ridges like this when I was a tad, me and Uncle Earl, and that's why I'd headed up this one.

I was near the crest, just easing around a thicket, when the foliage to my left chattered and a ball whuffed past my face to gouge bark on a tree trunk just beyond. The rifle's crack echoed up the slope and the roan sidestepped and danced. I dug in heels and jumped him out of that cover and into a clearing above a draw, leaning low and letting him bolt, praying that the fellow yonder had a God-fearing long rifle and not one of those swivel breech contraptions that can shoot six or eight times hand running. He fired again as I broke clear, but this time it was the thump of a pistol and I don't know where his shot went.

But it settled one thing. I'd had a sort of notion that I might haul left and go charging down on him before he could reload. His pistol changed that idea. If it was a revolver, he'd pick me off. Even with some practice, I wasn't a very good shot. So I went back to idea number one. I hauled right and that roan surged up that crest with the power of a hunting horse and I held my breath. If there was a sheer over that cap, we had both better sprout wings.

And sure enough, there was one — a break-off drop of fifteen or twenty feet with overgrown rubble below it. But we came up right at the edge of it and the roan did a switchback that would have made a weasel proud. It danced along the lip of that sheer and I clung for dear life and we thunked into a berry thicket just alongside it. Where Frank Kingston had got himself such a horse I never knew, but I never was so proud of a horse in my life.

The tight cover of the thicket calmed him, though he was still tossing his head and rolling his eyes when I got down. I patted his neck and said some things to him that a man wouldn't want anybody to hear him saying to a horse. Then I looped his reins and scrabbled my way out of that thicket.

The sharp edge of the sheer bit into the crest of the ridgecap to within about ten feet of its top, and I ran along the edge, bent low, listening. He had seen me heading for the top. He would be coming fast, to give me no time to lay an ambush.

Shoe-iron scrapes showed where the roan and I had crested.

I topped out and ran, the way he had come. Just below the ridgecap we had broken through a screen of scrub cedar. The limbs were disturbed, all laced upward, the way we had come. I put my head down and bulled through the other way, forcing them back. Below the cedars I paused. I couldn't see him yet, but now I could hear him coming. He was in the thicket, maybe fifty yards away. I went to the right, easing along, until I found a deadfall break that was fairly clear. Just as I stepped out, he came into sight below me, looking upward, and as I saw him he saw me. His revolver came up and he reined toward me, firing. The bullet cut cedar above my head as I went back through the screen, and he was right behind it.

I broke through at the crest, caught my balance at the edge of the sheer and veered hard right. I was just diving into cover as he broke through, going full tilt.

His horse screamed and set its hooves, trying to stop. It skidded, switching ends, scrambling madly, and its rider pitched out of his saddle, back over the mount's rump. Head over heels he disappeared over the edge of the sheer. The horse's rear legs went over and it clung with its front hooves, wild-eyed and snorting.

Then it lost its grip on the rock and disappeared.

I eased up to the break and looked over. The horse was just getting to its feet, slipping and sliding in the slope of rockfall. The man law sprawled to one side, flat on his back.

As I started down, the spooked horse panicked and went down the talus slope, skidding and bawling. When it found solid footing below it took off into the trees. It was unhurt and it was scared. It would cover some ground before it slowed down.

I slid down to the talus, then stepped carefully to where the bounty man lay. He was bleeding from several scrapes, writhing and moaning. I found his weapons, tossed the rifle away and stuck the revolver in my belt. It was a little like the one I had, a modified Paterson with a loading lever alongside its barrel. But I was used to the Dragoon.

The man was coming around. I squatted alongside him, just out of reach, and watched his eyes refocus. When he saw me he tried to scrabble away and slid a few feet further down the slope.

I pointed my gun at him and he froze, staring into its muzzle.

"How much am I worth to you?"

He just stared at me like he hadn't heard.

"The bounty you're after," I clarified. "How much is it?"

He found his voice then. "I don't know what you're talking about, mister."

"You aren't after Kingston's bounty?" I steadied the gun and drew the hammer back. "I guess you just enjoy tracking people and shooting at them, then?"

He stared at me. I shifted my point and shot the heel off his boot. Probably surprised me as much as it surprised him . . . I hadn't practiced all that much. "I do wish you'd talk to me," I told him.

He had a good sweat going. "It's five hundred dollars," he muttered. "That's what he's offering."

Now it was my turn to stare. "Five hundred . . . for me?"

"He don't like you," he explained. "Says you stole from him."

No wonder the tracers were out.

I thought about it, then got to my feet, standing careful on the shifting talus. "You got any broken bones?"

He studied on it, shifting this way and that. "I don't think so." He looked around. "Where's my horse?"

"Off yonder. It'll stop eventually."

"Are you going to shoot me?"

"I don't know. You got any bounty on you?"

"Not that I know of."

"This is a nice pistol," I said, drawing his modified Paterson. "You don't need it any more, do you?"

"Not if you shoot me," he blustered. Then he shrugged. "I guess I don't need it either way."

"Mighty generous of you." I put it back under my belt. "You know, it'd be a shame for you to go to all this trouble and not collect that bounty from Frank Kingston. What kind of evidence does he want?"

He shook his head. "Nothing specific. I guess just something of yours. Something you wouldn't give up easy."

"What's to keep him from welshing on you?"

He scowled at that, an ugly expression. "You got lucky, Frost. Generally I get what I go after. And I always collect."

"Yeah, I bet you do. Well, it would save me a lot of

trouble if you'd collect that bounty, mister. Why don't we just say I'm dead, and you go ahead and collect your money. I don't aim to go back that way again, anyhow. And I can surely stay out of sight long enough for you to get paid and get gone."

He was suspicious. "Why would you do that?"

"Why? Because I don't cotton to folks like you doggin' my backtrail, is why. Besides, I sort of enjoy the idea. If old Frank goes to setting bounties on folks, he sure ought to have the opportunity to pay off."

"What's your cut?"

"This fine pistol here. This is my cut. In advance. Take it or leave it, bounty man. It's better than a hole in the head."

He took a deep breath and nodded, skidding a little further down the slope when he did.

"When you get to the bottom of that slope, you go find your horse. When you find him you come back here. You'll find your rifle around here someplace, and I'll leave you some evidence up on the ridgecap that you can show to Frank Kingston."

That bounty man had a hard time getting down that slope, but he made it. When he was gone I climbed back up to the cap and retrieved the roan. I opened my pack and looked through my tools, hating to part with any of them but knowing that Frank Kingston would know that I'd hate to. Finally I picked out a good spokeshave that old Mr. Froehner gave me when I built my first wagonwheel. It was a sort of commemoration. It was the day I went from being an apprentice to being a journeyman wheelwright. Carl Froehner had carved my initials on its grip with his own hands, and had put on the date. I hated to lose it.

I left it there on the ridgecap. I wondered if Frank Kingston would ever appreciate what a fine thing he had bought

17

with his five hundred dollars.

Be a shame if he didn't, because I'd have to let him know sooner or later that that was all he bought.

It seemed to me that there were lines in the Good Book someplace, how a righteous man should take pity on fools and show them the error of their ways. Maybe that's in the Good Book. If it isn't, it ought to be.

II

Maybe there's merit to the notion that some folks just plain strike sparks, like whopping flint with steel. I admit I had no use for Frank Kingston, right from the first time I laid eyes on him. And outside of his cronies along the waterfront and that gaggle of paid toughs that old Bailey Kingston kept on to look after him, there weren't many folks around New Albany who cared for Frank.

He was a brawler and a troublemaker, and he took pleasure in hurting folks most any way he could think of. The story around New Albany was that Frank was old Bailey's way of getting even with everybody in general for the leg he lost all those years before when one of the Knob Hills farmers got fed up and shot him with a musket.

There were those who said, too, that keeping Frank around New Albany was the old man's insurance that Frank wouldn't be off hatching plots against the old man. Bailey Kingston didn't any more trust Frank than he did anybody else.

At any rate, Bailey Kingston raised his boy mean and idle and when he grew up he sent him off to a fine school for a time, then brought him back and set him up in New Albany—to keep an eye on him, or to devil everybody else, or both.

Those I heard talk about it at all allowed that Frank Kingston probably had done more that was hurtful in the years since than old Bailey had done in his whole life. Still, there never was much that could be proved in a court of law, and Frank had his backers too, so things just sort of went along like that.

New Albany was hitting its stride about then as the boomingest town on the river. There was plenty of commerce, and new lands opening up out west . . . people passing through and others settling in to supply them, and factories going up as fast as the materials could be docked and sorted. There were two shipyards on the river, laying up hulls and mounting steam engines. There were foundries and stamping mills, and a brand new glass factory. There was a carriage shop that had grown into a full-scale factory building wheeled vehicles, and across the alley from it was Carl Froehner's factory. Only one product came from Froehner's little place. Big overland wagons, modified to Carl Froehner's design, rolled out of the assembly shed at the rate of one per week.

Which is why I had come to New Albany. When it came time for me to choose a craft, I chose to be a wheelwright. There was a fair wheelwright at Hardinsburg, who had started as a ship's carpenter and taught himself the skills, and I signed on with him winters to help keep his shop and learn his practices. After three seasons I was doing as much repair as he was, and had outfitted a pair of surreys with trim wheels that brought a good price.

Still, there was more to learn. So when Uncle Earl's letter came from New Albany, about Carl Froehner looking for craftsmen, I was ready to go.

We gathered around the table in the evening, Pa and Ma and me and my four brothers and two sisters, and I told them it was what I wanted to do. Pa chewed on the matter for a few minutes, then shrugged. "It's man's work, Zack," he said. "A fine wheelwright can name his wages, but there are no second chances for those who lack the skill."

"I wouldn't go as a journeyman," I said. "But I would go to learn. Uncle Earl says this man is doing something new . . . a rig like the Conestogas, but fitted for the emigrant trade. I've never worked on anything so big."

My little brother Burl whistled. "Conestogas! There isn't any wagon anyplace as big as those!"

"Froehner's might be lighter," Pa allowed. "It seems to me that if a wagon is to go to the far country, too much weight would be a hindrance."

"The wheels would have to be stronger," I said. "Where there are no roads, they'll take rough treatment. And even with some timber weight shaved down, a wagon that size might still weigh a ton and a half empty. Then load all of a family's goods aboard . . . why, those wheels will have to test out to a ton apiece smooth rolling and twice that on the prairies."

"Can you make such a wheel, Zack?"

"I haven't done it. But I can learn."

"I saw the wheels you made for Judge Adcock's surrey," Burl beamed. "A man can do that, he can make any wheel there is."

Pa ruffled his hair. "Hush, boy. Zack knows better than that."

I did, for a fact. Setting wheels to a surrey frame is a neat trick, and I was proud of that. But surrey wheels are to overlander wheels as a pipestem is to a roof beam. A man might build a handsome shed who lacks the skills to build a cathedral.

"I've said I'd be a wheelwright," I told them. "I want to see the wagons Froehner will build. If they are as Uncle Earl says, then I'll be a wheelwright when I can make running gear that will serve one of them well."

"If *everything* were as your Uncle Earl says," Pa muttered,

21

"then this would be a most wondrous world."

Ma gave him a withering glance, "Earl Donovan has his own ways of thinking, Jedediah. You know that."

"It's a Lord's wonder any of us survived the raising of your baby brother," Pa stated. "It's because I know him so well that I have concern about this wonderful opportunity he has found for Zack."

"Earl wouldn't harm a hair on Zack's head," Ma said. "He has always taken care of him."

"Aye," Pa nodded, grinning. "And every scrape Zack ever got into—that I knew about—had the fine hand of Earl Donovan elbow-deep in the makings of it."

It was the sort of thing Pa liked to say about Uncle Earl. Partly, I think, Pa just enjoyed seeing the flash of Ma's eyes when he spoke plain about her baby brother. Pa had married late in life, and the years after that had never dimmed the wonder he felt every time he set eyes on his precious Mary . . . nor stilled for a moment the fun it gave him to taunt her now and then just to see her sparkle. And partly, he said such things because they were true. Though the peculiarities of my Uncle Earl had never interfered with Pa raising him and doing the best job of it he knew how.

They hadn't been married more than a few months, my folks, when my grandmother Donovan died in childbirth and left an orphan infant boy to be looked after. Pa never even waited to be asked. He got the news and he packed up Ma and they went and got him.

So, though I was their firstborn, I wasn't their first baby. Uncle Earl was. By the time I came along, he was already toddling around looking for new ways to put the world together to make it work his way.

And I knew as well as Pa did that, as the years went by, Uncle Earl caught on that having a baby nephew around—especially one who kept outgrowing his britches and tended toward the size and temperament of the men in Pa's family—could be a right handy asset now and again.

I had my share of thrashings from bigger boys when we were growing up, and I did my share of thrashing as I got the hang of it, and as often as not I had the feeling that the real beneficiary of the rough-and-tumble times was Uncle Earl.

One time when I was about twelve or thirteen, and just starting to get some size on me, Uncle Earl and I were on our way down to the creek to catch some fish and I was wondering how come Uncle Earl had toted along Pa's big old double-barrel fowler, but he didn't say. Alongside the creek four of the Stuckey boys were waiting for us, and they had their pa's best mule with them.

When we stepped down out of the brush, Buster Stuckey came forward and poked me with his finger, right in the wishbone. "Lay down them poles, Zack," he said. "I got to give you a lickin'."

Now, Buster Stuckey never was long on brains. That's why he and I were in the same grade in school, even though he was four years older than me and full man sized. And I had figured out before that when Buster Stuckey got a notion in his head it just stuck there and nothing short of thunder could shake it loose. So I handed the cane poles and the stringer to Uncle Earl and said, "I'm awful sorry you got to do that, Buster," and he hauled off and swung a fist that would have poleaxed me if I had been where it was.

It turned him about half-way around. I dodged aside and jumped him, landing on his back so hard that he ran a dozen steps to keep from falling. And I hung on. I got one arm around his neck and both legs around his middle. I squeezed and knotted and used my free hand to hit him as hard as I could, as fast as I could, anyplace I could reach.

He bellered like a bull and went to bucking and spinning, trying to throw me off, and his hands grabbing this way and that for some part of me he could grab onto.

23

Buster was strong. I'd seen him break a hickory bat just with his two hands. So I did my best to stay away from those hands. One of them came at me over his shoulder, going for my neck, and I bit him on the thumb. Even so, he like to have dislocated my jaw before I twisted away from his fingers.

Then he went to work on my feet, and had the left one twisted about half way around when I decided that was as much of that as I could tolerate. I leaned back, dragging knuckles across his adam's apple as I went, and swung the points of my knuckles into his armpit, then threw myself back as hard as I could. It threw him off balance and my shoulders hit the ground with him still pinned in my legs. I felt like all my ribs were grinding together, but I kept the motion going and he sailed over me, upside down, and landed on his head.

When I got my legs untangled from him and got up, he was just lying there, all crumpled up, and his brothers were glaring at me like hounds at a bayed hog. But Uncle Earl was between me and them, and he had Pa's scattergun pointed at them. He looked around at Buster, with that expression of his that's like a person might look if somebody told him England was on the moon.

"He isn't dead, is he, Zack?" he asked.

I surely hoped not. I didn't have anything against Buster. But when I leaned down to see if he was breathing, he snored. "I guess not," I said.

"That was a dirty trick, Zack," Omer Stuckey said. "You got him from behind."

Uncle Earl just shook his head. "Fair is as fair does," he said, and twitched the shotgun. "Back off and leave the mule."

When they were all out of jumping range, Uncle Earl handed me the shotgun. "Better grab up the poles and stringer, Zack," he said. "I don't believe the fish are biting today." Then he swung up on that mule and rode off, straight and sober as a deacon.

I checked out Buster again. He was sound asleep, and he seemed to be all in one piece.

"I'd help you get him home," I told his brothers, "except I can't walk very well. He like to twisted my leg off."

That wasn't the only place I hurt, either. My ribs felt near staved, my jaw ached and my head was throbbing. I could barely walk when I set out after Uncle Earl.

He was waiting up the path, still on the mule, walking it around in circles and leaning to look into its ears.

"How do you like my new mule?" he asked. "May not be the best mule around, but it's a good one."

"That isn't your mule," I pointed out to him. "It's Mr. Stuckey's mule."

He looked at me like I'd gone daft. "Well, not anymore it isn't. I won it fair and square. I bet Omer Stuckey that shotgun there against this mule that you could whip Buster."

Anyhow, that's how Uncle Earl always was. And as many times as Pa took him out behind the shed and laid the strap on him, it never made any difference.

One time when he was so sore he couldn't sit down, I asked him why he acted like he did, seeing as how it always got him punished.

He just shrugged and sort of grinned. "I guess life's like that, Zack. A fellow that wants to get ahead gets it behind."

"Pa's just trying to make you decent, Uncle Earl," I told him.

His grin went soft with understanding and good will, though he could hardly stand to touch his backside. "I know that, Zack. Your pa is doing a fine job of raising me up, and I'm beholden to him . . . though sometimes I wish he'd educate me a little easier."

There were times a'plenty as we got older, when I could happily have strangled my Uncle Earl—for a minute or

25

two. But he was family, and he did have a way about him. I could never stay mad at him for very long.

Well, I knew when Uncle Earl wrote from New Albany about Carl Froehner's wagon factory that there likely was more to it than met the eye. But, at the same time, I knew that Uncle Earl wouldn't outright lie to any of us. If he said there was a big wagon operation at New Albany and that there was a place in it for me, then at least we knew there was *something* there which might vaguely resemble the situation as he described it.

"You can take Lady Blue," Pa decided. "She's about too old to ride, but she can carry your gear."

Ma mended my coat and made me two extra shirts. Burl went and got his favorite pack and cleaned all the frogs and marbles and things out of it and brought it to me. He wanted me to take it, so I did. And little Lucy, the baby of the family, baked me a loaf of bread that would have foundered a herd of goats.

On a bright morning I set off for New Albany and whatever destiny had to show me there.

I didn't know anything about Frank Kingston then. Uncle Earl hadn't mentioned him. I had never thought much, either, about whether some folks just naturally strike sparks. Maybe if I had, though, it might have come to me that flint and steel don't strike sparks until somebody brings them together.

Somebody like Uncle Earl.

III

After I left the bounty man up on the ridge, I angled back down to the pilot road and let the roan stretch his legs for a few miles. That horse did love to run. There were some barges on the river—a string of three and a pair of separates. One of those was an old-style keeler, bound for Cairo or beyond, and after I had passed it and exchanged waves and hollers with the boatmen I went on another mile then hauled up and left the road, angling down toward the river.

I needed to disappear for a while, on the chance that the bounty hunter would do what I told him and go on back to New Albany to collect the bounty from Frank Kingston. He might do that, I knew. And I'd given him my word that I wouldn't be in his way if he did.

On the other side of it, there was the possibility that he might decide to come after me again. If he did, he'd be a lot more careful the next time. I never was raised in a velvet box. Growing up in the Knob country, there had been a plenty of rough and tumble, and I could usually take care of myself all right. But I wasn't brought up stupid, either, and I knew that playing games with a tracer is a good way for a man to get killed. Men who hunt men for a living don't generally make a mistake twice. I hadn't any doubt in my mind that that bounty man — and any others like him who might be trailing these hills looking to collect Frank Kingston's bounty — were a lot better at catching folks than I was at keeping them from it.

Those boats out there on the river, rough and nasty as they might be, had looked awful pretty from the road. Had it not been for Frank Kingston making me trade horses with him, I thought, I might have been on one of those very boats right now, just lazing along with the flow, all that was past behind me and a wide world opening fresh at every bend ahead.

When we were tads, Uncle Earl and me, we had gone to the river with Pa from time to time. There was an old timber dock there, and sometimes after a harvest folks would go down there and barter produce for the wares the rivermen carried.

I always liked to watch the boats. There would be flatboats and barges and rafts, all coming down from Clarksville and New Albany up by the falls, carrying all manner of people and things and all bound for yonder.

Uncle Earl liked the steamers best. They plowed along against the current, belching out great writhing ropes of smoke that lay on the winds like dark fog, going upstream. Uncle Earl had heard of places back east where they had railroads and street lamps, and even in those early times he had a craving to go there and see what he could see.

But the boats I liked were the ones going downstream — boats on the river bound for other rivers that would take them yonder . . . I'd sit on the riverbank and watch them pass and wonder what sorts of yonders they would find.

Now and again there would be barges carrying wagons. Conestogas, most of them were, great bright wagons as big as boats themselves, bound for the westering trade. They'd come down the river like bright parades, strings of sometimes six or eight barges, each carrying four big blue wagon

28

bodies two by two, wagons as long as a good cabin is wide, their high sides Prussian blue and their keels up-turned and jaunty as gondolas. Sometimes their bows were raised, and they arched above them ready to take canvas. Their big wheels would be stacked beside them, painted all bright red like their bolsters and axles.

They'd go down one river and up another, Pa said, and when they put ashore the people who would use those wagons would be there to meet them.

Where would they go from there, I wondered. I'd heard the men talk sometimes, looking off to the west. They spoke of Oregon and of Santa Fe, of the plains territories and the shining mountains and California. They read to one another from letters that had come back, about lands that stretched out so far they just went on forever, and about rich valleys and green meadows and cool-water streams.

I asked Pa where folks would go with wagons the like of those. Pa just grinned, and I always thought he looked a little sad. "Yonder, Zack," he'd say. "Way yonder."

Somehow, to me, the folks that were westering seemed to make more sense than all of Uncle Earl's prattle about the street lamps back east.

They were bright days back then, full of mystery and mischief. Uncle Earl and me, both just shirt-tail tads, we ran the woods sometimes, wild as a pair of Shawnee pups.

We'd fish from cutbanks and set snares in the thickets, and what we caught would be our dinner. We made bows and slings and wooden swords, and we stalked some critters that we should have fought shy of—like the cinnamon bear that treed us both one day, and like Mistress Darcy's milk-nanny. That bear never put the fear of God into me the way Mistress Darcy did.

Then sometimes we'd slip away and go up on the west ridge to run the crests. Uncle Earl was always looking for secret paths and shortcuts and pirate caves while I looked

29

for sheers and clear slopes where a body could stand and see forever.

The yonder places, to me, were out there . . . places far beyond the valley that sloped away down to the river, beyond the high hazy hills far off where the world was blue and secret . . . Beyond the climbing distances and the mists that blended with horizon sky.

Way out past there were the yonder places, and I couldn't imagine how far even when I tried. But sometimes I could almost see them from the ridge — faraway places that glowed with evening light, then took fire and drank the setting sun.

Sometimes the breeze on my face had a taste to it that I could imagine was the taste of way out there. Then Uncle Earl would go to fidgeting because he hadn't found any hidden treasures, and we'd head for home. I always liked to look back one more time, to see the first stars come out in the western sky. Where they were, it seemed they must be shining down on those yonder places.

We usually got our ears singed for being out so late and everybody being worried about us. But then, I don't recollect Pa ever taking the strap to us about that. He saved that for more serious business.

Like the time we shot off the anvils.

I was about seven at the time, I guess, and Uncle Earl maybe eight or nine. It was a plain wonder, looking back, that either of us ever got any older.

Uncle Earl had got off with Pa's best powderhorn, and we'd sparked us a piece of punkwood and been flashing bits of powder to see the smoke it would make. Then Uncle Earl got a better idea.

Out in the workshed, back of the barn, Pa kept a couple of big old anvils for the occasional mending of tack. One was bolted to his workbench, the other nailed down on top of a cut of oak stump just outside the door. Between the two of us, both puffing like turkey toms at a flocking, we managed to unbolt and lift the inside anvil. But short of harnessing a draft horse there wasn't any way we could budge the outside one. So Uncle Earl just shrugged and said, "Well, it'll be all right, right here."

We didn't know how much powder to use, so he emptied the horn on top of the anvil. Then we lugged the other one out and turned it upside down on the first one, with the powder between.

The more we looked at it, the more we didn't think it would be a good idea to just hit it with the flared punk, so we found a few inches of old fuse and set it, then lit that. Then we high-tailed for the corner of the barn.

I never in my life heard a noise like that. Like the biggest cannon you ever heard of, it was. They said later on that every chicken within a mile stopped laying for a week.

The noises that came after the first noise weren't nearly as loud, but they were the bad ones. I don't know how high in the air that top anvil had gone—the blast of it had knocked us both over backward—but I was already getting to my feet when I heard it come down. That was four separate noises: the sound of it going through the barn roof, the crunch as it went through the hayloft floor, the clatter as it demolished the tackle stall and that final, irrevocable thump as it buried itself in the good earth with hay sifting down to cover its grave.

Pa saw fit to use the strap on that occasion.

When we talked it over later, both of us still bright red low down and smarting, Uncle Earl said he'd bet that folks back east wouldn't raise such a ruckus about somebody just making a little noise. I remember thinking then that I'd bet that out west, there'd be a whole lot more room for an anvil to fall in without causing such grief.

I guess I had that westering notion in my blood way back then. But a lot of years had to pass before the time came to aim that way.

I'd learned to write and to read and to cipher. I'd got my growth and picked a trade and followed it. And in the past pair of years I had made wheels for overland wagons. I'd done more than that. I had *built* overland wagons, when help was scarce and Carl Froehner had orders stacked up. Generally it took four men two months to build a wagon and do it right. But for a time there, in that last season in New Albany, twenty-two of us had kept them rolling out of the assembly shed, one new wagon every week.

Even when Carl Froehner was on his death bed, taken down like a lot of people that year with the blackwater fever, we pitched in and kept his factory going for him and we didn't let up until his heirs and his creditors stepped in and cleaned up and there wasn't anything left to pay any of us the wages we had earned.

One of those creditors was Bailey Kingston. Pen Campbell, who had kept Mr. Froehner's books and handled shipping orders since the works started, told some of us that he thought that was odd. He didn't remember Mr. Froehner ever doing business with Mr. Kingston. But the court people who came in didn't ask any of us about our views on the matter.

They just came and closed us down. Or thought they did.

The thing was, there was a crew of us working to finish a pair of wagons for Caleb Tucker — a special order that Mr. Froehner had promised would be delivered to the boatmen in the spring. Mr. Tucker himself had come to the factory, all the way from Pennsylvania, to inspect Carl Froehner's product and place his order. He was a sharp-eyed, bearded man, maybe in his fifties, and he had toured the wagon works.

I'd been fitting a wheel onto its axle, working with the wagon jacked since it was fully assembled and no longer in its slings. He had paused to watch, then picked up a sixteen-pound maul and swung it with all his strength, right down onto the tire of the wheel I had just placed. On an ordinary wheel—one made for common draw—a blow like that might have bent the tire and shattered the felloes beneath it. It might even have split some spokes. But this wasn't an ordinary wheel. Carl Froehner didn't accept ordinary wheels on his overlanders . . . his "Froehnervagens," as he called them.

The maul rang and bounced, and Caleb Tucker winced as the shock of it went through his wrists. He put it down and peered at the wheel. There wasn't so much as a hairline separation between wood and metal.

He turned to Carl Froehner. "Who made this wheel?"

"I haf four vheelwrights," Mr. Froehner said. "Could haf been any of dem." He glanced at me. "Dis your vheel, Zack?"

I nodded. "Yes, sir. I just finished sweating on the tire."

Caleb Tucker frowned at me. "You do your own smithing, young man?"

"Yes, sir. We all do. Mr. Froehner says a wheelwright could get sloppy if he could blame his mistakes on a smith."

He glanced at Mr. Froehner and nodded, running his fingers along the iron tire. It was a good four-inch rim, the kind Mr. Froehner himself taught me to make. Then he knelt and counted the studded segments of the wood rim. "Six arcs," he said. "You always shape from the hexagon, young man?"

"Only the front wheels," I told him. "Six felloes, twelve spokes, rim diameter of three feet eight inches. For rear wheels we shape from an octagon . . . eight segments and sixteen spokes. Outer diameter with the tire is four feet and eleven inches, but it has the same load capacity as the front."

"How do you dish your spokes?"

"Deeper than some, sir. I like three inches on the front, four on the back."

33

"Why?"

I glanced at Mr. Froehner. He nodded. I said, "Strength and symmetry, sir. Any good wheel is dished. If it were flat, it would have no lateral strength. And where these wagons are going, people will be depending upon them . . . maybe staking their lives on them. I wouldn't want to think about folks coming to grief out in the far yonder just because I didn't dish a wheel the best way I know how."

He looked me up and down, then turned to Carl Froehner.

"That's why I came here," he said. "My family is important to me. I'll not put them to greater risk than I must."

He stooped again and looked at Abe Miles, who was under the jacked-up wagon, on his back, painting cross-members. "How much does this wagon weigh?" he asked.

Abe applied a deft stroke, his tongue sticking out from concentration. Then he looked around. "A ton and two, sir." When Tucker didn't respond, he said, "Ah . . . that's two thousand and two hundred pounds, sir. Empty weight."

"And what would happen to you right now if this wagon were to fall?"

"It won't, sir. The wheel's in place."

"But before . . . when the wheel wasn't in place?"

"It wouldn't have then, either, sir. We make our own jacks."

Benny Strother was fitting the tailgate with hardware, and Tucker walked around to watch. "What is the length of this bed?" he asked.

Benny slipped a ferrule into place. "Sixteen feet inside, sir. Add four inches for outside length."

"What wood is in the bolsters?"

"Hickory, sir. Same with the axles."

"And the hubs?"

Benny looked at me. "Black gum, sir," I told him. "It won't split."

Caleb Tucker would require two wagons. He ordered them and paid for them, and he and Mr. Froehner shook hands on the deal. Then he came back to where we were working and said, "There are great open lands out west, young sirs. Not just the goldfields, but many kinds of gold are out there, waiting for the right kind of men to gather them. Those of us heading that way now are mainly farmers and merchants. But there'll be a need for fine craftsmen. Had I the skills you've shown me here, there'd come a day when I would set my eyes on the west and never look back."

"You said you're going west," Benny said.

"Aye, even at my age." There was a stubborn pride about him then, with just a touch of sadness. "But it won't be quite the same. I've waited too long . . . I won't be able never to look back."

The Tucker wagons were a special order, and we worked hard to make them right. They were in assembly when Mr. Froehner died, and the people came to close the factory.

We didn't like it, not any of us. It wasn't the way Mr. Froehner would have had it be. But there wasn't much we could do.

There was one thing, though. We could finish those wagons that Caleb Tucker had paid for, and send them on their way before the foreclosers got their hands on them.

We worked nights for more than a week, all of us slipping through the back gates and bringing our own lanterns and tools. And when we had them assembled, tall and proud there in the back shed, and there was no proper paint for us to use, I told Uncle Earl about it and he went off somewhere and found paint for us.

It wasn't the Prussian blue and bright red that we'd had in mind, but it was good paint and it went on with a fine gloss that dressed up those two wagons just right. The beds of them were dark brown and the running gear bright yellow . . . the very same colors, Benny pointed out, that

35

Curly Joe had used to paint his sporting house.

We ironed tool boxes onto them, just back of the lazy-board, and keg braces on both sides. We outfitted them with jacks and tar buckets, and equipped the tool boxes with ax, auger, line and spare linchpins, and we stowed a hundred pounds of snowy canvas in each one, for rigging cover for the eight tall bows.

No two finer wagons had ever graced a wagon works. Mr. Froehner would have been proud of them.

Our problem then was how to get them out of the factory and down to the river to meet the barges. Nothing said that they were the property of Caleb Tucker — nothing except a handshake agreement with a man now dead.

Abe Miles said he could borrow horses and harness, and Benny Strother said it would be easier to dismantle the rolling doors than to break the locks. I was going to set up a diversion to draw the guards away, but as it turned out Frank Kingston made the diversion. He braced me when I led Lady Blue along the street, and one thing led to another and he killed Lady Blue. The diversion was what I did to him after that.

I never saw those wagons roll down to the river, but they were there when I crossed with Frank Kingston's roan, heading south and west.

And now I had seen them again. Among the things on those barges I had passed were a brace of proud Froehner-vagens with brown beds and bright yellow underpinnings.

So I sat the roan at the river's edge, waiting for them to come along, wanting one more look.

But it wasn't the barges that came into sight first. It was the keeler I had passed. It came along, close in, its crew walking their poles in double-time. And before I could so much as wave there were men on the bank behind me with guns in their hands.

"It's him, all right," one told the other. "He's the one." To me he said, "Just step down easy, mister, and put your guns on the ground. Captain Webb would like a word with you."

IV

They were burly, unkempt men with the flat shoes and corded forearms of boatmen. They held sawed-off large bore muskets with the hammers drawn. When I hesitated, one of them waggled his weapon at me. "Come on, get down. We ain't got all day."

Out on the water, the keelboat was hauling in toward shore. Some of the men at the front rail also held the sawed-off muskets. I got down and put my guns on the ground, then stepped back.

"That's good," the speaker said. "Captain Webb wouldn't like it if you got itchy and did somethin' dumb."

The keeler hove in close and slipped toward the bank sideways, grounding just a few feet out. Men crowded up to the near railing, looking down. Their tall poles stood above them leaning this way and that like a field of corn after a wind.

A bearded brawler with a red stocking cap shoved some of the others aside and squatted on his heels at the rail, for all the world like a big, ugly monkey wearing clothes. He squinted shrewdly at the roan horse, then glared at me. "What makes you worth three hundred dollars?"

Three hundred? The bounty hunter had said five.

When I didn't say anything he scowled more fiercely. "I

hope you appreciate that I wouldn't have took the time for a penny less."

"I can sure see how you wouldn't," I admitted.

"And not even any earnest money in advance. Cash on delivery. I hope you appreciate the trouble I'm goin' to."

"I don't see why you even bother," I said. "Why don't I just mount up and go my way and we'll say no more about it?"

"Can't do that," he said. "I give my word. You just ask anybody if Spider Webb's word don't mean something on this river. How do you think I got where I am today?"

"I guess you just followed the river," I guessed.

"That's exactly right! And if a man's goin' to follow the river, he better be good as his word. There ain't any other way." He stood and jostled crewmen aside. "Get some planking over there, you knotheads. You expect that horse to fly?"

There was a minute of turmoil aboard, then several heavy planks snaked out from the rail to form a sort of gangway to the firm bank. The boat swayed and sideslipped and men hurried across to brace their poles against the bottom.

When Webb was satisfied he jerked a thumb at me. "Well, come on, then! Lead the animal aboard. Time's wastin'." As I urged the roan up the planking, its eyes showing white at the unaccustomed footing, Webb squinted at the ground where it had been standing. "I hope you know how to use a broom and a scoop. We got no stablehands on this vessel."

He sent boatmen out with scythes and rakes, and they were back shortly with armloads of hay. Others had cleared bales and kegs aside on the foredeck, making a clear space virtually walled on both sides by stacked cargo. They spread the hay there and had me lead the horse around and into it.

"Whatever he does, you clean it up," Webb told me. Then

39

he handed me my guns. "You left these layin' on the ground back there. How's come you to get a bounty on you, anyway?"

"I guess I crossed the wrong man," I said. "But you know, Mr. Webb . . ."

"*Captain* Webb! Or Spider. But don't call me mister, not on my vessel, mister!"

"I . . ."

"The rest of these knotheads is 'misters.' I'm captain. Takes discipline to run a keelboat, and if you go to callin' me mister, how's these knotheads to know who to look to in their hour of need?"

I could see the sense of that, all right, and told him so. Then he was off, shouting and cussing around the deck, getting crewmen lined up with their poles, and I was busy keeping the roan calm, and when I got a chance to look around we were out in mid-stream, coasting down the Ohio just like I had seen folks do back when I was a tad.

My guns were still loaded, caps waxed to their nipples just like they had been. If I'd taken a notion to open fire right then, there wasn't anything stopping me. Nobody was paying me any attention, just a casual glance now and then when a crewmen crossed the foredeck.

I gave the roan a hatful of milled oats. The horse was steadying down, getting used to the rocking of the deck under its feet. After a while I climbed one of the cargo stacks to look around. We were a long way from New Albany, and going the wrong way if they intended to take me back. But then, on a river a keelboat only has one direction.

Where the river curved, the crew took up their poles and began marching back and forth along the shoreward rail — walking to the front, then ducking their poles and pushing against them all the way to the rear again — while Spider Webb manned the tiller and hollered insults at them. The boat edged outward into the current, away from the shoals. Looking back along the river in evening light—before the bend hid its course from sight—I thought I could see those wagon barges, but they were a long way back and I couldn't be sure it was them.

When the keelboat was out in the stream again the crew put down their poles and dispersed to various places around the deck, some lighting up pipes, some sitting on bales, some just watching the world go by. Spider Webb gave the tiller to one of them and came forward. He looked critically at the strawed deck under the horse.

"Them planks will bring a fair price, if you don't mess them up," he said.

"The deck?"

"Sure. I get to where there's a market for the cargo, I bust up the boat and sell the wood. Then I get me back up yonder and build another one. That's how this business works."

"Where are we going?" I wondered.

He looked at me the way a person looks at somebody who asks fool questions. "Down the river," he said. "Keelboats don't go anyplace except down the river. You don't know much about keelboats, do you?"

"I knew that much. What I meant was, where are you taking me?"

He climbed up on the cargo and squatted beside me. "Right where I said I would. Cairo, Illinois. Spider Webb is a man of his word. Anybody on the river'll tell you that."

"Then that's where you intend to collect? At Cairo?"

"That's what I said. Like my money in good coin, too. No bank drafts, if you please."

"If I . . . you mean you plan to collect from me?"

I stared at him and he stared back, and neither one of us knew what the other was talking about.

Finally he said, "That was the deal . . . wasn't it?"

41

"I don't know about any deal, Mr. . . . ah, Captain Webb. Aren't you out to collect the bounty?"

"How would I do that? The bounty's at New Albany. That's up river. I told you, keelboats only go downriver. The deal I made is to get you to Cairo for three hundred dollars. Feller said you'd pay on delivery."

A profound suspicion came alive in my head. "What feller?"

"Name of Donovan. Said he's your uncle."

"Yeah," I admitted. "He is."

Where did Uncle Earl think I was going to get three hundred dollars?

Spider Webb seemed satisfied then, that all was well and everything was understood. "Can you use those revolving guns?" he asked.

I shrugged. "I'm not much of a hand with them, but I've been practicing."

"That's good," he said. "We ain't the only ones on the river."

The evening sun sat on the tops of the forested bank ahead, and made it hard to look that way.

"Since you don't know anything about keelboats, I better explain the rules. Passengers get to ride easy. You don't have to walk a pole unless we ground. Cargo is off limits. You can sit on it or sleep on it, but don't open it. But if hijackers jump us, every man pitches in. If you didn't have your own hardware you'd get assigned a musket. Anybody that finds salvage gets an equal split of the proceeds, and every man keeps his own flotsam. Waylon—that's him back there with the tiller—he's purser and cook. If you got vittles of your own, I advise you to choose them. Waylon's a rotten cook." He pursed his lips, thinking. "Every man gets a share of grog when we make night camp, and whoever's standin' guards gets double the next day. Oh, and no jig-dancin' on board, and don't piss upwind. I guess that's about it. If I

42

make more rules, I'll tell you what they are. This here keelboat's name is . . ." he frowned with concentration, then turned and bellowed, "Waylon! What did I say this here keelboat's name is?"

Back at the tiller, Waylon knuckled his whiskers. *"Aunt Maude* . . . I think," he called back.

Webb nodded. "This here keelboat's name is *Aunt Maude*. For the sake of propriety, you ought to remove your hat when you say it."

"I'll try to remember that," I told him. "Uh, Captain Webb, did my Uncle Earl say anything? Like any message for me, or anything?"

"Not that I recollect." He stood and pointed, accusingly. "Look what your horse just done!"

"Don't worry about it," I told him. "I'll clean it up."

Captain Webb made it very clear during the hour after sunset that stopping off to pick me up had cost him valuable time and probably would cause *Aunt Maude* to be late in fetching down to Snag Island, which was where he planned to make camp. Further, arriving late at Snag Island meant arriving at dark. He spoke gloomily of shoals and grounding, of waiting hijackers and problems with finding firewood . . . and especially of the dire consequences of not getting a full night's rest.

I didn't hear a lot of it, because he was expounding at length as he went about the business of running his keelboat, and all I heard was what he said in my vicinity.

For my part, I was busy tending Frank Kingston's roan horse — *my* roan horse, I had to keep reminding myself. I got his saddle and bridle off him, rubbed him down, painted tallow poultice on a raw spot where his headstall had galled him behind the ear, and worked for a while at readjusting the headstall. And I tried to keep *Aunt Maude's* deck austere. The roan was a big, healthy horse, his systems fully functional, his eliminations enthusiastic and unhesitating.

I wondered where Uncle Earl expected me to come up with three hundred dollars to pay for this ride down the river. I was pretty sure he knew I didn't have much in the way of money. We'd talked about that before he went off to steal paint from Curly Joe so we could finish those wagons. Still he had made a deal with Captain Spider Webb, so he must have had something in mind. It had been my experience all my life that Uncle Earl always had something in mind.

Being my ma's baby brother, Uncle Earl took after the Donovans. Even when we were little kids, I remember Uncle Earl being small — smaller than me as we grew. Lithe and small boned. Sometimes he seemed delicate and underfed. Other times he reminded me of a weasel — all quick and slinky and whipcord tough. He generally seemed whichever way suited him at the time. But he always had a reason for anything he did.

One time he set out to learn to chunk rocks — not just the ordinary rock-chunking that all little boys try their hand at from time to time, he set out to be the best rock-chunker anywhere around. Everytime we turned around, seemed like, Uncle Earl was bouncing rocks off stumps and taking aim at knotholes in the shed wall. Got so he just never missed. He could put a rock through a maple gap from forty yards. He could hit a pump handle right or left and tell you where the rock was going next.

When he could, he'd set up chunking contests with some of the boys over on Caldwell Road and win all their marbles from them. He told me that was why he had learned to chunk rocks, was because good marbles were hard to come by and he intended to go into the marble business and make a lot of money. But mainly, I think, he'd figured out that an expert rock-chunker doesn't get braced much, even by the bigger kids. A fellow that can chunk a mean rock can pretty well tell everybody else how the cow ate the cabbage.

Later on, when we had some years on us, Uncle Earl learned that a man with a gun can do the same thing—if he's the best there is around.

For a person who could just naturally charm the beard off a billy goat, my Uncle Earl used to spend a lot of time developing other powers of persuasion.

It was like old times . . . not knowing what he had in mind.

The sun cast tree-shadows out across the river and the shaded bank took on that secret blueness of evening light. Dark waters whispered along the stained sides of the keeler, carrying us along on a fair current where the tiller's only use was for trim—sweeping now and then. Just enough to keep the front of the boat ahead of the back of it.

Crewmen lounged around, smoking their pipes and watching the world go by, and Spider Webb was asleep on a pile of cargo. Waylon came ambling forward, along the right-hand catwalk, and stood for a few minutes with his fists on his hips, studying the roan horse. Waylon was a big, lurching hulk of a man, crag-faced behind wild whiskers, and I wouldn't have wanted to get crosswise of him. He would have made two of Buster Stuckey.

After he had looked the horse over pretty good, he climbed up on a tarp-covered stack and sat there, giving me the same scrutiny.

"What do you do when you ain't bountied?" he wanted to know.

"I make wheels. I'm a wheelwright."

"That a fact?" he looked at me with renewed interest. "Never tried my hand at that, though I've done a bit of cooping in my time. Ever done that?"

"No, but I've watched. A good cooper at work is a fine sight. How come you to quit?"

"No market for good barrels any more." He shrugged.

"What with tradin' ships goin' to steam nowadays, they all use iron casks for their water an' lockers for the vittles. Nobody buys barrels except the breweries, and they don't hire decent coopers. They just ring out rough staves and seal 'em with calk."

"Well, I been building wagons for Carl Froehner, and I can tell you a man that would calk a keg for an overlander would suck eggs."

"That a fact? Wagon people still use good barrels?"

"Those going west do. There'll be places out there where folks could die for want of a tight waterbarrel."

"Wagons is a good business. How come *you* to quit?"

"Mr. Froehner died and we got shut down. I figured I might try my hand out toward the territories someplace. Maybe Springfield or Westport. That's where the big wagon companies make up to head for Oregon or California . . . places like that."

Places like that. The yonder places that I had dreamed about all my life. When I got to where those westering folk assembled their trains, would I stop there?

Waylon had a far-off look in his eyes, just like I probably did. "How many barrels do you suppose each of those wagons would carry?"

"I don't know. Conestogas that I've seen generally are ironed for two. But we paired up the strapping on Mr. Froehner's wagons so I guess they could carry four if they wanted to. The wagons themselves are lighter than Conestogas by close to a thousand pounds."

"I never been west of the Mississippi," he said. "Well, except for doin' a little tradin' and carousin' at Hannibal and New Madrid and places like that. And New Orleans. I guess you could say New Orleans is west of the Mississippi . . . it's west of the rest of it."

"Some places out there," I mused, "the sun doesn't go down until it's already stone dark here."

For some reason that notion upset him and he scowled at me. "I don't like to hear that kind of talk."

Somebody back in the stern had brought out a fiddle and started playing on it, and now there was a rhythmic thumping from back there, and voices raised in laughter. Up on the cargo stack Spider Webb snorted, sat up, looked back and bellowed, "Here, now! Cut that out! I don't hold with jig-dancin' on my boat!"

The river ghosted around a long, lazy bend where the breeze played with evening mist, and ahead was the glow of firelight. Up on the cargo stack, Spider Webb rubbed his eyes and stared, then yelled at the stern, "Hard alee! Hard alee!"

The crewman at the tiller squinted up at him. "What?"

"Turn it right, dammit!"

Waylon thumped to the deck, shaking his head. "Wind's from the right, for heaven's sake. Alee is left." He ran toward the stern.

Somebody had done something back there, because the keelboat began to turn. I held the roan's halter and watched the forerail swinging across the view ahead, then a bank with darkened woodlands above it, then I was looking up-river.

"Waylon!" Spider Webb roared from somewhere. "Get that tiller moving. We're going backward!"

As a crewman rushed past, waving a long pole above his head, I caught his arm. "What's that all about?"

"Hijackers!" he said. "They're waiting for us on Snag Island!"

V

It sounded like all hell was breaking loose in the stern of the keelboat then, but all I could see from the front deck was high stacks of cargo and the wrong end of the river. I snugged the roan's halter rope to a crate lashing and climbed.

We were floating backward down the Ohio, stern-on toward a wooded island off the left bank, and there was firelight there. Waylon had the tiller, sweeping mightily to turn the boat while some of the crew ran along the right-hand rail, bulling into their poles, and Spider Webb danced at the stern rail and shouted curses: The gist of it was that Snag Island was *his* layby and everybody on the river knew that, and if the blackguards just *had* to hijack *Aunt Maude* then they ought to come out and meet him on the river like decent God-fearing pirates.

Those of the crew who weren't plying poles were hauling sawed-off muskets out of the little deckhouse and passing them around.

Webb glanced around and saw me up on the stacks. "Stand by to repel boarders!" he shouted.

The island was a few hundred yards away and coming up smartly. With obvious reluctance, *Aunt Maude* swung until we were approaching sideways. Webb shouted and the polemen reversed their steps, pushing now toward the right-hand shore.

Now that we were close, I could see a lot of people on that island, fanning out along its near end. There were puffs of smoke, and something went past my ear like a hornet in a high wind. A ball smacked into the lashed crate just below my foot and I baled off there so fast I lit half-way across the roan's back. He whuffed and danced and I slid down and pulled one of my revolvers. Crewmen came over and around the cargo stacks, taking cover, and began returning fire with their muskets. The firing from the island diminished as those over there scrambled for cover behind trees and stones. I heard a rumbling sound that seemed to carry through the deck, and thudding feet behind me. Looking up and around I could see poles rising, falling and rising again on the upstream rail, as men pushed under shelter of the cargo.

Aunt Maude had been dead on the current for a moment, but now she was alive again and I could feel the slight, rhythmic swaying of her as somebody managed the sweeping tiller. I wondered who could be brave enough — or crazy enough — to be standing back there on that exposed rear deck. I climbed again to the peak of the center stack and peered over. The little deck house had been sheared from its moorings and skidded across to the rearward corner, right up against the rails. In its shelter, Spider Webb sat cross-legged, big hands gripping the tiller bar above his head. He swayed from side to side as he worked the sweep.

As I watched, Waylon darted from the cargo stacks and took the tiller, his big shoulders giving it power enough to skid the boat's stern from side to side as he pulled. The firing had picked up again, musket balls and buckshot whining around us as the crew returned fire.

I took another look over the left stack. The island was less than a hundred yards away, bearing down on us, but *Aunt* ·

Maude was moving as well—angling past, making for mid-stream. Spider Webb scrambled down into my slot and came up beside me.

He looked at the pistol in my hand. "It's all right for you to shoot at them folks over there," he said sourly. "Matter of fact, it's recommended practice at times like this."

"What's going on?" I wanted to know. "Who are those people?"

"Offhand, I'd guess that's Buckeye Pearce and his varmints. They usually show up along this stretch. Can you hit anything with that there handgun?"

"Sometimes."

"Then raise up here and try your hand at it." He peered over the top as I raised up to join him. He pointed. "You see that little tree right past the fire, there? With the two fellows behind it? Well, that ain't two fellows, it's just one, bent over. Shoot either end of him you'd like to."

I shrugged and levelled the revolver. *Aunt Maude* lurched as Waylon began another sweep. I had held on the man's shoulder, but when I fired he shrieked and straightened up, dropping his firearm. His hands went to his haunches and he hollered again, then rolled into the darkness of the brush.

"That's not bad," Spider allowed. "Been me, I'd have gone for the top of him. It's more permanent."

"Any of your people hit?"

"Yeah," he scowled. "Willie Carmichael's got a ball through his leg." He raised and fired his musket, and someone on the island howled. "What I can't figure is how come them to be on Snag Island. They can't take us from there less'n we run aground, and they know better than that."

I raised up to snap another shot. We were standing out from the island now, almost abreast of the tip of it and angling to point downstream. It was dark enough that the island was just a shadow against the pale sheen of water, the tops of its trees dim silhouettes against a fading sky. I had an impression of furtive movement over there—people moving from cover to cover to flank us—but could see no one clearly enough for a target.

But there was something else, and I grabbed Spider's arm and pointed. Growing from the far end of the island was a boxy silhouette on the river, extending outward. A boat, coming out into the current.

Spider snarled. I saw his teeth glinting in the dusk, the slitting of his eyes. "So that's how it is," he muttered. "He set a trap for me. Damn his mangy hide!" Shaking his head like a wounded animal he rammed home another load and fired it in the general direction of the boat ahead. It was a waste of powder at the distance.

"Does this happen all the time?" I asked.

"Not exactly like this. Usually they just pole along with us for a mile or so and we all do some shootin'. I guess Buckeye is gettin' smarter in his old age." He turned toward the stern and yelled, "Waylon! Boat ahead! Make for the main current!"

Aunt Maude responded to another surge from the sweep, turning slightly to the right. I saw a flash ahead, on the boat, and a ball kicked up deck splinters a foot from the roan's hind hoof. I swung around and braced the revolver with both hands and fanned three fast shots at the place the flash had been. A sort of gurgling moan floated back across the water, followed by a splash.

"Hey, now," Spider said. "I believe you're gettin' the hang of it."

"I wish I could see who I'm shooting at," I said. Since New Albany, I had a real poor attitude toward people who shot at horses.

Both boats were drifting in the current now, with Snag Island crawling by to our left. The pirate boat was pushing for midstream, a course to intercept ours. The distance between diminished slowly.

"He's never tried anything like this before," Spider said. "I don't know . . ."

"What are you carrying in this cargo?"

He swung toward me in the gloom. "That ain't any of your business!"

Business or not, it stood to reason that there was something on this old keelboat that those people wanted worse than usual.

One of the crewmen, crouched below the bale where we were perched, muttered, "We ain't going to make it past them. They got poles workin' behind barricades."

I wished I could see what was going on over there. I wriggled around and slipped, sliding down the stacks until my feet sank into the pile of hay at one side of the roan's slot.

"Captain Webb . . . is there any way you can stop this boat?"

"Stop? You mean like not moving?"

"Yeah."

"Hell, no. Best we could do would be to slow it down a little. But why would we do that?"

"It's just a notion. Don't you have some barrels of oil back there someplace?"

"It isn't oil. It's coal oil. All the way from Pennsylvania. Why?"

"Go get a barrel of it."

"Look, I'm kind of busy here, if you ain't noticed. I got to figure how to get us out of this mess."

I climbed back up beside him. "Captain Webb?"

"Yeah?"

He turned and I poked him in the gullet with the muzzle of my revolver. "I said I need some coal oil. I mean *now!*"

He swallowed. I could feel his adam's apple jiggling the pistol. "Since you put it that way, ah . . . how much of it do you need?"

"A bucket full would do just fine."

He turned carefully. "Waylon! Send up a bucket of coal oil!"

From the stern came, "Do what?"

"Don't argue with me!" Spider roared. "Send me a bucket of coal oil! Right now!"

"All right! You don't have to shout!"

A minute later a crewman came around the stacks, ducking for cover. "Here's your coal oil, captain. What do you want me to do with it?"

Spider shrugged.

"Set it down there on the deck," I said. "Then gather up a bundle of that straw—a good armload—and twine it tight."

"What are you goin' to do," Spider growled, "burn my boat?"

"No, I'm not going to burn your boat. But if I'm going to shoot at people I want to see them." The man had a bundle twined up and I told him, "Now douse it with coal oil and toss it in the water, right there under the front rail."

"Do like he says," Spider said. "He's crazy."

The oil-soaked bale bobbed along a few feet from the rail, a dark patch on the water. "Throw a match on it," I said.

"Hell, that thing will set the boat on fire," Spider yelped.

"Not if your people get on those poles and slow the boat."

With my pistol still tickling his throat, Spider Webb threw back his head and roared, "All hands! Poles down! Back water!" Boots thumped, poles clattered along both sides and *Aunt Maude* shuddered. Water swirled and gurgled along her sides and there was a visible wake spreading from her forerail.

"Throw that match," I told the crewman.

The match flared, arced and went out in the water a foot from the oiled bale, which was drifting away from us now.

"I missed," he said.

Another match flared, arced and lit on the bale. It lay there, a tiny spark in shadows, then flame grew from it and within seconds the floating bale blazed happily. Its light gave the people on the other keelboat a good look at us, and their guns began talking.

I picked out points of light and fired back, and some of *Aunt Maude*'s crew were answering with their muskets. With my revolver no longer at his throat, Spider Webb emptied a pair of smoothbores across the water and started reloading. "You're doin' more for them than you are for us," he complained.

But the poles were holding and *Aunt Maude* swayed and gurgled, restrained from the current that was her life. The flaming bale was a bonfire on the water, and as the pirate boat crept out ahead of us it closed on it cheerily, lighting the faces of men at the barricaded rail. I got out my other revolver. Now there was something to shoot at.

"It's goin' to hit 'em," Spider breathed, wide-eyed.

"Well, when it does, let's see if we can't keep them away from it long enough for it to burn some wood."

That proved to be a popular idea. As the bonfire neared the other boat, whose sweep was boiling water trying to get away from it, Spider's crew concentrated their fire on the area where it would strike. In the light of the flames, the splinters flying from rail and barricades over there were like feathers at a henfight.

"Whooee," somebody said. "Look at 'em dance."

That cheery little floating fire snugged itself right in under Buckey Pearce's deck rail, just a bit forward of center, and in a minute or less there was a good fire going there.

"By God," Spider snorted, "that ought to keep 'em busy."

Between the effect of our firing and the confusion caused by the burning deck, the hijacker boat was dead in the water, its poles tangled and holding it like a many-legged shoal.

"Get me a powder keg," I suggested. "Not a full one. About half is good enough. And a coil of that rope back there."

"That's not rope," Spider snapped. "On a boat it's called *cable*. Nobody on a keelboat calls cable rope."

"I don't know anything about keelboats," I reminded him. "Just get it up here. And an open keg half-full of powder."

He sent a crewman scurrying to fetch it, and glared at me. "You go playin' with powder you'll blow up my boat."

"I'm not going to blow up your boat. Just keep those people busy."

The crewman was back with powder and rope. Cable, then. The same one who had lit the haybale. "What are we gonna do now?" he asked happily.

I snugged a good lash around the squat little barrel, then stepped to the forerail and bent far over to place it in the water. *Aunt Maude* was straining at her poles, the current fighting her. But some of the near polemen were getting the drift of what I was doing, and passed it back, and the poles creaked and bowed with renewed effort. I believe for a minute or two there *Aunt Maude* was actually going backward, upstream.

I paid out rope—cable—as fast as the current would take it and the powder keg bobbed along toward the burning keelboat. I handed the rope to the happy crewman. "Float this over there and see if you can guide it right into the fire."

He grinned at me, his teeth glinting. "Fourth of July," he said.

The powder keg homed on the other boat and headed for it, a little black shape on moon-silvered water. I stood and watched its progress, feeling very pleased with myself. The fact was, I realized, I was having a grand time. Getting right into the spirit of things.

The very same way I always used to get caught up in the spirit of whatever weird idea was in Uncle Earl's head at the moment.

The boatman with the keg line glanced around. "My name's George," he said. "Any more of these notions you happen to get, I'm your man."

"This is all working out very well," I admitted.

There are times when even the best of us sort of overlook the obvious. I take no pride in that, but it is a fact. The obvious was that my roan horse was a high-spirited animal who had managed, somehow, to stand quietly through at least fifteen minutes of running gunbattle between keelboats. The obvious was that he was standing there on a quivering deck, his tail to the forerail, and a halter rope holding his head so that he couldn't look around to see what was going on. The obvious was that there were people firing muskets over him, under him and along both sides of him, and that there were balls whining past him from the other side.

The obvious was . . . I was standing right behind him.

One hoof took me just below the right shoulder. The second one caught me in the seat of the pants. Right then I didn't know all that, but I was keenly aware of those exact locations for a good long time thereafter. All I knew right then was that something on the order of seventeen Buster Stuckeys hit me from behind and a month's worth of stars came out and danced and the world went away to be with them. I was looking at flowing water, then I was looking at an upside down keelboat diminishing in the distance, then I was looking at the sky. Then ice cold water slammed me about half silly and followed up by trying to drown me.

It was one of those experiences a fellow thinks a lot about . . . later on when he has the time.

I came up gagging and gasping, and just sort of rode the waters for a spell, trying to get some air into my lungs. It seemed like a long time, but eventually I got around to wondering where I was.

Off in one direction was a shadowy hulk standing tall above the river, a big thing with the shape of tall, lashed stacks upon it and poles waving above it, and bright flashes erupting here and there. Much nearer was another big shadowy shape, coming closer as I watched. It was like the first one, with the poles and flashes, but it seemed to be on fire. And off to the side, not very far away, was a little, squat round shape floating in the water, keeping pace with me. It looked like a half-submerged keg with a rope lashed around it.

I was dazed and confused, and part of me wondered what Uncle Earl had been up to now.

The noises I was hearing began sorting themselves out. There were gunshots, shouting voices, rippling water and crackling flames. It was all sort of confusing and I wondered why I was in the water. I looked at the squat shape nearby, pacing me in the water's flow. A powder keg. That's what it was, a powder keg. And it was heading right for the burning part of a keelboat a few yards away and when it got there all hell was going to break loose. As clearly as if it had been yesterday, then, I remembered the time we shot the anvils. I guess it took that to get it through my head that something very loud was about to happen.

I must have milled water like a gator on the prod that last few yards to the pirate boat, because as I went up over the rail there were men gaping at me from all around and backpedaling away as fast as they could.

I pointed. "That keg is going to blow."

They looked where I was pointing and there was a mad scramble for the far side of the deck. I heard people bumping other people off into the river. There was just a lot of splashing over there.

The fire was burning merrily on the right-hand rail — the one I'd heard Spider Webb call "starboard" on his boat, but that was his boat and this wasn't — and it gave a good light there on the deck. Enough to see the three coming at me from the stern.

The first one was a big man with eyebrows like thornbushes. He swung a musket at my head and I ducked. I came up with a boat pole and prodded him in the belly with it. He backed off and bumped into the second one, who was waving a curved sword. The third one got past them and took a swing at me with a club. I dodged aside and got my feet all tangled up with my boat pole and fell on my back. All three of them came at me.

That keg couldn't have come at a better time.

Next to a half-keg of gunpowder set off between a keelboat's catwalk and a river, a horn of powder between anvils is about as exciting as shelling peas.

A wall of white fire shot up alongside the boat, with a roar that would put thunders to shame. The deck pitched, its right side rising as though something very large had come from below and knocked hell out of it. Plank barricades splintered and crashed inward, pieces of them flying clear across the boat to splash into the river beyond. I was lying flat on my back, and the deck threw me into the air and then came up and swatted me. The three men around me were thrown around like rag dolls. The big one with the musket crashed against the little deck house and flipped clear over it to land on the other side. The one with the sword dropped his blade and clung to a boat pole which rose up majestically from the deck, then went right on up and over. I heard the splash beyond as the man and the pole both hit the river.

While the boat was still dancing on roiled water the big man across the deck got to his feet, paused just long enough to say, "Jesus Christ!" and took a running jump over the far rail.

I don't know where the third one with the club had gone, but as I got to my feet he came from somewhere, flailing that club at me. Some people do have real one-track minds. I dodged and swatted him upside the head, then swung him around and put a boot right on his tail-bone and pushed. He cleared the far rail as handy as could be.

I'd like to make it clear at this point that all of this happened according to my plans, and that I was acting with cool logic throughout. I really would like to. Trouble is, that isn't how it was. By the time anything resembling a lucid thought got itself arranged in my head, I was sitting on the deckhouse of a burning keelboat bobbing along down the Ohio River at a good clip, sort of wondering where everybody was. It seemed as though there were things somebody should be doing.

The whole deck of the boat was a litter of junk—poles and overturned kegs, two or three guns, a curved sword, broken planks and barricades, all kinds of things, a weird chaos in the firelight. The big steering sweep wagged this way and that in the current, its tiller bar gone.

I don't believe I was thinking at all right then. I just sat there and wondered. I wondered whether the Dragoon revolver there on the deck was mine. I wondered where my horse was. I wondered whether I had stowed a supply of grease in the Tucker wagon toolboxes after packing their hubs . . . forgetting a thing like that can give a wheelwright a poor reputation. I wondered why the little hatch on the wheelhouse was opening.

What got me straightened out was a voice. It said, "In my opinion, if you don't put out that fire very soon, this boat will sink and we will drown."

I don't know whether it was the logic of those words that got me to moving, or whether maybe it was how she said them.

VI

It took me a while to get that fire put out, and it left quite a hole in the keelboat's superstructure. But the only water we seemed to have taken on was what I used dousing the flames.

When I finished, I trudged back along the deck, tired and sore and stumbling over things in the dark. The girl was a shadow atop the deck house.

"It seems to me," she said, "that you should have saved a portion of that fire. It is so dark without it, I don't know how you intend to mend the tiller."

"Why should I mend the tiller? This isn't my boat."

"No, I thought not," she said. "You don't seem to know much about it. The tiller is that long wooden handle . . ." she pointed, ". . . that is supposed to be attached to that large swivel thing there, but isn't . . ."

"I know what a tiller is," I snapped. One of my natural reactions to prolonged stress and confusion. I tend to become cranky.

"Then you know that its purpose is to steer the boat."

"I'll steer the boat in the morning."

"In my opinion," she said, "if this boat isn't properly steered it is likely to run aground."

"That sounds all right to me."

"If it runs aground at this velocity, we shall likely be killed."

I looked ahead at the pale expanse of river, stretching off into the night. "Our present velocity is because we are in the main current. In order to run aground we would have to be out of the main current, in the shallows, in which event our velocity would be reduced."

"Oh?" She seemed to brighten. "Then we could run aground gently and wait for help to arrive?"

"Exactly." My head was throbbing unmercifully, and I had a knot on the back of my skull that I was just beginning to notice. I figured it came from either a horse's hoof or a boat deck, but I didn't know which.

"In that case," she said, "I believe you should get us out of the main current."

I shook my head, partly to see if anything was rolling around loose in there. "I can't. The tiller is broken."

"But you have poles. Can't you pole us aside? I have seen that done."

"Oh, all right. I'll try."

I found a sturdy boat pole and made my way to the front rail. Holding the pole midway, I poked it into the water. Nothing happened. I couldn't find the bottom. I gripped the pole three-quarters of the way up and tried again. Still nothing. Only water and more water.

I decided to try it one more time. Kneeling at the edge of the deck I thrust the pole downward as hard as I could, hand over hand until I was gripping the last six inches of it. I leaned down to get as close to the water as I could.

The Ohio River does have a bottom. It is one pole's length below the surface at mid-channel, and it has a tenacious grip. The pole snagged, jerked me forward and down, and the keelboat shrugged me off and passed over. I could have counted the moss streamers on its bottom had there been light enough to see.

By the time I got my grip loose from that wedged pole, the stern of the boat was passing overhead. I surfaced just in time for the wagging sweep to catch me a clout on the ear. I caught it and held on, catching my breath. Then I hauled myself to the stern rail and climbed up on deck again. I was soaked, chilled, stunned and tired and I was learning to hate keelboats.

The girl was gone from the deckhouse cover. After a moment I spotted her, a dim silhouette crouched at the front rail, peering into the water.

The little deck house was only about three feet tall, but beneath it was a well cut into the deck. In there, in the darkness, I found a couple of smelly blankets and wrapped them around me. Then I groped forward and found a bench running along the side.

I lay down there and went to sleep

Sunlight on my face and the bright sounds of morning woke me, and for a time I couldn't figure out where I was. All the incidents of yesterday seemed remote and blurry, like fever dreams half-remembered. The aches and pains I had accumulated were real enough, but even those were tolerable since I had rested.

I lay there until I was fully awake and had things sorted out in my mind, then got up and crawled out of the deckhouse.

The boat was right of mid-stream, out of the main current now but still floating steadily along, the water burbling contentedly under its rails. The deck was no longer the tumbled clutter that I recalled. Poles had been laid carefully along the sides, overturned kegs and bales had been righted, and there was a neat stack of weaponry in one corner — muskets, clubs, a Dragoon revolver, a curved sword, three or four knives and an assortment of hats.

The girl was sitting at the far rail, watching the wooded shore go by. She wore a dark dress with a stained white collar and voluminous skirt that spread around her, and her dark hair was pulled back severely and tied in a bun. Sitting there, facing away, she gave the impression of someone very prim and stern, and the voice I remembered—haughty and scolding—confirmed the picture. Young, I decided, small and exceedingly plain. Undoubtedly awkward and bony, I decided, probably endowed with nothing more rewarding than a sharp tongue and an impatient disposition. I decided all that in a glance, and threw in the probability of close-set, suspicious eyes, a hatchet nose and a mouth molded on the taste of green persimmons.

All that and a pirate as well.

Well, it didn't matter. I was only here temporarily. I turned to look back, upriver, wondering how long it would take Spider Webb and his crew to catch up and retrieve his paying passenger from this hulk. The river curved away behind, but as far as I could see, squinting against the morning sun, we were the only vessel on it.

When I turned back the girl looked around and I revised my earlier estimates. Severe, yes. Suspicious and impatient, yes. Haughty and imperious, probably. But the face framed by that severely-tied hair might have graced a pixie. And the figure molded by that dark dress did not give the impression of boniness.

"Well," she said coldly, "I dare say you have never been bothered by any great sense of responsibility."

"What do you mean by that?"

"I mean that you have slept the night away and never gave a thought to the welfare of this boat or its passenger. What would Captain Pearce say to that?"

"I haven't the vaguest idea. Captain Pearce is a pirate."

"That is obvious. But I should think that even among pirates there would be some sense of responsibility."

"I'm not a pirate," I pointed out. "You are. I just got here."

She came to her feet, dark eyes blazing. "Sir, I am not a pirate. I am a Presbyterian. And I shall demand an accounting from your Captain Pearce, I assure you."

"He's not *my* Captain Pearce. I told you, I just got here last night."

"What are you, then . . . a passenger?"

"Not intentionally. Actually I seem to be a passenger on Captain Webb's boat—that's the one you people attacked—and that isn't intentional either. What I'm really doing is traveling west . . . on horseback."

Her eyes went wary and she backed off a step. "On horseback?"

"Yes. You see, I am a wheelwright . . ."

"Keelboats of my acquaintance do not have wheels."

"Not keelboats. Wagons. Overland wagons. In fact, there are two of them on this river somewhere right now that I helped to build."

"Wagons. On the river."

"Yes, they belong to Mr. Caleb Tucker. He and his party are to receive them at Cairo, then I suppose they will journey west to join a wagon company at Westport or somewhere." I shrugged and pointed west. "Yonder."

"There are wagons on the river bound for Westport and you yourself are traveling by horseback."

"That is . . ." I nodded, realizing that all of that might be a shade hard to grasp. "That is essentially correct. Except that I was kidnapped by Captain Webb's men and taken aboard *Aunt Mauda* as a passenger. Captain Webb had an arrangement with my Uncle Earl."

She looked at me even more strangely. "Are you all right? Would you like to sit down? Maybe you should sleep some more."

"I'm quite rested, thank you."

"Then what, exactly, *is* the matter with you?"

"Well, I don't know for sure. I was helping to stand off the attack when you and your pirates . . ."

"I am *not* a pirate! I am a passenger!"

"Oh. Well, then, when your host attacked us. And I believe my horse kicked me off that boat and onto this one."

"Are you telling me that that awful noise I heard—when everyone was shooting guns—are you saying that was *you?*"

"Yes, after a fashion, I suppose it was."

"Then possibly you know what became of Captain Pearce and all of his men?"

"They all went overboard, I believe." I looked back up-river again, shading my eyes. "I don't suppose you have seen anything of *Aunt Maude*, have you? Or my horse?"

"I haven't seen a living soul," she said, with something like sympathy in her voice now. "No aunts or uncles, no wagons, no horses galloping by—really not anyone at all. Perhaps if you would select one of those hats over there to shade your head, then go and sit down somewhere and rest . . ."

The hat was a good idea. I had no notion of where my own had gone. I picked out one that seemed to fit, and while I was at it I put my revolver back in my belt where it belonged. It seemed undamaged and its loads seemed secure. I had no idea where my other one was, but this was the best of the two.

She had gathered up all the broken planks from the blown-out barricades, and stacked the wood neatly in a corner of the deck. I went and picked up an armload and began arranging it on the foredeck. She came and peered at what I was doing, a deepening frown on her face.

"What are you going to do, set this boat on fire again?"

"If I set it on fire again, I'll put it out again. I noticed that there are tins of tea in the deck house, and that keg yonder should contain fresh water. Do you know how to brew tea?"

I had to extinguish the deck twice — by sluicing water under the fire — but we came up with a fair tea, which made us both feel a little better.

"My brother and I are traveling to Vicksburg," she explained. "Ezra intends to help the Reverend Cooley establish his church there. Ezra says it is his understanding that Vicksburg is in need of enlightened ministry."

"So that's why you were a passenger."

"Yes. Two days ago Ezra arranged for Captain Pearce to take us to Vicksburg. He paid him handsomely. Fifty dollars for each of us . . ."

"Fifty dollars?" I almost choked on my tea. "Fifty dollars is what it costs to ride a keelboat?"

"Ezra felt it was exorbitant," she explained. "Usually these boats will take passengers for thirty dollars. But Captain Pearce was the only one available when we boarded."

"But *fifty dollars?* I thought the fare was three hundred!"

"Oh, my, no. Why, Ezra says that for seventy dollars a keelboat will take a passenger all the way to New Orleans."

When she said it, I believed it. And somehow I couldn't picture Uncle Earl not knowing that.

I drank some more tea, then asked, "What became of your brother . . . of Ezra?"

"Well, that is the really irritating part of it all," she said. "No sooner had we gotten settled on board and a few miles downstream, than Captain Pearce's men came and threw Ezra overboard and locked me in the deckhouse."

"Did they . . . ah . . . molest you in any way?"

"No. I was concerned about that. But when one of them tried to force entry I quoted scripture to him and threatened him with damnation . . . as well as with an axe. That took care of that for a time. Then there was quite an uproar. Someone was hailing from the shore, and the boat put in, and there was a lot of excitement, then the boat cast off again and everyone sounded very busy. And after a time they began shooting. Why, there were bullets coming right through the deckhouse walls. I got down in the deck well and stayed there. And then there was that awful noise, and a lot of scuffling and splashing, and the deckhouse door came loose so I could go out and look around, but there was no one there but you."

"I see," I said. I had been thinking that I was the one who'd had an adventure. "I am very sorry about Ezra. Possibly he managed to . . ."

"Oh, God takes care of Ezra. He'll be all right. I am only concerned that he must be terribly worried about me."

I was crawling around in the stuffy little deckhouse, taking inventory, when she came to the door and knelt to look in. "I think you should come out here," she said.

"Just a few more minutes," I told her. "There are some things here that . . ."

"In my opinion you should come out now," she insisted.

I turned and started toward the door, crouching because the space was only about five feet high, well and all. "All right. What's the matter?"

"We are approaching a . . ."

When a keelboat is moving on a wide, flat current, you don't really notice that it's moving. When you notice is when it stops. This one stopped abruptly and she plummeted headlong into the well where I was trying to stand. We both tumbled head over heels the length of the little space and fetched up against the far wall as tangled as two tabby cats with only one mouse.

". . . snag," she finished. We started trying to get unwound from each other. She wasn't anywhere near as bony as I had first supposed. "Behave yourself!" she hissed, pulling loose. "Honestly!"

The snag was a big old jutting stump that had washed down the river some time in the past, then bedded itself in the bottom. The boat had plowed right into it, head-on, and the current held it there. I tried pushing us loose with a pole, but all I could do was bob one corner around a little, and as the boat shifted against the main branch of the snag it edged over and lodged itself against a second one.

"I suppose this is as good a place as any to wait for *Aunt Maude*," I told her.

"In my opinion this is a very bad place to wait for anything," she said.

"Why?"

She shaded her eyes and pointed upward, where one large, bare branch of the second snag stood tall over the deck like a huge, skeletal finger. Near the top of it was a large, active hornet nest, swaying precariously with each nudge of the current-pushed keelboat.

"You know," I allowed, "I believe you are right as rain about that. This is probably a good time to see if I can put a tiller bar on that sweep."

VII

It took close on to an hour, using four of the boat poles strapped together in a cluster, binding them on with rope — or, as Spider Webb called it, cable — before I had a working tiller bar in place. And through it all that big hornet's nest swayed and shook above us, angry residents growling out from it at every motion.

If it fell, I knew we'd have a cloud of hornets on us in seconds and there would be no place to go except the river.

The girl fussed around while I worked, making suggestions and complaining when I ignored them. And she had picked up the curved sword and kept swinging it around nervously and glaring at the hornet's nest. I mentioned to her that trying to stand off hornets with a sword made about as much sense as sending chickens to church, but she didn't quit.

Finally I had a working tiller, and it was time to try my hand at keelboating. I tried to remember how Waylon and the others on *Aunt Maude* had positioned themselves, and gave it a tentative pull. The boat shuddered and swayed, grating against the snags, and the hornet's nest gyrated viciously.

"Gently!" she chirped. "Gently, please!"

There isn't anything gentle about a keelboat's sweep.

Either it sweeps or it doesn't. I put my shoulders to it and dug in my heels, swaying the boat's tail out toward the middle of the river. Timbers squealed, the snag vibrated and we began to move.

"In my opinion . . ." she started.

"In my opinion," I hissed through clenched teeth, straining at the big sweep, "it would help if you'd pick up one of those poles and push."

"I don't push," she said. "I am a passenger."

"So am I, Miss, but if the Good Book doesn't say that Presbyterians push poles in situations like this, then it ought to."

She picked up a pole and pushed, and between us we got the boat's corner to the current and she began to swing. I sighed with relief and gave her one more sweep for good measure. She cleared the snag and slid sweetly into the current, sideways.

I glanced up and saw the snag shuddering with a final shiver. And the hornet's nest parted company from it and hit the river a few feet away, mouth up and a cloud of angry insects spiralling out with murder on their minds. They saw motion and went for it and we were it.

The girl dropped her pole and started looking around for her sword, and I swept her up under one arm, tossed her headlong into the gaping deckhouse and piled right in on top of her. As I closed the little door I could hear the thumps of hornets hitting it from outside.

"Get off me!" she fussed.

"Get out from under me," I told her. "I'm busy."

"I can't. You have your knee in my stomach." She struggled, pushing my leg away.

"Quit that. The only thing keeping this door shut is me. Hold still and behave yourself." I was astraddle her, then, on my knees, and I raised as high as I could so she could slide out of there.

"How long do you intend for us to remain in here?" In the darkness of the stuffy little box, her voice was harsh with suspicion.

"As long as it takes for those hornets to go away."

"And how long will that be?"

"I haven't the vaguest idea."

I don't know what she was thinking about, there in the dark together like that, just the two of us alone in the wilderness, floating down the river on a keelboat. But I know what I was thinking about.

I was remembering the time Uncle Earl and I found the bee tree out in the woods — way out past where we were allowed to be at that age.

He had been watching bees work around a baneberry thicket.

"I bet if we'd follow the bees we'd find a treasure," he said. "A pirate treasure, for sure."

"Bees don't lead to treasure," I told him.

"Now you don't know that for sure, Zack," he scolded. "Why, I bet some bees build their hives right where Indians and pirates hid all their diamonds and gold. I bet that's why most people never find secret treasures, is because they don't think to look where the bees are."

So there was nothing for it except that we had to follow those bees and find their hive. But when we did, it wasn't in a pirate cave. It was in a hollow stump, up near the top . . . as big a hive as you ever saw.

"I bet that stump is just bulging with honey," Uncle Earl decided. "I heard folks on the river will pay a dollar a pound for good comb. Or maybe it's five dollars a pound. Let's see how much of that we can get."

"We're going to get stung," I reminded him.

"Bees never sting folks that look them right in the eye," he assured me. "Everybody knows that. A person that just walks right up like he owned the hive, and looks the bees

71

right in the eye, why, he can take all the honey he wants and they don't mind."

"I don't think that sounds right, Uncle Earl."

"Well, it *is* right. But don't worry about it. I'll get the honey. You just help me carry it home. I bet between us we can carry home a hundred dollar's worth."

So we went and looked over the stump, and sure enough, it wouldn't be any great trick to shinny up there and get plenty of honeycomb . . . as long as the bees didn't mind.

I was looking at it, waiting for Uncle Earl to start climbing, when there was a thrashing in the thickets alongside. I couldn't see what was in there, but it made a fearful noise and suddenly Uncle Earl came running out of the thicket, pointing back. "Zack, there's a bear in there. A real big one. I bet it's here for the honey."

I was ready to make tracks right then, but he stopped me. "I'll tell you what, Zack. That's an awful fierce bear in there, but a fellow that can't outsmart a bear has got no right to honey money. So here's what we'll do. I'll go in and tend to that bear while you get as much honey as you can out of that hive. Just remember, look them right in the eye and don't let on that you're scared of them."

"How are you going to tend to a bear?" I wanted to know.

"The very same way. I'll just look it right in the eye and tell it to behave itself, then I'll lead it away far enough so it won't notice you taking the honey. Bears aren't any smarter than bees. Everybody knows that."

I came out of that scrape with about three pounds of comb and some good bruises from falling off the stump, and I was sick for ten days from all the stings I got. But Uncle Earl did all right. I remember thinking later, though, that he was wrong about one thing. Bees are a lot smarter than bears. They don't hold still long enough for a body to look them in the eyes.

I had been thinking about Uncle Earl a lot lately. There

was something about the offhand way he decided not to go with me when I left New Albany . . . as though it wasn't any big thing and he'd just think about it later. Of course, Uncle Earl had never been keen on westering the way I had, but we had talked about it from time to time and I had thought that when I headed out he might tag along. I guess that was habit from all the years. It seemed as though, looking back, I was usually the one who decided which direction we were going and what we were going to do. Uncle Earl was the one who decided how far we would go and what would happen when we did.

Him just deciding like that, in that offhand way, that I should go ahead and start west and maybe he'd be along later . . . well, it just didn't fit too well.

And that whole business about Captain Webb's keelboat. Why did Uncle Earl decide after I had gone that I needed to be picked up by a keelboat? There was the business of Frank Kingston's bounty, of course, and that had come up after I was on my way. So he might have been taking a hand to help me out. But why the keelboat? I'd never known him to have any dealings with keelboaters. And why on earth had he told Spider Webb that I'd pay three hundred dollars to get down the Ohio to Cairo? He knew I didn't have three hundred dollars.

But then, when we first followed those bees, we didn't have any honey, either. But maybe Uncle Earl knew all along that we would.

After a time the hornet's nest drifted away, bound down river on its own separate course, and the hornets went with it. We came out on deck and the first thing I saw, looking off upriver — the keelboat was floating backward again — was another vessel just coming in sight around a distant bend. It was too far away to make out, just a dark dot on the sun-dazzled water, but it looked good to me. We hadn't found anything decent to eat on the pirate boat, and the dried meat, hardtack and dried berry-bark in my pack on Spider Webb's boat had begun to seem like a feast.

And I had been worrying about my horse.

I went forward to the sternpost, hauled the tiller and began sweeping. Sedately, the keelboat swung in the current, first sideways, then finally floating forward as a civilized boat should. Then I looked ahead for a likely place to pull in to shore. A few hundred yards away, on the right bank, a cove opened and I manned the sweep to head us toward it.

The girl peered ahead at our course, scowling. Then she turned. "In my opinion, you are not steering straight with the river. We are heading for the bank."

"That's right," I explained. "There's a boat back there and I want to pull over and wait for it. I think it's Captain Webb's keelboat."

"Why do you want to wait for it?"

"Well, so I can get on it again. I'm supposed to be his passenger."

"If you get on that boat, who is going to steer this one?" She seemed suddenly troubled. "How am I going to get downstream?"

"I guess you can get on Captain Webb's boat, too. There's enough room."

"But my passage is paid on *this* boat, not that one. And I don't have any money. Ezra has all of our funds."

"Neither do I, to speak of. But we'll work something out." What was it that Spider Webb had said, when he told me the rules aboard *Aunt Maude?* "Do you know what salvage is?" I asked her.

"Of course I do. Salvage is the act of mercy of setting a lost soul back on the course of redemption . . . the fulfillment of the divine promise through intervention . . ."

"That's *salvation,* for God's sake . . ."

"Of course it is for God's sake. Charity of the highest sort,

74

a mission worthy of the most devout . . ."

"You sound just like your brother."

"You don't know my brother."

"I think I'm beginning to. What I asked about is *salvage!* As in: 'anybody that finds salvage gets an equal split of the proceeds.' That kind of salvage."

"Oh," she said. "You are speaking in purely secular terms. I suppose salvage is anything of value that one might find aboard a wrecked or grounded vessel. Something like that."

"That's what I thought. How about flotsam? In secular terms, please."

"I'm not sure." she furrowed her brow, thoughtfully. "I think that would be things like cargo or wreckage that are found floating on the water. As opposed to jetsam, which would be things washed ashore. Why?"

"Just a notion," I said. "Uncle Earl sort of left it to me to figure out how to pay for this trip."

Working the sweep, I guided the boat toward the cove, an opening in the bank of the river where little willowed banks shielded flat water beyond. "Go forward and watch the water," I said. "Tell me if it looks too shallow. I just want to stop, not run aground."

"All right." But she hesitated, staring back upriver. "In my opinion, that boat approaching us is not a keelboat," she said.

I was concentrating on navigation and didn't look around. "Why do you say that?"

"Because if it is a keelboat, it is afire. In my opinion, that is a steamboat back there."

I looked around then, and she was right. The boat was much closer than the first glimpse I'd had, and its plume of dark smoke was clearly visible, streaming upriver on a westerly breeze. A two-deck double sidewheeler, coming fast under a head of steam, it seemed to take up the whole right side of the river.

"We had best get out of the way," she said.

I agreed, changing my mind about the cove. But looking back, I realized that I wouldn't have time to swing across into the clear current. And if that steamer was going as fast as it seemed, its wake would toss the keelboat around like a cork in a rainspout. I didn't want a wreck to deal with. I had other ideas for this boat.

So I hauled the sweep again and headed for the cove. In there behind the cut bank, we would be shielded from the wake. It would be a nuisance getting out again, but it was better than being overrun by a river volcano. The big riverboats had driving rails and sturdy bottoms, and from what I had heard a lot of their captains didn't hesitate to overrun lesser craft if they got in the way.

Sedately, swaying her backside like a temptress as I hauled the sweep, the keelboat edged into the cove.

"Go right a little," the girl called. "I think it's deeper over here." Then, "Quick! Turn left! There's a log!"

I felt it rumble the entire length of the right-hand rail as we sideswiped it, and a snag projecting from it grabbed the burned-out hole there and brought the boat to a skidding, turning stop. But we were in the cove then, behind the sheltering bank.

The girl was nowhere in sight. I ran to the front and knelt at the rail. She was about five feet out, just getting to her feet in chest-deep water, spitting and sputtering. A cloud of bottom-mud spread around her, turning the turgid water brown, and the top of her head was caked with mud, clear back to that silly bun. She must have gone in head first and straight down.

"Are you all right?" I asked.

Dark eyes hot enough to shape horeseshoes flashed at me. "I am not!" she advised me. "Why on earth did you do that . . . stop like that?"

"I couldn't help it. We hit a snag."

"Well, you can stop laughing this instant and give me your hand!"

"Why don't you wash off your hair before you come aboard. You really are a mess."

"Oh!" she fumed at me, then splashed water on her head, patting it and looked at her hands. "Oh, gracious!"

She began fumbling with her bun and I said, "Let me know when you're ready. I'll help you out."

I walked over to take a look at the snag, then back to the stern to drive a pole into the bottom and lash it to the post. I didn't want us drifting aground.

From the river came a distant thumping, sluicing sound that grew in volume, and beyond the willows the steamboat came in sight. I was very glad that I had pulled out of its way. That big boat was going full-steam and not about to stop for anything. It was tall and elegant, with bright-painted trim and polished fittings, and the wheelhouse was a good forty feet above the water. Big sidewheels drove it, moving water with enormous ease, and its bow wake was a high froth that became crashing waves as it passed, battering the cutbanks, showering through the willows.

There were people at the rails, strolling the decks, gazing casually here and there . . . elegant people who probably were involved in serious travels but appeared to be simply enjoying an outing.

They passed so close that I could see faces.

As the noise receded and the waves lapped at the toes of the willows, I heard the girl calling me.

I was deep in thought as I walked the length of the little keelboat to help her aboard. I had guessed wrong about the bounty man, the tracer I had left atop a ridge a long way back. I had assumed he would go back to New Albany and report to Frank Kingston there to collect his claim. But that

77

wasn't how it was at all. One of the faces on that steamboat, right there at the rail, was the bounty man.

And the face next to him was Frank Kingston.

VIII

Girls look better with their buns down.

She had taken me at my word, and let her hair down and washed it. And while she was at it, apparently she had taken a bath and done her laundry. That severe dark dress with its funny little collar was laid out on the forerail to dry in the sun, along with her lace-up shoes and dark stockings.

When I hauled her up onto the deck she was wearing a shift and holding a petticoat in front of her, and she wasn't the least bit bony . . . just trim. With her hair down, her face seemed softer and her eyes rounder. If she'd had that hair pulled back any tighter it would probably have broken her nose. She looked just a whole lot better this way.

I guess I was staring because she blushed . . . a sort of pink on blue, like embers among the chillblains. It went clear to her forehead. "In my opinion," she said, flustered, "a gentleman who leers is no gentleman."

"I never said I was a gentleman," I pointed out. "I said I was a wheelwright. And you said you were a Presbyterian, but right now you don't look so much like a Presbyterian as you did before."

"A lustful heart is the devil's playground," she said. "Turn your back, please."

"I will in a minute. First, I think we should be properly

79

introduced. My name is Zachary Scott Frost. Generally folks call me Zack."

"How do you do. My name is Priscilla Lawrence. You may call me Miss Lawrence."

I offered to shake hands and she almost did, then she grabbed that petticoat tighter and backed away. "Now please turn your back."

"Oh, all right!" I turned away and headed for the stern. I guessed we might as well get back out in the river where we could look around . . . maybe just drift the boat past the willows and pole it down there. Sooner or later, Spider Webb should show up. Keelboats don't go anywhere except down the river.

I unlashed my anchor pole and pushed the boat off its snag, then began easing it out, setting the pole against the sunken log when I could. With a solid object to push against, I could really get my shoulders into it.

Priscilla sat on the front rail in her wet shift, washing the mud off her feet and waiting for her clothing to dry. Not that I was looking at her, of course. I never said I *wasn't* a gentleman, either. But I *was* getting it through my head that on a keelboat a fellow ought to keep an eye on his passenger. That comes under the category of duty.

Slowly, as I began to puff and sweat, the boat eased back toward the channel cut. When we were clear of the log I poled the front end sideways, bringing it around to where I could use the sweep.

I had just got it lined up with the cut and laid down my pole when white smoke puffed in the brush behind the little cove and a ball whanged off the roof of the deckhouse beside me, howling as it ricocheted away across the river.

The blast of the musket was followed immediately by another and by the sounds of men yelling and pushing through brush. Priscilla Lawrence yelled, did a backroll on the front deck and scampered for the shelter of the deckhouse, grabbing up the curved sword as she went. I gave the sweep a heave that started us moving, then shifted for another push.

They were coming through the brush across the cove, only sixty or seventy yards away, a dozen or so men brandishing various implements—hayforks and bludgeons, sickles and knives . . . a couple of them had muskets. They pounded out onto the bank of the cove and splashed into the water, heading for us. I dropped the tiller long enough to grab a musket from our stack and spray them with water. I don't know whether I hit anybody or not. Then I went back to the tiller, bulling right and left on its bundled grip, hauling that sweep around with a will that made the boat sway like a chorus dancer at Curly Joe's as its front rail crawled toward the cut.

They were coming on, meaning to come over the stern rail as soon as they could get to us. But when there wasn't any more shooting, Priscilla came out from behind the deckhouse and came to perch precariously on the rail, her bare toes curling over its edge. With one hand on her hip and the other waving that sword around she shouted, "Behave yourselves! God is watching you!"

One of those nearest, a huge bull of a man straining to breast the water and carrying a sickle, grinned as though he had seen an angel and renewed his efforts. Whether or not there had been anything on board that he really wanted before, there was now.

"Miss Lawrence!" I snapped, hauling the sweep desperately, "Get out of the way!"

The big man was ahead of the rest, powerful legs pushing him through the water. He reached for the sweep and missed it, and came on toward the stern deck. We were moving, but not fast enough. I eased off on the sweep, drew my revolver and pointed it at him. "Get back! Just back off!"

He was beyond listening to reason. He reached for the deck rail and I fired, just as his feet slipped in the mud and he went under. One of those behind him howled and grabbed a bleeding shoulder.

"All of you, back off!" I yelled at them.

They had stopped where they were, shouting curses at me but not wanting to face the gun. As the keelboat edged further away I put the pistol in my belt and resumed the tiller. I hauled it around, started to reverse the sweep, and Priscilla screamed. A huge hand came from the water below the rail, grabbed my ankle and flipped me on my back as though I were a snared chicken.

Well, hell, I thought. This imbecile is worse than Buster Stuckey. I reached for my revolver, but he still had hold of my ankle and he twisted, flinging me over.

Before I could recover, he came over the rail, vaulting it on great arms, water streaming from him. He still had his sickle and he grinned happily as he raised it over me. Then something flashed in the sun and he jerked back, dropping the sickle. With a slow look of awful accusation spreading across his face he stepped back again, holding a bleeding hand.

". . . and don't come back ever again!" Priscilla finished whatever she had been saying. He glared at her, ducked and his foot missed the rail. He toppled backward off the boat, his impact raising a prodigious splash.

It got my feet under me and gave that tiller a swing like I never had before. The sweep thumped into the big man and his weight added leverage to pull. The keelboat edged past the willows and into the eddying shallows of the river. Two more sweeps and we were away, heading downstream.

"If you had been more efficient in getting us under way," Priscilla snapped at me, "We could have avoided that."

She turned on her heel and stalked away toward the foredeck, the shift twitching around irritated but no less interesting hips and thighs.

I gulped air into my aching lungs, shrugged and concentrated on the river, pausing only briefly to kick a bit of salvage over the side. It was a large severed thumb, and I didn't see any reason to point it out to Priscilla. It would only have upset her.

We had gone only a hundred yards or so when I heard someone hallooing from across the river. I shaded my eyes. A man stood on the far bank, waving at me. He held the reins of a horse, and even at that distance he looked familiar. I glanced back upstream. We were fresh out of steamboats, so I hauled the sweep and started to see if I could get across.

We passed him in mid-stream, floating jauntily down the river sideways, the boat trying to decide whether to respond to me or the current. I saw him shake his head and shrug, and a few minutes later I saw him riding along the high bank, heading for wherever I might make landfall.

I knew him by then. It was the helpful crewman from Spider Webb's boat. The one who called himself George. And the horse he was on was my roan.

We had gone another mile or so before I got the keelboat across the river and slung a line over a stump just out from the left bank. By that time Priscilla had her clothes on and was Miss Lawrence again, bun and all. And I felt like I was really getting the hang of keelboating. The trick I had tried had worked. I'd angled that boat across and looped a floodwater stump set out from the bank. Then as we came abreast I ran back with a pole and plunged it down alongside the right rail just as the boat began to swing on its line. Then when the boat was still I lashed down the pole and there we were, snug and secure.

And when I looked up, George was there on the bank, in the saddle of my roan horse. He touched his hat brim, then caught sight of Miss Lawrence and tugged his hat off his head. "How do?" He said. "Taken on a passenger, did you?"

"She was already a passenger," I told him.

"Nice goin'. What was you doin' over at the right bank? Keelboats generally don't ever go near the right bank along here. It's dangerous."

"We noticed. Who are those men? Hijackers?"

"Democrats," he said. "I expect you are wonderin' how come I have your horse. Well, it's because Captain Webb sent me to find you. He said. 'George, you go find that fella an' if he's still alive you look after him 'til we get there.' That's what he said. So I said, 'I sure will, Captain Webb, but how am I supposed to catch up to him because if he's still alive I expect he's gone on down the river by now.' That's what I said. And he said, 'That's his horse yonder, messin' up my deck. You take that horse and find him.' That's what he said. So I taken the horse an' here I am an' here you are with Captain Pearce's keelboat an' a passenger. How do, Ma'am."

Democrats?

"I got your pack here an' I been noticin' your vittles," George added after several deep breaths. "Looks like better food than what Waylon slops out on *Aunt Maude*."

With the keelboat secured, then, we went ashore and George built a little cook-fire while I unpacked food and said a few private words to the roan—something to the effect that if he ever even thought about kicking me again I would personally shoot him in the head.

Then George had to hear all about what had happened on the pirate boat after I got there, so I told him. And Miss Priscilla Lawrence was all ears, too.

"That awful noise was powder blowing up?" she repeated. "In my opinion, Mr. Frost, you could have done dreadful damage with that."

"That was what he had in mind, Miss," George assured her. "And I helped. I played out that line just like he said.

Man, that sure was pretty! It looked like the whole boat was goin' to stand on its side. I told Captain Webb later that we ought to try that again sometime."

Webb had put *Aunt Maude* in at a cutbank after the fight, and his men had picked up a pair of Buckeye Pearce's hoodlums. It turned out that somebody had told them that there were valuables aboard *Aunt Maude*—some unusual cargo of some kind—but they didn't know exactly what it was. At any rate, that was why *Aunt Maude* hadn't showed up so far. They had been busy chasing overboard pirates.

"George," I asked him, "How much would you say a keelboat is worth?"

He shrugged. "Big one in good shape, maybe a thousand dollars, more or less."

I indicated the battered and scorched pirate boat bobbing on its leash. "How about this one?"

"I don't know. It ain't so big, and it's pretty beat up. Word is that Buckeye has been draggin' that boat upriver and floatin' it down for two-three years now, piratin'. But maybe it'll bring six-seven hundred. You claimin' salvage on it?"

"No. I'm claiming it as flotsam."

"That ain't flotsam," he pointed out. "That there is a keelboat. Flotsam's stuff you find floatin' down the river."

"That's where I found it, and that's what it is. Flotsam."

"I don't know," he said "Captain Webb . . ."

"Captain Webb told me that every man keeps his own flotsam. He said that's a rule. He also said that Spider Webb's word is good on this river, so I guess he'll stand by what he said."

George scratched his head. "You got a point there, all right. Who do you plan to sell it to?"

"I plan to sell it to Captain Webb, if he'll buy it. Otherwise I'll lash it on to the front of his boat and he can deliver it to Cairo for me."

"I don't think he'll want to . . ."

"It's up to him," I said. "Buy it or deliver it. I'm his passenger and this boat is my flotsam."

One thing about my Uncle Earl. I never knew him to go back on a promise to anybody. What he promised, he always delivered, even if it half killed me.

Priscilla Lawrence was glaring at me across the little cookfire. "I hope you aren't overlooking your responsibility, again," she said.

"What responsibility?"

"Your responsibility to your passenger. I have paid for passage down this river, on *that* boat. I intend to be delivered at Vicksburg on *that* boat . . . as agreed."

"But I'm not going to Vicksburg, ah . . . Miss Lawrence. I am only going as far as Cairo. At that point I intend to divest myself of all responsibilities not of my choosing . . . including keelboats, bounty hunters, unpaid fares and other people's passengers. From there I intend to go where the wagons go."

"Where's that?" George asked.

"I don't know. Yonder."

I guess I was expecting an argument from Priscilla Lawrence, but she didn't say anything more. Yet as the lazy hours passed, waiting there by the river, I saw her looking at me several times, and her expression was odd . . . as though she were turning some idea over in her mind, looking at it from various angles, exploring it. As though, if she decided on whatever she was thinking about, by the time anybody else ever knew what it was, it would be too late to do anything about it.

In midafternoon the string of barges crept by—the same ones I had seen before—and there was no mistaking the brown and yellow pair of bright new wagons that sat proudly on their decks, big wheels stacked beside them. With those wheels set to their axles and canvas on their bows, those would be tall, proud vehicles. Vehicles for the yonder places. Wagons to take folks as far as they wanted to go. Wagons born to see new sunsets.

Slowly, ponderously, the barges paraded by. Nobody ever bothered barges on the river. They were big and slow, but the cargo they carried was consigned cargo, not easily taken or easily cashed in. And they carried deck guns. Keelboats might have problems with river pirates and the like. Barges didn't.

I watched them pass, and when there were far down the river I was still seeing the colors of those overland wagons. And when I turned, Priscilla was looking at me again, in that strange way.

The sun was on the river when George got to his feet and pointed. "There she is. *Aunt Maude.*" He grinned, splashed out to my flotsam and tied a cloth to a pole to start waving them in.

IX

When Uncle Earl left home, he was eighteen years old and his life had gotten a little complicated. There was a river gambler named Claude Ledet who had been hanging around Hardinsburg, and Ledet considered himself a fast man with a card or a gun. Nobody questioned that very much. Enough of the hill folk had lost their summer wages to him at the gaming table that there wasn't any doubt of the former. And there were some dark rumors from upriver that kept anybody from wanting to try him at the latter.

But then one morning Uncle Earl came home with a pile of money in his poke, and Ledet started spreading the story that Earl Donovan had cheated him at cards and that he intended to kill Earl Donovan on sight.

Far out as our place was, I guess it was a while before the story got to us. But when it did, Uncle Earl strapped on his pistol belt and set fresh loads in his Dragoon. "If I wait," he told me, "that thieving Frenchman will be out here directly and it's hard to tell who might get hurt."

"Will you face him?" I asked.

"If he'll face me, I will," Uncle Earl raised a brow. "But I don't believe he will. If you learn how a man plays the cards from his deck, then you know how he'll play other games as well. I took his money because he cheated at cards . . . and because he thought nobody else could do that better than he could. I don't expect he'll change."

"You *did* cheat him, then?" I asked.

He nodded. "The second time he dealt off the bottom I palmed a pair of treys and let him win. So he did it one more time and I kept two deuces and let him deal me another, then I cleaned him out with his own hand."

"Then that's why he wants to kill you. You made a fool of him."

"He made a fool of himself. And I believe he will do it again if he has the chance."

"They say he has killed men."

"That may be," he said, "but I expect he dealt from the bottom to get it done."

It was hard on Ma—and hard on Pa, too, I think—when he said he was leaving. But he was of an age then, so they just wished him well and watched him on his way. I would have gone with him, but he wouldn't have it. "You grow yourself a little more, Zack," he told me. "I'll be in touch."

A week later we heard that Claude Ledet was dead. They'd found him hunkered in an ambush pit alongside the river road, with an empty gun in his hand and a bullet hole in his head. And I kept thinking of the last thing Uncle Earl had said. "I couldn't have won his money if he hadn't cheated on the deal. I expect I won't be rid of him unless I let him cheat on the shoot."

Uncle Earl didn't come home again. But we had letters from him now and then. One was from back east, posted out of Hudson Bend, New York. He said he had come to the conclusion that all the treasures to be found in the east already had been found, and all the money to be had already was had, but he had some notions how it was done.

The next we heard he was in Ohio, doing well in the land business and thinking about how to franchise pack trains to the territories.

Later he was in Virginia, and he didn't say why he was there except he expected to come into some money soon.

And it was the next season that the letter came from New Albany about Carl Froehner's wagon works and how it was time for me to take up a high trade. Of course, Ma had written to him, too, so he had kept abreast of what I'd been doing. And the chance to make wheels for overland wagons just fit right in for me.

Though he didn't say so, we all just assumed that Uncle Earl was associated with Mr. Froehner — in business with him or working for him, or something. I was a little surprised when I got to New Albany and found out that Mr. Froehner had never heard of Earl Donovan. But he *was* looking for wheelwright apprentices with experience, and he *did* intend to vest a few good craftsmen with journeyman status, so everything worked out.

In those short seasons that I was with Carl Froehner, I hardly ever even saw Uncle Earl. He was around, now and then, and I'd look him up occasionally. But New Albany was a growing and lively town, and we didn't have much contact.

Uncle Earl never had steady employment, though he never seemed at a loss for sustenance. He frequented Curly Joe's and a few other houses, and when he was hitting a good streak he was always easy enough to find. When his luck ran bad he would disappear — sometimes for weeks — and then show up again with a stake and start all over.

I always had the impression that most of what he was doing in New Albany was waiting and listening. Having a river and a rail, and being the most westerly point of any real civilization at the time, New Albany gathered news the way a dung beetle gathers horse manure. I recall Uncle Earl saying one time that information was like sand, blowing around in the winds grain by grain. "Zack, everybody knows something," he said. "Some people know a lot about some things, but most people just know a little about a lot of things. And you see, the less folks know about anything, the more they enjoy talking about everything. So if a fellow wants to know a lot about something, he has to listen to everything anybody says about anything, and the best place to do that is a place where everybody knows a little about a lot of things . . . and that place is New Albany. That's why we're here."

"*I'm* here because Carl Froehner is building overland wagons here," I corrected him. "You know that. You sent for me."

"Yes," he said, as though he had just remembered something, "What I meant was, that's why *I'm* here. Naturally you don't have anything to do with that."

"With what?"

"With why I'm here. Zack, you ought to pay attention. Paying attention is what I've been talking about. You ought to pay attention to what folks say."

"Why?"

"So you can tell me."

You'd have to have grown up with Uncle Earl to understand how ordinary a conversation that was.

I thought about what I'd heard folks say lately, and recited some of it . . . something like, "Well, Tom Baskin said if you soak hickory dowel in coal oil for a month you can double the strength of it. And Mr. Morton Cope allows that Adam's last name was Cope. He says the scriptures bear him out on that. And Harry Milam believes that if you boil down wild onions the elixir will cure colic and kill ants. And Milt Downey says . . ."

He looked sad and shook his head. "You're not gettin' the hang of it, Zack."

". . . says his brother Tim is an escort for gold shipments across the Mississippi, bound for Philadelphia."

"Now you're gettin' the hang of it, Zack."

Sure, I got the hang of it. It was like a puzzle that had a thousand parts and maybe five or ten of them fit. Like when I read about the gold shipment that had been lost out in the Missouri Plains—that was in the newspapers, of course—it sort of reminded me of what Milt Downey had said about his brother, Tim. Then a few months later, when Milt Downey was talking about how his brother had disappeared somewhere out west and the family didn't know where he was, that reminded me of those other things. I remember laughing at myself about that. Zack, I told myself, you're getting as bad as your Uncle Earl.

When we were little kids running the ridges, just most anything could set Uncle Earl off on a treasure hunt. He'd find a scar on a tree trunk and decide it might have been a sign carved there by pirates so they could come back and find whatever they had left . . . wherever they had left it.

One time we found a little stone cairn off in the hills. It had been there long enough that the rocks were leached out on top, and their dark undersides said they had never been disturbed. The cairn pointed toward a breakaway ridge, and sure enough, we found another one there, pointing to a ledge where we found scrapings done by human hand. Uncle Earl was fit to be tied, he was that excited. At the base of the ledge was a rockfall and we worked half a day moving rocks, uncovering a little dug-out hole like a shallow cave.

But what was in it was no pirate treasure. It was just a little pile of age-rotted furs with an Indian pipe lying on top of them. And when Uncle Earl lifted a corner of the old furs, there were old, dark bones beneath.

I was all for taking the pipe, but Earl said no. His eyes were as big as saucers. "Leave it there, Zack," he said. "It belongs to him."

The thing was, not all the trails that Uncle Earl thought he had found were false. We followed some real trails in

92

those days, and we found some things. They just never turned out to be treasures. But Uncle Earl never stopped trying.

And when I ran into Uncle Earl in New Albany and mentioned about Milt Downey's brother Tim being disappeared, he got that old look about him and I knew he was off again . . . following trails.

It's how he always was. Pa had said it would take an act of God to change Earl Donovan, and I guess he was right.

I never heard much more about the Downey business. Sometime after all that Milt Downey left New Albany and nobody seemed to know where he had gone. And a few days later Uncle Earl joined me for dinner at *Eats,* which was the name of Gabriel Polucci's place down the street from the Froehnerworks, and happened to ask whether I had heard anything about some of Frank Kingston's men asking around about Milt Downey. Which I hadn't.

By that time Mr. Froehner was on his death bed and I wasn't paying much mind to anything except trying to get wagons finished. So if there had been more to hear, I don't guess I would have heard it.

But I was thinking a lot about things like that as we worked to lash two keelboats together, end to end, like one long boat with sweeps at both ends, and set off down the Ohio River toward Cairo.

I was thinking about that because of what I had wangled out of Spider Webb. A man can learn a lot in the process of selling a burn-damaged keelboat as flotsam.

I had learned, for one thing, that not all the cargo on board *Aunt Maude* belonged to Spider Webb. Some of it was consignment goods, including a couple of crates that belonged to one Earl Donovan and were consigned for delivery to that same Earl Donovan at Cairo.

Also I had learned about that three hundred dollar passenger fee. The deal was, Spider Webb had agreed to watch for Earl Donovan's nephew along the way and, if he found him, to take him aboard as a passenger—whether he wanted to go or not. It had been explained to him as an act of mercy, Spider said, because I had a bounty on my head and needed some protection. They had agreed on three hundred dollars with the understanding that they would split the proceeds between them when I was delivered at Cairo. A hundred and fifty for Spider Webb and a hundred and fifty for Uncle Earl. All I had to do was come up with the money.

"I don't intend to pay you three hundred dollars," I assured Captain Webb while we were lashing the front beams of the two boats together.

"A deal's a deal," he glared at me.

"But I don't intend to ride the rest of the way on this boat," I told him. "I shall ride on *that* boat, along with my horse, my gear and my passenger. In return for the pleasure of *Aunt Maude*'s company, I shall allow your crewmen to walk my rails when they pole. At Cairo, when you pay me six hundred dollars for my flotsam, I will return to you one hundred and fifty, which is what you would have received anyway."

"But I promised to split with . . ."

"Don't worry about that. If Uncle Earl wants a hundred and fifty dollars from me, I think he should come to me directly for it. Don't you agree?"

Webb shook his head. "A deal's a deal. I don't feel just right about this."

"Don't worry about it," I reassured him. "It's a family matter from here on . . . between me and Uncle Earl."

It was something else Pa had said. "Earl Donovan may never change his ways, but he *is* family, and it wouldn't be right not to at least *try* to break him of sucking eggs."

When we put into the current, Spider sent George up to man the front sweep while Waylon worked the rear one. It was an odd-looking craft that wended its way westward along the big river. Especially when they ran the poles. *Aunt Maude* was a big keeler, full-loaded and handsome as keelboats go. My flotsam was a little keeler, battle-scarred and burn-pocked, not carrying much of anything except a tall sorrel and my gear. But when the poles were at work it was the flotsam that was hauling the load, and not the other way around.

Priscilla Lawrence had listened intently to the entire transaction, visibly approving of the part of it that let her remain a passenger on the flotsam, visibly confused at a lot of the rest. Late on the second day of tandem travel she came to where I was sitting on the deckhouse sharpening my tools and leaned there beside me.

"You have a strange sort of family, in my opinion," she observed.

"You mean my Uncle Earl? He's all right. He just doesn't generally plow the same fields as other people."

"So I gather," she said. "But I wonder if he is the strange one, really, or whether it is his nephew whose furrows tend to wander."

I looked up from what I was doing. "What on earth makes you say a thing like that?"

"Oh, I don't know," she shrugged. "One draws observations from one's experiences."

It was always Pa's belief that, to a woman, having the last word on a subject is a thing of great value. One way they manage that is to phrase that last word in such a way that there just isn't any reasonable response to it.

The problem with that is, once the last word has been said, either the subject gets changed or the conversation ends. I guess I was feeling a little lonely, out there in the wooly wilds on a river that only stopped where yonder started, but I didn't want her to stop talking to me. So I changed the subject.

95

"Speaking of family, I surely do hope that your brother Ezra is safe and sound and in good health."

"It is charitable of you to hope so," she admitted.

Actually I didn't hope any such thing, except for her sake. I didn't know Ezra from Adam's off ox, and from what little I had heard of him I judged that his wagon was probably running on less than four wheels. But it kept us talking.

"In my opinion," she continued, "Ezra is capable of looking out for himself. Ezra is beloved of the Lord Almighty and . . ."

"He's what?"

"He has a . . . an arrangement with God. They take care of each other . . . so to speak. What I worry about is that he—Ezra, of course—may not know where I am and may be distraught with worry for me. He is not used to having the responsibility for another person, you see."

As far as I could see, that ended that subject. But she wasn't through talking. "Ezra has his calling, you see," she said.

"His calling?"

"Yes. God has given him a ministry upon earth. But the Lord works in mysterious ways, and after our parents were gone Ezra was required to sell the house to raise funds for the needy. So when the Reverend Cooley came along and Ezra decided to go to Vicksburg, I insisted upon going with him . . . against his better judgment, I'm afraid."

"Then you have a calling, too?"

"Not at that time, though I had waited for it to come. I have never doubted that somewhere there is a ministry for me, if I recognize it when I see it. God can provide suitable work for any person who is willing to undertake what He suggests."

"Well, don't worry about it," I said. "I'm sure your calling will come one day."

"Oh, it has. In God's good time, it has."

96

"Oh?" I lost track of what I was doing. "When?"

"The day before yesterday."

"You got your calling two days ago?"

"I believe so. Possibly I was slow to recognize it, because it is hardly your typical ministry. But I believe the Lord has made it quite clear to me . . . in His mysterious ways."

"Oh. Well, congratulations. Does that mean you won't go to Vicksburg?"

"Probably not." She tipped her head, raised one eyebrow and studied me like she was candling eggs and I had a lumpy yolk. "As I understand it, someone has offered a large sum of money to have you, ah . . . killed."

"Frank Kingston doesn't like me," I nodded.

"Is that why you are emigrating?"

"I'm not emigrating. I just sort of always wanted to see what's out there, so I decided to go and take a look."

"But you have a trade."

"A craft. I'm a wheelwright. Actually a little more than that. I'm a wagonwright. But people understand better when you say wheelwright."

"You don't look like a craftsman."

"What do I look like, then?"

"Actually, you look a lot like a bear. But that isn't what I mean. Just from appearance, I would have judged you to be a . . . I don't know, maybe a policeman, or a pirate, or a gambling person . . . or possibly a soldier of some sort. And the way you evicted those horrid people from this boat . . ."

"That just sort of happened."

"And fought off those Democrats . . ."

"Democrats?"

"That is what Mr. Bullard called them."

"Mr. Bullard?"

"Your friend. George."

"Oh."

"And the way that Mr. Bullard and Mr. Gibbs, and even that Captain Webb . . ."

"Mr. Gibbs?"

"Your friend. Waylon Gibbs."

"Oh, sure. Waylon."

"The way they all seem to . . . well, sort of follow your lead when you insist . . ."

"I haven't noticed that."

"Of course you haven't. In my opinion, it is your nature to be obtuse."

"To be . . ."

"At any rate, I believe the clue is in the Scriptures. Possibly Second Samuel, though I don't remember exactly. But it has to do with champions of the Lord's work. Something to the effect that they shall arise from among the innocent and be beset on all sides by the wicked, and by this sign we shall know them, and we are to attend and nurture them and walk with them in their way."

Somewhere along the way, quite a ways back, I had lost the drift of whatever she was talking about, and I decided it was best if I fess up to it. "I don't know what you're talking about," I said.

She pursed her lips and nodded, patiently. "Precisely. Well, I believe there is little room for doubt."

"About what?"

"About my calling. My mission." She sighed. "But I must say it isn't going to be easy."

"What isn't?"

"To attend and nurture you and walk with you in your way. In my opinion, Mr. Frost, you are going to require a great deal of divine guidance."

I finished sharpening chisels, then put them away and went to find Spider Webb. "How far are we from Cairo now?"

He looked at the river banks and at the sun. "Eight days

. . . maybe ten. Why?"

"How far cross-country, by horseback?"

"I don't know. Half of that, maybe. Why?"

"I need to exercise my horse. Put me off at the next bend, Captain Webb. You have my flotsam as security. I'll look you up in Cairo."

X

While Webb's crewmen poled us toward the bank, I saddled the roan and laid back the lashing straps on the saddle skirt. Priscilla Lawrence came from the deck house and stared at what I was doing.

"Mr. Frost, are you going somewhere? Why are we putting ashore?"

"I told Captain Webb I need to exercise the horse," I explained.

She hovered around suspiciously while I got the roan ready to ride and watched crewmen run out planks when the double boat sidled up to the bank. I led the roan ashore, then looped his reins to a willow limb and walked back aboard. My gear, all packed and ready to go, had been lying by the deckhouse with a blanket thrown over it. I picked it up, stepped across the deck, tossed it ashore, pulled in the planks, took a running start and jumped. On the bank I turned and waved to Webb. "Take her out, Captain! Thanks for the ride!"

Polemen pushed off and the flotsam drifted toward the current, *Aunt Maude* swinging sedately along behind it. As I picked up my gear for lashing to the saddle I heard an angry shout from the river.

"Mr. Frost!" She stood at the near rail, angry fists on her

hips. "You are making this very difficult!" For a second there I thought she was going to abandon ship, but a couple of crewmen blocked her with crossed poles.

I swung aboard the roan, and I think he was so glad to have solid ground under him that it never crossed his mind to try to throw me off . . . which he usually did on first mounting. And I was just as glad as he was. I had never thought I'd be so relieved to get off a keelboat.

But I had things to do and places to go, and all the yonder I'd dreamed about was waiting out there someplace. I was free and unencumbered. I had salable skills and a stake to begin. I also had a bounty on my head and an enemy somewhere ahead of me, not to mention Uncle Earl — who might be anyplace by now, but wherever he was I knew he was cooking up something that I would be better off without. But even with all that, I was satisfied. Somewhere ahead, about where yonder started, tall wagons were assembling and folks were looking west, and I wanted to be there when they rolled out.

Many were the nights I had lain awake, thinking over and over the words Caleb Tucker had said. Words about the west. Words that carried visions in them and that spoke directly to all I had ever wanted from life.

Maybe Priscilla Lawrence was right, about one thing. Maybe I *was* the odd one in my family. Maybe I was an adventurer. As peculiar as Uncle Earl could be, still every path he followed had a reason to it and every goal he dreamed about was something a man could put in his pocket. Not so with me. If a trail led yonder, that was reason enough to take it. The goals I dreamed about were as elusive as smoke on the wind. But they were glorious. To be there and to see, to know the song of the breezes and the taste of the land in those places where the sun went down.

At any rate, I was on my way, with a good horse under me and a wide world ahead, and the last thing I needed was to be anybody's ministry.

That roan was ready to run and I was ready to ride. I snugged my hat tight, put heels to him and we started putting miles behind us. I held west by the lowering sun, skirting the hills and the deepwoods regions, drawing away from the river. The land here was new to me, but not much different from what I was used to, either around Hardinsburg or up at New Albany. In the way that most lands have, it was deceptive. Mostly unsettled except for an isolated farmstead here and there, generally untraveled except for the occasional itinerant peddler and a few less social folks, the land seemed wild and hostile. By comparison, the river seemed placid and welcoming. And in that was the deception. It was really the other way around.

In these days of restless movement, of shifting settlements and great migrations, the river was the artery of life. It attracted people. And where there are people, there is trouble. For a man with a horse and a gun, the wild lands are far more friendly.

Though spring was upon the land and the days were warm, the chill of night still clung to the high lands like a last breath of winter. I built my small fires in secluded places where a cutbank or a ledge could trap the heat. And though I slept well, I kept an eye on what was about me. Even the remote places, in wild lands, can sometimes bear surprises.

Above the Ohio, the Wabash was running full and I followed it northward until I found a ferry at Wickes Cross, then angled south of west away from the settled areas, preferring the solitude of the ridges and the solemn loneliness of the old Shawnee forests.

I thought for a time of cutting north, heading for St. Louis. Once across the Mississippi up there I would have been into the Missouri wilds and once and for all free of any last entanglements upon me. No more Frank Kingston, no more bountymen on my trail, and no more Uncle Earl with his endless schemes and maneuverings. I thought about it. But I was short on cash money and short on supplies, and it would be a comfort to have the money Spider Webb had promised for the flotsam boat. And to collect, I would have to stop over at Cairo.

Four hundred and fifty dollars would be enough to see me across Missouri in fine style, and enough left to set up shop at Westport or Independence or Olathe—all places that were just names to me, but were the places where the big wagons assembled to begin their migrations to yonder.

"You're a fool to go to Cairo, Zack," I told myself. "You have no less now than what you started with." But the logic of it said to go on down to Cairo and finish my business there. I chose to follow my logic.

So I angled south of west and gave the big roan its head to put tireless miles behind us. It was good to be away and free and on my own . . . except for a little feeling I had now and then, a sort of notion that Uncle Earl—wherever he was—somehow would have known that I would be tempted to shake the dust from my heels and go off on different paths; and that he would have known that I'd decide against it, and that I'd go where he would expect me to go and be there when he expected me to be there, and no matter what private decisions I made for myself the end result would be just what he had figured on.

And thinking that, I almost turned north again until the silliness of that set in. And then I felt that he might have known how that would come out, too.

All of my life, I had known how a marionette feels, dancing on its strings. Generally it feels that it is in charge of its own affairs and making its own decisions, because it can't see the strings that are on it. But if a marionette pays attention, it will notice now and then that there is a pattern to the random things it does. And if it keeps track of things like that, it may notice eventually that its patterns invariably contribute to the livelihood of that fellow up there in the shadows with those funny-looking sticks in his hands.

The marionette idea wasn't mine originally. It was Pa's. My pa was always a man to vote when election time came, and he read everything he could get his hands on to read, and he took a keen interest in politics . . . very much the way a man trapped in a small room with a rattlesnake takes a keen interest in that snake.

But when Pa talked about marionettes he was talking about the taxpaying public. When I thought about marionettes it usually involved Uncle Earl, and the marionette was me . . . shooting anvils and robbing honey trees.

There was cargo on *Aunt Maude* that belonged to Uncle Earl. I hadn't the vaguest idea what it was, but I was pretty sure that when the keelboat landed at Cairo Uncle Earl wouldn't be very far away.

I had no idea where Frank Kingston had gone. I had seen him on that passing steamer, but all that meant was that he wasn't in New Albany. For all I knew he could have been bound for St. Louis or New Orleans . . . or hell, for that matter. It bothered me that the tracer had been with him. Somehow or other, that hadn't worked out the way I'd hoped. But it didn't necessarily have anything to do with me.

But Uncle Earl did. I made up my mind then and there that whatever he was up to, I wanted no part of it. I would complete my deal with Captain Webb, make Uncle Earl do a few parlor tricks for the hundred and fifty dollars he thought he was going to get from me — and then give it to him if he really needed it. But after that, all bets were off. If he wanted to go on west with me, on my terms, I'd be pleased to have him as long as he could behave himself. If not, I'd just say, "Uncle Earl, it's been nice knowing you." And that would be that.

There is a place down there in the toe of Illinois where a road has been built, curving around boglands and winding up the slopes of facing hills to crest on a bald ridge where a body can see for miles in any direction. The road is overgrown in places and seldom traveled. Someone had told me it was once a military road, maybe built by the Spanish or French to provision some long-forgotten outpost back in the Shawnee strongholds. I followed it for a time, because it went the way I was going, and on a bright spring morning I looked out from that crest and far away, shining like a little silver thread, was the lower Ohio.

The river curved toward me on an inward bend, and a mile of it was visible as it bent back toward the south. Another day or so, I reckoned, and I would be at Cairo.

There was something on the river—just a bright speck of color—and I shaded my eyes for a better look. It was a string of barges, tiny in the distance but clear enough to the eye that I could make out the yellow and brown of the big wagons resting there. Caleb Tucker's wagons, riding down the river . . . big, handsome wagons on their way to someplace where their wheels would be mounted and their canvas tied on, where teams would be hitched to their traces and people would climb aboard.

Somewhere out there those wagons would come alive and their wheels would roll and they would take whatever roads there were that led to yonder.

Maybe Priscilla Lawrence was right about me, in a way. Maybe she understood that I wanted to be where those wagons staged up, and I wanted to see them roll out. And maybe she had the notion that I wouldn't be satisfied with that, either. Maybe it seemed to her that I would want to go with them when they went.

Maybe she was right.

* * *

Cairo was an ugly place. It sprawled and tumbled and spread around its long docks and up the slopes behind — a brawling, blustering cluster of every kind of building, all thrown together. I had seen river towns before, but never one so boisterous, so seething with the feral vitality of trade.

There were craft of all kinds along the docks, but none that I had seen before, and I wondered about the barges with Caleb Tucker's wagons. But then, looking around the town, I saw them. Cairo occupied a thumb of land jutting down between the final sweep of the Ohio and the double channel of the Mississippi where it flowed around a wooded island. Just below, the two rivers joined.

The island was a staging ground for the transfer of floating goods to road docks on the Missouri side. Pole butts and cable winches lined its banks. Tugs and push-boats, tough little vessels with blunt prows and big steam engines, worked along and around it.

The main street across Cairo went from water to water, from docks to docks. Eastward, it aligned with a wagon road on the far side of the Ohio, in Kentucky. Westward it led down to the Mississippi, emerged again in mid-river as a cleared strip across the staging island, and emerged again on the far shore, running back and away from off-loading docks and assembly yards on the Missouri side.

The string of barges had been broken up, some of them probably joined with other strings bound downriver toward New Orleans. But the ones with overland wagons as cargo rested at anchorage beside the island. I counted fourteen wagons over there, most of them blue with red running gear in the traditional manner, though two or three were of other colors — tan and apple-green were favorite colors of westering folk in that season. And clear among them were the two big Froehnervagens, dark brown beds on bright yellow bracing, the exact colors of Curly Joe's Sporting House at New Albany. Who else but Earl Donovan would steal paint from a sporting house?

I felt a deep kinship to those wagons. Maybe it was the effort we had gone to, to complete them and make good on Carl Froehner's promise. Maybe it was the satisfaction of having put one over on the receivers when they shut down the old man's factory. Partly, I think, it was a special pride at knowing the craft that had gone into their assembly.

I found a stall and grain for the roan, at a boarding stable above the river road. A bathhouse and barber cost me two bits, and dinner that much again. Like all busy towns with people passing through, Cairo was mighty proud of its goods and services.

It was still early, so I walked around for a while, seeing the town, listening to folks talk, catching up on the news. When I got the feeling that somebody was watching me I eased into a shadowed wagonway and surveyed the street from there. A lot of people were out and around in the evening hours, but I didn't recognize anyone. So I put it down to general goosiness and went on.

Uptown, away from the riverfronts, there were some decent looking hotels and I was trying to decide which one to discuss credit with when I heard a familiar voice and looked around.

Two men had stepped out of a doorway, and I knew one of them. It was Caleb Tucker. They turned toward me, intent on their conversation, and almost bumped into me before they noticed me standing there. They glanced at me curiously, started to go around, and Tucker stopped.

"Don't I know you?" he asked.

"Yes, sir." I pulled off my hat. "I'm Zack Frost. I used to work for Carl Froehner."

"Froehner . . . yes. You do look . . . ah, yes. The wheelwright. You told me about the dishing of spokes. Very impressive. Did you come down with my wagons?"

"No, sir. But I see they arrived all right. Are you pleased

107

with them?"

"Abundantly," he said. "I inspected them this morning, with Captain Rawlings . . . by the way, let me introduce you." He turned to the other man, a wide-shouldered, craggy gentleman of middle years. "Judd Rawlings, may I present Zack Frost. He's a very competent wheelwright."

"Wagonwright," I corrected, then took the other man's hand. "How do you do."

He nodded and shook.

"Frankly, I was surprised to see the wagons arrive," Tucker said. "Captain Rawlings had word that Mr. Froehner had passed away, and that the factory was closed."

"It was," I said. "But some of us thought it would be a shame if your wagons weren't delivered, so we . . . ah . . . well, we expedited the project."

"You were in on that," Tucker's cheeks twitched. "I heard a little about it from the bargeman . . . and others . . . how those two wagons were smuggled out of a court-closed facility and turned over to him for delivery without documentation. He almost didn't bring them."

"I'm sorry," I said. "I guess we didn't know about the documentation. We were damned . . . pardon, sir. We were lucky to get them finished, much less get them to the barges. We worked nights after they closed the plant down."

This time he went ahead and grinned. "Marvelous. I'd like to hear that story. Possibly . . ."

The door opened again and a crowd of people emerged onto the boardwalk. Four or five men and at least as many women. I was glancing at faces, then I stopped glancing and probably stared. She was young, maybe eighteen or nineteen, with tawny hair flowing from the lace of her bonnet, and the biggest blue eyes I had ever seen. She saw my stare and blinked, then averted her face.

"It looks as though everyone is ready," Tucker said. "We were just on our way to have a meal, Mr. Frost. If you'd care to join us . . . ?"

I found my tongue and shook my head. "I've eaten, thank you. I was just . . ."

"Well, never mind," he said, slapping me on the shoulder. He turned to the others. "This is one of the young men who rescued our wagons for us. Zack Frost, may I introduce my sons Tom and Samuel, my wife, oh, and these are the Pattersons—they'll be traveling with us—and the Holstons, and my daughter Mindy . . ."

He went on naming out names, but I wasn't listening. Mindy. I didn't think I'd ever heard a prettier name.

". . . around tomorrow morning," Tucker was saying. "We're staying at this hotel. I would like to hear about those wagons, first hand. It's very nice meeting you again. Come along now, everyone. Mr. Frost, I shall look forward to our visit in the morning."

Like a sheepdog with its flock, he had them rounded up and on their way down the street, and I was still standing there mutilating my hat and wishing I had said something intelligent to Mindy Tucker. Something memorable. Something dashing and gallant and worthy of attention. *Anything* but "How do."

The man Tucker had called Captain Rawlings hung back for a moment, looking me up and down. "You don't look much like a wagonwright," he said bluntly. "Are you good at your craft?"

"I built for Carl Froehner," I reminded him.

"Yes . . . well, what are you doing now?"

"Nothing much. Just sort of heading west. I expect I'll find work out there."

"I expect you might," he nodded. "Good evening, then, Mr. Frost." He hurried off to catch up with the rest of them.

Mindy. Mindy Tucker. Where had I seen blue eyes like those? Sometime I had, a long time before, and the memory of them was sweet and puzzling.

I walked and thought and when I got around to paying attention again I was back near where I had started, on the river road. And I still hadn't arranged a place to sleep.

I turned at a cross street, started back uptown, having that feeling again . . . like I was being watched. But now there was no one around. The street was dark and empty. The sounds and the lights were behind, on the street that I had left.

Glancing back I saw two shadowy forms behind me, walking rapidly. There was an alleyway ahead and I aimed for it, just being cautious. I'd step in there, out of sight, and let them go by. No sense inviting trouble in a strange town.

I was three steps from the dark way when a man stepped out, facing me. Even in the half-light I knew him, and there was no nonsense about the gun he held, pointed at me.

"I thought you'd show up here," he said. "I've been looking for you."

I kept my hands where he could see them. "I thought we had a deal, back there on the ridge."

"You thought what you wanted to think. In my line of work it doesn't pay to claim a bounty that isn't earned."

"In that case, I want my spokeshave back."

"Don't get smart, tough guy. I'm the one holding the gun now. I set out to collect on you, and that's what I aim to do."

I heard the other two come up behind me, felt their presence, knew they were with him. "Look," I told the tracer, "We ought to be able to work something . . ."

I never finished the thought. Something hard and blunt collided with my head, right behind the ear, and I didn't have any thoughts at all.

XI

Those blue eyes were like Yolanda's eyes.

Yolanda . . . yes. Yolanda Van Ney. Yolanda with the blue eyes like morning sky. Yolanda with the braids that were heavy ropes of spun gold. Yolanda with the homespun dresses that couldn't hide the brand-new curves beneath them. Yolanda . . . twelve years old and suddenly becoming a woman while I was still just an awkward kid getting bigger and more puzzled every day.

Those blue eyes never looked at me much, but I looked at them. They didn't see me now, but as they came closer I felt I was drowning in them. Then they just slid away and I was coughing and strangling and someone unpleasant was telling me to wake up.

"Douse him again," someone else said. "Hell, Charlie, did you have to half kill him?" A familiar voice. The tracer.

"He's a big one," another voice said. "I don't take chances."

Cold water sluiced over me and I choked and struggled. I couldn't move.

"He's coming around," the tracer said. "He's alive. I guess you won't need me any more."

"Stick around," the first voice growled. "You might learn something." I should know that voice, I thought. I shouldn't ever forget . . .

The cold water soaked my clothes, but my face and shoulders were hot. I managed to get my eyes open and saw glowing coals, a bed of them in front of me, glowing and wavering in their heat.

"He's come to," the tracer growled. "Now pay me, Mr. Kingston. I've done what I said I would."

Kingston.

"Don't be in such a hurry," Frank Kingston said. "The fun has just started."

I turned my head away from the glowing coals and a hard hand crashed against my jaw, turning me back.

"Hello, Frost," he purred. "You've caused me too much trouble."

I was bound hand and foot, tied to a chair, and the chair had been tipped forward so that my chest rested against the kiln-brick of a smithy forge. The coals in its bowl were cherry red, just right for shaping wagon tires.

"Just so nobody can say I didn't ask you politely," Kingston said, "where is my horse and where are the letters?"

"You don't have a horse," I said, groggy. "We traded."

The hand rocked me again, this time from the other side. When I could see again I looked up at him. Folks had always talked about what a handsome man Frank Kingston was. Those that didn't know better had always been impressed by his chiseled features. But now he didn't look quite the same, up close.

"Did I do that to you?" I wondered.

His hand went to his flattened nose and his eyes burned with the light of the forge coals. "You're going to wish Slater had just shot you outright, Frost. I'm going to see to it. I'll ask you one more time. Where is my roan horse, and where are those letters?"

"And I'll tell you one more time, you don't have a roan horse. I do. And I don't know about any letters."

The cold smile that spread across his face was as ugly as anything I ever saw. "I'm going to enjoy this, wheelwright. I'm going to enjoy it a lot." To someone behind me he said, "Loose his right arm. Carefully. Keep a good grip on him, he's strong."

I felt hands at work on my bonds, hard hands holding my arm. I let it hang limp until the bonds fell away, then put all my strength into it and tried to swing. I think I lifted the one holding me off his feet, but that was all I could do.

"Hold him," someone spat. "Damn it, hold that arm!"

Two of them had me by the arm, bringing it up and around. Beyond Kingston, the tracer backed away. "I want no part of this," he said. But the rest ignored him.

"I wonder what kind of wheelwright you'll be after today," Kingston said. Then to the others, "Put his hand in those coals. Hold it there."

Now come *on*, Frank, I thought, noticing how giddy I was from being hit on the head too much . . . you're carrying all this *way* too far. But when the skin of my fingertips started to sizzle and my hand was inches from those coals, it was time to get over being giddy.

A boy raised up in the Knob Hills the way I was, cutting fencewood from the day he can swing an ax, has a good bit of meat on his bones. In my time I had cleared about a hill and a half and grubbed out the stumpage so we could plant corn.

I hollered like a boar hog turning on hounds and surged against that fire-pit with every bit of strength I had. My elbow came unsprung and gouged into the belly of the man on my right, my shoulder bumped the one on my left and we went over in a rolling tangle, all three of us and the chair.

It was a good cane chair, but not that good. As I rolled across one of them, trying to get at the other with my free arm or my teeth, the chair disintegrated into snapping withes and splinters, and my feet came free. I rolled again, into the shadows beyond the lamplight of the shuttered smithy, and a bullet whanged off a crib brace beside me.

"Don't shoot!" Kingston yelled. "We don't want company!"

"Then you handle him yourself," the tracer snorted, and I heard footsteps and a slamming door.

One of the men who had held me was writhing on the dirty floor, making bleating sounds. But the other was coming at me, a burly man but cat-quick in his movements and crouched low like a wrestler. I scuttled back behind the bins and he came on, boxing me into the tight space there. He paused, put a hand to his boot and came up with a slim knife that glittered in the forgelight. I backed away, around the corner of a little alcove that was in darkness, and felt around for a weapon. I'd had in mind a piece of strapping or chain, but what I found was a wrecker's sledge, sixteen pounds of iron on a hickory handle. It was too big to swing in the alcove, so I headed out of there and met him at the corner, swinging sideways. I don't know what he might have expected, but it wasn't a wrecker's sledge. The big hammer flung his arm aside as though it hadn't ever been there, and squashed into his chest with a sound like a dropped melon. Even before he fell, I knew I had killed another man. I went right over him, looking for Kingston.

He was just coming into the bins, reaching to draw his gun, and I bulled into him with a shoulder, carrying him back toward the forge. He fell, rolled and came up again, but his gun was gone. I raised the sledge, then dropped it and backhanded him across his face. He stumbled backward and I followed him, going on pure rage. He braced himself and swung a hard fist that made me see little bright things all around. He was as big as me, but always having other folks around to do his dirty work for him had cost him the edge. I blocked his next swing and punched him in the

114

gut, then doubled over and brought a backhand clear up from the floor. It lifted him, turned him completely around, and he staggered and bumped into the firepit. He tried to catch himself, but his hands hit the coals and he flung his arms wide and fell face-down in the cherry-red glow.

I hope to God I never hear a scream like that again.

I grabbed his collar and dragged him out, sizzling and smoking. He collapsed to the floor, gibbering.

"Go home, Frank," I told him. "Just go back home and don't ever bother me again."

The tracer was gone. One of Kingston's thugs was whining on the floor and the other wouldn't ever whine again. His chest was crushed.

When I got out of there and looked around, it took me a while to get my bearings. The place was a shuttered smithy sitting on the rise above the high docks on the Mississippi side, remote and private. I must have been out for a while, to have been brought this far.

I ached all over, but by the time I had walked back to the boarding stable where I left the roan, I felt better. I washed up at the rainbarrel and looked in on the roan, then I went through my gear piece by piece, item by item. My tools were there, all as they should be. My Dragoon was there where I had left it and I made up my mind that I would keep it at hand from there on. I'd need a holster, but that wouldn't be hard to make. I held the sleek revolver in my hand and it was a comfort, just the way any good tool is a comfort to the hand that will use it.

I went through pack and saddlepockets, bedroll and duffle, and everything was where it should be and there wasn't anything there that didn't belong. And that was puzzling. Frank Kingston had been serious about wanting me to give him some letters. But I didn't have any letters, or have the vaguest idea what he was talking about.

Idly, just because it was a thing I was accustomed to

wondering, I wondered if Uncle Earl might happen to know something about all that.

I was putting things away when the hostler came in, yawning and carrying a lantern. He looked at me and his eyes widened.

"You look like somebody dropped you in the river and forgot to fish you out," he said. "Things lively uptown to-night, are they?"

I pointed up at the loft. "Any objection if I throw my roll up there tonight? I didn't get myself a bed."

"If you got beat up like that over a bed," he decided, "then beds must be in high demand. No, I don't mind. You've paid for a stall. Loft privileges come with it. Just don't snore too much, and don't bother Homer."

He started to turn away. I asked, "Has anybody been around here being curious about my horse or my gear?"

"No, not that I noticed particularly." He paused. "There was one feller . . . but he just looked in and went on his way."

"What did he look like?"

"Dandified, I reckon. Took him for a riverboat gambler or a sportin' house man. Regular banty rooster type, with a curled mustache. Somebody you're lookin' for?"

I nodded. "If you see him again, don't trust him. Lock up your valuables. Bolt your women-folks in the root cellar. Don't take your eyes off him and don't listen to anything he says."

"Sounds like he's somebody you know," he said.

"I ought to. He's my uncle."

Pa used to say the only way to be sure that Earl Donovan was around was to look after supper and see if his plate was empty. He'd say something like that and it would get Ma started, and she'd tear into him for always accusing Earl of being sneaky. Then his eyes would twinkle and he'd say, very sober-faced, that he did *not* consider Earl Donovan sneaky. He considered red Indians sneaky, he'd say. And ferrets, and politicians and pickpockets and the widow Smith. But not Earl. No, he'd say, the word sneaky fell woefully short of applying to Earl Donovan.

Well, I wasn't going to go looking for him. If he had "looked in" here, as the man said, then he knew where to find me. More than likely, he had probably known where I was every minute since I got to town.

The more I thought about that, the madder I got. When I finally got to sleep, in the loft, I could have shod a horse just by spitting nails at his feet.

First light through the open bay brought me awake, and I wished for a few minutes that it hadn't. I was so sore I could barely move. A strained shoulder, as best I could tell . . . bruises in a dozen places, a cut lip and an eye swollen partly shut . . . burns on my right hand, not deep but painful . . . and a knot behind my left ear. Had there been choice in the matter, I wouldn't have cared whether school kept or not.

But it was time to be out and about. So I hauled myself down from that loft, looked in on the roan, washed up at the rain barrel and put on my one and only set of clean clothes. The shirt I'd been wearing was torn and bloody and one of its sleeves was burnt. I cleaned my boots with it. When I was dressed, I got out the Dragoon Colt and put it in my belt. When I had time, I would make a holster for it from a piece of tanned hide. It would be more comfortable to carry that way. But I didn't intend to be without it again.

I built a little fire in the hostler's grate and made coffee in a tin cup, and when he showed up I shared it with him.

"You look like you been through a stampede," he observed cheerfully. "First time in Cairo, I take it?"

"I'll heal," I said.

"Sleep good, did you?"

"Fine . . . just fine."

"I fretted half the night, wishin' I'd told you about Homer. Hope he didn't bother you none."

"If he did, I didn't know it. Who's Homer?"

He looked relieved. "Good. Couple of times, fellers sleepin' here have tried to kill Homer, just for gettin' cozy. But he can't help that. It's his nature."

"Who's Homer?"

"He's . . ." he looked around and pointed. "Here he comes, now."

Winding down from the loft was about the biggest snake I had ever seen. It was at least eighteen feet long, and its head was the size of a wagonjack. It slithered to the floor, staying clear of the stalls, and came toward us. My hand went to my gun.

"Best mouser I ever had," the hostler said. "Feller I traded him off from called him Annie Condo, but I like Homer better. Don't see many rats around here any more. Cats either, for that matter."

Or sleeping customers, I decided.

"Hate to rush off," I said, "but I have things to do."

I never held with snakes, nor saw any the size of Homer. I didn't say so, but if I came back and my horse was gone, I was going to check Homer for lumps.

The sun was just pinking the roofs of buildings uptown when I got to the hotel where the Tucker party was put up, and I expected to wait. But Caleb Tucker and Captain Rawlings were out on the front porch, smoking cigars and watching the day start. Tucker waved at me as I crossed the street, then both of them stared at me.

"I assume you came by those markings honestly," Tucker said, not assuming any such thing but just being polite. Rawlings didn't comment. He just looked at me with eyes that didn't miss much.

"I didn't have much choice in the matter," I explained.

"But it's done now."

"Did you win?"

"I must have. I'm still here."

The less said about any of that, as far as I was concerned, the better. I knew I had killed a man the night before, and the fact that he and two others were trying to kill me . . . or worse . . . didn't do a whole lot to make me feel any better about it. I wasn't raised up to be opposed to killing. In the Knob Hills, folks that raise their kids that way wind up outliving their kids. But I wasn't raised to favor it, either. And I never had.

Tucker seemed curious, but Captain Rawlings just nodded. "That's answer enough for a man to give," he said.

They were on their way to breakfast, and I went with them. It was a clean little place run by an Irishwoman who served up good portions of potatocake and side meat, and coffee you could stand a spoon in.

What Caleb Tucker had in mind was to hear about how his wagons were built and what they would stand, and how they got out of the factory after Carl Froehner died. So I told them that, and answered their questions.

Captain Rawlings, it turned out, was a wagonmaster who had been west past the shining mountains with an emigrant party, and now was organizing another party to go again. The Tuckers would be in that party, assembling at Westport in three weeks. Others were coming by other routes to join them there.

"We expect to have forty wagons," Tucker said. "Maybe more. And it might interest you . . . Captain Rawlings knows of at least six vehicles that will be with us, that were built in your shop."

"Carl Froehner's shop," I corrected. "Froehnervagens, he called them. I may have helped build some of them."

"Yes. We believe, though, that my two wagons are the only ones painted brown and yellow."

I just nodded and looked away. "Curly Joe chose the colors, sir. We did the best we could."

With coffee in hand, then, I turned the subject to what I had in mind. "Mr. Tucker, I mentioned that I am on my way west. I wonder if I could travel with your party . . . at least to Westport?"

He glanced at Rawlings, who shrugged. He looked back at me. "I would have no objection, I suppose, if you want to ride along with the wagons. Certainly you would be a welcome addition, Mr. Frost. But my . . . ah . . . party is not traveling with the wagons to Westport. We just stopped here to inspect them. We will take more comfortable accommodations through Missouri, and meet them there."

"But your wagons? . . ."

"Oh, I've hired drivers to take them across Missouri. Two young men who applied to me some time back. But as I said, I have no objection if you would like to accompany them. You mentioned that you have a horse, and I can see you have a gun. I'm sure you would be welcome out there."

"In Missouri," Captain Rawlings breathed, as though he were talking to himself, "the more guns the better."

I stalled around for a while, hoping for a chance to stare at Caleb Tucker's daughter again. But soon there was no more excuse for stalling so I went my way and they went theirs. I didn't even find out when they were leaving, but I did learn that if I wanted to ride along with the wagons, I should be at the west bank docks across the river when the wagons were barged across from the island, which would be whenever their drivers showed up. Tucker had handsome six-up teams of draft horses waiting across there. He would add more animals at Westport, he said. Animals were cheaper out there than back here.

I turned toward the corner of the street leading downtown, walked a short distance, then stopped and drew my gun. I was barely aware of the gentry skittering off in all directions when I did it. My whole attention was on the horseman in the street ahead, and his eyes were fixed on me.

But he didn't make any hostile moves. Instead he raised a hand and walked his horse forward. It was the man Frank Kingston called Slater. The tracer.

"You can put that away," he said. "I'm finished with this business."

I hesitated, but when he made no move to raise a gun I slid mine back into my belt. I didn't think he was going to shoot me down right out here in the street in broad morning.

"You did a job on those men," he said. "I hung around and went back after you left. I took two of them down to find a doctor. The third one was dead."

"You'd have been better off if you'd kept our deal before," I told him. "That way you'd have been paid."

He grinned, the cold grin of a man who knows no humor except the pain of others. "I've been paid. In full. Kingston had the cash money on him. I took my bounty. It was due."

"Then why are you still here?"

"I just wanted to see what you look like in daylight. Now I see, I guess I should tell you. Kingston will find a way to kill you, Frost. If it's the last thing he ever does."

I shrugged. "I don't know why. That's a good horse I own, but it isn't worth that."

"Next time you see him you'll know why," he chuckled. "Look at his face . . . if he gives you the chance. Then you'll know."

He didn't say any more. And when he turned and rode away, down the road toward the Kentucky docks, he never once looked back.

XII

I spent two more days just waiting around in Cairo, but I didn't see anybody else I knew. A steamer had docked, up from New Orleans and bound for St. Louis, and the Tucker party was on it when it resumed its journey. If Frank Kingston and his busted-up henchman were still in town they kept to themselves and I never saw hide nor hair of them. And although I had about half expected Uncle Earl to turn up, he never did — though I was sure it was him that the hostler had seen.

I took a room at a hotel — not one of the fancy ones uptown, but a clean enough place without too many rats running loose. I didn't really mind the rats. After seeing Homer, I had taken a liking to rats. And I surely wasn't going to sleep in the stable loft any more.

I thought seriously about moving the roan, but that stable was the best-tended one I saw. There was a high-grass pasture out behind, and the hostler was good about turning the stock out to romp and graze each day. And he didn't skimp on the oats.

The first day when I went back to check him, the roan was out in the pasture and there were slats kicked loose in his stall. But he was in good shape and fine spirits, and the hostler didn't remark about the whole thing. I assumed, therefore, that after first meeting my roan and Homer got on all right.

But I would like to have seen that first meeting . . . from a distance.

I went to a bank and used the roan as collateral to borrow a few dollars for hotel and stable costs, and to buy a few things I would need. At a saddlery I paid a dime for a span of good tanned hide, and borrowed the saddler's tools to make a holster for my Dragoon. I fit the leather to the gun wet, holed it with an awl and stitched it like a glove along the backside, then brought a belt-loop over and stitched that. When it dried and I oiled it, the Dragoon rode in it like it was meant to live there, and it was a comfortable weight on my hip.

Then I found a smithy where the trade was brisk and the jobs stacked up, and I stood in the doorway looking around. One smith and two devils worked the place, and at the time they were all busy making chain. The smith glanced up when he saw my shadow. He squinted at me. "If you're sellin' something, go away. If you're buying, the stock's yonder by the wall. If your animal needs a shoe, go find a farrier, for we have none here, and if you have smithin' to be done it'll wait its turn like all the rest." He spat in the direction of his glowing forge and turned back to what he was doing. He had good hands, and had never missed a lick all the time he was talking. I decided I liked him.

"There's a smithy across town," I said. "back from the north docks, all by its lonesome. Do you know who tends it?"

He didn't look up. "Nobody tends it, far's I can tell. Not anymore. Poley McGovern used to, but he took to runnin' with river trash and he don't even open now 'cept once in a blue moon. That's why I'm buildin' this here bear twine instead of fittin' tires onto Dr. Humphrey's coach like I promised to do."

123

So that was how Frank Kingston had come to have a smithy at his disposal. He just found one empty and walked in.

Dr. Humphrey's coach was nowhere in sight. But its wheels were . . . proud, lacquered wheels standing near the door, waiting for attention. They made my thumbs itch.

I looked over the available tools, stoked up the forge, selected strap-iron from neat bins and went to work.

Several times over the next few hours the smith paused to stare at me, a little puzzled at why I was working in his shop, but he didn't make an issue of it. I measured and cut, heated and hammered, welded and trimmed until I had four bright new iron tires assembled. Then one by one I set the wheels up on a hub pivot, roll-heated a tire for each one at the forge, doing it the way I had learned at Carl Froehner's shop, and sweated them on, cooling them in place in a trough of cold water, sealing the iron to the rims. Each hot tire melted away the wax I had painted on the wooden rim, but the sand I had mixed with it remained and the cooling tires tightened down to bed it into the wood like teeth. Dr. Humphrey might wear out those tires, but he would never throw one off.

I was finishing the last of the wheels when the smith said, beside me, "That's good work. Damn good."

"Yes," I agreed. "It is."

"You plan to stay on here?"

"No. I'm just passing time. Waiting for a keelboat."

"Sorry to hear that. Well, I'm obliged, and I'll pay you what that work is worth to me. If you see anything else around here that you'd like to fix, just have at it."

Just for passing time, wheelwork always did beat lying around. It was pleasant there in the smithy, the sweet breezes of spring wafting through to mingle with the honest scents of sweat and hot iron, the music of hammer and anvil, bellows and tempering through. And from the open

124

front of the shop I had a clear view of the bend of the Ohio and the docks along its bank. The day's work had ironed the kinks and bruises out of me, and I felt good.

As evening shadows spread across the river below, I put edges on a pair of scythes and repaired a hand auger, then I washed up, put on my coat and started uptown. But it was still early for sleep, so when I passed a place with bright lanterns flanking its open doors and the sounds of mild revelry coming from inside, I went in.

It was a long, breezy room with a plank bar along one side and maybe twenty tables with chairs. The men, thirty or more of them, were an easy mixture of what I took to be locals and travelers. The voice of the place, that I had heard from outside, was the pleasant discordance of a dozen conversations against a background of fiddle music played by a black man in a raised box off in one corner.

I glanced around, and several men glanced at me, but I saw no one I recognized, nor any hostility in their glances. I was just another customer.

Bottles and jugs of spirits lined the back counter behind the bar, but most of what was being served up was tall mugs of yellow ale, cool as though stored in a cistern and hoisted a keg at a time. I bought a mug and leaned back against the counter, just relaxing and listening to the good sounds. And remembering blue eyes.

About the time I first started noticing Yolanda Van Ney — when I was about twelve — was when Pa started explaining to me about the birds and the bees, as he called it. Actually, except for introducing the subject, he didn't talk about birds and bees at all. But he did talk about bulls and cows, and how calves came to be, and then he went through the procedure again with regard to dogs, and he really hadn't told me anything I didn't know until he explained about analogies. And that led him off into more comfortable subjects, so that what we wound up talking about was

125

James Fenimore Cooper's writings. The upshot of what he wanted me to know, though, was that little girls turn into women because God took a look at the world after he had created Adam, and found it sadly lacking in both beauty and confusion. With Eve, He added large measures of both. Most of the dumb animals didn't give a flip about that "two by two" business, he assured me. Wolves and eagles tended to pair off and stay that way, but they were exceptions.

But what the Lord had in mind for men, he explained, was women . . . one for each. And He tried to insure that arrangement by giving the fair sex the means to keep a man warm by night and aggravated by day, so that he wouldn't have time to think about wandering off. And all of that was so the babies would be tended and raised up in righteous ways.

God, he said, isn't going to think much of a man who goes after women the way a bull goes after cows and never gets the hang of cherishing.

I felt kind of sorry for Pa right then, he was trying so hard to civilize me when what he really wanted to talk about was James Fenimore Cooper and Washington Irving. And all the time Uncle Earl was sitting on a cider keg over in the corner of the barn, shaking his head and looking inscrutable.

Later on, Uncle Earl took it upon himself to straighten me out about the ways of the world. He was fourteen then, and thus possessed all knowledge.

"Think of life as a millpond," he said. "What you want to be is the stud duck."

I never managed to be Yolanda Van Ney's stud duck, though she was a major player in some of my more improbable dreams in those days. I was Romeo to her Juliet. I was Lancelot to her Guinevere. I was Natty Bumppo to her Alice. The problem was that while I was dreaming, Yolanda was fishing. She cast her hook for Will Fedders, who was seventeen and a man grown and was farming eighty acres of good bottom land. By the time I had begun molding the skills of courtship, Yolanda was Mrs. Fedders.

I took a vow of celibacy and practiced it faithfully until I was at least thirteen.

All these years, and I still hadn't decided whether I preferred Pa's version of the birds and the bees, or Uncle Earl's. But just seeing Mindy Tucker's eyes — so like Yolanda's eyes — had me seeing Natty Bumppo visions again.

With darkness, activities along the waterfront had slacked off. And the tavern crowd had grown. The various conversations were a pleasant mosaic of sound set to the fiddling of the black man in the box, only bits and pieces coming clear above the general babble.

One of those pieces, right next to me, came across as discordant.

". . . necessary to go among the sinners and be as one with them," a voice intoned, strident with imbibery.

"They stray that they may be brought to righteousness," another answered. "Which shall we try now, brandy or whiskey?"

"Whiskey," the first answered, matter-of-factly.

"A bit of wine for the stomach's sake," the second agreed. "Innkeeper, two whiskeys!"

"And none of your rot-gut!" the first demanded. "We'll have the honest nectar, if you please! Good lord, but these ruffians do crowd."

I hadn't been crowding anybody, but I edged over to give the complainer a little more space and turned to see who I was favoring.

They both wore austere black coats with stained collars, and their black hats sat squarely atop their heads. The nearest one was a distinguished-looking gentleman with silvery curls around his ears and the eyes of a squawking jay. The one next to him had features I had seen before, but not on that face. I stared at him, making up my mind, then nodded. "Are you, by any chance, the Reverend Ezra Lawrence?"

He hesitated, wondering if he knew me, then nodded. "I am. But I don't believe I know you."

"Well, you don't. But I have wonderful news for you. About your sister."

He blinked. "Who? Oh, yes. Priscilla. Yes. What is it?"

"The pirates didn't rape her."

"They didn't . . . sir, you are being absurd. Nobody would . . . my sister? Priscilla?"

"She escaped unharmed and in excellent voice. She should be along directly."

Somehow it seemed to me that the news didn't thrill him the way it should. I had the impression that, far from being distraught about her, he had sort of forgotten her entirely.

"I knew you'd be pleased," I told him, wishing I hadn't brought it up at all.

"What is this about your sister, Ezra?" the jay-eyed one interrupted. "I thought that was all behind you."

"I thought it was," Ezra said, still staring at me. "You must be mistaken, sir. My poor sister was captured by river pirates. I'm sure she is dead by now, God rest her soul."

"You told me that Captain Pearce would . . ." the jay-eyed one insisted, to Ezra.

"Hush, Phillip," Ezra snarled. "If what this . . . gentleman says is true, then the Lord be praised, Priscilla is still alive."

Jay-eyes hiccupped. "And we're out a hundred dollars." He swallowed his whiskey raw and in a single gulp, then licked his lips. "The wages of sin," he said. "I'll take another of these, my good man. Then I believe I shall try the rum."

Ezra scowled at him. "The Reverend Cooley is preparing himself for our Vicksburg ministry," he explained. "Possibly we have tried to learn too much in too short a time."

"What did he mean, you're out a hundred dollars?"

His eyes shifted, became furtive. "Ah . . . I suppose he meant the funds that we paid to a keelboat captain—in all good faith—to deliver my dear sister and myself down the river."

"In that case you're only out fifty, because your sister is due for delivery on that very boat."

The Reverend Cooley, swaying slightly, turned jay eyes in my general direction. "They are bringing her here? That bla'gard promised . . ."

"Shut up, Phillip!" Ezra hissed at him. Then he smiled for my benefit. "The Reverend Cooley is suffering for his piety, sir. Pay him no mind."

"Are you fellows Presbyterians like your sister?"

"Well, actually, no. The Reverend Cooley believes that a mission of mercy such as ours is most productive if it is ecumenical."

"Denominational trappings play hell with the profits," Cooley chirped, banging on the bar. "More rum over here, if you please! And some brandy!"

The stink of charlatan was so strong about them both that it was like a real odor. As little use as I had for Priscilla Lawrence, I decided she was far and away better than her brother.

"How did you get here?" I asked, casually. "To Cairo, I mean."

"By horseback," Ezra shrugged. "The Reverend Cooley received two fine horses for us, from a pious gentleman anxious to promote the Lord's good work."

"I guess he was nearby with the horses when you were thrown off the boat?"

Ezra's eyes shifted again and he gulped down another shot of whiskey. If he was going to try to pace the Reverend Cooley, I thought, he'd have to hurry. Cooley had a long head start.

He didn't answer my question, but it didn't matter. I'm like the fellow with the blisters on his hand. It doesn't take me long to look at a horseshoe. These two had a scheme in mind, to fleece the believers in the town of Vicksburg, and they had decided that Priscilla's presence there would be a liability. Among her other irritating qualities, she probably was honest.

The last thing I needed right then was to go to worrying about Priscilla Lawrence. But I couldn't help feeling sorry for her. With a brother like Ezra, well . . . she'd have been better off with boils.

It seemed pretty clear to me that they had paid a river pirate to take her off their hands.

"It is a real inspiration to me," I told them, "to witness with my own eyes two men of God who have the courage of their convictions."

The Reverend Cooley hiccupped and tried to look pious. Ezra just blinked.

"What I mean is," I said, "it must be difficult to do what you are doing . . . to actually immerse yourselves in the realms of iniquity, to personally sample the sins of the fallen, so that you will know first hand what you must deal with."

"Terribly difficult," the Reverend Cooley belched. "But someone has to do it."

"I suppose you will want to sample the . . . ah . . . the carnal sins as well," I suggested.

Cooley braced himself with both hands on the bar and leaned toward Ezra to whisper, "What did he say?"

"I think he wants to know if we want a woman," Ezra whispered back.

Cooley turned toward me again, balancing himself carefully. "One does what one must in the service of the Lord, sir. Just lead the way."

I sidled closer to them, speaking low and earnestly. "I feel

130

a call," I said, "to do something to be of assistance to you. I happen to know someone here who is . . . well, all I can say is that she can provide you both with a truly memorable experience."

Ezra's eyes glittered. "Both of us?"

"Both of you."

"Where is she?"

"When you have finished your inspection of the devil's concoctions here, I will lead you to a place I know, where you can spend the night. She will come to you there when she's ready."

"What's her name?" Ezra asked, beginning to pant.

"Oh, she's been called various things, but you can call her Annie if you like. Annie Condo. I promise you, you will never forget this night."

It was just a notion that had popped into my head, but it did seem like the thing to do. It was the least I could do for Priscilla Lawrence, to sort of make amends for the fact that I had no intention of being her mission.

And Homer might enjoy having somebody to sleep with.

XIII

They'd have plenty to preach about in the days to come, those ecumenicals. Their bout with the devil there in that tavern in Cairo left them in sad shape. The Reverend Cooley passed out on the floor before we left, and I had to carry him over my shoulder clear across town. Ezra wasn't in much better shape, but his feet were working so all I had to do was navigate him.

I didn't see any sign of Homer, but I figured he was around someplace. I got them stowed in the loft, and when I climbed down carrying their coats and hats they were both snoring. I removed all the money from the Reverend Cooley's coat and put it in Ezra's coat. Then I hung up the Reverend Cooley's coat and hat, had a look at my roan, and started to leave when I heard a sound and turned. Homer had appeared from somewhere and raised his head above stall level to look at me with gimlet eyes four inches apart.

"You just stay away from me," I told the snake. "Go on, now, go to bed." I pointed at the loft trap. "There are warm folks up there for you to cuddle with."

He just stared, so I backed off and headed for the door. When I looked back he was heading for the loft, great coils seeming to swallow the ladder as he slithered upward. "Offer them an apple," I said over my shoulder. "They'll appreciate that."

Above the waterfront, Cairo had gone hushed and dark. The hour was late, and I was tired, and tomorrow would be another day. I had just reached the hotel when I heard the distant scream. Thin and lingering, from a long way off, it was just the sort of sound a man might make if he woke up to find three hundred pounds of snake in his blankets.

At dawn I climbed out of a lumpy hotel bed, washed, shaved and dressed, and went out and bought myself a breakfast. From there I went back to the smithy and spent some time fitting end-irons to a set of wagontrees.

There was a chill in the air that made it pleasant to work with forge and anvil, and before I noticed it several hours had passed. The sun was high when I stepped out to look at the river docks.

Aunt Maude and the flotsam were there, snugged alongside a trade dock. I scrubbed at the smithy's rainbarrel, put on my coat and hat, and shook hands with the smith.

"If you come this way again," he said, "there's always work."

George was on the dock, keeping an eye on *Aunt Maude,* and he grinned when he saw me. "Captain Webb's lookin' for you, sir," he beamed. "Said if you showed up, that he'll be back directly."

The flotsam's deckhouse opened and a bunned head appeared.

"Might ought to watch your step with the missy," George cautioned. "She didn't take it kindly, you abandonin' ship like you did."

She came out of the deck house and stalked across to the near rail. "So there you are," she pointed out.

I tipped my hat. "Yes, mam. Good morning."

"Good morning yourself, Mr. Frost. I've been intending to have a word with you." She stepped up on the rail and from there to the dock, and I caught her hand to keep her

133

from falling.

When she was on the dock she pulled her hand away quickly and looked me squarely in the eye. "In my opinion, Mr. Frost . . ." she noticed the extra coat and hat I was carrying ". . . What do you have there?"

"These are for you, Miss Lawrence. I met your brother Ezra last evening, and relieved him of these. I thought you might want to return them yourself, when you find him."

"You took his hat and coat?" she stared at me. "Why did you do that?"

"I thought it might ensure his staying around here until you could find him and rejoin him on his quest for God's abundance. Frankly, Miss Lawrence, I don't care much for your brother and I care even less for the Reverend Cooley. But I didn't want him to leave here without you. And I don't think he would leave without his coat — and what it contains."

"What it contains?"

I handed them to her and she dug around in the coat's pockets, her eyes going very wide. "My word!"

"Yes, mam. There is a lot of money there, for a fact. My guess is, it includes the proceeds from your house, as well as the proceeds from a pair of horses that your brother and his partner bilked some poor farmer out of — or stole, possibly — and the proceeds from whatever other shady dealings those two have been involved in."

She was gaping at me. "Ezra? I . . . I don't believe it."

"It doesn't matter whether you believe it or not, Miss Lawrence. I know it for a fact . . . that and more besides, which I don't think you would like to hear."

"Did you hurt my brother?"

"No, mam. Matter of fact, I saw him safely to bed — him and his friend — with the best mouser in Cairo to watch over them in the night. Then I kept this money, for the purpose of handing it over to you."

134

"What . . . what am I supposed to do with it?"

"That is entirely up to you, mam. But if you want a suggestion, I recommend that you keep it firmly in your personal possession, and that you take your brother as far away from the Reverend Cooley as you can manage, and make it your mission in life to break him of sucking eggs. Being dishonest and a hypocrite are not your brother's main failings, Miss Lawrence. The main one is, he's stupid."

And that, I guessed, took care of that. I didn't want Priscilla Lawrence trying to follow me around, however holy her reasons. I had enough to worry about, not knowing what Uncle Earl was up to, and wondering if there was any truth in what the bounty tracer had said about Frank Kingston, and needing to get my business settled with Spider Webb so I could get on over there and join up with the Tucker wagons and go west.

I didn't need a Presbyterian on top of all that. Besides which, though I did have a sort of warm feeling about her — maybe two or three warm feelings when she'd been fresh from the river and had her hair down — Still I had the notion that I wanted to learn a little more about Mindy Tucker. Whatever came of that, it wouldn't be helped along by the presence of a ministering Presbyterian.

But now, with one inspired maneuver, I had resolved all of that. There just wasn't any question about it. Priscilla would go away and devote herself to civilizing her brother, and that was that.

I just wished she had chosen some other way of thanking me. When her lip started to twitch and those big dark eyes brimmed with tears, I had the feeling that I hadn't handled things just all that well.

She didn't say anything, just turned away and walked off along the dock, head bowed and clutching her brother's whiskey-smelling money coat to her bosom. She looked awfully small.

"You certainly got yourself a real way with the ladies," George said. "Yes, sir."

"Well, she needed to know about her brother."

"Oh, she already knew. Waylon and me, we told her how her brother sold her off to Pearce's pirates."

"You knew about that?"

"Sure. Couple of them that the boys picked up, they talked about it. So we told her, so she wouldn't feel so bad about how she thought *he* might be feelin' about *her.* You understand?"

"Well, then, if she already knew, why is she crying now?"

He looked at me like I was about eight cents short on the dollar. "Because *you* told her. And because you fixed everything up so she's stuck with that no good brother of hers, instead of with you. She had her heart set on lookin' after you, Mr. Frost."

"I know," I said. "That was the whole problem."

"Seems to me a man could do a lot worse," George muttered.

Spider Webb showed up a little later, with a sharp-eyed boatman in tow, and got right down to business. "You owe me a hundred and fifty dollars," he said, scowling as though he expected an argument. "A deal's a deal, whether or not you decide to ride."

"I'll not debate that," I assured him. "All deals hold. I owe you a hundred and fifty and you owe me six hundred, for that flotsam there."

"You do drive a hard bargain," he said, scowling at the damaged keelboat. "But, like I said, a deal's a deal." He pulled out a wad of currency and counted. "The difference bein' four hundred and fifty dollars to make us even."

"That's how I count it, too," I assured him. I took the money and stowed it away, feeling relieved to have the deal done. I was pretty sure I had skinned him on the price of the flotsam, and I'd been afraid he'd change his mind.

We shook on it, and it was done.

Webb turned to the sharp-eyed boatman standing beside him. He pointed at the flotsam boat. "There she lays, Charlie. See for yourself. Three planks and a dollar's worth of square nails, and she'll be a fine little craft to take your hides to New Orleans."

"I reckon," Charlie nodded. "A thousand, you said?"

"Only because I don't have time to stay around and dicker," Webb said. "You know she's worth more."

"Maybe so, but a deal's a deal. One thousand dollars it is." He shelled out currency which disappeared into Webb's heavy coat.

A thousand dollars.

Webb stalked past me and faced George. "I wish you'd change your mind, George," he said. "Good crew's hard to come by."

George shook his head. "Sorry, cap'n. But we talked it out and decided Mr. Frost here is right. Out west is the place to be these days."

"Well, you got wages coming," Webb shrugged. "Waylon, too. Where is he?"

"Gone into town to get us gear and possibles. You can pay me for both of us."

Again money changed hands, and Webb turned to frown at me. "Now don't you forget, it's up to you to clear with your uncle about that money. A deal's a deal."

"A deal's a deal," I agreed. "But I don't know where he is."

"Well, he better show up pretty quick. Two of them boxes on deck are his, but I can't wait around for him."

"That's fine," I said. "When he comes to get his boxes, you tell him he'll have to see me about the money you promised him."

He nodded, still glaring at me—the sort of glare people reserve for folks who flog mules or drown puppies.

Finally I asked him, "Captain Webb, do you have something on your mind?"

"Not particularly. I just don't hold with proselyters."

"With what?"

"Proselyters."

"I don't even know what that is."

"Sure you don't." He glanced around at George. "Well, you sure enough proselysed George and ol' Waylon."

"Like hell he did," George erupted. "Nobody does nothing to me that sounds that way, no, sir!"

Webb ignored him. "Mr. Frost, I don't hold it against you that you proselysed Miss Lawrence . . ."

"Who said I did that?"

"She did. But I put that down as natural and normal, her bein' a fine-lookin' young thing and all. Any man might. But when a man goes to doin' that to keelboat crews, I say he ought to be ashamed."

Outside of maybe Uncle Earl on occasion, there haven't been many people who ever caught me at a loss for words. But I was then.

"I just don't consider it natural," Webb concluded. He turned and stalked away toward *Aunt Maude*.

"Do you know what he's talking about?" I asked George.

"Not lately. Ever since him and the missy got to visitin' over supper on *Aunt Maude*, Captain Webb's been talkin' peculiar. I guess she taught him some new words. But I'll stand witness, if you want. Not you nor anybody else has ever done nothing like that to George Bullard. I'd have decked you if you'd even tried."

"I should hope so."

At any rate, I was doing what I had set out to do—shedding responsibilities, obligations and burdens the way a duck sheds water. I was square with Spider Webb and out of the boat business, with money in my pocket to show for it. I had put the Reverend Cooley's ill-gotten gains into good hands, along with Ezra Lawrence . . . and with her hands

138

that full, Priscilla Lawrence wouldn't have time to worry about nurturing me. I had seen the last of Frank Kingston . . . despite the bounty tracer's dire predictions, I couldn't see any future business he might have with me. If Waylon and George wanted to go west, that was fine. They were free agents and no concern of mine.

I went to the bank, paid off the loan and got my horse out of hock. I paid my hotel bill and topped off my supplies, adding a few things I hadn't thought of that caught my eye.

I walked across to the Mississippi side of town and there before me, just a river away, was the beginning of yonder. Out there, beyond those forested banks, somewhere I might find the sundown places and hear unbreathed winds singing far songs. Westport waited, and the promise of blue eyes. And maybe beyond there, if the spirit moved me. Pa told me once that those grand words, "Go west, young man, go west," came from a newspaper up at Terre Haute. But if they weren't in the Good Book, they should have been.

The wagon barges were no longer at the staging island, but had been moved across to the Missouri side for unloading. That meant Caleb Tucker's drivers had showed up, and that meant it was time to move.

"There are great open lands out west," Caleb Tucker had said. "Not just the goldfields, but many kinds of gold are out there, waiting for the right kind of men to gather them."

The right kind of men. Was I? I didn't know, but I'd been wanting to find out since I was a shirt-tail tad running the ridges and seeing yonders beyond the sunsets.

"There'll be a need for fine craftsmen out there," Caleb Tucker had said. "Had I the skills you've shown me here, I would set my eyes on the west and never look back."

Some drunks had crawled into the stable loft during the night and got involved with the hostler's snake, and the hostler was fit to be tied.

"Homer's used to bein' shot at now and again," he com-

139

plained. "He's been rassled around some, too, and he don't mind that. It's just good clean fun. But he ain't used to bein' called names, and I ain't used to bein' told I'm in league with the devil. I'm a God-fearin' man and Homer's a good snake. And they didn't pay for board, neither."

I shared with him all the sympathy I could come up with, and in fact it did seem to me that Homer, all curled up back in the shadows behind the grain sacks, had a hurt expression today. But it's hard to tell with snakes.

I bought out my roan and saddled him. He was feeling his oats and I had to knee him in the ribs to get him snorted down enough to secure the cinch rings. Before strapping on my gear, I led him out to the pasture and swung aboard. His ears turned back and his head went down and his rump went up and it was all I could do for the next few minutes to stay on top of him. But after he got that out of his system, everything was all right.

"Fine, spirited animal you got there," the hostler admired. Even Homer had come out to watch.

"He's all of that," I panted. "He sure is."

Back in the stable I strapped on my gear and was set to travel.

Across that river it would all be new. There were routes out there, and I had read about them. Trails that had become roads because folks followed them . . . trails that went from one place to another, little threads across a great land, footsteps of the explorers, marks of the surveyors . . . trails that folks heard about, and probably some they didn't.

And there were places where no trails were known, all the places that the maps showed blank. Little lines of ink on paper that showed the mile or two along the known routes where what was there had been seen . . . but between the little lines were the vast uncharted places, and it was places like that that a man wanted to see.

All my scores were settled, all debts paid and all burdens

left behind. As free and unhindered as anyone could be, I stepped up to my saddle and rode down to the river to cross.

Nothing can go astray faster than a noble notion.

There was a crowd waiting for the ferry, and most of it was mine. Ezra Lawrence, looking pale and surly, glared at me from the seat of a surrey. His sister sat beside him, prim in bun and bonnet, the reins taut in small, businesslike hands.

"In my opinion, Mr. Frost," she said, "those who dawdle are doing the devil's work."

Just beyond, Waylon Gibbs sat perched on the high seat of a freight wagon, holding its team in check. He grinned at me and jerked a thumb at the pile of traveling gear in its bed. "We probably got enough supplies here to get us across Missouri, providin' we add a bit of game along the way. Those big wagons yonder, are those the ones we're travelin' with?"

George Bullard looked uncomfortable atop a sturdy gray horse, but he clung like an able seaman. "Them two boxes there belong to your uncle. Captain Webb said to bring them along, so you can deliver them."

After that, it wasn't especially surprising to find out who Caleb Tucker's hired drivers were. Abe Miles and Benny Strother had worked on those wagons, just like I had. And they had heard Caleb Tucker's words the same as me. If I had stayed around New Albany—after we finished Carl Froehner's business—long enough to ask them what they planned to do next, they would have told me.

PART TWO

THE OVERLANDERS

XIV

It was a good small caravan that set out that day from the west bank staging yards. Six big overlanders in all, counting the brown and yellow pair, along with a surrey, a brace of spring wagons and seven men on horseback . . . nine vehicles lined out on a road that was no road at all but only a trail angling away from the stepped banks of the Mississippi, up the rising hills that buttressed the Ozark mountains.

Will Posey had the map and the trail orders. He had been a scout once, he told me, for survey parties exploring the Osage territories. Now he worked for Captain Rawlings, assembling emigrant parties and leading them west.

He was a hard-eyed, tight-lipped man. He carried a big plains rifle always at hand, and his eyes seemed to miss nothing as we rode.

"I've guided for some men," he said as we rode together. "Some dreamers and some fools, along with some decent folk. This Tucker, now, he'll do to ride with."

"That was my opinion," I said. "Mine and some others, too."

He nodded. "You ever seen the shining mountains, son?"

"No. Might like to, though."

A mile or so along we topped out on a bald ridge and

Posey waited for me to catch up. He pointed to the west, where the land climbed away toward purple tops that looked like jagged teeth against the orange sky. "Ozarks," he said. "Mountains they is, an' plenty for some. There's caps yonder a quarter mile high, and there's holes in there so deep a man could spend his life and never see the sunrise. But those ain't mountains to a man that's seen mountains."

"Like the shining mountains."

"Like nothin' else."

"Is that where you're going? To the shining mountains?"

"Tucker didn't say?"

"He just said west. I'm not in his party, just tagging along to Westport. I'm a wagonwright."

"Well, the shining mountains is where he aims, and that's where we'll take him. They've built a town out yonder, on Cherry Creek. Call it Denver City. Not far from Pike's Peak. That's where our train is goin'."

I just nodded, trying to picture a place I had never seen.

"Some folks go to the gold region to make a killin'," Posey said. "Tucker's got a different notion. He's goin' there to make a *livin'*."

"Farmers and businessmen."

He glanced at me. "What's that?"

"Farmers and businessmen. Mr. Tucker said that's who's going."

"The miners are already there."

Up now and away from the riverbottom lands, the country was easy and rolling, wooded in some places, open in others. A good land. But Posey warned all the men to keep a sharp lookout and keep our guns at hand. Missouri had its wild places, and its wild places held men who knew no law.

Our segment of the Tucker company plodded north by northwest with Will Posey in the lead, heading for the south river road, one of two great emigrant trails crossing Mis-

146

souri. Nine vehicles, twenty-four people, we left one river and headed for another.

When the Tucker party assembled at Westport, it would be a full company, ready for the open plains. But now with the chill of spring in the air, its parts still were coming together.

All six of the overland wagons were new. The four which had joined were from wagonworks in Pennsylvania and up-land Ohio. The brown and yellow Froehnervagens driven by Abe Miles and Benny Strother and one of the others were, as Posey put it, "in transport." That meant they were not yet delivered to their final users. A young Pennsylvanian named Mahlon Krause was driving the third of these, hired by its owner.

The other three overlanders were already in possession of those who would take them west. The Maddens, man and wife and four children, rode high and proud in a Conestoga, while Buck Honeycutt walked alongside a much smaller, prairie schooner style wagon, driving its teams as they say a'shank's mare, now and then glancing up at his pretty Betsy and their two little girls.

Then there were the Conways, the brothers Paul and Todd and their sisters Catherine and Charity, with their mother, the widow Bessie.

Six overlanders, and among them rolled two supply wagons and a sturdy little surrey driven by a bright-eyed Presbyterian and transporting a sullen ecumenical.

Those of us who were mounted—Will Posey and myself, and either Waylon or George, taking turns—rode scout, flank, wide guard or drag . . . whatever position Will Posey set us to, depending upon the land we were crossing at the time.

These were backcountry lands, mostly untamed. Little clusters of settlement clung in random places, here a valley with rich soil and ready water where a man could make a

147

crop, there a tight cluster of sheds and tents where men mined for lead, elsewhere a trading post at the crossing of wild trails. But these places were few and far between. In most of the old Spanish lands between St. Louis and New Madrid, law was words in a book somewhere far away. Where people gathered — or traveled — they must be their own law or there was none.

Captain Rawlings and Will Posey had chosen our route carefully, a course midway between the wild hills of the Ozarks and the unpredictable bottoms and bluffs of the big river's course — a path that would not wear out people or stock, nor cripple wagons, but that fought shy of the habitats of the local folk.

We were transporting things of value — the stock, the goods and supplies, the wagons themselves would draw the attention of those who saw us pass — and it was better if we held ourselves aloof.

Will Posey said it in his way. "I've fought the heathen redmen on the plains and I've stood off Missouri bandits. Of the two, I'd rather face the redmen."

Six days, he said, or maybe eight, then we'd swing west on the traveled road that followed the Missouri up to Westport. "With luck," he added, "we'll join up with some more of our folks there, enough for a strong party. Central Missouri isn't too bad, but there's bad blood to the west over the free state issue. Bad blood draws a bad crowd."

In that first day of caravan we covered nearly twenty miles and camped the night on a hogback ridge with good graze and a sweetwater spring.

I was riding alongside the Conway wagon as we approached the site, sort of staying handy to have a glimpse of the sisters Catherine and Charity whenever the opportunity came up — though Todd Conway kept making it clear by his manner that they didn't know me from Adam's off ox and their red-haired sisters were not along on this trip for my amusement. When we came to the bedding ground Posey had selected, Paul—who was driving at the time—angled off looking for the best place to make night camp. The other wagons were doing the same, each driver deciding that this or that other area looked to him like where he wanted to stop.

The clear top of that hogback was maybe a quarter-mile square, and we were spread out all over it, each family or driver becoming a separate unit with the approach of nightfall.

Will Posey had gone off ahead somewhere, looking at the next morning's trail, but now he came back and when he topped the ridge you could have heard his yell a mile away. Everybody on the hogback hauled up and looked around to see what was wrong.

I had my gun out, and I guess every other man among us did, too. Out at the crest, Posey put spurs to his horse and came charging in among us, shouting curses and waving that big rifle around like a twig.

"Gather in!" he shouted. "Everybody! Gather to me!"

Todd Conway's eyes were as big as saucers. "Indians?" he wondered.

"Maybe outlaws," I suggested, trying to look in all directions at once.

Away off, over near the swale where the ridge dropped down to woodlands, Mahlon Krause was hawing his big team around, cutting a nice turn to head our way. Paul Conway was doing the same thing, getting up a good roll to head in on the shouting Will Posey. Elsewhere Thomas Madden was barking at his horses, getting them moving again from a full stop, and Buck Honeycutt was swinging onto the back of his wheelhorse while Besty handed out his rifle from the bow gap. Abe Miles and Benny Strother came in at a quick-trot, their brown and yellow wagons neck and neck. Waylon Gibbs was coming with one of the supply

149

wagons, the other following close behind . . . and a quarter mile away, off the trail, the Lawrences's surrey stood beside a copse of dogwood, its horse ground-reined and its people nowhere in sight.

The hackles on my neck probably raised my hat an inch off my head. Forgetting all about the Conway sisters and Will Posey and the rest of it, I heeled the roan around and lit out at a gallop.

I saw them just before I got there. They were beyond the copse, Priscilla standing in that rigid pose of hers — hands on her hips and her chin thrust out like the prow of a small but pugnacious keelboat — while Ezra paced back and forth, his hands behind him and his mouth going a mile a minute.

The roan nearly swapped ends getting stopped, and they both stared at me. "What the hell do you think you're doing?" I yelled at Priscilla.

Beyond her, Ezra glared at me. "We are having a family discussion, sir, and I'll thank you to go on your way."

Priscilla had turned red, and I realized that Presbyterians aren't partial to casual references about hell and damnation and the like. But that was beside the point.

"Why did you stop?" I was still yelling, and trying to see in all directions and still hold her attention. "Get in that buggy and get it moving!"

"Ezra doesn't want to go any further," she explained. "We are debating the issue."

I didn't know what the emergency was, but I had faith in Will Posey and this was no time for a family debate. I wheeled the roan again, circled around them and pointed my Dragoon at Ezra. "Get in that surrey or I'll shoot you. Now!"

He went white as snow and got his feet tangled, but he went. He was already climbing aboard when Priscilla got her mouth closed enough to say, "*Mis*-ter Frost! What on earth are you . . ."

150

"You get in too," I said. "Now! Or I'll shoot your brother."

She kept a little more dignity than Ezra had, but it didn't take her long to climb aboard.

"Drive!" I yelled at her. I reined alongside, leaned and got a handful of their horses' headstall, and away we went.

All the wagons were just coming together in a tight clump, right in front of Will Posey, when we got there. He included us in a general glance up and down the line, and I never saw a man look sterner in my life.

Horses stamped and harness jangled and axles creaked and children babbled, and he just stared. Gradually the sounds faded, and it got so still you could hear the breeze tickling the grasstops.

He let it linger for a few seconds, looking from one driver to the next, missing nobody. Then he said, very quietly, "What were you all doin'?"

We all just sort of looked at one another. Paul Conway cleared his throat. "We thought we'd camp right over there, sir," he said. "The grass looks good, and . . ."

"Shut up," Will Posey said. He pointed a stern finger at Benny Strother. "You. What were you doing?"

Benny shrugged. "Getting ready to stop for the night, sir. Abe and me, we thought we'd rig down over there where we could get the breeze."

"Damnation," Posey said, drawing out the word enough for it to have covered the Book of Revelations.

Thomas Madden raised a tentative hand. "You *did* say we would camp here tonight, didn't you, Mr. Posey?"

Posey took a deep breath. "Yes," he said. "That was exactly what I said. I said we would camp here. By that I meant . . . here!" He pointed at the ground in front of him. "Right here! Not in this general vicinity. Not spread over half of eastern Missouri. Right by God here! Where do you people think you are? Baltimore? Don't you remember anything I told you about staying close and keepin' your eyes

151

open? God almighty, was I a yayhoo like some around here, I'd have myself some fine new rollin' stock right this minute and half of you wouldn't be alive to tell about it!"

Mahlon Krause shrugged and kicked in his brake. "We camp here," he said to nobody in particular.

Posey spent several minutes then, drilling everybody on where they were supposed to be and how the wagons were to be placed and where the ropes went to hold the stock, and a few other pointers. When he had them all working he edged over to me and fixed me with angry eyes. "What were you doin' off yonder?"

"Picking up stragglers," I admitted. "You like to scared the fool out of me when you came up yelling like that."

"I hope I scared the fool out of everybody," he said, relaxing just a mite. "Where these folks are goin', fool's what gets people killed."

Since it was the first night on the trail, and since Waylon had experience as a keelboat cook, Posey put him in charge of the evening meal.

"Small group like this," Posey said, "we'll share meals to save on time and supplies. Those that have their own vittles," he looked around at his motley group, "can contribute to the pot if they want, and get credit in the company account. Anything the cook needs, that anybody has, he gets. Until we get to Westport—or join a larger party—I'm the captain of this outfit. Anybody who doesn't like that can pull out right now."

He looked around, giving anybody who wanted to have a say the chance to.

Only Ezra, off in the shadows leaning on a buggywheel, spoke up. "I don't like it," he said.

Nearer the fire, Priscilla turned. "Hush, Ezra. The gentleman isn't talking to you."

"I'm talking to everybody here," Posey said. He glanced at me. "You got Mr. Tucker's permission to ride along with us,

Frost. These others you brought, do you speak for them?"

"I didn't bring anybody," I insisted. "They just came."

"You did, too, Mr. Frost," George Bullard piped up. "You're the one told Waylon and me how we ought to go west."

"I didn't say you ought to go west, George. I said *I* was going west."

"Well, you told Waylon there'd be a place for a cooper." Posey's eyes narrowed. "He's a cooper, you say?"

"He is that. And me, I'm a fair carpenter, myself."

"Then it could be Captain Rawlings may want to offer you both passage when we make up at Westport. He'll decide that, but I'll take you on for the transport run if you'll sign a pledge."

"What pledge?"

"The same one every member of this company is going to sign before we pull out of here in the morning. It'll oblige every man here to share and share alike, work and work alike, and do as the captain says. That's me. How about it, Frost? Do you speak for the people with the surrey?"

"I don't speak for anybody but myself. I didn't invite anybody along on this jaunt."

Priscilla's mouth dropped open. "Why Mr. Frost, shame on you. That was a fib."

"Miss Lawrence, I didn't ask you along. You just came."

"But you did so! You instructed me to take my brother as far from the Reverend Cooley as is possible for me to do. The farthest locale within my ability to reach is wherever you are going. Also, we agreed days ago that I am to follow in your way, to attend and nurture you . . ."

"We didn't agree on any such . . ."

"Frost, what have you been doing to this young lady?" Posey was eyeing me coldly. "I don't hold with . . ."

"That's the way me and Waylon understood it, too," George Bullard offered, helpfully.

Ezra Lawrence had come forward, into the firelight. He pointed a shaking finger at me. "I shall thank you to refrain from making unseemly advances toward my sister, sir!"

Catherine and Charity Conway, firelight dancing on their red hair, were taking it all in. They blinked big eyes at me in unison as their brothers edged between them and me.

But Ezra wasn't through. "I do not intend to go anywhere with this man," he said, still pointed at me. "Not only has he led my dear and only sister astray, he robbed me as well. And he robbed the Reverend Cooley, and he tried to feed us both to a messenger of the dark angel . . ."

"Ezra, that isn't so!" Priscilla shouted at him. "He gave the money to me!"

". . . led my own sister from the paths of righteousness and then had the gall to steal from me to pay her . . ."

"What did you feed them to?" Mahlon Krause wanted to know.

"That money was mine to start with!" Priscilla declared. "You sold my house, Ezra. You know you did!"

Will Posey's head seemed to sink down between his shoulders. "Shut up!" he roared. "Everybody shut up! All we're supposed to be doin' here is organizin' a six-day journey, for God's sake!"

Whatever else he had to say was interrupted. Over by the supply wagon Waylon began banging on a washtub. "Vittles is on!" he shouted. "Come and get it or I'll throw it out!"

"He's cooked for boaters," George said, admiringly.

After supper, most of the party took a vote and presented their petition to Will Posey. They voted against asking Waylon to cook any more.

The upshot of it was, every man among us signed the pledge—the *obligation*, as Will Posey called it—except Ezra, who refused.

It seemed to me that my problem was resolved. Will Posey would have no choice but to exclude the Lawrences, to send them back. But Posey had other ideas.

"Men without families is assigned to tendin' the livestock," he announced. "Teams of two, two-day rotations. All except Mr. Frost. Frost, you're assigned to tend Ezra Lawrence, for the duration of this obligation."

"Ezra isn't livestock," I pointed out.

"He ain't a signed man of the company. The manifest only declares for folks, critters, rollin' stock and goods. Now it's clear that Ezra ain't rollin' stock or goods, an' I sure won't declare him as women and children, so all that's left is livestock. He come with you, so you're in charge of him. You see to it he gets fed and watered and does a share of the haulin'. And if he stampedes, it's on your head."

XV

Nothing very much was resolved, except for staying close and keeping an eye out for trouble. But I don't think Will Posey worried too much about the rest. He was a scout, not a wagonmaster like Captain Rawlings. And what he wanted to do was deliver us safe and sound to Captain Rawlings at the earliest opportunity so he could wash his hands of us.

I couldn't blame him. I knew very well how it was to be encumbered by unrequired persons.

I'd had misgivings about signing his pledge. It would have been a lot simpler just to wish them all well, saddle my roan and head for where the sun went down. The problem was Uncle Earl's boxes. They wouldn't tote handy on a horse, and I wasn't of a mind to try to find a pack animal at that point.

Once again, just like so many times before, Uncle Earl had created a situation that left me obligated, even though I had no idea what the situation was.

One time when we were tads, Uncle Earl hired out to Mr. Cruikshank, down by the Derby cutoff, to lay stepping stones across his creek for him so it would be easier to get back and forth to his hay meadow.

156

The creek was shallow at that point, with a good rock bottom, but it was about forty feet across. Uncle Earl agreed to do the job for three dollars. I didn't know about it at the time.

Then Uncle Earl went to Mistress Thorne, who had a place on the ridge back of the cutoff, and offered to carry her eggs to market twice a week for a dime a trip. Well, it was four miles by road from her place to the crossroads where they had market, but less than a mile as the crow flies. Nobody went the short way, though, because of that creek.

Then Uncle Earl came around and found me and said, "Zack, I know how a fellow could make himself some money."

When I said how's that, he said, "You know that creek crossing over there by old Cruikshank's place? Well, I'll bet I could get Mistress Thorne to pay a nickel a trip just for taking her eggs to market, and if you went by way of the creek it wouldn't take any time at all."

I thought about it and it sounded all right except for the creek crossing. I'd been across that creek many's the time, and it was tricky business. About half the time I tried to cross, I fell down. Carrying eggs across there just didn't seem like a good idea.

But he had an answer to that. "Why don't you go and lay some stepping stones across there, Zack? That ought to do it."

Well, I got the stones down in about a week of hard work, and sure enough, next thing I knew I was toting eggs. I'd made three trips before I found out that Uncle Earl was collecting a dime and only paying me a nickel, but when I did I raised him clear off the ground by his galluses and said, "Uncle Earl, you are doing wrong."

He just grinned in that sideways way of his and said, "Why, Zach, I thought I told you. That fifteen cents I kept was my finder's fee. From now on, you can collect direct and keep it all. After all, I did put you onto this good thing, didn't I?"

It wasn't until about three years later that I happened to find out how Mr. Cruikshank had paid him three dollars for the stone crossing, and by then it just didn't seem to need redress.

But then, I never did tell him about the insinglass shelf I found when I was breaking out stepping stones. And I didn't share the seven dollars I got for it with him, either. It just never crossed my mind.

On the other hand, now that I thought about that, it *was* Uncle Earl who told me about the peddler who came through Hardinsburg now and then, who paid good money for pyrites and moonstones and insinglass and things like that. He even knew his name and where to find him.

Or maybe it was like the time I was on the way home from cabin school, and I took the shortcut that led up the rise to where I could see Yolanda's house — the way I usually did about then — and right there beside the trail was a bale of shingles just lying there, with "Property of Earl Donovan" written on the bale in chalk.

Well, that was a dilemma. It was clouding up, and anybody knows baled shingles will curl if they get rained on. But Uncle Earl wasn't anywhere around, and I had no idea how those shingles got there or why they were his, and it was about three miles to home. My shortcut past Yolanda's added about two miles to the trip.

So there wasn't anything to do that I could see, except take them on home.

A bale of shingles weighs thirty pounds, thereabouts. At least, that's what it weighs when a body first picks it up. After a mile of toting it weighs nearer fifty, and by the time I got home it had gained another fifty on top of that. I was purely tuckered when I got that bale of shingles into our barn.

Then I had cows to milk and stalls to clean, and I was back in the toolshed honing scythes when I heard the barn door open, and Pa and Uncle Earl came in. They went right to the shingles.

"Here they are," Earl said. "A whole bale, just like you said you needed."

Pa looked them over and nodded. "Well, I don't know how you did it, Earl, but a deal's a deal. I'll pay your price for them . . . though if I ever learn you came by them in some shady manner, I'll take the strap to you."

Uncle Earl seemed offended. "Sir, I traded for these, fair and square. You just ask Mr. Van Ney. He made them, and he traded this bale to me for three setting hens. All I'm trying to do is just make a fair profit on my investment."

"Well," Pa said, hesitantly, "I can't fault a lad on that. Very well, then, the deal is done." He knelt again to look at the bale. "Mr. Van Ney is a hand at splitting shingles."

"Yes, sir, he is," Uncle Earl said. Then, with the exaggerated confidentiality of a boy of fourteen sharing deep secrets with a man maybe going on fifty, he said, "You know, I believe Zack is kind of sweet on that girl of his, Yolanda. But you don't need to worry, sir. I'll keep a sharp eye on Zack, like I always do."

Some things don't ever seem to change. Somehow those shingles got right where Uncle Earl wanted them, when he wanted them there. And somehow, I figured his two boxes from the keelboat were going to do the same thing.

At least this time I wasn't toting them three or four miles on my back. But they were like that bale of shingles. When it came to it, I just couldn't leave them out in the rain to curl.

So I signed Will Posey's pledge, with the resolve that whatever happened next — whether Uncle Earl showed up to claim his possessions or not — when we got to Westport that was where those boxes would stay . . . whether or not I did.

I hadn't started out really thinking of anything beyond the makeup areas — Westport or Springfield or wherever the big wagons staged to begin their treks westward. I was a wagonwright — a wheelwright and beyond, thanks to Carl Froehner — and those staging grounds offered opportunities for a man of my craft.

But the more I watched those overlanders roll, high and handsome on their bright wheels, tall wagons with the look of far places about them, the more I mused about how it might be . . . those prairies out there, vast without end, they said, yet rising ever up and on, and then one day a low cloud on the horizon that was no cloud at all . . . a rim of ragged blue that grew a bit each day until it filled the western sky and changed the very sunsets to patterns of its own design. The shining mountains. The Rockies.

Could I set out to see the yonder and stop short of seeing *that?*

I would think on it again, when I saw the staging grounds and could decide what it was I wanted to do. That was the practical thing, the way Pa would have told me. Make your decision when you know what is involved . . . what you gain and lose by going on, and what you gain — and lose — by staying.

I would think on it again. Of course I would. I would think on it every step of the way, just like I always had.

We had pretty well run out of settled places now, and the hills our trail led through were wild and beautiful. In some places the land looked as though a great hand had rested upon it at one time, then had casually shifted its weight, pushing up ripples alongside each mighty finger so that shallow valleys fanned out from broad meadows, with blunt wooded ridges separating them into secret places. Game was plentiful, and we crossed some streams that were so ripple-clear a body could count the pebbles on the bottom and see the fish hanging in the currents.

We followed one of the finger-print valleys for several miles, and came up out of it at a place where spreading oaks grew so close that we had to wind our way among them, single-file with the big wagons' wheels riding up on roots at either side.

The two Froehnervagens, carrying almost no load, danced nimbly along without problems. It was tougher going for the Madden and Conway wagons. Fully loaded with the goods of families and whatever else they carried, those Conestoga-types bumped along, fighting the trail while their teams strained in harness. In the last half-mile of climb, where it was roughest, George Bullard and I got ropes on their timbers and added our saddle-horses' strength to pulling them, one at a time.

Finally we had them on level ground, and Will Posey came back and got down to look at the tracks they had left. "You folks are carrying too much weight," he told them. "It's up to you, but somewhere along I think you're going to have to lighten the load."

Madden looked worried. "Here?"

"No, you'll be all right along here, I guess. We can put some of your stuff in those empty wagons. But after Westport, there won't be any empties. You folks be thinkin' about that."

He had decided on a night camp over the next crest, several miles away, and one by one we moved out, as they were aligned. The Froehnervagens went ahead, with the two supply wagons following, then the pair of Conestogas and the transport wagon after them.

I was up in my saddle again, coiling my tow rope, and looking back down the trail. Several minutes passed before the surrey came into sight. Ezra was driving it now, and he whipped the reins angrily as they cleared the crest and came out of the oak forest. Priscilla was looking back the way they had come, and both of them were arguing a mile a minute.

". . . no skin off my nose," Ezra was saying. "Their problem, not mine."

". . . could at least have stopped and offered a hand," Priscilla was overlapping him. ". . . the charitable thing to do, Ezra. In my opinion . . ."

"What's the matter? I asked, coming alongside. "And where are the Honeycutts?"

Priscilla pointed. "They're still back there. One of their wheels came apart."

"Right where the trail is narrowest," Ezra rasped. "I had to drive off into the woods to get around them."

I looked ahead, where the rest of the train was moving away. I drew my Dragoon and fired a shot into the air, and a minute later I saw Will Posey and George heading back our way at a run.

"What did you do that for?" Ezra wanted to know.

"To stop the others, to get some help back here."

"For what?"

Priscilla stared at her brother, her lips so tight they showed white at the corners. "Oh, Ezra, shut up."

He opened his mouth to say something more and I beat him to it. "Ezra, thank your sister."

"Thank . . . what for?"

"For probably saving you from being thrashed for another day."

"By whom?"

"By me, Ezra. Like she said, shut up."

The Honeycutt wagon sat aslant on the climbing trail, its sheared left rear hub hanging a foot above the ground. Pieces of wheel were strewn along the road for thirty feet behind it. Buck looked pale and frightened, and Becky stood close beside him, their two children clinging to her skirt. I could almost hear the thoughts in their heads . . . abandon the wagon, abandon their possessions, abandon their dreams . . .

"Well, don't just stand there," I told them. "Get all those parts picked up. And don't miss any. You can't assemble a wheel without wheel parts."

Buck looked at me as though I had made the sun come up. "You mean it can be fixed?"

"We'll never know until we try."

When Will Posey arrived I showed him the problem and asked if we could camp where we were. He shook his head. "The stock need water. We've still got a few miles to go. Is there any way to get them that far?"

"I reckon," I said. "How about getting Abe and Benny back here. Tell them we need axes, strapping and a saw."

The Honeycutts were gathering up spokes and felloes, and I looked over what they had found. Without its tire, the wheel had simply fallen apart. Two of the spokes were broken and one felloe was split, showing the part of the wheel that had taken the impact when the hub dropped. I inspected the hub. Except for one socket being gouged, it seemed firm. It was of good black gum wood, well seasoned. I looked over the other wheels on the wagon and found them to be sturdy and well-fitted, except for a looseness in the tires. So, likely, there wouldn't be any spoke shrinkage to deal with.

Abe and Benny came trudging back from the Froehnervagens, carrying two axes, a saw and a roll of harness strap. They walked around the crippled wagon, looking it over, and Benny crawled underneath to see the hounds.

"Nothing broken below," he said.

"What do you think?" Abe asked. "Can the wheel be fixed?"

"I've seen worse," I shrugged. "It's worth a try. But first we have to move the wagon. Mr. Posey doesn't want to camp here."

"Drag pole, then?" Benny suggested.

163

"I guess."

While Benny and Buck got out the wagon jack and began raising the axle, Abe and I found a tall, straight young ash tree with a diameter of about ten inches and cut it down. With ax and saw we trimmed it to a stout pole more than twenty-five feet long, and brought it back.

With the sheared axle raised higher than the others, we positioned the pole so that it rested under the axle and extended out maybe ten feet behind the wagon, its end resting on the ground. The pole angled upward along the sideboard to the front corner post, rising to almost its top.

While I lashed the pole in place with harness leather, Benny and Abe rigged a turnbuckle between front corner posts to give them all the strength possible.

When we eased off the jack, the wagon settled down onto its drag pole and rested there, level on three wheels and a crutch.

"Move 'em out," I told Buck. "Let's see how she drags."

He whipped up his team and the wagon rolled. The drag pole furrowed the ground where it was soft, but it supported the wagon.

"He can make a few miles that way," I told Will Posey. "Then we'll see about the wheel."

The drag pole didn't have any more trouble clearing the top crest than a wheel would have, and we headed out in the clear toward where the other wagons waited.

Will Posey started ahead to get his charges aligned again, then he reined up and turned back. He came straight to me. "I don't want you to get the notion that I don't appreciate you all pitchin' in to rig a drag pole on that schooner wagon," he said. "And for a fact I'm hopin' you can repair them folks' wheel. But out in this country just because a man does most things right don't cut it if somethin' is wrong."

I didn't know what he was talking about. "Did I do

164

something wrong?"

"Pitchin' in to help others don't relieve any man of his own personal responsibilities," he said.

"So?"

"So, look yonder." He pointed ahead to where the wagons waited. "Mr. Frost, where is that surrey?"

XVI

"He just said he didn't have to stand for such treatment," Priscilla said. "Of course, Ezra always says things like that, so I didn't pay particular attention. But then we all stopped, and the Honeycutt wagon was missing and everybody wondered what was wrong, and anyway the next thing I knew my luggage was lying on the ground and the surrey was gone and so was Ezra."

"Probably making for the river," Abe said. "Fellow like that usually heads for towns or rivers. What do you want him for, anyway, Zack?"

"I don't want him. Far as I'm concerned he can go to the river and jump in. Good riddance."

"Well, it seems to me like somebody ought to go get him and bring him back," George looked at me accusingly. "After all, he *is* the Missy's brother. And that surrey and horse belong to her, too."

"Likely he'll never make it to the river," Will Posey shrugged. "That's Table Rock over there. Sheer bluffs, and breaks beyond, and there's yayhoos in the bottoms out there that might jump an army if they took a mind to."

"Ezra will be all right," Priscilla pursed her lips. "God looks out for Ezra. But if I am to change his ways, I do need him close at hand." She looked up at me, with the wide-eyed, innocent, trusting expression of a woman who intends to have her own way if it hare-lips half a state. "Only for that reason, Mr. Frost. I *would* take it kindly if you would go and fetch him back."

It isn't difficult to trail a surrey over broken terrain, which I did for three or four miles. Even a light vehicle leaves a clear impress where the ground is soft or sandy, and its wheels make parallel furrows in high grass, crisp little lines that a body can see from a distance.

Even with the start that Ezra had, I didn't think it would take long to catch him. The only question was whether I should take him back unhandled or whether maybe a few judicious thumps might shake some sense into him. I came out on a brushy crest and saw the twin lines of surrey wheels like snake tracks going away, wending down the slope of a long meadow toward wooded bottoms below. He was angling southward a little, toward the shoulder of that feature Will Posey called Table Rock. He saw it in his way and was aiming to go around it, which told me that Ezra hadn't the vaguest idea of the terrain below. Breaks, Will said. Sheer caps and rubble slopes and winding gullies, feathering toward the distant Mississippi bluffs. There might be roads near those bluffs—Will didn't know—but there were no roads across the breaks. Maybe Ezra and God would manage to get a surrey through there, but Ezra alone was never going to make it.

Another mile and the country was becoming rougher. It wouldn't be too long, I thought, before I'd see him coming back my way, cut off by the breaks. Either that, or maybe I'd find him at the bottom of a gulley all tangled up with his wrecked surrey and no longer a problem for anyone this side of the pearly gates. That was a cheerful thought. One way or another, Ezra was going to solve his problems.

Dying would be a nice, direct way to go about it.

But that wasn't really as comforting a notion as I wished it would be. There was always Priscilla. And though I had no use whatever for Priscilla Lawrence—barring maybe that she did catch a body's eye when all she had on was a wet shift and her hair down—still I didn't want to be the one to haul a corpse back to her and say, "Here he is, Miss Lawrence, here's your brother and my, but isn't he gone quiet now."

Better he just explore the edges of the breaks for a bit, then turn back so I could take him home.

I was nearly to the bottoms when I saw another trail coming in from the right, fresh prints of two horses swinging east to fall in behind, their marks overlapping the surrey's. A quarter-mile ahead, all the marks disappeared into forest. Ezra had more company out here than just me, and whoever it was, they weren't our people.

Back when Uncle Earl and I were tads, the folks always had plenty of critters around. Not just all of us kids, but other kinds, too. We always had a couple of milk cows, and usually an extra horse or two, and of course chickens—everybody always had chickens, and ours produced yard eggs over nest eggs two to one—and usually some pigs for slaughter in the fall. But there were also dogs and cats. Pa was never without a brace of potlikker hounds, and Ma always liked to have her fice, as she called it. And we had barn cats and house cats.

I guess we learned some things from the critters, and I believe Pa knew it. He used to point out how well dogs and cats get along together, as long as folks don't interfere. A dog and a cat will chum up just fine unless somebody teaches one of them to take offense at the other. It's dogs and dogs that are likely to fight, or cats and cats. Pa used to say that in the hierarchy of things living, dogs and cats ranked right up near to folks, well above the descending order of critters, beasts, brutes, hogs and varmints. He said that some folks in other places held to the notion that every live thing lives more than once, and what they are in this life depends on how they conducted their affairs in the last one. He said if that was so, then dogs and cats probably would be folks next time around if the Lord was charitable.

Then sometimes if Ma was there—especially if her fice or one of the cats was curled up on her lap—he'd look at her and allow that maybe he had that wrong. Maybe if a man lived a Godly enough life, he said, he could come back curled up on Ma's lap like that.

But what Uncle Earl learned from cats and dogs—and he pointed it out to me, and sure enough he was right—was that they have different ways of approaching a situation. He began studying on that the day a badger wandered into our dooryard and Pa's potlikkers took after it and got themselves chewed up for their trouble.

"You see how those hounds went for that badger?" Earl said. "They just saw it and made a beeline for it."

Later on he went off into the woods and came back with a bullsnake, and told me to come on out to the barn.

He set the bullsnake down on the barn floor and ran out and came back with a cat and put it there too. "Now watch," he told me.

So we watched. That cat spent the better part of a half hour working up to that snake. It would stalk along until it got close, then it would veer away and sort of sneak past it, on the diagonal. Then it would approach again from another direction, and do the same thing again. I could have cut a wheel pattern just from the lines of approach that cat made, homing in on that snake. It went at it from every side there was, methodically, one angle at a time. Of course, bullsnakes being the way they are, it saw the same thing from every angle—a beady-eyed bullsnake looking at it and flicking its tongue.

"You see what it does?" Earl got excited. "By the time it gets ready to make its move, a cat knows every inch of the terrain and every angle of attack."

It didn't come to anything. The cat used up all its angles of attack and that thing there in front of it was still the same fat bullsnake, so the cat changed its mind and went off to do something else.

But we did learn from that. I've always wondered whether what we learned was the same thing, because when Uncle Earl mentioned it later and I told him my idea about how to pattern spokes and felloes, he seemed disappointed.

But I thought of it now, and it didn't seem like that cat had such a bad idea. Whoever was behind Ezra was in those woods where his tracks led, and I was coming down on them across an open meadow.

Anybody who's ever caught a bullsnake knows you don't come at it head on.

There was some scrub off to my left, poking up from a shallow wash, so I headed over there and got down into it, turning left at the top so it would look like I was going the other direction. It wasn't a trick that would fool anybody much. Yayhoos generally are country boys, and they know a man doesn't leave a fresh trail to circle blind for sign. But if somebody was watching, that little turn-back at the wash might have left him wondering just where I might come out.

When I had cover between me and the forested bottoms I heeled the roan around and headed for them, following the wash. Whoever was down there, for whatever reason, I didn't want to give him time to think much about me if he had seen me, or to get very far away if he hadn't.

The wash widened, the cover deepened, and pretty soon I was past the pummeling of brush and into forest. I edged right, at an angle, and estimated I was four or five hundred yards from where the surrey tracks had entered the trees, and a little bit beyond.

If the people following Ezra had in mind to stop him, they wouldn't have waited very long after they were in the cover of the woods. And if they were owlhoots, as I suspected, Ezra's time was growing very short. He had no gun, which might give him a few extra minutes—if he'd had one and they intended to accost him, they'd shoot him rather than give him a chance to use it. As far as I knew he had no money, which wouldn't buy him time anyway—real yayhoos will kill a man quicker for being broke than anything.

All he had to defend himself was a surrey which couldn't outrun anything in woodlands, and his general disposition which wasn't going to do him a hell of a lot of good because people out to rob don't usually want to hear a sermon.

Trees muffle sound, so I gambled on being where I thought I was and headed full-tilt toward where I expected Ezra was. Had I been the yayhoos and seen me coming along, I'd have split up. One of me would have gone ahead on to catch Ezra while the other one waited just back of tree-line, looking for a clear shot.

That's what I would have done. If they hadn't done that, then I was fixing to be in about as much trouble as Ezra was. But I'd played cat as long as I could. My plan now was simple—light into them hell for leather and hope to God they weren't both at the same place when I got there.

Dragoon in hand, I snugged my buckle against the saddle horn and gave that roan its head.

One instant I saw the clearing coming, the next I was in it and all hell broke loose. The surrey was there, Ezra sitting in it stiff-shouldered and white as chalk. The other man had a pistol in one hand and his saddle-horn in the other, one foot in the stirrup and the other just reaching for the ground. He might have heard me coming, just in that last second, but his horse hadn't. It reared and spun and sent him sprawling, and I reined the roan around to go after him. He was on his knees, scrabbling for his gun in the fallen leaves. I started to raise mine, but suddenly Ezra was there, clinging to my arm, jibbering "They're robbing me . . . don't let them hurt me . . . stop them . . ." and his grip was the iron of blind panic. I tried to shake him off and lifted him clear off the ground, still bleating like an idiot.

Beyond, the fallen horseman had his gun. It rose, levelled and thundered, and Ezra wasn't on my arm any more. As the gunman was cocking his hammer for a second shot I pointed and fired, and he dropped his gun again. He tried to pick it up but his right hand wasn't working. He went for it with his left and I fired again. Leaf mold exploded at his knee and he toppled over on his side. I thought he was down for good, but he rolled and again the pistol was pointing at me, waving wildly. It thundered and I heard his ball whiff past my ear. I gritted my teeth, fired and saw bark fly off a tree beyond him. I fired again. He slumped, cursing, then staggered upright, his good hand still holding that damned gun. I fired two shots as fast as I could trigger them and he went over backward. He lay for an instant, then twitched and I cocked and triggered again but nothing happened. Just a loud click in the sudden silence.

Still, he wasn't getting up. Except for that one spasm, he hadn't moved. He just lay there and the sunlight filtering down through spring-green branches glistened on bright blood.

The roan was dancing and pawing, and I was twisting this way and that, still pointing an empty gun at the man there on the ground. I started to lower it and something hit me in the back — something that whistled and smoked and seared like hellfire. Thunder came with it, and I swung around. The other one. There had been two.

He sat easy in his saddle, yellow teeth glinting as he grinned at me, and I heard his hammer click back. He raised and pointed, then stopped still and his eyes went

172

wide. He swayed in his saddle, and I heard the echoes of a gunshot. A red spot appeared, dead center on his shirt, then he shuddered as another joined it, not an inch apart. I just sat there feeling dazed and stupid and watched him tip slowly to one side and fall from his horse.

My back felt cold and numb. I was dazed and I knew it, but that didn't make it go away. I heard somebody moaning and saw Ezra rolling around on the ground, nearly under the roan's feet, holding a bloody arm. There were two other men on the ground—the hillyers—but they weren't moving at all. I had done one of them, but not the other. So I looked around some more.

He was just coming out of the trees off to my left, a slim gray dandy on a sleek gray horse, putting away a fancy gun and sort of grinning at me in that sideways manner I had seen all my life.

"You took your own sweet time showing up," I told him.

"You were doing just fine 'til you ran out of loads," he shrugged. He walked his horse around behind me and paused. "Got yourself a crease there, Zack. That's going to smart some by tomorrow." He came alongside and looked down at Ezra. "Who's he? Anybody that matters?"

"Not to me, but I came out to bring him back. His sister wants him."

"Oh. Fair looker, is she?"

"She's a Presbyterian."

He twitched his reins and rode over to where the second yayhoo lay. He looked down at him, then went to the first one and paused there, looking. When he turned back toward me he was shaking his head. "Sloppy work, Zack. Lord, you shot that one all to pieces. If he was a deer he wouldn't hardly be fit to eat."

"If he was a deer he wouldn't have been shooting back."

I had been saving up for weeks to have some harsh words with Uncle Earl, but right then they didn't come to me. I stepped down from the roan and started to put my Dragoon away.

"Load that before you do anything else," Uncle Earl said. "There's been enough noise out here to attract every owlhoot in twenty miles."

I reloaded, then put it away. Uncle Earl was still in his saddle, looking around and taking inventory. "Two saddle horses with saddles and gear," he said. "Couple of guns, maybe some other odds and ends . . . a hundred, maybe a hundred and fifty. I say we split the proceeds right down the middle. That all right with you, Zack?"

"Are you going to help me get Ezra's arm bound so he'll stop leaking?"

"No. He's your friend's brother, not mine. But I'll collect the stock and the leavings while you do that. While you're at it, see if you can't get him to shut him up, will you? I hate to hear a man carry on like that." He stepped down, tied his reins to the surrey and set out to gather up the yayhoos' horses and valuables. I had to swat Ezra to get him to hold still so I could wrap his arm. He settled down a mite, but he still whimpered. The ball had only nicked his shoulder, not much more than a scratch, but the way he carried on a body'd have thought he was at death's door.

"Don't worry so much, Ezra," I told him. "You'll live. And if we have to amputate I'll sharpen up a felling ax and do the job myself."

Things went easier after that. Ezra fainted.

I couldn't reach the gouge on my back to fix that, so Uncle Earl tended it for me. And I remembered part of what I wanted to talk to him about.

"I paid that keelboat captain a hundred and fifty dollars," I said. "But that's all I pay. If you expected a share, forget it, Uncle Earl."

"Oh, that's all right, Zack," he assured me. "I never intended to take money from you . . ."

"No, you intended to get it from Spider Webb."

"That would have been another matter. But I didn't really think it would work out that way."

"Then what did you tell him that for?"

"Well, Zack, I thought it would be nice if you could have a ride on the river, like you used to talk about. But I was a little short on funds, so what I figured was, I'd just set things up so you'd have the incentive to raise the money yourself. You know how you are. If it doesn't have to be done, generally you don't do it. This way, you did. And look what it got you . . . a nice, leisurely cruise down the river in style and comfort."

He fussed over the crease on my back for a few minutes, then decided it needed stitching so he dug around in his saddlebag and came out with a cobbler's awl, some twine and a tin of Doctor Proctor's Herbal Liniment like we used to swab the hogs with.

By the time he had me ready to travel I was soaked with sweat and my eyes kept crossing. But he got it done.

When I could talk again I asked, "Uncle Earl, what's in those boxes?"

He smiled like an angel. "I'm not just real sure, Zack. I got kind of busy back yonder, and never had time to look. But I believe they contain the key to a lost fortune, and you and I are going to find it."

I just looked at him for a time, my head swimming. Then I said, "A pirate treasure? Another damn pirate treasure? Uncle Earl . . ."

He raised a hand. "No, not like that at all. Do you remember Milt Downey, Zack? Back in New Albany? The one whose brother disappeared out west someplace?"

"Yeah."

"You recollect that Tim Downey — Milt's brother — used to escort gold shipments . . ."

"Yeah."

175

"And Tim Downey wasn't all that disappeared. A gold shipment did, too."

"I heard about that."

"Yeah. Well, Milt Downey's gone, too. One day he just wasn't there any more."

"Maybe I heard about that, I don't know."

"It was about the time you fellows were building those last two wagons. You were busy. Anyway, Milt Downey disappeared, and it was funny, because some of old Milt's belongings wound up over at Frank Kingston's place . . ."

"Those two boxes?"

"Sure. That's where I got them. I hauled them out of Kingston's while you were pounding on Frank and trading horses with him."

"Uncle Earl?"

"Yes?"

"Do you suppose there are letters in those boxes?"

"I wouldn't be surprised. I never had a chance to look. Why?"

"Uncle Earl, supposing Frank Kingston was to have some notion of who got off with those boxes, who do you think he might think it was?"

He grinned that odd grin of his. "Why, I guess he might have thought it was you, Zack. But don't worry about a thing. I'll look after you."

I just stared at him for a minute. Maybe I thought he would at least drop his eyes, the way a man who's ashamed of himself ought to. But no, not Uncle Earl. He just stared back, the picture of innocence with a grin on its face.

Through gritted teeth I said, "Uncle Earl, I don't know what kind of rat's nest you got going, and I don't want to. But this time it's your rat's nest and not mine. I stayed along with those wagons this far because I felt responsible for your boxes. I hadn't made up my mind about anything else. But now I have. You've got your boxes and I'm through. I have

176

a wheel to fix, and after that I'm gone."

"Now, Zack . . ." he started.

"Now, Zack, nothing! If Frank Kingston or his tracers come at me again, maybe that's your fault and maybe not. I'll just do what I have to. But whatever else you're up to is your own lookout. Maybe I'll head on up to Westport and maybe not. But I'm taking my own trail from here on, Uncle Earl, and whatever you're slopping around in, you can just count me out."

XVII

It took some explaining to Will Posey—how I had gone out to fetch one fellow and then fetched back two—but when I told him about the yayhoos out there he nodded sagely.

"They'd have killed him as quick as look at him," he said. "There's decent folks in Missouri these days, but a body would have to get directions to find them."

I introduced Uncle Earl around and he howdied everybody, letting an appreciative gaze linger on the wagon with his boxes inside, the Conway sisters and Priscilla Lawrence, in about that order. To Will Posey he said, "I guess I picked a good time to show up. My nephew sure enough would have been a dead man if I hadn't happened to be there."

Posey glanced at me, then back at Earl. "I had a notion he could look out for himself."

"Oh, he can, most ways," Earl said. "I taught him practically everything he knows. It's just that I haven't finished teaching him everything *I* know yet."

Priscilla had wandered around behind me as I was getting off my horse, and now she squealed, "Oh, my Lord."

I whirled around. Her face was white, and she was biting her lip. She sidestepped to stare at my backside again. "Mr. Frost, you are bleeding!"

"I shouldn't be. Uncle Earl sewed me up." I tried to turn my head far enough to see what she was looking at, but I couldn't.

Will Posey came around to look. "No, he isn't bleeding. He already bled. That coat's a mess, right enough, but it's mostly dried."

"It's just a crease," Uncle Earl said. "No real damage."

But everybody around had to come and look, anyway, and that set Ezra off. He wandered around moaning, holding his scored arm out in front of him, and he developed a limp. He carried on until Priscilla snapped at him, "Oh, Ezra, shut up!" Then he went off somewhere to pout.

"I'll be glad to ride along with you folks for a ways," Uncle Earl told Will Posey in a tone that said he had just solved all of Will's problems. Then he dismounted, tied the gray's reins to the tailgate of the Conway wagon, winked at Catherine and Charity, and went off to look at the two boxes he had shipped to himself from New Albany.

"Since he's your uncle, I guess you vouch for him," Will Posey said. He turned away then, saving me the trouble of explaining to him that I would sooner wrestle bears than have the responsibility for what Uncle Earl might or might not do.

Priscilla had Ezra in tow, getting him aboard the surrey, but when he was in place she came back. "When we stop for the night I shall mend that coat for you, and give it a good cleaning . . . though I don't know whether blood stains will clean properly with camp washing."

"Well, thank you," I told her. "I appreciate that."

"In my opinion, it was Ezra's fault that you were injured. I expect I should have a look at that, as well. Possibly I could assemble a poultice."

"Tell me something, Miss Lawrence. You have assured me that God takes care of Ezra, but it seems to me that if it weren't for folks taking extreme measures to keep him out

179

of trouble, your brother would be in a heap of it most of the time. How do you account for that?"

"The Lord moves in mysterious ways his wonders to perform."

"Yes'm. But I have to tell you, if Ezra requires any more mysterious intervention you'll have to find somebody else to do the Lord's work because I probably won't be around."

I expected her to take offense at that, but she didn't. She just peered up at me with those big eyes in that little face all pulled taut by her bunned hair, and clicked her tongue. "I must say you don't *resemble* an instrument of the Almighty . . . at least as I might have envisioned one. But the facts speak for themselves, Mr. Frost. You *have* been instrumental in the preservation of my brother . . . and possibly even of myself. There is little room for doubt that my decision was correct. You require attention, Mr. Frost."

With that she returned to the surrey and wheeled it into the forming line of wagons. The two Froehnervagens were already rolling, and I could see Uncle Earl in the bed of the second one, probably looking through his boxes. The Conway wagon followed, with his gray horse still tied on behind, and then Mahlon Krause with his overlander, the Maddens, the surrey and the supply wagons. The Honeycutt wagon was last, placed there by Will Posey so that its drag pole wouldn't spook any following team.

George had ridden on ahead with Will Posey, and when the Honeycutts pulled out there wasn't anybody left there but me. I stood on the hillside, holding the roan's reins and watching the line of wagons going away. There wasn't anything in the world right then holding me to that outfit. Uncle Earl had his boxes. Waylon and George had their dreams. Priscilla had her brother, and Will Posey had as many guns — counting Uncle Earl — as he'd had before I set out to retrieve Ezra. Uncle Earl had two extra horses and some hardware that he considered half mine, but I didn't need them.

All I would have to do, I realized, was just climb up on the roan and point its nose west and go. By the time they knew I was gone, there wouldn't be a chance in the world of any of them ever finding me again.

And I was remembering the look on the bounty hunter's face in Cairo, when he told me that Frank Kingston wasn't going to give up until I was dead. "If you'd seen his face," he said, "you'd know."

A man alone in lonely country can get lost. He can lose himself so thoroughly that not a soul can ever find him — not a friend or an enemy, not even God himself. All it would take would be to just turn west.

But if I did, who would repair Buck Honeycutt's wheel?

I looked off to the west, where the Ozarks rose toward the lowering sun and beyond were lands so wide that nobody could say for sure what all was there. Then I took a deep breath and climbed into the roan's saddle.

When I came up to them, the Honeycutt wagon was staying with the others, its drag not impeding it much on the downhill haul. Buck was walking alongside his wheel-horse, driving from there, and three bonneted heads were framed by the looped canvas above the tailgate. Besty, little Penny and the baby, Anna. The tykes were watching in wonder as the long pole grooved the sod behind them, and Besty was telling them how it would be in the long years ahead, out west in the new lands, when they could look back and recall their wagon's crutch making its mark across Missouri.

As I neared, Betsy smiled a bright smile for me and began telling the tykes how Mr. Frost was going to repair their broken wheel so it would be just like new. And I was glad I hadn't turned west just then.

Of all the things that can postpone a man's search for yonder, being needed is one of the strongest. I'd mend their wheel. Then tomorrow I'd say my goodbyes. Not even Uncle Earl could get me entangled between now and tomorrow.

There were others at the place Will Posey had chosen for the night camp. Four men and a woman, with a couple of little boys aged somewhere between tad and tagalong. They had an old wagon, a hitch of mules and three gaunt horses, and from the looks of their camp they had been there a few days.

We eased around to the west and pulled in about half a mile away. And this time Will didn't have to tell anybody to keep close and watchful. Our two extra horses trotting along behind Waylon's wagon—horses that just hours ago had belonged to men who were now dead (victims of terminal lawlessness was how Uncle Earl had put it)—were a vivid reminder that in this part of Missouri it didn't pay to be trusting.

Where Posey waved down the lead wagon, the others spread and formed into two wings with the trailing wagons closing the gap behind, and every man of us had a gun near at hand when we stopped.

For a time, as our folks set about making camp and tending the stock, we ignored those others over on the opposite slope. There was a little stream between us, and a quarter mile of rising ground either way. We looked across at them and they looked back at us, but nobody made any moves out into the land between.

Like us, we guessed, they were travelers bound for somewhere, and we had no mind to bother them if they didn't bother us.

Abe Miles set a brace under the tailgate of the first Froehnervagen—the one he had started calling *General Jackson*—and I got out my tools and set up shop there. My left arm was sore and stiff from the cut on my back, but that didn't matter much. The way the Lord put me together, generally my left hand is just for holding onto things while my right hand uses tools on them. And as long as I could choose my position, the injury didn't bother my grip any.

Buck and his family had collected all the pieces of their wheel. I laid them out and there were none missing. The major damage was a pair of busted spokes, a split felloe and a gouged socket in the hub. It would take two repairs to make it right—one now with what was at hand and another later, with seasoned wood.

While I was laying out my tools, Benny and Abe took off to find a likely tree. Hickory was my preference, but I'd settle for straight ash if I had to—or even pecan or white oak in a pinch. Within minutes we heard the sound of axes over in the shadowed thickets.

I pried a gate-brace off Buck's wagon to cut pins from, and had just started on that when Priscilla Lawrence showed up.

"Give me your coat," she said.

The coat was torn across the back where the ball had furrowed me, and the edges of the cut were stiff with dried blood. I handed it to her and turned back to my work.

"And your shirt," she said.

I was inclined to argue about that, but the light was failing and I didn't want to waste the time. I peeled off my shirt and handed it to her. She wrinkled her nose at it.

"In my opinion," she said. "This is hardly worth repairing."

"I'll need it tomorrow, Priscilla," I said quietly. "I'm leaving."

She looked up at me and blinked, then stared at my chest. "You *do* look like a bear," she said. "My goodness."

I shook my head and turned to the tailgate again, and she gasped. I had seen Uncle Earl's tailoring work on human hides before, but I guess she hadn't. She hurried away and I started dressing the ends of the good spokes.

She was back in less than a minute. "Hold still," she said. Something cold touched my shoulder blade, then spread across the sore place. Cold, but warming rapidly as it soaked into my skin.

"Mustard poultice," she explained. "It will keep you from mortifying."

Between the bullet crease throbbing, the mustard beginning to overheat and the surprisingly gentle touch of her small hands on my skin, it was hard to concentrate on wheel spokes. She tore strips from a bolt of linen and started trying to bind over the cut. She stopped.

"Sit down," she said.

"Where?"

"On the ground, if you please. You are very hard to reach."

"Is this going to take long? I'm busy."

"Only a minute, if you will cooperate. Sit down."

I sat, and she marched around and around me, wrapping linen, having me hold my arms this way and that. Where she tied it off was right in the middle of my chest, square on the wishbone. She made a knot and started to pull it to, and I flinched and yelled.

"For heaven's sake," she complained. "No one should have so much fur."

"It's been a long winter," I pointed out. "Come summer, I'll probably shed."

Uncle Earl had come over to watch, and now he started chuckling. "When Zack was a tad, it was all we could do to keep him out of berry thickets," he said. "He liked to hole up in them and growl. Of course, that was only in the summer. In the winter, he hibernated."

"Uncle Earl," I snapped, "I wish you'd take that mouth of yours and . . . ouch!"

184

"Pardon," Priscilla said.

"You're doing enough of that for both of us," Uncle Earl added, cheerfully.

When it came time to unwrap that bandage, I was going to have to shave off the knot. It had as much chest hair in it as it did linen.

When I was back on my feet, Priscilla walked around me, looking at her handiwork. "How do you feel now?"

"Cold," I told her. "Cold and half-naked and mustard-raw, but I'll live if I can get on with this job."

"Well, you'd best wrap in a blanket. Your garments won't be ready until at least morning."

Abe and Benny came in with a six-foot length of straight ash trunk, and I had them quarter it into bats. Two of them I tied onto the Honeycutt wagon, along the bedrail where they would get plenty of sun.

"Cure the wood," I explained to Buck. "These will make good permanent spokes when they're dry."

The other two I shaved down to rough proportion with a hand-ax, then went to work with a rasp. When the light failed, Buck and Benny brought out lanterns and hung them above the gate where I was working.

The wheel wasn't dished the way I preferred, but it did have a one and three-quarter drop from hub, so I shaped the spokes against the undamaged ones, then dressed down the ends with lamp-oil and bound them in sacking. Two or three times a day, until cured spokes were available, Buck would need to slosh some water on these so they wouldn't shrink.

The felloe was split cleanly, and I bound it back with canvas and pegged it through with seasoned pegs from the gate-brace. Starting on the hub, I set the first spoke in the gouged socket and aligned it with a cut of gate-brace to get it firm. Then one by one, using tar to set them, I replaced spokes in the hub to form half a wheel plus one, and set it upright on the tailgate, bracing it with the tarbucket and a chunk of rock. By lamplight I worked the felloes into place, straining against the standing spokes, bending them back until, one by one, their ends chunked into their holes and the felloes sat firm forming a half-ring of wooden rim.

I stood back to get my breath, sweat drying cold on me in the cooling night air. Someone handed me a blanket and I looked around. Almost everybody in the band was there, watching as though I were the best entertainment to come along lately.

"You see how those felloes set around the edge?" Benny asked Waylon Gibbs. "That's the sign of a wheelwright. You can see where they come together, but if you run your hand along it you won't feel a seam. Ordinary wheelmaker, he'd have to take a rasp to that round to get it smooth. But not Zack. He does it by fit."

"Fit and eyeball measure," Waylon nodded. "They're the marks of a cooper, as well."

Little Anna Honeycutt was peering from behind her mother's skirts. She pointed a tiny finger and said, "Pretty."

Maybe it's in the Good Book somewhere that a man's satisfaction is in having his work admired. If it isn't, it ought to be.

"The evening air is quite cool, Mr. Frost," Priscilla said. "Tie that blanket around yourself before you take a chill."

I wrapped it like a robe and tied it around my middle with a bit of rope, then went back to work.

"We'll have to wedge the tire on with shim," I told Abe Miles. "There's nothing here to make a forge."

He looked doubtful. "We looked for a hickory tree, Zack, but there's none around. Softer wood won't hold a shim."

"Hedgeapple, then? The heartwood might work."

He shook his head. "None around here. There's walnut, and pecan and ash. Chestnut, elm of several kinds . . . plenty of oak, but oak won't sliver for a shim."

"Then we'll take it from a wagon," I decided. "Abe, do you think you could trim some shaving from the mainbrace? I have a short ripsaw over there . . ."

"This wagon's brace is pine," he shook his head.

"Well, the Froehnervagens have hickory. Take a shave from one of them."

But Will Posey held up a hand. "Now just hold on. Those wagons belong to Caleb Tucker. I don't believe . . ."

"You laid down the rules for this outfit, Will. If one needs what another has, it's shared. And this wheel needs hickory shim if it's going to make it to where there's a proper forge."

"Zack's right, Mr. Posey," Abe chimed in. "That's what you said."

"But Mr. Tucker's wagons . . ."

"Won't be harmed a bit. We built those wagons, Mr. Posey. We know what they can do without."

Posey sputtered a bit, but he subsided. We knew what we were doing, and he knew it.

"Slice it fine, Abe," I said. "A sixteenth, three wide, cut to . . . ah . . . six-inch lengths. I'll pare them with a drawknife."

"Just like old times," Abe grinned. "Ordinary folk settle for ordinary shim, but not Zack Frost. Oh, no. For him, the bits must be reeds you could tune for a pipe organ."

"Fine wonder we ever made a wagon to roll," Benny agreed, but there was a pride in his tone. The thing we all shared—and had since Carl Froehner's wagon works—was a love of our craft.

And it turned out that we weren't alone. As fine as Abe could slice shim, George Bullard could refine it with a carpenter's blade. And when it came to thinning the ends of the little panels of wood, Waylon Gibbs with his cooper's eye was a master at it.

I had the wheel turned and the remaining spokes and felloes set, and was fixing to rim the iron tire into place with a mallet when there was a commotion in the group—a few startled voices, then everybody went silent. I looked around.

There were strangers among us. The four men from the stranger's camp were a few steps away, just at the edge of the lamplight. And each of them held a rifle in his hand.

"Easy, now," the tallest of them said. "We come to talk."

XVIII

The four were brothers. Their name was Altman, and they were one of those tribes Pa used to point out, where if you've seen one of them you've seen them all. Tall, stringy men with big hands and feet, hatchet-blade noses and bobbing adam's apples, they shared the look of worn leather and sun-crinkled eyes of palest blue. The tallest was the eldest, and he gave his name as Julius Altman. His brothers were Cassius, Brutus and Marcus.

"No offense intended," Julius said, "comin' in on y'all that way. But we been shot at twice now and it makes a man cautious."

"No offense taken," Thomas Madden allowed. "Provided you're friendly, then you're welcome here."

"What we needed to know," Altman said. "Little caution wouldn't hurt y'all none, though. Had we come to rob, we'd have what we come for by now."

"I don't think so, at all." Will Posey stepped from shadows to their left, his big gun on his arm. Todd Conway was right behind him, carrying a shotgun. "Out here," Will said, "it'd take a fool not to keep a lookout."

"Seen your lookout," Altman drawled. "Knowed where you was all along. What I said stands. But we come friendly so no matter."

"It matters that you're still alive," I pointed out. Will Posey had gotten himself into a game of last-word stare-down that wasn't going to do his temper any good.

Altman glanced around at me. "What?"

"My Uncle Earl doesn't care for owlhoots." I pointed. Above and behind the four, Uncle Earl sat grinning on the high wagon box of General Jackson. His revolver glinted in the lamplight.

All four Altmans looked surprised, and Will Posey smiled.

Julius Altman shook his head and glared at his brothers. "I told y'all these folks wasn't the greeners ye tooken 'em for." He turned back to Will, assessing him as the man in charge. "We got us some fresh backstrap yonder, more'n we need, but we done run out of flour. We come to see if y'all would consider a swap."

"We could spare a bit of flour." Helen Madden nodded. "Thomas, why don't you take a lamp and lead these folks' wagon over here. We can share supper."

Will Posey looked concerned. "Missus, I don't . . ."

"Phaw, Mr. Posey! Didn't you see? There's a woman and babies out yonder. You said yourself this is a lawless land."

"Yes, but, Ma'am . . ."

"I see no harm in that," Madden nodded at his wife. "There's a comfort in numbers. Where are you folks headed?"

"West," Julius Altman shrugged. "Someplace where there's land to work that a man can't get kicked off from."

Carrying lanterns, Thomas Madden and Todd Conway started out across the bottoms, with Marcus and Brutus Altman.

"Best get cookfires started," Will Posey told some of the others, still looking worried.

Out of curiosity, I waited until he was off by himself, watching the lanterns in the distance, then I sort of eased over to where he was.

"You think those folks are a problem, Will?"

"Maybe not," he shrugged. "They're tenant farmers, not outlaws."

"Well, you look unhappy."

"Folks in general are a problem," he admitted. "Train can get out of control, mixin' with strangers."

"Where's the harm in being neighborly? Seems to me, those are seasoned men. Not bad folks to have around on a night camp."

"I don't think they're goin' to rob us," he said. "There'd have been better ways, if that's what they had in mind."

"Then what's wrong?"

"I think they plan to join us, is what I think."

"You have the say on who joins and who doesn't."

"Do I?" He looked at me pointedly, then glanced around, his eyes lighting on Waylon and George, then on the Lawrences, and finally on Uncle Earl up on his wagonbox, looking at papers by lamplight. "Do I, really?"

"Would you turn away a lone wagon, with a woman and kids, out here in the wilds?"

"If they endanger the train I'd have to." He squinted at me in the dusk. "You and your friends, you have a look at that thing they're driving. Then you tell me whether they can keep up, and for how long. Tell me that, then I'll decide."

All my life I've noticed that every time I open my mouth somebody pokes in a wad of responsibility for me to chew on. Even when Uncle Earl and I were tads, he always was good at avoiding things like that. But I never was.

Like the time that little spaniel pup turned up in our dooryard back home, just a small handful of wiggling dog, barely weaned and smelling to high heaven and needing a place to stay. I already had a good dog and didn't need another, but that potlicker nuzzled up to me and I told Ma

191

that if we could keep it for a while I'd tend to it.

I didn't want to wetnurse a spaniel pup, but I did, for several months. Even old Scrofus, a long-legged hill dog who was my best friend at the time, pitched in and helped. Come summer, that pup was a frolicsome hound big enough to tend to itself, and Uncle Earl stepped in and took over.

I heard later that he'd sold it and four others just like it — all of them had turned up on different porches around those parts just about the same time — to Squire Murcheson for a dollar apiece.

I never did get the straight of that, but it was an example of how an innocent comment always led to me having chores to do.

When Will Posey handed me another chore now, I was used to it, so I went back to work on the Honeycutt wheel and told Abe and Benny that we were going to be in the wagon inspection business directly. It didn't matter to me. I'd still be leaving tomorrow, when it was done.

I don't like to shim a wheel if there's any other way to do the job. Shimming is exacting work, and even the best job of it will lead to a tire rolling out of round. But with no forge at hand, nor any way to approximate one, there was no way to resize the Honeycutt's iron tire and sweat it into place. So I did the best I could.

Coming from the bolster of General Jackson, those narrow shims were of good, seasoned hickory. I got the wheel assembled and laid out rim-down on the tailgate, then wrestled the tire into place over the rim, using a mallet and clamps to make it fit. Then I paired and pared shimstock — top and bottom, right and left — and set them in the crack. Going around the rim, alternately rasping and tapping, I worked them down until just a hair's width remained. One more tap on each one — top, bottom, right and left — and they were in place. The wheel was sturdy, but when I hoisted it against the light—it weighed about sixty pounds—there was visible separation for an inch or two past each shim.

Julius Altman had been hanging over my shoulder, watching every move, right along with Buck Honeycutt. Now the stranger squinted at the cracks I was clucking over and said. "Was it me, I'd peg it too."

Abe Miles frowned at him. "Mister, Zack is a first-rate wheelwright. He knows how to build a wheel."

It didn't bother Altman any. He just shrugged. "Buildin' is one thing. Fixin' is another. Back yonder folks learn a heap about make-do."

"Where would you peg it?" I asked him.

"Here and here," he pointed. "Drill and drive, push the rim out."

"I never tried that before."

"Reckon you never had to. Field ain't like factory."

Abe was ready to argue with the hillman, but the more I thought about it the more sense it made. I'd always shrunk the tire to grip the wheel. But without a forge I couldn't do that. With pegs, I could expand the wheel to grip the tire.

"Where are you folks from?" I asked Altman.

"Carolinas," he shrugged. "Virginia. Tennessee. Kaintuck. Wherever."

"Farming folks?"

"None better. Farm and hunt. What our Pa raised us to do."

I had asked about as much as was polite, but he hung around while I rigged my drill.

"Hear tell there's places west," he said, "where a man can claim land for his own and raise crops for hisself, and no landlord to answer to."

"That's how I hear it, too."

"Anyways, our kind never held with slavery, an' now it's so that all the planters are throwin' out their sharecroppers

193

and puttin' nigras to the fields, so it's best we go someplace else."

I drilled my holes while George Bullard worked the rest of the hickory down to little tapered dowels, wheel-wide. Then I tapped them into place with a mallet — one top, then one bottom, then right and left, and so on, preserving the round. When it was done it was a busy-looking rim, with eight extra pegs through its felloes. But there was almost no gap between rim and tire, even alongside the shims.

Julius Altman peered at it with me, and his mouth twitched at the corners, under his beard. "Heap of how-to in this world that a feller don't learn in shops," he said.

Uncle Earl had repacked his boxes and come down from the wagon box, looking puzzled. I asked him what he had found and he said he'd be damned if he knew.

Benny brought grease and we dressed Buck's axle and put the wheel back in place with a shiny new linchpin from Buck's own toolbox. Betsy and the babies looked at it admiringly, holding a lantern to see its contours. I took a look at the other wheels for loose tires, but they all seemed solid.

"I want to thank you for that," Buck Honeycutt said when it was done. "Betsy and me, we have all we own in that wagon. When we broke down, well, I tell you, I was lookin' my bad dreams right in the face. I don't know what we'd have done if we had to abandon now."

"Enjoyed it," I told him honestly. "But the first place you come to where there's a good forge, you get that tire sweated on right. Any wheelwright can handle it, or a blacksmith that's worth his salt. There's one trick I like, treating the rim with wax and sand before the hot tire goes on. Makes it grip like nothing else I know."

"Maybe you can do that, when we get someplace," he said. "I'd pay you for it, what I can."

"I don't expect I'll be around then," I told him. "But any wheelwright can handle it for you."

I wandered off to find a pan of water and some soap, and Julius Altman tagged along after me. When we were alone he said, "I caught your name back there. Are you the one the bounty men are out for?"

I peered at him in the gloom, wondering where he'd heard about that and what he intended to do about it. "There may have been some," I allowed. "But that was back yonder. I think it's behind me now."

"None of my business, 'cept I like a man who'll help folks out now and again. But it ain't behind you, mister. Somebody is out for your hide, sure enough. You might want to watch your backtrail."

"I'm obliged," I said. "Anything more you can tell me?"

"Just that a feller has got things stirred up in Cairo, and ain't makin' bones about offerin' money for you, delivered. Heard about it clean up at Sally Run, comin' across."

"Your folks are coming in," I told him, hearing the creak of a wagon and stamp of hooves in the darkness beyond the ring of canvas tops.

"Heard 'em," he nodded. "That's Lib drivin'. She's Marcus's woman. Easier hand on the reins than he has. The rest'll be bringin' the stock."

"If you're going west, you ought to join this party," I suggested. "But Will Posey would have to say aye to that. I guess he heard you say you'd been shot at back yonder. He's a cautious man where trouble for his party is concerned."

He looked at me with eyes deep-set and shadowed. "Expect a man to be that. I'll talk with him. But I wonder, does he know he has a bountied man here?"

"No, but it doesn't matter. I don't plan on staying. You think people will cross the river looking for me?"

He nodded. "Reckon they already have. You made yourself a bad enemy seems like."

"Yeah. His name is Frank Kingston, and I guess he has reason not to like me. But I thought I put a stop to that at

Cairo."

"There may be a mite more to it than you know about, Mr. Frost."

"And you know more than you've said." My hand had wandered near the butt of my Dragoon, but he saw the gesture and shook his head.

"I mean you no harm," he said. "But I know. You probably recollect a cousin of our'n. Name of Slater?"

Slater. Yes, I knew the name.

"That's the one," he said. "My brothers and me, we don't hold with his line of work, but he's a fair enough man for bein' a tracer. It was him we met outside of Sally Run. He told us, how you had him dead to rights back yonder, but you done him fair . . . and about what you done to that Kingston when he caught you."

"And is your cousin one of those after me?"

He shook his head. "He's had enough. You won't see him again. But I reckon you'll see Frank Kingston when he's on his feet again. Slater said you burned off half his face and stole some letters from him."

"I didn't steal anything from him. The rest of it . . . that was his own doing."

"I reckon. That's how Slater saw it, too. But he'll be comin' soon enough. Slater said that."

"Well, I'll tell Will Posey about it, and then I'll head off on my own. But you folks ought to stay with the party if he'll let you — at least to the river road where there's traffic."

"I reckon," he said. "Be up to him."

"We already had one run-in with owlhoots."

"I heard." He rested his rifle across his arms and leaned against a wagon-wheel. "It's this slavin' business that's done it. Ever'body in lawful parts is choosin' up sides, seems like. An' ever'body in the backlands has gone wild. Folks are talkin' war some places. Things get that way, it just sets the bad 'uns loose."

196

"I heard you say you folks had been shot at."

"Yeah. Back yonder. Just local politics was all. Democrats."

The Altmans' wagon pulled in—not into the circle but just alongside—and I could hear them unhitching their team and tending stock. I dried my face and hands on a blanket, and when I looked up Julius Altman had gone off to lend a hand.

"You heard all that, Uncle Earl?" I asked quietly.

He came down from the bows of the transit overlander, making almost no sound. "You've got yourself in quite a mess, Zack. I'd be careful if I was you."

It wouldn't have accomplished anything to explain to him that it was *him* who'd got me in this mess. I had learned a long time ago that with Uncle Earl, the facts of any matter were as he chose to see them, and there was no changing his mind. But I was curious. "Frank Kingston was after me about some letters, Uncle Earl. He still is. But I don't know about any letters. What did you find in those boxes?"

"Nothing much. Just odds and ends, Milt Downey's stuff. I wouldn't be surprised if old Frank had him killed just so he could see what was in his room back there."

"You think Milt is dead?"

"He disappeared, and Frank had his stuff. It seems likely."

"So now you have his stuff and Frank thinks I do."

He shrugged. "Seems like." He wasn't looking at me. He was turned half away in the shadows, gazing across at the people making camp—going here and there, figures by firelight. I knew he wasn't going to tell me anything. Uncle Earl had never in his life drunk from the same stream as other folks, and most folks never knew how to take him. I usually did, but it didn't help much.

Most folks, when they know something they don't intend to tell, become evasive or aloof. Uncle Earl never was either of those, but Pa had a word for him that always seemed to fit. He was obtuse. Evasive is to aloof as the pullet you can't catch for dinner is to the rooster on the barn roof that isn't worth bothering about. Obtuse, on the other hand, is like when you're hungry and there just plain aren't any chickens around.

Even as a tad, Uncle Earl was like that. When he chose not to enlighten a body, there just weren't any chickens around.

But I had never learned to quit trying. "Uncle Earl, what was in those boxes?"

"I told you. Odds and ends. Milt's Sunday suit, some shirts, a busted watch, pair of old boots. Not worth the bother."

"Uncle Earl, were there letters in the boxes?"

"A few. Letters from homefolks and like that."

"Uncle Earl, were there any letters from Milt's brother Tim?"

"There were a couple, but they didn't say anything about gold shipments. Stop ragging me, Zack. You know I wouldn't keep anything from you."

"Sure. Like you wouldn't spirit away the apple pie at a church social."

He leaned nonchalantly against a wheel and his mustache lifted as he smiled. Catherine and Charity Conway were fussing around a cookfire a little ways off, and I could read his mind as well as I could read mine.

"This is a good looking outfit," he said. "You know, Zack, I've about come around to your way of thinking. I believe the thing a man should do is go west in search of his fortune."

"You do."

"I do. I believe you had the right notion all along about that. And after talking to Mr. Madden and them—about how they plan to set up in business at that new town out there, that Denver, well—that strikes me as the place a man might want to go."

"It does."

"For a pure fact, it does." He was still eyeing the Conway girls. Now he pulled out a little comb and slicked back his mustache. "Might go see what's cooking," he said.

As he started away, I retied my blanket and wondered about supper. That and one other thing.

"Uncle Earl?"

He glanced around.

"The letters from Tim Downey. Where were they mailed from?"

"Denver, Zack. See you around."

I saw Priscilla across the camp, carrying a steaming pot. For this camp at least, Will Posey had assigned her to take charge of the cooking.

XIX

Presbyterian or not, Priscilla Lawrence turned out to be a hand at cooking. With just trail provisions to work from — a fresh deer the Altmans provided, flour and saleratas from the Maddens' supplies, a bucket of fresh milk from Charity Conway's cow, a little molasses and salt and a bit of spice from Betsy Honeycutt's wares — and with some of the other women toting pots and tending a dutch oven, she put out a feed that would have done a Spaniard's *cocinero* proud.

When everybody's plate was full and folks were spreading around to eat, Will Posey ambled across to where I was squatted on my heels and hunkered down beside me. He had a plate in one hand and his knife in the other, and was packing away grub like he'd been starved.

"Don't know why that woman didn't speak up before, when we first looked for a cook," he grumbled. "We never would have had to set tongue to that slop of Waylon's if we'd knowed about this."

"I don't know why," I agreed. "But then, I've been through a firefight and three free-for-alls with Miss Priss and to date I have yet to understand anything about her. Did Altman talk to you about joining up?"

He nodded, shoveling in another blade of meat and dumplings. "Fyed hing abah't."

"What?"

He chewed, screwing up his face for patience, and finally swallowed. "I said I'd think about it. Lordy, if man was meant to eat and talk at the same time he'd have two blow-holes on his face. I said I'd think about it, but first I want you and them drivers to have a look at that old wagon. I want to know is it sound."

"We'll look at it, first light. But I think you could do worse than to have Julius and his brothers along. Strikes me they're folks that carry their own weight."

"My thinkin' too. 'Course, it'll be up to Mr. Tucker and Captain Rawlings whether they can sign on past the makeup at Westport. Generally, folks pay passage to join a train. But sometimes they can pay in kind. That's what I expected you were plannin' until you all signed up a little bit ago."

"They might hire as guards or scouts. They're good men, I . . . until what?"

"What?"

"What you just said. Who 'signed up'?"

"Why, you did. Cash money, on the barrelhead. I already got you on the roll. Didn't he tell you?"

"Who?"

"Your uncle. You know, I'm danged if I can see how that young feller is your uncle. I mean . . ."

"He's my uncle, all right. And two years older than me to boot. But he can't sign me on. He wouldn't pay the price if he had it, which I doubt."

"Well, he did. Cash money, up front, for the Frost-Donovan party. Listen, Zack, I don't know what it's all about, but I already signed you into the passage register. It's done. If you got a problem, you can talk to Captain Rawlings about it at Westport. But unless he says otherwise, you and your party are part of the Tucker company now. I hope that's clear."

Yes, it was all very clear. Like lantern light through a

rathole. I had left my gear stowed in General Jackson, and when Priscilla had taken my coat and shirt, I had put my wallet there, too. With my flotsam money. And that was where Uncle Earl's boxes were, and where he'd gone to poke around in them. What was it I'd been telling myself, just hours earlier? That I'd stick around just long enough to fix the Honeycutts' wheel, then I was gone. Not even Uncle Earl . . . so I had told myself . . . could change that between then and tomorrow . . . could he?

Can crows fly? If I left now, I'd leave flat broke.

Will couldn't give back my money, because that would mean revising the register and only the wagonmaster can do that, and Captain Rawlings was wagonmaster but we wouldn't see him until we got to Westport—or at least to the river road—because we were just a partial party in transit.

Once more, just like always before, Uncle Earl had taken it upon himself to guide my steps along paths of his choosing.

The realization of it rose up in my throat and Will Posey shied away so fast he like to have dropped his plate. I glanced around and he was edging away, his rifle at his hip pointing my direction.

"Drop that bore," I told him.

He hesitated, then lowered it, balancing rifle in one hand and plate in the other. "Well, all right. But damn, Zack, when I hear a growl like that comin' from a critter the size of you, I just naturally think bear."

I set my plate on a tackle box and turned away.

"You haven't finished your eats," he said. "Don't you want the rest?"

"You eat it if you want it. I have to go find Uncle Earl and do him bodily harm."

I made a pair of rounds of the wagon camp, with people scattering ahead of me, gawking at me just like Will Posey did and probably thinking bear. But Uncle Earl wasn't to be found. I checked out my tack, and sure enough my money was gone. All I had left was in my pocket. Uncle Earl's boxes were there and I rummaged through them but there wasn't a letter anywhere—not so much as a scrap of paper.

His gray horse was in the slung corral with the rest of the stock. So were the two owlhoot horses he had brought in. His saddle and gear were where he had stacked them. So he hadn't gone off anywhere unless he went on foot. But I couldn't find him.

I started another round and hauled up short to keep from bowling over Priscilla Lawrence. She had come from someplace to stand directly in my path, holding a roll of cloth in one hand and a little clay pot in the other. Her feet were braced wide as though to turn a storm and she gazed up at me from about the level of my wishbone. When I stepped aside, she moved too, blocking me.

"I do wish you would stop blustering about," she said. "You are frightening the children."

"I'm not blustering. I'm looking for my Uncle Earl. I intend to whack him upside the head several times."

"Apparently you are angry with him," she said. "In my opinion, anger accomplishes very little in dealing with people. Sit down."

"What?"

"Sit down," she repeated. "I want to redress your wound. I've made a fresh poultice. Remove your blanket and sit down."

"Where?"

"Right here. Sit on the ground so I can reach you. And for heaven's sake, stop scowling. You look like a cranky bear."

"I feel like a cranky bear. When I get my hands on Uncle Earl . . ?"

"Sit down!"

I sat and peeled off my blanket. The air was cold.

"Now hold still," she ordered. "This will do wonders for you."

She removed the earlier, makeshift bandage and cleaned the stitched cut, muttering to herself about the quality of sewing that had been done there.

"I killed a man today," I said to nobody in particular.

"Yes, I heard all about it," she said. "You saved Ezra's life. Under the circumstances, I'm sure God will forgive you."

"Speak for yourself, Miss Lawrence. Ezra isn't God's brother."

She clamped her mouth shut and slathered on cold poultice, none too gently.

"Not the first man I've killed, either," I complained.

"Stop hunching your shoulders like that. Do you want to pull these stitches open?"

The poultice started to warm and she painted on a second layer.

"All I wanted to do was take a look out west," I said, bitterly. "Just pack my things and go. Just see what's beyond the hills and across the rivers. That's all. Just . . . simply . . . go."

"That doesn't sound very responsible," she noted.

I ignored her. "That was all I wanted to do. Just go west, alone and free and nobody dogging my trail or weighing me down or tagging along or . . ."

"In my opinion, a man without responsibility is apt to get into trouble."

"Trouble! My lord, woman, since I . . ."

"Hold still!"

"Just . . . peaceably . . . minding my own business . . . quietly go west. That's all. But no. I have been kidnapped, ambushed, shot at, beaten, threatened with bodily injury, shot at, belabored by hypocrites, attacked by hornets, kicked into a river, blown up, shot at, accused of larceny, sent on fool's errands, misdirected, lied to, tricked, shot at, robbed, hounded, ah . . . did I mention being shot at?"

"Several times. Hold still."

"I have been burdened with responsibilities I never wanted and that are none of my doing, I've had a price put on my head, I've been preached at and sworn at, and every time I see my way clear to get shed of it all and head west . . ."

"In my opinion, we *are* going west."

"Not *we! Me! I* want to go west. By myself. Alone. I want to just ride away and not look back, and go see what's yonder."

"You are hunching your shoulders again."

She laid on a compress and wound bandages over it, skittering around me like a waterbug around a lily shoot while I sat there with my arms sticking up.

"All I ever wanted," I muttered. "Just to go west and be a wagonwright. But can I get it done? Oh, no. Everywhere I turn there are pirates and keelboaters and Democrats and Presbyterians and ecumenicals and tracers and Frank Kingston and people's idiot brothers and the last thing I needed was Uncle Earl to boot. Where is he, anyway? I need to stomp his butt for him."

"Who?"

"Uncle Earl."

"He was around a little bit ago. In my opinion, Mr. Frost, you would benefit by looking to him for guidance. Such a mannerly gentleman. My! Is he really your uncle? You must be twice his size, at least. And so different. I'm sure *he* would never bluster and carry on like . . ."

"He's a damned thief, is what he is."

"Mind your tongue, sir! The Lord . . ."

"The Lord never had Uncle Earl to put up with. He stole my money! He just flat up and took it! And then had the gall to sign me on with a wagon party. I don't even have a . . . what are you doing back there?"

"It's all this hair on your back. I got my finger caught. Hold still. Heavens!"

"Well, that hurt."

"I'm not surprised. There. You can stand up now, and for heaven's sake put that blanket on again. You'll catch your death and offend the ladies."

When I was bundled up again she said, "I washed the blood off your shirt and coat . . . most of it, anyway. I shall mend them in the morning."

"Good."

"In the meantime, if you like, you could come and sit by the surrey with me and tell me what's troubling you."

"Tell you what's . . . ?"

"Well, you do seem aggravated."

"What do you think I've been doing here? I've *been* telling you."

"You have been blustering. I make it a point not to listen to bluster."

"Oh, for God's sake!"

"Yes. Exactly. Ah, Mr. Frost . . . ?"

"What?"

"Thank you for not letting those people shoot Ezra."

"You're welcome."

"I have pointed out to Ezra that he owes you his life. I believe he is very contrite about the whole thing."

"Good. I . . ."

"I made it very clear to him that from now on he is to be on his best behavior where you are concerned, and that he is to assist you without complaint when you convert our surrey."

"When I what?"

"Convert our surrey. Mr. Posey said you will have to reinforce its hounds and construct a weatherproof containment to make it fit to travel. He said some of the Mormons have used surreys in their travels, but they require conversion."

"The Mormons?"

"Probably, although he was referring to the surreys."

"Does he intend for me to do that before or after I inspect

the Altman wagon?"

Thomas Madden had wandered across, smoking his pipe. "Speaking of that," he said, "do you know anything about Conestogas? My lazy board is stuck."

"Mine does that, too," Paul Conway spoke up from his fireside. "I didn't want to mention it while you were just a guest, but now that you all are members of the company, do you suppose . . ."

"I need to see if Waylon can patch my water barrel, too," Madden added. "It doesn't seal."

"Like Mr. Posey said," Todd Conway recalled, "share and share alike."

I gave up looking for Uncle Earl and went and found Will Posey. "I can't be a member of this wagon company," I told him. "I don't have a wagon."

He raised a brow, then pointed at Waylon Gibbs' wagon. "What do you call that?"

"I call that Waylon Gibbs' wagon. It isn't mine."

"Well, it's part of your registry. They came here with you. Same with that surrey over here. By the way, you ought to reinforce the hounds on that before we hit rough country. I've seen Mormons do that, and it worked out fine."

"I want to see the register, Mr. Posey."

"You can see it, but like I told you, I can't change it. Bring a light."

He dug out his logbook and registry and watched me closely while I read the entry there, signed for me by Uncle Earl. The Frost-Donovan party was duly recorded as a part of the Tucker Company, in transit to Westport for emigration to Colorado. The Frost-Donovan party, it said, consisted of one bow-rigged freight wagon, one surrey, six draft animals, five head of riding stock, various articles of equipment, five able-bodied men and one woman. The men were Earl Donovan, Waylon Gibbs, George Bullard, Ezra Lawrence and me. The woman was Priscilla.

As part of the articles of entry, I was named as responsible individual for the whole shooting match, and each of us was assigned a job with the transit group. I was named as wagonwright, Waylon as cooper, George as carpenter and stock tender, Ezra as chaplain and Earl as roving guard.

I felt as though smoke was going to come out of my ears any minute.

"You saved a mite of money by takin' on these jobs," Posey assured me. "Whole passel would have calculated out to near six hundred dollars, but I let you on for four-fifty."

"I think I'll kill him," I growled.

"Who?"

"Uncle Earl."

"Not while you're with this company," he said, sternly. "I won't stand for any such thing as that."

XX

Looking back, I guess my ill temper that evening was the result of several things. Being hoodwinked, outthought, misdirected, shot at and stitched with a cobbler's awl, all in one day, is enough to make a man surly. And then Uncle Earl showing up like he did and right away stealing my money and consigning me to a transit wagon party, well, I guess it just set me off. For a fact, I wasn't fit to be around at the time. But after a good night's sleep, maybe I could see things a little more reasonably. I still meant to nail Uncle Earl's hide to a barn door, but I'd got past growling at all and sundry.

It wasn't everybody else's fault, after all. And it wasn't like I wasn't headed where I meant to go. I had been set on going to Westport since the minute I saw Mindy Tucker's eyes and they put me in mind of Yolanda's eyes. And sure enough, that's where the transit company was bound. Westport. It was just a cumbersome way to travel for a man with a fast horse and no obligations.

But I slept on it and thought about it. I could still leave. I could leave broke, but I could leave. I might sell his horse . . . It was just the principle of the thing. If Uncle Earl could just have behaved himself that one time, I could have made my own choices. But, I guessed I still could.

I knew from childhood that fretting about Uncle Earl's

behavior was about as productive as fretting over why goats eat wash-line flannels. No amount of soul-searching ever made a goat quit being a goat, and no amount of fretting ever changed Uncle Earl.

When I woke up with dawn in the Missouri sky and spring birds a-spangle in the chilly air, he was squatted there beside me with a hot mug of steaming coffee in each hand and a cheerful grin on his face. I took one of the mugs. "You owe me four hundred and fifty dollars," I told him.

"Heard you raised a ruckus last night, Zack," he said.

"I was looking for you. Where were you?"

"I told Will Posey I'd take a turn now and again as night guard, so that's what I was doing."

That hot coffee tasted good, and it sort of took the edge off. So all I said was, "You owe me every dime of that money you took, Uncle Earl. Every last dime."

"Just consider it an investment, Zack. Trust me. Have I ever failed you?"

"Yes. Just about every time that I can remember that you said for me to trust you."

He grinned again and tilted his head. "Nice to think about those old days when we were kids," he sighed. "But we don't have time for reminiscence now, Zack. We have work to do."

"Like what?"

"Well, for starters, you promised to inspect the Altman wagon for Will Posey. Then you need to reinforce the hounds on Miss Priscilla's buggy . . ."

"It's a surrey, Uncle Earl. Buggies only have one bench."

"Surrey, then. Better see about the axles, too. And it seems like it would be a good idea if you'd rig curtain ties on it, so those folks won't get wet when it rains. Hate to see a lady like Miss Priscilla get wet."

"I've seen her get wet. She's not bad."

"Have you, now?" He arched a curious brow. "Anyway,

both of those Conestogas have stuck lazy boards . . ."

"Comes of their being painted shut. Germans built them."

". . . and I told Mahlon Krause that you'd be along to move those boxes of mine over into the freight wagon."

"Do it yourself, Uncle Earl."

"All right. I'll do that part of it before I leave."

"Leave?" I glared at him. "Where are you going?"

"Oh, I'll be back directly. Thought I'd ride part way back along our trail. Have a notion there may be people back there, being curious about us. I'll go take a look."

He wasn't going to say any more than that, and I knew from knowing that he wouldn't that there probably was a whole lot more to it than what he said. It comes of knowing Uncle Earl. The more he knows the less he'll say about it, and the less he says the more you know he knows. It gets to the point that being around him is spooky, because you feel like he knows all there is to know about every single thing that doesn't get mentioned.

He went off to move his boxes out of the transit over-lander—the last time I'd seen them they had been in General Jackson, but that didn't seem worth even wondering about—and I was finishing my coffee when Priscilla came with my shirt and coat and another steaming mug.

"I hope you're not still in a snit this morning," she said cautiously. "You already have about half of these people afraid of you."

"I am just fine this morning," I assured her, sampling the fresh mug. "What is this?"

"Herb tea. It relieves constipation."

"I may relieve Uncle Earl's constipation with a boot."

"That's how you were talking last night. You were quite cross, you know."

"Small wonder."

"Take off that smelly blanket and let me see your bandage. Sit down."

"Again?"

211

"Again."

I sat on the ground and she mused over my repairs until she was satisfied, then I put on my shirt and coat. They were neatly mended and clean. "Thank you, Miss Lawrence."

"It was nothing, Mr. Frost."

Little threads of pink cloud off on the eastern hills said it would be a bright day, and the birds were all agreeing on that. All around the circle the wagon camp was waking up, coming alive with the sounds of people getting set to face another day. And it was a sizeable camp, it seemed to me. Counting the Altmans, they numbered ten vehicles — the two big Conestogas of the Maddens and the Conways, the two Froehnervagens which weren't quite as big and heavy as the Conestogas but were trim and racy with the look of far places to them, Buck and Betsy Honeycutt's prairie schooner, the tall transit overlander that Mahlon Krause was delivering to Westport, two plank-sided freighters, Priscilla's canopied surrey and the Altmans' weathered old wagon.

Ten rolling vehicles encircling the road camp of thirty-five people — sixteen men, eight women and nine children in all. And a sizeable slung corral just beyond where men were coming to tend the stock and Uncle Earl was saddling his gray. Forty-six draft horses were there, with nine saddle horses and three mules, and in a pen alongside two milk cows waiting for their milkers.

I tried to imagine what the emigrant camps would look like, when all the parts of the train had come together and were rolling west, aiming for yonder. How many wagons would there be then? How many bowed tops of white canvas to catch the morning sun? How many big wheels ambling over distant miles, stout hubs radiating bright spokes that would gleam and flash as they passed?

Yes, I thought, it would be worth seeing.

Abe Miles and Benny Strother came from the pair of

generals and we walked across to the gap between the Conway wagons and out to where the Altman wagon stood.

It was not pretty like the others there. It was not bright and new. Its paint was weathered and its sideboards patched, its bow-stretched canvas stained and motley with old repairs. Yet it stood proud and tall, square on its axles, old hubs black with grease and soil yet still firm.

"Come to see if we're fit to roll?" Julius Altman asked, standing beside a rear wheel that came to his shoulder.

"Will Posey wants to know," I said.

"Then have a look," he shrugged. "She's seen more of God's country than all these others put together, but I reckon she's sound."

And she was. We went from tailgate to doubletree, Benny bouncing around looking at axles and centerfits, Abe crawling underneath to inspect the massive midpole and the hounds and braces while I went from wheel to wheel, scraping hubs to see the raw wood, testing spokes in their sockets, squinting at the tires.

I learned a few things about wheel repair in those few minutes. Julius and his brothers hadn't always had a wheelwright at hand when they needed one. But they had made do, and the sense of their efforts was plain.

"Make you a deal," I told Julius. "If you'll teach me how you side-banded those felloes on that rear wheel, I'll show you a trick about troughing the hub rim to make your axle tar last longer."

He only nodded, but there was pride in his eyes.

Benny had gone forward to look at the tongue and trees and inspect the breeching. Abe Miles came from underneath and crooked a finger at me. "Come look at this, Zack. I never saw anything like it."

I went, crouching to look at the front axle where the tree hammer was attached. Instead of the swinging pivot that should have been there, connecting the doubletree to the axle frame, there was a closed oval of rusted metal and I

213

had to look twice to see what it was. It was octagon iron, and would have been about four feet long straightened out. It was a rifle barrel.

"That used to belong to a night rider," Julius drawled. "One of Colonel Darcy's Regulators he was. The last ball that gun ever fired was the one that made that hole in the tailgate yonder."

Abe shook his head in wonder. "Well, it works."

The brake shoes were hickory, and had been tended with care. Their harness was dark with age and dappled with patchwork, but it was oiled and sound.

"You folks have done some travel," I allowed, tipping my hat to Lib Altman as she came from her cookfire with a rack of seared meat. She was a trim young woman, fine-featured behind the windburn on her nose and cheeks, but there was a solid toughness about her that was a match for the whipcord intensity of her husband and his brothers.

She set the meat rack up on a shelf on the wagonside and lashed it into place. A day of good sunshine and the dark strips would be jerky. "We've wandered a mite," she said. "Horatio there," she pointed at her oldest boy. "He was a year old when we drug up the first time. He'll be five soon. And Hannibal yonder, he's three. He was born in the back of this wagon."

"Do you know where you want to go?"

"Yonder," she shrugged. "Someplace where my Marcus can put a plow to the soil and make a crop . . . and where nobody will have call to run us off."

Her husband Marcus was squatting nearby tending harness, listening. Now he looked up. "They say out yonder a man can claim land and prove up on it, and it's his own. That's where we aim to go. Folks don't get run off land that's their own."

I compared notes with Abe and Benny, then I told Julius Altman, "You folks strike whatever bargain you can with Will Posey, and don't worry about this rig of yours. It'll take you where you want to go."

The three of us walked back to the camp circle and Abe wagged a thumb at the two Conestogas. "Stuck lazy boards," he grinned. "Do we fix 'em the Froehner way or the other way?"

Benny was slicking back his hair and gazing at the Conway sisters, their bonneted heads bright as new pennies as they put away their camp gear. "The other way," he said. "What else?"

Abe glanced at me. "You up to snaggin' lazy boards, Zack?"

I shook my head firmly. "You two show off all you want, but I've snagged my last snag. Do you know what those planks weigh?"

"Thirty-one pounds, nine ounces," Benny extolled, already showing off.

"I'll clear the area," I conceded. "But I'm not going to catch them."

A stuck lazy board is like a stuck breadboard in a German kitchen. Nine times out of ten, when they're new they're stuck, and the reason is that Germans who build things generally are more concerned about a fine coat of paint than about how a thing works. Carl Froehner was one of a few exceptions.

I won't fault the work of the German wagonwrights in Pennsylvania. Every Conestoga I ever saw was built there, by them, and the Conestoga is a fine wagon, for all of being too big and heavy for overlander work. Those Germans are fine craftsmen and they use their skills abundantly . . . right up the point where the paint goes on. Then nine times out of ten they paint it shut and leave it that way. Maybe it's against Teutonic principle for a man to ride a lazy board when he drives a team, instead of walking alongside or riding the wheelhorse. Maybe it's the same thinking that makes them never mount seats in Conestogas—not even a sideboard plank. People who want to sit in their Conestogas

215

to drive them have to put the seats in after they buy them. The Germans won't.

Carl Froehner had a preferred method of releasing the painted-over lazy boards on Conestogas. We were to carefully carve the paint from the grooves on each sideboard, then apply a turnbuckle to the righthand side until the board popped loose, following which we touched up the paint job, sanded and waxed the lazy board, and put it back in place. Worked slick as goose droppings on a tile floor.

Benny and Abe, though, developed a method of their own. They'd clamp an iron extender to the right hand end of the stuck board, then haul off and drive a 16-pound sledge against it, full roundhouse swing.

One time, on a bet, I caught one of those planks as it came shooting out from its slot. I won the bet. I also never did it again.

Now while Abe and Benny went to get their extenders, clamps and sledges, I cleared everybody away from the left sides of those two big wagons and set men in cordon to make sure nobody got in the way. And when they had it set up, and swung their sledges, and those big planks came flying out to thud onto the hard ground, I believe the entire crowd was impressed with the skills of Abe Miles and Benny Strother. I know for a fact that Catherine and Charity Conway were, which was just what Abe and Benny had in mind.

There is a lesson in that. When it comes to making an instant impression on the fair sex, a man can study for years and work for hours to assemble the best wheel the Good Lord ever saw fit to tolerate on his good earth . . . he can do all that and not hold a candle to a couple of grinning showoffs with sixteen pound sledges.

If there isn't something in the Good Book about that, there ought to be.

By the time the sun was on the hills, we were rigged and rolling—ten various vehicles, seven outriders and the extra critters. And though I kept looking at the lonely hills to the west and knowing I should be there instead of here, I had to admit to myself that it was a grand sight to see those wagons roll, and a grand feeling to be part of them.

I had slung a packsaddle on one of the owlhoot horses, and borrowed an axe and a saw, and I rode out from the train in search of a hickory tree of a certain size. If a man intends to convert a church-social surrey into a working overland cruiser, he might as well start with timbers that will stand the strain.

It was mid-morning before I found what I wanted, and I was out ahead of the train and a couple of miles off the trace when I did. I worked for an hour cutting and trimming hickory bolsters to sun-cure and then work down for reinforcing timbers, then I loaded what I needed onto the pack horse, climbed aboard the roan and headed for the wagon trace.

As I topped a little rise with a deadfall crest I saw them coming, rolling high and proud with the good sun on their canvas, still a mile off but a handsome sight even at the distance.

But the wagons weren't all I saw. Not far away, between me and them, horsemen sat their saddles in the shadow of a breakaway ridge. I couldn't see how many, but I counted six for sure, and they were well-mounted and armed to the teeth.

They hadn't seen me, as far as I could tell. They had their eyes on the wagons. But I could see them, and even at the distance I recognized one of them.

Even with his face mostly covered with gauze plasters, and big wadded bandages on his arms and one of his hands, there was no mistaking him. It was Frank Kingston, and he had manpower to back him up.

XXI

Any hound dog that has ever brought home a fresh rabbit knows what to do if he finds hostiles between him and where he's going. He backs off as quietly as possible, makes a long circle around, and goes home some other way. Then, of course, as a matter of honor once he has delivered the goods, he goes hunting for the cause of his extra travel and kills it if he can.

I've heard of a halfbreed mastiff that went out and tackled a black bear for no other reason — as far as folks could figure out — than the bear was in his way when he was bringing home a haunch of venison that he had stolen from the neighbor's shed.

There isn't any question that that old dog acted right on the first encounter. Burdened by a haunch of venison, he did the logical thing and went around the bear, avoiding trouble. As to whether he was right in what he did next, that is debatable. I expect that where honor is concerned, tackling a bear might be something a dog just has to do. In his dog mind the issue probably was simple. That bear had caused him to backpedal, and that was a humiliation, and therefore his honor was at stake and the bear had to be punished if it was the last thing he ever did . . . which, by the way, it was.

It was a thing Uncle Earl and I had debated for hours, back then. To me, it was simple. It was over and done and whether the dog was right or wrong didn't make a whit of difference to anybody. No amount of moralizing about it was going to make the dog be not dead, or assure that some other dog wouldn't do the same thing some other time. But Uncle Earl just couldn't leave it alone. He acted like that old dog's last hurrah was a personal affront to him and needed to be picked over and philosophized about.

"It's not just dogs," he insisted. "People are the same way. If it wasn't for harebrained concepts of honor, wars wouldn't have battles."

Most anybody else might have lost the thread of it all right there, but I had been raised with Uncle Earl since we were tads, and I'd picked up a trick or two about following his reasoning. I had also figured out that the way to wind him tighter than a fouled millrope was to be obtuse in response to his best reasoning.

So I asked, "What good would a war be without battles?"

"You see?" he shook a finger under my nose. "You see? That's just the kind of thinking that killed that halfbreed dog. Battles are what's wrong with wars, Zack. Can't you see that?"

"Seems to me like wars are what's wrong with wars," I offered. "Battles are just a lot of shooting and stabbing. Wars are dumb."

He screwed up his face and stamped his foot and stared at the sky. "Zack, what am I going to do with you? Do you know how silly what you just said is?"

"About wars?"

"About wars. Zack, wars are how folks are. Everybody wants something somebody else has, and if the somebody who wants it makes up his mind that he's going to have it but the somebody who already has it makes up his mind that only over his dead body is the somebody who wants it ever going to get it, then you . . ."

"What?"

"I said, if . . . tarnation, Zack, you understood exactly what I said! There's nothing wrong with wars except that folks get hurt in them, and it's the battles where they get hurt. Battles are dumb, not wars."

"Why have either one, then?"

"Because without wars folks who want something and can't get it wouldn't have any way of getting it anyway, and folks who have something somebody else wants would just keep it and never really know what they wanted it for to begin with. That's clear enough."

I figured his millrope was sufficiently fouled by then, so I decided to give him a hand straightening it all out. "Let's take particulars, then. Say you want something Buster Stuckey has and Buster Stuckey won't give it up for any price. Does that mean you go to war with Buster Stuckey?"

"Exactly."

"Then what happens?"

"Then I get what I want or I don't, and it's decided."

"You get it how? By sending me out to beat the tar out of Buster Stuckey?"

"Only as a last resort," he conceded.

"So that's a battle for the sake of a war."

"Like I said, that's a last resort. There ought to be a better way."

"I've always thought so, too. Maybe it would be better if you didn't go to war with Buster Stuckey in the first place, Uncle Earl. Did you ever think of that?"

"Then how would I get what I want from him?"

"Steal it?"

"There's that, of course. But folks who steal things get a bad reputation."

"And those who go to war don't?"

"Hardly ever. It's how folks are." He looked smug.

"I guess that's because wars are matters of honor."

"Almost always," he nodded.

"But battles aren't?"

"Battles are folks fighting over somebody else's honor, not their own."

"Yeah, I can see how that is. If it wasn't for harebrained concepts of honor, battles wouldn't be wars."

"Yeah. You see, you . . ." he stopped and glared at me. "That isn't what I said!"

"Isn't it? What *did* you say, then, Uncle Earl?"

Like I said, that went on for hours. We never did resolve whether or not that old dog should have gone out after that bear. What we did resolve, though, was that going around the bear the first time—long enough to take his prize home—was pretty smart thinking for a halfbreed mastiff.

When it comes to thinking, I guess I'm the equal of any halfbreed mastiff. I looked over the situation there on that trail through the Missouri backwoods, and decided the thing to do was to go around. If I had time.

I eased back up the rise, keeping to cover and knowing how that old halfbreed mastiff must have felt when he went around that bear. I was worse than irritated about Frank Kingston being out here where he never should have been. I was downright aggravated. I'd had all the pleasure of Frank Kingston's company that I could stand, and I'd thought I made that pretty plain to him. People had died in the process of me making that plain, and he and I were both the worse for wear from it. But here he was, a long way from his habitual stomping grounds, dogging my trail just like he'd been doing—him and his bounty hunters—since the day I left New Albany.

I recollect Pa's expression the day I came home from thrashing the Bailey brothers. They were all three of a size and all as big as me back then, but that didn't much enter into the complaint the folks got from the widow Bailey after I cleaned their plows for them. Pa was waiting for me when I got home and he looked me over, counting bruises and scrapes. Then he asked, "Son, why did you beat up on the

Bailey brothers?"

And I told him straight out, "Because them beating up on me just isn't any fun any more."

That's how it had come to be, being hounded by Frank Kingston and his hired thugs. It just wasn't any fun any more.

Our run-in in Cairo should have made it all plain. But no, he wasn't through. Here he was again.

The wagon train was coming on, making good time through the backwoods hills, and there wasn't any short way back around that cutoff ridge, so I turned north when I had the rise behind me, and gave the roan a whack on the rump and let him have his head. I concentrated on towing the pack horse along behind, while it concentrated on making its strides long enough to take it where its bridle bit was going. We covered a quarter mile in the time it takes to tell about it, then I angled right and ran another one, barely seeing the overgrown trail where we crossed it. Beyond was good brush, so I hauled up and headed south again, staying out of sight of the trail but knowing where it was.

When I judged I was past the place where the armed men waited, I eased off and closed in for a look. Through budding branches I could just see the ridge, and I hoped they were still there. I went on a little further and looked again, being as careful as I knew how. I didn't know who might be around, or where, but anybody interested in our wagon party enough to watch it from a distance would be concentrating on the head of it.

Somewhere close by, hard to judge because of the forest distorting sounds, I could hear wagons—clink of trace chain, squeak of wheels, the rustling of canvas and the rattle of loaded beds. I stepped down and tied off the horses in a deadfall cove in a thicket, then crouched and worked my way toward the trail. The brush was thickest alongside the traveled way, where sunlight got through the trees and nourished the lesser plants.

I got down low and wormed through, just far enough to get my bearings. The trail seemed clear, with no wagons yet in sight though I could hear them moving, and nobody else around that I could see. I backed away into the brush, raised and started to turn, and froze. The bore of a big plains rifle may be only a little more than a half-inch of air, but staring into the business end of one can knock the stakes out from under a man—especially if he thought he was all alone.

It seemed like a lifetime that I stared into that hole, but I guess it was only a second, because then it veered away and there was Will Posey behind it, looking pale and angry.

"Do you know how close I came to blowin' your fool head off?" he demanded. "What are you sneakin' around out here for?" He eased his hammer down with a white-knuckled thumb, and I put a finger to my lips, wishing he'd hush. "Stupidest thing I ever seen a grown man do!" he shouted, a foot from my face. "If I hadn't saw that it was you . . ."

"Hush!" I growled at him and he backed away, starting to raise the rifle again.

"What the devil do you mean . . ."

"Hush!" I roared, and could hear echoes trailing off through the woods. In the silence that followed I whispered, "Will, I was coming to warn you . . ."

"Sneakin' up ain't the way to warn a body!" He blared. "Jesus God, Zack . . ."

"Hush!" What good that did, I didn't know. We had already made enough noise to bring every owlhoot in the county down on us, even the deaf ones. "We have company ahead," I whispered. "At least six, waiting by the trail. They're not friendly."

Will had finally gotten the notion of it. "How do you know?" he whispered.

"I saw them. I don't think they saw me, but . . ."

"Where are they?"

"There's a breakaway ridge a little ways on. I saw them

223

there. One of them is Frank Kingston."

He squinted at me. "Who's Frank Kingston?"

"Bad news," I assured him. "He's been sighting on me for weeks now."

"Why?"

"I don't believe I know for sure. But they're all hardcases. What do you want to do?"

"Protect the wagons," he shrugged.

"Where's your horse?"

"Yonder. I'll get him."

We met on the trail, took one long look north, then turned south just as General Jackson's lead team came in sight around the near bend.

"We got to get out of these thickets," Posey decided. "Wagons can't fort in thickets. You been ahead, what's there?"

"The nearest clearing is right under that breakaway, where I saw Kingston and his men."

"Field of fire?"

"Maybe four-five hundred yards from center."

"Then that's where we'll go. You, Miles!" he shouted. "We got owlhoots ahead! Follow me and haul up when I tell you!"

Abe nodded and slapped his reins. Posey wheeled his mount. "You bring 'em up," he told me. "Wing wedge where I stop the first one, teams inside."

He heeled his horse and was gone, with Abe Miles dusting the rumps of his teams to pick up speed after him.

Benny Strother was close behind, driving General Ames four-up.

"Let 'em out!" I yelled. "Wing wedge in the clearing yonder, and keep your gun handy!"

George Bullard, riding alongside General Ames, waved his musket and spurred his mount, heading out to share the lead with Will Posey.

The two Conestogas came next, three teams each of big draft horses hauling their loads, and I repeated the order, adding—to Thomas Madden and Paul Conway—"get the women and kids down in the beds. There may be trouble."

Thomas Madden hauled out his lazy board and clambered up, then from there to the front gate of his wagon, and behind him Paul Conway was doing the same thing. It delayed their start, and I hoped that Will Posey would notice and wait for them to close up. Damn those German wagonwrights, I thought. Didn't it ever occur to them that a wagon might have to run?

The Honeycutts didn't have that problem with their prairie schooner. Buck was already up in his seat, and as he snapped his reins I saw Betsy burrowing the babies down among the gear inside. Mahlon Krause had heard the order and he vaulted aboard his wheelhorse, agile as a big monkey, and got them to running as soon as the Honeycutts were clear.

I signalled Waylon Gibbs to hold up, and tied my pack horse to the tailgate of his freighter, then went on past Todd Conway with his supply wagon and caught the reins of the surrey's wheelhorse at the headstall. "Hold tight!" I shouted. "We have to move!"

As I led them out at a run, past the two waiting wagons, I heard her voice behind me, startled and wind-whipped. "Why?"

"Because there are bandits after us!"

"Oh, merciful heaven!"

When I glanced back, Ezra was clinging to the dash and all I could see of Priscilla was her white-laced rear over the driver's seat backrest, dark skirts billowing around it. When I looked again she was smoothing her skirt around her with one hand and brandishing her sword with the other. I hadn't even realized she still had it.

We passed the Gibbs wagon and I guided her team back onto the trail and released the reins. "Go!" I shouted. "Follow the wagon ahead! Stop and pull in when they stop!"

She took the reins at a run and the surrey bounced and

flew along the narrow trace, chasing the transit overlander.

I waved Gibbs and Todd Conway ahead, repeating Posey's orders, then hauled aside as the Altman wagon rumbled by, Marcus at the reins and Lib unlimbering a rifle. Julius, Cassius and Brutus Altman fanned out to ride flank and Julius paused for a second.

"Them your bounty hunters up ahead?"

"Yeah. Sorry."

"They know you're here?"

"I don't think they saw me."

"Then you hightail for cover and stay clear. I'll tell Posey."

He drummed away, heading for the front. His brothers were riding flank guard and pushing the loose stock, and the precision of them said they had seen a few scrapes before. They knew what to do.

Quickly, I counted noses as I had seen them. All present and accounted for . . . all but one. Uncle Earl was gone, and I recalled that I hadn't seen him since morning.

XXII

"I'll ride back along our trail," he had said. "Have a notion there may be people back there, being curious about us."

When would I ever learn that it doesn't pay to not pay attention to what Uncle Earl says? "I'll wager you that I can lift a cow on top of the barn," he told Pa one time, back yonder. Had it been me, I'd have had a tongue lashing for offering Pa a wager. But then, I was his son. Earl was his brother-in-law, and Pa allowed some differences in standard.

"What will you wager, Earl?" Pa asked him.

"I'll wager my silk hat against your belt ax," Earl said.

"But you don't have a silk hat, Earl."

"Well, I'll wager my winter coat against your pot gun that if I don't win the wager about lifting a cow on the barn, I'll pay you off with a silk hat."

Ma sort of huffed around about all that blatant wagering taking place in her house, but she tolerated most things that Pa tolerated and since Pa was tolerating Uncle Earl right then, well, so did she.

"You're saying," Pa said, "that you will give me your winter coat if you don't come up with a silk hat to give me if you don't win my belt ax by lifting a cow on the barn."

"That's right," Earl nodded. "Except if I don't win on that, but come up with a silk hat, then you have to give me your pot gun."

"That sounds simple enough," Pa said. "Let's see you lift a cow on the barn."

So we all went out and Earl looked up at the top of the barn and said, "Where's the cow?"

"Take your choice," Pa said. We had six or seven cows at the time.

Uncle Earl pointed at the nearest one, a brindle that Ma had named Lady Felicity because of its bad temper. "That one will do." Then he clasped his hands behind him and stood there gazing at Pa with his head cocked to one side.

Pa stared back at him for a while, then said, "Well?"

"It isn't on top of the barn," Earl said.

"You said you were going to lift it up there."

"Well, I can't lift it on top of the barn unless it's on top of the barn, can I? You put it up there, and I'll go up and lift it."

Pa's mouth dropped open. "Well, I'll be damned," he said.

Ma said, "Mind your mouth, sir." Then she giggled and went back indoors.

"That was a treacherous wager," Pa told Uncle Earl, "And I declare it void. You should be ashamed of yourself, Earl Donovan."

Earl didn't blink an eye. "Then I don't win your belt ax?"

"Certainly not!"

Earl dug around under the porch and came out with a tow sack. He opened it and extracted a dusty silk hat. Ceremoniously, he handed the hat to Pa. "You owe me your pot gun," he said, "because you wagered it against my winter coat that I wouldn't come up with a silk hat to give you if I didn't win your belt ax."

They went on for an half-hour or so, Pa blustering and growling like a big old bear with a bad tooth, before Ma came out and handed him his old pot gun.

"He has the right of it," she said. "From now on, I would suggest that you pay close attention to what any Donovan has to say."

Pa still fumed, but he handed the pot gun over to Uncle Earl.

Later I asked Uncle Earl what he had wanted Pa's belt ax for in the first place and he said, "I didn't want the belt ax, Zack. I wanted this pot gun. I've a wager with Seth Toliver. He's going to pay me six dollars for this old gun if I can make it shoot backward."

"It isn't worth but a dollar, and it won't shoot backward," I explained.

He just grinned in that slantwise way of his. "That's what makes wagers, Zack. That's what does it, every time."

Incidentally, about the kindest thing most folks ever said about Uncle Earl was that he took a heap of getting used to.

But right then I didn't know where he was, or why, and the best two notions I'd heard lately were from Will Posey about protecting the train and from Julius Altman about me staying out of sight. That being Frank Kingston yonder, the second was probably the best way to do the first. Trouble was likely if those scutters saw me, but it might not be if they didn't.

I gave the roan some running rein and lit out of there toward the rise where I had been when I saw them the first time.

I made a wide circle and came up to the high ground from the west.

They were still there, moved around a little but in the same shielded place back of the breakaway ridge. Now I could count them. There were six, including Frank. Three of the others were familiar, men I had seen now and again around New Albany and identified as Kingston men — toughs who did the things that Frank Kingston wanted done. Names came to mind. Bo Singer — bucktoothed and feral, a knife-fighter they said. The blocky one was the one they called Hantz, a powerfully-built man bigger than me though not as tall. And Waverly, the duelist—a known killer sheltered by the Kingston connections.

The other two were lanky men who looked like hill people, hardbitten and mean, the way hill people are when they go bad.

I was taking a better look at Frank Kingston's plasters—it looked as though someone had fashioned a cast that covered his neck and half of his head, stiff bindings running across his nose and his upper lip—when I saw movement beyond them. Will Posey and Julius Altman trotted their mounts out of the forest and into the rough clearing, with George Bullard a few steps behind.

They paused, looking around, then spread as the first of the wagons emerged in the clear. Abe Miles had always been a good teamster, and he showed it now. Those big horses pranced and wheeled smartly as Will Posey pointed the way, and General Jackson rolled along as though about to fly.

Ten feet behind was General Ames, then the Maddens' big Conestoga with its six-up hitch, its canvas billowing in the wind.

The Kingston bunch had seen them when I did, and they closed up at the foot of the breakaway, ready to move. The second Conestoga cleared the woods with the prairie schooner right behind it, and by the time the surrey was in view General Jackson was out in mid-clearing with Abe Miles hauling reins to turn the rig in a tight half-circle, Benny Strother swinging General Ames out to form up next to him

In massive motion, the transit train began closing itself into a tight, defensive formation.

Julius Altman had ridden to within a hundred yards or so of the breakaway, and George came up to flank him, carrying his short musket. When Julius reined in, hard eyes on the men half-hidden by the ridge, his posture said no man was going nearer to those wagons than where he sat his saddle—not without dealing with him first.

Out in the meadow Will Posey was everywhere at once, waving his plains rifle, sprinting his pony this way and that, shouting orders. For the purpose of this train, his job was wagonmaster. Now he was putting his charges into place.

The little surrey came in right on the heels of the Honeycutt wagon. Priscilla was driving with both hands on the reins, cradling her sword on her lap while Ezra clung to the dashboard and his wide hat. Mahlon Krause veered the transit overlander left, overtaking the surrey with a surge of power and swinging in to close the near flank of the wing wedge formation and neatly throwing the surrey into the middle of the group where it was surrounded by wagon walls. Waylon Gibbs and Todd Conway spread apart, neck and neck, then corrected course and drew rein as their lead teams disappeared behind the overlander, and Marcus Altman plugged the final gap with his teams. What had been a line of wagons rolling along a wilderness trace now was something else entirely. It was a fortress in a meadow, a bastion of heavy sides and gates, of tall wheels and standing canvas, surrounding people and animals packed tightly within.

The Kingston bunch had ridden part way out toward where Altman and George Bullard stood their ground, but now they hesitated as gunbarrels sprouted from the wagons facing them, and Will Posey rode out followed by Brutus and Cassius Altman. Five armed and mounted men now faced the six, and the five had firepower behind them.

And I couldn't stand it any more. I wanted to hear what was said. I needed to know what was going on.

With the breakaway for cover, I galloped the roan down to the last thicket before open ground, then led him in and tied his reins. I had a hundred feet of open ground yet to cross to reach the ridge, but Kingston and his bunch were facing the other way and I made it without being seen.

Climbing the ridge was tricky. Mostly it was just a steep, brushy slope, but the breakaway ledge atop it and all down its south face was an erosion shear. I worked my way up to its wall, then had to edge northward until I found a place where I could reach the top and pull myself up. I was on a little tabletop peak then, a quarter mile long but narrow, like the blade of a hatchet. I kept low and crossed to the other side, belly-down right at the edge. The whole meadow spread below, and I could see among the wagons, teams in harness all facing inward, the surrey among them and just about enough space for men to move among them to keep them quiet.

Will Posey and his guards were about fifty yards out from the base of the crest, and the Kingston bunch was off to my right, an easy rifle shot away . . . had I had a rifle and been inclined to snipe.

". . . intend to search those wagons for stolen property," Kingston was saying, shouting across the space between the groups. "I have a road warrant that says I have the right."

"Road warrant from where?" Posey shouted back.

"Issued by a court officer at New Albany, Indiana," Kingston said. "It's legal."

"Not out here, it ain't. I expect you know that. Now you all just turn around and light out of here. We don't want trouble."

"You already have trouble. You're harboring a fugitive, among other things."

"Oh? Who's that?"

"Name of Zachary Scott Frost. He has a bounty on him."

Will Posey seemed at a loss for words, but Julius Altman spoke up. "Who set that bounty, mister?"

"I set it, and I intend to have him."

"Mister, you know private bounties ain't legal. Not even back where you come from. Now do like the man says and get on out of here, while you still can."

"Is Frost with those wagons?" Kingston held his ground,

his bull voice demanding.

Will Posey started to answer, but Julius Altman cut him off. "Mister, there ain't anybody named Frost with those wagons there. You have my word on that."

"Then where is he?"

"Not with the wagons. That's all I mean to say. Now you all git!"

"What are you going to do if we don't?" It was Bo Singer's drawl, slow and deadly.

"Law of the road," Will Posey erupted. "These here wagons are in transit, an' anybody that jeopardizes them is fair game." He levelled his plains rifle. "I don't cotton to shootin' first, but I can make an exception."

Three other rifles and a musket aligned with his, and the Kingston five exchanged glances.

I had a bad feeling about this. The whole thing just didn't seem right to me. Frank Kingston was a man to bull his way through right enough, and there were teeth behind his bluff and bluster. But it didn't seem like he ought to be out here like this, confronting a forted wagon company with five men. Somehow, it didn't seem like his way.

Maybe they hadn't expected the train to fort. That was reasonable. They didn't know they'd been seen, so they might have just thought they'd ride right in among the wagons while they were on the move. And maybe they didn't know about the Altman brothers being along . . . but still the odds were wrong.

Frank Kingston wanted his horse back. And he wanted me because I had humiliated him in New Albany, and probably a lot more now because of those plasters on his face and the burns beneath them. It wasn't likely, considering how those coals had glowed, that Frank Kingston would ever again be called a handsome man.

But there was more than that. Uncle Earl had taken something from him, and he thought I had that something, and he wanted it back . . . or maybe he just wanted in the worst way to know that I was dead so that I couldn't do whatever that something—letters, he had said, and Uncle Earl had found letters—might enable me to do. Uncle Earl knew a whole lot more about what was going on than I did, but trying to learn anything from Uncle Earl was like trying to wrap a rope around smoke.

Still, Kingston wasn't likely to get past Posey and the Altmans—or even George—without a fight, but there he was, still out there crowding them . . .

As though to hold their attention!

All I had to do was raise my head to see it. Beyond the wagons, to the east, the thickets converged downward toward a sort of triple draw, a little pattern of runoff breaks that were head-high or more in brush. The three draws led up toward the wagons, and became one draw that curved back to the south, not forty yards from the tailgate of General Jackson.

And there were men in the draw now, mounted men moving quietly, hidden from the people at the wagons.

Frank Kingston hadn't changed. It was his way to take whatever he wanted, whenever he wanted it, and he always made sure he had the means to do that. Now he was going to take the wagons, and some good people were going to get hurt because they weren't ready for a massed attack from the far side. From the ridgetop I could see the deployment inside the wagon formation. All the guns were on this side. Back there, where the attack would come, were the women and children—Helen Madden and her brood, the Conway sisters and their mother, Betsy Honeycutt with her two babies . . . and Priscilla Lawrence with her idiot brother and that silly sword, crouched by the surrey, not seeing the danger just beyond them.

I did the only thing I could do. I stood, in full view of those below, and emptied my Dragoon in the general direction of Kingston and his men. If I hit anything I couldn't tell it, but the bullets sang around them and they wheeled and scattered, and I saw Waverly's horse whirl and pitch, throwing him off. I pointed and yelled, "Will! Behind you! They're going for the wagons!"

It was as though my shots had set off a chainfire. Some of Kingston's men were firing then, and the air around me was alive with whining lead. I saw Julius Altman's rifle smoke, and one of Kingston's hillmen was slapped from his saddle. And in the echo of it I heard Kingston's voice somewhere shouting, "It's Frost! I want him! Get him!"

Will Posey was already heading for the wagons, his pony at a dead run, and the Altman brothers right behind him. There was nothing any of them could do for me. What they had to do was protect the wagons and their kin.

I turned to run and something stung my leg and I found myself face down in the grass. When I tried to get up my left leg folded under me and I fell again. I tried a second time and hobbled to the back side of the ridge, and when I fell I went over the edge. I was rolling, tumbling, the slope battering me and nothing making any sense except pain. Then a gulley wall hit me and knocked the wind out of me. I lay there gasping, trying to steady down the world that kept spinning around me, and a way off in the distance I could hear guns, and people shouting.

Running hooves drummed hard ground and became a roar. I raised my head an inch and looked to the left. Horsemen were coming around the breakaway ridge, at a gallop. Bo Singer came first, then Hantz and a hillman, then Frank Kingston, roaring and waving a gun.

They went right past, not even looking my way. If my Dragoon hadn't been empty I could have shaved the odds then. But it was, and they passed, and I saw why they weren't looking. Beyond, ahead of them, was the natural slope of the ridge and that's where I should have been. Any man would have been there . . . unless he was shot and fell over the ledge.

But they would look, and then they would turn, and it

wouldn't take them a minute to find me.

And that was why the halfbreed mastiff went after the bear, fogged words in my head told me. Because he knew the bear's mark was on him and if he didn't go after it, it would come for him.

Frank Kingston wasn't ten yards past me when I hauled myself out of that gulley, and I think the only thing that kept him from seeing me was the plasters on his head. I wanted to finish the job right then. Somehow I wanted to pull him down off that horse and make it so that he could never again endanger innocent people . . . could never again pose a threat to Priscilla Lawrence. Vaguely I wondered why I was thinking that. Of all the disjointed thoughts swirling around in a world of pain and confusion, why did that come to mind?

I was moving then, dragging a leg that wouldn't do its work, and I never in my life moved so slowly it seemed. Time passed—dull, noisy time that didn't mean much except that I should be going somewhere. I kept moving, and when I fell there was brush around me and men shouting in the distance. Things came into focus for a moment then. Kingston and his riders were at the slope, just hauling rein and spreading out, looking up toward the top. But it would be only minutes before they came back . . . and where I had crossed the open ground was a trail of blood, little bright beads of red shining in the sun like rubies on a chain.

Where had I left the roan? For a moment I couldn't remember, but even while I was thinking about it I was moving again. A giddy time that seemed like an hour but must have been only a few seconds, and thicket growth closed around me.

I bumped into something and it shied away and I clung to it while I studied what it was. It was a saddle, and the horse under it was Frank Kingston's roan . . . *my* roan.

I don't remember a lot after that. Just that I was in the

saddle, and it was important not to fall off, and it was important to put as much distance behind me as that racing horse was good for . . .

And the distance had a direction that was important too. Away from the wagons. Away from all those people who would be hurt if I stayed, because there were men who would hurt them to get at me . . . away from it all, and lead the shooters away so far that they would never go back.

Away from the memory of Mindy Tucker's eyes that seemed to be Yolanda's eyes but kept fading away and coming back changed—dark and somber and always looking at me. Eyes that were wide and almost slanted, eyes that were gentle and learned to smile when she released that tight bun of hair behind them.

XXIII

Zack Frost doesn't get hurt. Don't worry about Zack, he takes care of himself. You need something done, count on good old Zack. He'll manage. Nobody stops Zack. Nobody hurts him.

I had lost blood, and the world was a shifting, changing place, racing past as I clung to the roan. Hills and ledges, thickets and meadows, canyons that were there and then someplace else . . . and voices that talked around and around in my head, reassuring.

Zack Frost doesn't get hurt. Nobody had ever said that, at least that I could recall. But it seemed like everybody had always known it. I was always the biggest one . . . first-born but not first child — that was Uncle Earl back then — but always bigger than the rest. Come rough and tumble time I was the one who was in it because I was the biggest, and everybody knew that. And I grew and learned, and the feeling was just always there. Zack doesn't get hurt. Look to the others, protect them because they can be injured. But not Zack. Nobody hurts Zack. Everybody knew that, and I knew it right along with the rest of them. Nobody ever said it in so many words, but we all knew.

How many times had I heard Uncle Earl say, "Don't worry about Zack, I'll look after him like I always do"? And his saying that was expected and it was all right because we all knew I didn't need looking after. Everybody else might, but I'd be all right.

And Pa would say to Ma, "Don't worry about Zack. He's got his head on straight. He can take care of himself." It was what he needed to say, and it was good. And Ma telling the widow Talbot, "Of course I worry about them when they're out like that, but who can keep boys at home? Besides, they look out for each other, and you know Zack isn't going to let anything bad happen."

"Earl is the oldest, isn't he?"

"Yes, of course, but Earl is frail sometimes. But not Zack. Just look at the size of him."

Nobody hurts Zack. I believed it. All the years that we were tads, there was always somebody who would try. And half the time Uncle Earl was encouraging the whole thing because he believed it, too. We all did. Nobody hurts Zack.

Bull-strong, Pa said I was. Like Pa's brother Jacob, he said. I wonder what ever became of Jacob.

Kids growing up in the Knob Hills learn the rough and tumble. It just comes naturally. But when you're big for your age—at any age—there's that much more opportunity. Everybody comes at you one time or another. The big ones come because they are big and they don't want somebody to be bigger, and if they can put you down then that makes them the biggest. The little ones are worse. They come because they can't lose. If they get lucky and whip you then they've whipped the biggest one around and nobody will give them trouble. But if they lose they really don't lose because it wasn't a fair fight because you are bigger.

Nobody hurts Zack. Sometimes I'd come home so cut and bloodied that I'd hide in the barn until the worst of it went away, and I never let Ma see me bleed. It wouldn't have been right, because then somebody would have hurt Zack, and we all knew that nobody did that. The time Uncle Earl and I fell off the top of Twin Peak bluff, when he broke his arm, I brought him home and fetched water for tending him, then I went out in the woods and bound up my ribs and never told anybody that for six weeks I couldn't stand to breathe and I had to sleep sitting up.

The voices went around and around, in time with the running hooves beneath me and the weird world swirling by. Somebody was after me, and I couldn't remember who it was but I knew they mustn't catch me or somebody would get hurt.

From a high place I saw some of them, combing the canyons where I had been, and I knew what it meant when one of them stopped and waved the others in. He had found blood. The bleeding had slowed, but still I was leaking and that was getting me into trouble. I took off my coat and tied it around my leg, and went on.

Somewhere back there I remembered wagons, and people about to be attacked by other people, and it brought an anger that steadied the world just a little. Those people didn't deserve to be attacked. They didn't need to be hurt. They hadn't hurt anybody.

I kind of wondered why that mattered. With me gone, they would be all right, wouldn't they? *I* would be all right. I was always all right. Nobody hurt Zack Frost. Everybody knew that. So why did they matter, those people? They shouldn't have mattered. Uncle Earl owed me money, but the rest of them didn't owe me anything and I didn't owe them anything. The best thing I could do for them was to be gone. They didn't matter to me.

Did they?

I would have to do something about the bullet hole in my leg. I couldn't go too far like this. But I couldn't stop, either. If I did, those others would find me. Oddly, it seemed as though I couldn't let that happen because if it did somebody — somebody else — would get hurt. Not me. I never got hurt. But somebody. It didn't made any sense, but then nothing did.

I lay-by the base of a walnut tree for a while, wondering how I got there and where my horse had gone. I couldn't remember getting off, or falling either. After a while there was movement on the slope below, and I squinted to make it out. It was the roan, wandering among brush thickets. I could just see him, legs and belly visible below the greening tops, his head showing now and then as he nuzzled at the patches of sunsweet grass beneath. But the sound wasn't coming from him. I heard hooves on gravel, but they were behind me.

It was one of Kingston's hillmen. He had his eyes on the roan in the thickets, and he rode up right beside me before he saw me there. He was raising his rifle, aiming at the roan, when I moved. He looked down, but I was already coming up at him and he saw me too late. I didn't have the strength to jump him — to go over his saddle with him and carry him down. But I did have the strength to grab and hold, and the weight to pull. I dragged him off his horse head-down, his rifle between us, and when he fell I rolled on him to keep him from using it. I heard a dull snap and abruptly he didn't move. I raised myself, the world swimming around me, and looked at him. His rifle had been across his neck when I rolled. His neck was broken.

I tried to stand, then, to go and get the roan, but the ground tilted and threw me rolling.

I hurt. I hurt all over. But I didn't want to hurt. Folks who get hurt — not me, of course, but those who do — and let on that they are hurt, they begin to believe that they are hurt and when they know they are, that's when they are. But as long as they don't let on about it to themselves, they really aren't hurt because they don't know about it. And that was a thing to hang on to, a notion so important that nothing else mattered except to cling to it. I wasn't hurt. Maybe I felt like I was, but I wasn't. Zack Frost doesn't get hurt. Not Zack.

But the voices kept talking to me and one of them was a

voice that didn't belong in my head. It didn't know what it was supposed to say, and what it said was wrong. The voices said Zack Frost doesn't get hurt. Zack Frost is always all right. No sense worrying about Zack Frost, nothing happens to him. All of them except the one that didn't belong there. You need attention, it said. You need someone to look after you . . .

. . . to attend and nurture you and walk with you in your way.

In my opinion, it said, you need help.

I shut my eyes and shook my head. Zack Frost doesn't need help. Whatever it is, Zack Frost can handle it . . . or get away from it if he doesn't have people hanging on to him all the time.

In my opinion you are very much mistaken.

How can I be mistaken? Everybody knows Zack Frost doesn't need help.

I don't know it, the voice said.

Then back off and watch. I'll show you.

The sun was a bright bird spreading its wings over dark peaks and I rode westward, using it as a beacon. I didn't remember recovering the roan and I didn't remember getting on its back. But I remembered when I had to do that, because if I didn't I'd never hear the end of it.

The voices kept talking to me, but her voice was silent now, just nodding and waiting, being smug.

In my opinion . . . just an echo among the voices in my head, but it made me wince.

I'm all right, I told it. Just shut up and leave me alone. I don't need any help.

Which was just as well, because there was no one there but me.

XXIV

Somewhere along a dark trail I managed to pack the hole in my leg with pieces of my shirt and tie it off with twine. At least, I guess I did that because when I noticed it later there wasn't anybody else there but me. I can't rightly say I remember doing it, though. Half-passed-out aboard a racing horse is no fit way to see Missouri. I don't recommend it as a mode of travel. You miss a lot that way.

I do remember lying on my back beside a coldwater stream, looking at the shadow outline of a horse standing over me and wondering whose horse it was. I remember stars winking in frosty air, and a bright moon that always seemed to be in a different place each time I looked. I remember being so cold that my teeth chattered, and so hot that I was soaked in sweat, and I remember movement . . . somebody moving around, doing things that needed to be done, and that must have been me because I remember how my leg ached with each movement.

I remember sunlight and thirst, and how cold the water was to drink, then I remember stars again and huddling beside a little fire that sometimes blazed and sometimes was just coals.

I woke from dreams that had tumbled over one another in breathless haste, and morning sunlight was on my face. I was half-starved, sore all over and aware of being alive.

I was in a tiny valley surrounded by high hills. Its floor was tall-grass meadow that sloped down to a pebbled stream. Gray ash said there had been a little fire beside the creek, and the way it was scattered around said I hadn't been in very good condition to tend it.

My saddle and day-packs lay a few feet away, saddle blanket and headstall beyond them, and the roan was grazing nearby. When I sat up he raised his head to look at me with curious bright eyes.

What I could see of the valley from there was maybe a quarter of a mile long and about a hundred yards wide, like an old loamed-up river bed with low cliffs bounding it and steep wooded hills climbing away all around. In the west, there were higher hills beyond the hills. I had come a good piece, because the Ozarks were closer now. Obviously, I had escaped from Frank Kingston and his men. Obviously, also, I had been here for a while. But most obvious of all was the fact that I needed to be moving. Kingston had hillmen with him, and they would be able to track a man on horseback.

I stood up . . . and fell down. I sat in the grass, panting and trembling, weak as a day-old kitten. Well, I'd get to moving, all right, but it wasn't going to be real soon.

I found jerked venison in my day-pack, along with some stale bread that I had put there before I went looking for timbers to toughen the surrey's frame. I ate all there was, chewing it slowly while I cooked coffee over a little fire. I had a little piece of sugar loaf, and I melted it in the coffee, then drank it down.

Within minutes, my stomach hurt so that all I could do was just lie there and groan and eventually go back to sleep. The roan woke me past noon, nuzzling me to see if I was still alive. The food had done its work. I felt a little better.

I was still weak, and my left leg didn't work too well, but with a crutch cut from a pine sapling I could get around. It was an hour later before I had found everything I needed, and the last thing I found was my gun. It was out in the grass, hidden and beginning to rust. I cleaned it with a piece of bandage and buffed it with the inside of the jerky bag to get some oil on it. Then I loaded it and put it on.

The roan cooperated when I put his headstall on him, and stood like a trooper to receive his blanket and saddle. For once he didn't even puff himself up. I loaded my packs aboard, braced myself with saddlehorn and crutch, and climbed aboard. Then I gritted my teeth and waited for the inevitable. He hadn't been ridden for at least a day or two.

If there isn't something in the Good Book about the pure cussedness of highbred horses, there ought to be. That roan went into a spasm of rearing, bucking, dancing and crow-hopping that lasted a good three minutes before he settled down. It was by the grace of God and nothing else that I was still on top of him when he finally got it out of his system.

I don't know if I would have had the strength to climb up again.

I held west, staying with the meanders of the little valley until it curved away to the south, then just riding by the westering sun and the lay of the land. I didn't have any real clear idea of where I was, except that I was somewhere west of the wagon trace and somewhere south of the Missouri River. I wasn't looking for roads and I wasn't looking for company, so I kept a sharp eye on the terrain and just kept moving.

Moving . . . and thinking about those strange thoughts I'd had back yonder when I was in no shape to think. All that about how I couldn't ever be hurt. Of course I could be hurt. I was hurting now, and not too proud to admit to it. But in a funny, foggy way, all those thoughts had been kind of right. Like the time Pa and I were out in the hills running trap lines and the widowmaker fell on us. It was a great, tall old snag that probably had stood through storm and wind for years, just quietly rotting away. But when its time came to fall was when there were folks under it. Old snags do that. It's why they are called widowmakers.

Well, it fell, and it knocked me tail over teakettle and like to broke my back. But after I had sprawled in the nettles and ached for a while I heard Pa moaning. He was pinned under the main trunk of that old tree, and bleeding from a gash on his head.

It wasn't like I had the strength right then to hoist that weight off him and pull him out, because I was stove up pretty bad and that thing must have weighed three or four hundred pounds. The thing was, I couldn't *not* do it. So somehow I did.

It took me a day and a half to get Pa home, because his head was injured and he was about half blind. But we made it, and he came out of it all right. But it was just one of those things that was part of our family. It wasn't any surprise to anybody that I wound up with just some bruises and a limp, or that I had got Pa out. Everybody knew, come something like that, that I'd come through. And I knew it, too, because that was how it was supposed to be. If I had carried on about how much I hurt, then nobody would ever have felt quite as peaceful after that.

Everybody grows up with some basic understandings, and that was one of mine. I was like Uncle Jacob, and I learned by doing what that meant.

Near sundown I came across a feral hog backed up in a thicket, and killed it for food. It took me five shots to put it down, and only two of them hit it.

I slept that night in a hollow in a cutbank and came awake at first light, chilled and shaking. A cold mist had moved in during the night, cutting visibility to twenty or thirty yards and soaking everything. I got a fire kindled and ate again, wolfing down seared bits of sizzling pig. I needed strength. Seeds from spiny bur limbs added to the meal, along with bits of bark from willow shoots and a tea made from sassafras root. I cooked strips of ham, layered them with hog tallow and wrapped them in folds of seared pig-skin. Searching in vain for berries, I found a span of wild cabbage and ate it raw. I collected resin from a gum tree and chewed on it, letting the bitter sugar dissolve and flow down my throat. Then it was time to move on.

The bullet hole in my leg was a wide, raw scar, but a thin scab had formed. I rebound it, using more of what had been my only shirt, then rubbed down the roan with the rest and saddled him. The dismal fog had dampened his spirits. He didn't try to throw me this time.

In a gray world where every limb dripped cold rain we set off, holding a course that I remembered being west. Within a mile, veering this way and that as the land dictated, I was reading the moss on trees to keep a sense of direction.

I couldn't have told within fifty miles where I was. Maybe not within a hundred. All I knew was that I had to keep going west, although the rising lands pushed me northward as the Ozarks rose around me.

Twice I found roads—maybe the same road twice but I believe they were different roads. Once I smelled wood-smoke and heard the lowing of cows, but I eased around and went on. The ones searching for me wouldn't have quit this soon, not when they had come so far. I wondered if Frank Kingston had gone mad. Maybe he had, with his face burned. But there was more to it. Something had brought him as far as Cairo, at least, and it wasn't the loss of his horse. He thought I had Milt Downey's letters from his brother Tim. I knew Uncle Earl had them, but Frank Kingston thought I did and there wasn't much I could do about that. I'd already told him I didn't have them. It wasn't up to me to send him looking for Uncle Earl. If he could pick up that track on his own, more power to him and it probably served Uncle Earl right. But I wouldn't do it.

Hours passed and the mist held, a chill blanket of dull white hiding everything around me.

Then there was another road—no more than a wagon

247

trace, but this time going north. I started to pass it by, then changed my mind. It might be a market road, where there would be farms. And if the bounty hunters were following me west, maybe they weren't north. In any case, I needed some things. I needed medicine if I could find it. I needed linen for a fresh bandage. I needed food and a place to rest, at least for a little while.

The trace wound among steep hills for maybe three miles, then angled downward to switch back on a giddy slope. At a second switchback there was a shelf of level ground and signs of many camps. More than a farm road, then . . . the trace was a commercial route. There would be towns on it, somewhere. Again I hesitated. Kingston's men could be anywhere. They could be everywhere, and I was in no shape to deal with them. I could leave the trace somewhere along and go on toward the west, as I had been doing. Somewhere, eventually, I would find my way.

Still, my leg throbbed constantly and the stitched cut on my back chafed with every movement. Both wounds needed attention. Clean cloth, soap and the makings of a liniment or poultice — I had nothing for that.

I let the roan graze, and rested for an hour, making myself eat more of the cooked ham. It was cold and greasy, with a wild taste to it, but it was food.

An hour before dark the mist turned to rain — cold, gray and monotonous. The trace swung to the left, under the shoulder of a receding ridge where little runnels sluiced down from above to become a running stream underfoot. Once or twice I thought I heard other sounds, sounds not a part of the wild land around me, but they came and went and could have been the clatter of gravel shifting itself on the sodden slopes. Solemn clouds lay low upon the hills, darkening as dusk fell on the land, and the trace went on, meandering toward the sawtooth end of the ridge.

I closed my eyes and let myself rock with the motion of the saddle. I wanted to sleep. When I looked again, the ridge had tapered away and another road was there, coming in at an angle—a wider road, with traffic on it.

I eased back into shadows, coming awake with a start. A tall wagon had passed just ahead of me, a shadow in the darkness with lanterns front and back. A man on horseback passed, glanced toward me, then turned and stopped. Behind him another wagon was rolling toward us.

He leaned, peering at me. "Almost didn't see you there," he said. "Are you one of us?"

I shook my head. "Just passing."

He turned his head toward the wagon, now only a few feet away. "Mr. Smith, hold up there, will you? There's something wrong here. Bring a lantern." He turned back to me. "You've been hurt. Are you ill?"

"I don't get hurt." I said it and it seemed to me the funniest thing I had ever heard. For a moment it brought back the giddy feeling of being lost and out of my head. I grabbed my saddle horn and braced to keep myself from falling. I had come too far since resting. I should have stopped again, but with the rain and all . . .

"Mr. Smith," he called again, "bring a lantern here, if you please."

Then there was light and I squinted against it, trying to see.

"Don't I know you?" the man asked. There were others there, too.

"I'm just passing," I told him. "Leave me alone."

"I *do* know you. You're the wheelwright. But what's happened to you? Answer me!"

"I don't know you." I shaded my eyes, trying to see past the lantern. It was nearly dark, and I felt woozy. I needed to rest.

"This man has been hurt," he said. "You men, give me a hand. Mr. Smith, please drop that tailgate."

The lantern moved aside as he spoke to them, and I *did* know him. "Where are we?" I asked.

"You don't know? How far have you come like this, son? This is the south river road, just east of Twin Bluff Camp. Two days from Westport."

Hands were on me, strong hands pulling me over, easing me down from the saddle. I got my feet under me and braced on my crutch, and I shrugged them off. "Leave me alone. I'm all right."

"All right, nothing. You can hardly stand up. What on earth happened to you, son? I thought you were coming up with some of the wagons."

"I can stand!" Again I shook them off, and almost fell doing it. "I was with the wagons, Captain. With Will Posey's group. But they were attacked . . . back yonder. The men were after me. I got away, but I couldn't go back because they're still after me. I don't know what happened back there. I tried to lead them away . . ."

I wasn't standing any more. I was sitting on the wet ground, hurting, and this time I didn't shake off the hands that lifted me.

"Put him in this wagon," Captain Judd Rawlings told them. "Let's have some light in there, and some blankets. Tory, please go and fetch Doctor Haynes. He can tend him while we roll. Step it up, now. We've lost our light already. We'll sort it out at Twin Bluff."

PART THREE

TO SEE THE
SHINING
MOUNTAINS

XXV

I guess I saw Twin Bluff Camp. It stands to reason that I was there. But all I can relate about it is lantern light and the inside of a big wagon bed. That's what I saw when I was awake. People came and went, people I didn't know except for Judd Rawlings. I told him what I could about the Kingston bunch and the forted wagons—everything I could recall about how it was, and a little about why.

He asked some questions, about how the wagons had been forted and the lay of the land, about the Altmans, and who was where. Then he puzzled on it, and came back later and asked more questions. There was a doctor with the train, and he fussed and clucked over me. Then I heard him outside, talking to Rawlings.

"Two bullet wounds," he said. "Both are flesh wounds, but the one on his leg is deep and he's lost blood. It's a wonder he could keep going."

"Two gunshot wounds?"

"Yes, but at different times. The earlier one is healing. Somebody did a barbaric job of stitching him up, but it has held. In addition, he has fourteen various contusions, scrapes and cuts, and some residual burn scars on both hands. Whatever that young man has been doing for the past month, I recommend that he never do it again."

"Will he recover?"

"I would say so. He needs rest and plenty of nourishment . . ."

I suppose there was more, but I don't remember it. I couldn't stay awake for sleeping.

With dawn, Rawlings came again. Beyond him were the sounds of a wagon camp making up for the day's travel. Just as he entered the tailgate I heard a rush of hoofbeats, mounted men on the move, going away.

"You sent men to see about them?" I asked.

He nodded. "Tory will find them, then we'll know. How do you feel?"

"I'm all right." I started to sit up, but he waved me back. "A little weak, I guess. But I need to move on, Captain. I've brought enough trouble. Those men . . ."

"You aren't going anywhere for a while. Relax."

"But they won't stop looking for me. They'll come."

He cocked his head to one side, looking at me the way a panther looks at a bear. "You consider yourself responsible for whatever happened back there?"

"I brought the trouble with me, I guess."

"Maybe you did, but I don't think you know very much about it. Kingston, you said. From New Albany. Any kin to Bailey Kingston?"

"Well, sure. Frank's his son."

"And Frank thinks you have some letters that belong to him."

"Far as I know, yes, he thinks that."

"But if you don't have them, why does he think you do?"

There wasn't any truthful way to answer that unless it was to tell the truth, so I just didn't answer. What was between me and Uncle Earl was family. I might take me a notion to bust Uncle Earl's face the next time I saw him, but I wasn't going to have anybody else do that.

Rawlings waited a minute, then he shrugged. "Something to do with gold, most likely."

That caught me off guard. "Why do you say that?"

"Just a hunch. Generally whenever the Kingston name comes up it has to do with gold."

"I never heard that. Why?"

"That's the business he's in."

"Gold?"

"Gold transport. Kaygee Freight is the biggest bullion transport operation in the west. Bailey Kingston owns it."

"Kaygee . . " Pieces of the puzzle came together. "That's the outfit Tim Downey worked for."

"Who?"

"Tim Downey. His brother Milt lived at New Albany. Both of them disappeared. That's whose letters Frank Kingston thinks I have."

"But you don't."

"No. He just thinks I do."

"So he put a bounty on you."

"Well, I thought that was because I thrashed him and took his horse."

"But he's after you himself now?"

"Yes. Of course, I burned his face for him."

"But he was already after you when that happened?"

"Wouldn't have happened if he wasn't."

I don't know if Rawlings was as puzzled as I was. It seemed like the more I learned the less sense it made.

Teams were being hitched. Trace chains rattled and the wagon quivered as the wheel team pranced in their breeching and traces tugged against the singletrees. I heard the swing team being hitched, and the lead team coming up. Pole straps were snapped on and the big wagon lurched like a thing alive, its canvas flapping against the high bows above my bunk.

Rawlings stepped down, closed the heavy gate and tightened the pucker strings. Then he looked in again. "We're moving out. You stay put and rest. We'll talk some more."

"Captain?"

"Yes?"

"With the transit train . . . well, my Uncle Earl might be there. And a couple of people with a covered surrey. I'd like to know if they're all right."

"I'll let you know whenever I hear."

What in God's name had Uncle Earl gotten us into? If Bailey Kingston owned the outfit that lost that gold shipment, and the Downeys were in on it . . . and where *was* Uncle Earl, anyway? When Frank and his bushwhackers hit the train, he wasn't there. He hadn't been there all day.

Reins snapped and whips cracked and I heard wagons rolling. Then the one I was in was rolling too. A half-oval of rose dawn light swayed across the boxed and baled cargo ahead of me, coming through the puckered canvas above the gate. Cool breezes drifted through, fresh with new spring and recent rain. Eight wagon bows held the canvas taut above, the end bows leaning outward. An overlander, obviously. Maybe a prairie schooner, by the slope of the bed, but it was hard to tell. Not a Conestoga, not even as large as a Froehnervagen, but a good sturdy wagon, fresh from some eastern works. I wondered how many wagons were in this company . . . how many already occupied by their parties and how many in transit. This one carried goods of some kind, stores for the prairie trail or for the stores and shops beyond.

Maybe this was another of Caleb Tucker's wagons, coming from St. Louis or points beyond. I wished I could see more of the train, but when I sat up I became dizzy. So I lay down again.

And slept. Slept, and dreamed again of far places yonder. Vast open spaces, going on and on, the places where the sun went. The places I wanted to see. And maybe I would, one day. Yet when I dreamed of going to those places, I was alone. Wagons rolled in the distance and I could see them out there, catching the western sun on bright canvas, going away and tiny with distance, strings of pearls on a prairie that didn't end until the shining mountains rose ahead. But I couldn't be with the wagons. Dark shadows rode the trails, searching for me. Sometimes in the dreams those shadows were men with guns. Then they would be baying hounds bounding after their game, and their game was me. I couldn't go with the wagons because if I did those dark shadows would be there too.

Westport was a grand sight. By the time we came into view of it I was hobbling around some, with padding on my crutch to ease the ache of using it. When the river trail curved around the base of that last hill before the bluffs, and the little town spread before us, I was up on the wagonbox beside the driver. Four wagons were ahead of us and nine behind, a mix of styles and sizes but all good rolling stock bound for the staging grounds. I was still bedding in the same one, a freighter driven by Percy Smith. When I pointed at the little town ahead he scowled at me.

"Not much of a town," he said. "A few cabins and some pole barns. I've sure seen better."

"Not the town," I told him. "Look past it. Just look at that!"

There was a river there, between us and the town and winding away around the toe of the settlement like a bright road. But beyond were wide, cleared flats, past the curve and on our side. And on those flats there must have been two hundred wagons, all sorts of wagons clustered here and there with the smoke of cookfires rising among them and spreading in the clear air to form a haze above. The town of Westport may not have been much, but its staging area was a city on wheels.

Groups and parties gathered there. Settlers for the Kansas lands with farm wagons rigged to roll for a few weeks with their stock in herd around them, then to serve as quarters until a cabin or a soddy could be built . . . those were in abundance. Small, sturdy wagons that appeared tiny next to

257

the tall overlanders, but would serve well the purposes of their owners. Pole corrals were everywhere around them, and beyond were pastures where men patrolled, tending the stock. Just at a glance I could see a thousand head of draft stock, or maybe twice that . . . ordinary stock for the ordinary wagons, and big Conestoga horses, Orlovs and Oldenburgs, Hanoverians and Percherons and here and there teams of Clydesdales, all for the far-ranging overlanders that would roll across the plains.

Tents and sheds dotted the staging grounds, clustered on the high places and wherever there were trees. Emigrants waiting for their wagons to arrive, I thought. Those and vendors set to serve the needs of makeup parties. Artisans and craftsmen . . . smiths, carpenters, stock tenders, farriers, harnessmakers, tailors, cobblers and coopers, hunters and packers — if such a place could not provide employment for wheelwright or wagonwright, what place could?

Judd Rawlings and his scouts led as we entered the staging ground. They waved the wagons in and we wound our way through the grounds to the bluff springs on the west side where big wagons assembled at head of trail.

Where more than a dozen overlanders were grouped in company assembly, Rawlings led his train and formed a second ring around them, then gave the order to unhitch and corral the stock.

"Two more groups on the way," he said, turning in his saddle so all the drivers could hear. "Transit train from Cairo, and a string of freighters coming down the Star City trail. When they're here we'll assemble and move out. Until then everybody stay close, tend the stock and keep guards on the wagons. This side of the river, whatever law there is, is us."

The transit train from Cairo. We should hear something soon. Three days had passed since Tory and his riders had gone back to look for them.

I counted wagons. In this company now, just those assembled here, were twenty-seven wagons, mostly big overlanders and slab-sided great freighters with just here and there a smaller rig. Leaning on my crutch, I went to have a look around. Side by side in the first circle stood a pair of matched Conestogas decked out with brass trim and bow bells. Driving seats had been rigged atop their front gates, and even the tar buckets suspended from their rear axles were polished. In a wide pole corral attached to them were their draft stock — sixteen perfectly matched brown Shires, every one of which stood near 18 hands at the withers. I had seen magnificent horses, but never such a set of teams as these. Immense and strong they looked, dwarfing even the tall Oldenburgs and feather-legged Clydesdales in nearby lots.

The bright Conestogas carried inscriptions on their gates: "Talbot Emporium, Denver City."

"Impressive, aren't they?" The voice was beside me and I turned to look down at a fancy-dressed individual with a round hat and a spotless buckskin jacket. He was big-nosed and scrawny, but his grin lit up his face like candles in a narrow window. "Rich folks' rigs," he nodded. "Half go and half show. Not enough just to get there, you know. Need to impress the folks along the way. Are you impressed?"

"I am impressed," I assured him. "Whose are they?"

He aimed a thumb at the nearest gate. "Talbot's. They're merchants. Papa struck it rich in Boston, and the oldest son is going him one better in St. Louis. These here are baby brother's outfit, bound for Denver City with the Tucker party. He figures to get in on the ground floor out there before the war starts, and make twice as much money as papa and big brother ever dreamed of."

"Power to him. What's he going to sell?"

"Dry goods, millinery, haberdashery, everything that's in those wagons there. Maybe five tons of foofaraw at twice what it's worth. What business is all about. What happened to your leg?"

"Somebody shot me. I wonder if this Talbot knows he's not going to make it to the mountains?"

He blinked at me. "He won't? Why?"

"Those hubs. See the gap there, above the spindle? Baby brother may have paid a sight of cash for these wagons, but he didn't bother to check the play in his linch pins. The way that's wearing down, another hundred miles and he'll be falling off his wheels."

He stooped to squint at the nearest hub, fingering the dark gap at its spindle. "For mercy's sake," he muttered. "How come you see that and nobody else has noticed it?"

"It's my business," I told him. "I'm a wheelwright."

He straightened and looked me up and down, suspiciously.

"Don't let appearances fool you," I said. "I've been seeing Missouri the hard way. But I know what wheels are about." I held out my hand. "My name's Frost. You see those three wagons off yonder? The long ones with the curved bottoms? I helped build those. They're called Froehnervagens. There should be some more here directly. I hope. Anyway, if I wanted to talk to baby brother Talbot about his wheels, where would I find him?"

His face lit up again, a grin that made his ears bobble getting out of its way. He shook my hand. "You just did," he said. "I'm Solomon Talbot. These are my wagons."

We looked over the Conestogas together. Their lazy boards were painted shut, as usual, but since they had driver seats that didn't matter much. Aside from loose hubs, they were in good shape.

"I can fix these," I told him. "The hubs are sound. It's the spindles that are in trouble. I could replace them, but it would be better to sleeve them and replace the linch pins with bore bolts and nuts. They're stronger that way, and they can be adjusted on the move."

I set him a price and he offered half of it and I raised the original price. He changed his mind about haggling and I went back to the first price and we shook on it. "Can't help myself, sometimes," he apologized. "It's the family tradition."

He called a man over—one of his drivers—and had him lower the tailgate on the second wagon. Then he clambered up into the bed and looked down at me. "Some of this foofaraw is pretty decent clothing. I'd suggest a modest advance for your services in the form of stock in trade. What sizes might you wear?"

"Not at twice what it's worth," I said.

"Craftsmen make formidable adversaries," he shrugged. "All right, my cost plus ten per cent." He glanced past me at his holding corral. "I would estimate that anything that fits one of my horses would be a shade large for you, but it's a starting point. So let's see. You'll need shirts and britches, a coat, decent boots . . ."

I decided I liked Solomon Talbot.

"One thing," I told him. "There's a fellow who shows up now and then, claiming to be my uncle . . ."

"Claiming to be? Who is he?"

"He's my uncle. Anyway, just in case he should show up here, no matter what he says, I want my money paid to me, not to him. And any deals he wants to make are his own deals and I have no part of them. And if you want to practice your family tradition on him, have at it with my blessing. Maybe *you* can cure him of sucking eggs."

XXVI

Honest, paying labor may or may not have curative powers. But time does, and labor is a better way to pass time than sitting around fretting. There was a blacksmith with the Tucker party, a little rawhide fellow named Anson Griggs heading for the far lands with a wife, a passel of children, two farriers and a rolling forge. With Solomon Talbot paying the bills we got the forge stoked and glowing, and Griggs and I went to work making spindle sleeves for the emporium Conestogas. Those Germans in Pennsylvania never put sleeves on their spindles when they built the big wagons to sell, and I never understood why. Every German I ever knew who drove a wagon of his own had sleeves on it. We put them on every Froehnervagen as standard equipment.

The second morning we began jacking up the wagons and remounting the wheels. I was up to my elbows in axle tar when Captain Rawlings sent word for me to come to the crew wagon. It was a much-traveled prairie schooner outfitted for trail supplies and bunks. I scrubbed at Solomon's bench keg, got down my coat, Dragoon and crutch and headed that way. It was at the far side of the Tucker party's grounds, and I stood aside for supply wagons coming through from the town on the bluff. A neat buggy followed them. I glanced at it, started on, then stopped. One of the men riding in it was Caleb Tucker. The other two might have been his sons, but I wasn't sure. Back there at Cairo, when the introductions were being made, I wasn't looking at anybody much expect Mindy . . . seeing Yolanda's eyes.

The buggy rolled past, the men deep in conversation, and I went on. When I reached the crew wagon the buggy was there. I went around to the other side, then stopped. The Tuckers were there, with Judd Rawlings and some of his crew. So were Will Posey and Julius Altman.

Altman spotted me first and thumbed up his hat. "There you are," he said. "Passin' glad to hear you wasn't killed. Some of us thought maybe you was."

"I thought so, too, Julius. What happened to the wagons back there? Is everyone all right?"

"What did you run off like that for?" Will Posey wanted to know. "We spent a whole day lookin' for you, when we should have been rollin'!"

"I already told you that, Will," Julius said. "Them outlaws was his outlaws so he run off to lead them away. Man keeps his private affairs to hisself when he can." He glanced at me. "That's how it was, wasn't it? You tell this hardhead."

Caleb Tucker was staring back and forth from one to another.

"What's all that about?" he asked Rawlings. "Has something happened to my wagons?"

"Is Priscilla all right?" I asked Will. "And Uncle Earl, did he . . . ?"

"Reckon so," Julius intervened. "What business is that uncle of yours in, anyway, Zack? That's a mean bunch he runs with."

"What bunch? Where is he?"

"Ain't he here? Thought he might have been. He . . ."

"Judd, what's going on?" Caleb Tucker was wide-eyed

with confusion. "Where are my wagons? This young man was with them . . . wasn't he?"

Rawlings had stepped to the wagon wheel. Now he lifted a rifle that had been leaning there, pointed it into the sky and fired. Echoes rolled around the staging grounds.

"Shut up," he suggested to one and all. "Joseph, haul some chairs and benches out here, if you please. Some of you boys help him. There seems to be a mite that needs discussed."

Conversation is like a wagon train. Without a wagonmaster it is only a crowd of disconnected parts going off in all the wrong directions. Judd Rawlings was a wagonmaster. He guided that inquiry with the implacable singlemindedness of one who knows how to use a whip, a gun and pure diplomacy . . . and exactly what each is for.

The wagons were all right. A couple of bullet holes in end gates, nothing more. Mahlon Krause had a scratch on his cheek from a splinter, and Waylon Gibbs was crippled up from a horse stepping on his foot. Ezra Lawrence's nicked arm had a second scar on it now, a saber cut inflicted accidentally by his sister.

They were on the road and should arrive within two days. Tory was bringing them in. Will Posey had come ahead to report to Judd Rawlings.

It was the first Caleb Tucker had heard of any of it. He and his party had just arrived in Westport by steamer, and he and his sons had come out to see the staging grounds. The rest of his group would be out later.

And finally we got around to what had happened out there.

"We thought at first there was only six or seven of them jaspers," Will reported. "Zack there, he spotted 'em first and let us know, so we forted the train wing an' wedge. Turned out there was better'n a dozen of them, but we didn't know that. Well, Julius here, he held off the ones we knew about so we could get out there an' talk to 'em. The

264

main one was a big dandy with plasters on his face . . ."

"Frank Kingston," I said.

"Yeah. Well, they claimed to be after Zack because of a bounty that Kingston had put on him. Said we was harborin' a fugitive and they had a road warrant . . ."

Rawlings snorted. "Road warrant! The highwayman's favorite tool."

"The same. Well, we told 'em to git an' leave us alone. Told 'em Zack wasn't with us, which he wasn't. 'Course, we could see him up on the ridge in back of 'em, but they didn't know that. But then the rest of 'em, that we didn't know about, they come up on our blind side an' I guess they'd have been amongst us except that Zack, he stood up and started shootin' and pointin', an' we saw what was goin' on. Then we hightailed back to the fort an' Zack took off an' them fellers took off after Zack."

"But there was shooting," Rawlings coaxed.

"There was. Mostly just wild. They couldn't get in, so they rode around out there a while, keepin' us busy. Got a mite too close once, an' Julius here, he dropped one out of his saddle with that there long gun. Better'n three hundred yards, we paced it. Then they hung back, an' by'n-by that plastered one come back and got what was left of 'em an' they all took off. I figgered Zack was a goner for sure, with that bunch on his tail."

"Did he threaten the party any further after that?"

"Don't rightly know. He hollered somethin' about there ain't any law past Westport, but then that Earl Donovan — Zack's uncle — he come chargin' in with that rough crowd I told you about, an' them hooraws taken off."

"*What* rough crowd?" I couldn't stand it any more. The last time I had seen Uncle Earl he had been alone.

"Marshals an' detectives," Will told me, as though I should already have known. "Private security. Meanest lookin' bunch I ever seen."

Judd Rawlings looked at me with a quizzical expression.

"Tell him whose private security they said they were, Will."

"Kaygee freight company. That's what they said."

Kaygee freight company. Bailey Kingston. What was Uncle Earl doing with . . . "What was Uncle Earl doing with *them?*"

"He didn't say, Zack. Then when they left he went with 'em. I sorta figured they'd be here, though none of 'em said where they was goin'."

Rawlings was still staring at me, the way a man does when he expects a body to be surprised at something and will be surprised if he isn't. Or the other way around. Now he sort of relaxed and nodded. I was surprised, and he didn't have any doubt of it.

And I knew that, because a body raised from tads with Uncle Earl just naturally expects folks to expect skulduggery. They'd be dumb if they didn't.

Caleb Tucker had relaxed after he learned that his wagons and his transit party were safe. But he still looked worried, and I didn't blame him. For a law-abiding man, heading west with his family and everything he has in the world and all his dreams ahead of him, even a brush with the chaos that lawless people bring can be a shock. Caleb Tucker was a civilized man—a man of order and enterprise, a man whose ambitions didn't pivot on taking from others, but on building futures. He had cause to be worried. Trouble had touched his bright world, and might again. And that trouble had come with me.

Solomon Talbot and Anson Griggs showed up and stood around for a bit, listening. Then Anson said, "Zack, I got the forge hot to temper those bore bolts. You gonna sit around here all day?"

When everybody looked around at me, Solomon grinned at Tucker. "Morning, Caleb. Hope you folks had a good journey. I suggest you hang onto this fellow. He knows how to make wheels work."

Rawlings interrupted whatever Tucker was about to say.

266

"That's something we need to discuss a bit later, I think. You all go ahead with what you need to do. We'll get back and talk some more."

Pa told me an old story one time about a man in India who was given an elephant as a gift. It followed him around wherever he went, and pretty soon he got to be downright unpopular because most folks just don't have room in their parlors for folks that have elephants tagging along.

I wasn't sure what kind of elephant I had, or where I got it—except that Uncle Earl had a lot to do with it. But I could surely understand how Caleb Tucker and Judd Rawlings might have reservations about me bringing it into their parlor.

Those dreams I'd had kept flitting around in my head. A long string of big wagons rolling westward, toward the shining mountains. A string of bright beads on the sun-washed prairie, going west, going out . . . going away. And me watching them go. And I realized then why the dreams hurt the way they did. It was because I didn't want to watch them go. I wanted to go with them. I didn't want Uncle Earl's elephant. I wanted to be part of what these people here were all about.

I stood and got my crutch under my arm. "Let's go put nuts on those wheels," I said.

Over on the west side a string of high-side freighters was pulling out, nine tall wagons with long double strings of mules in front of them. Even as they rolled out of their space, there were other wagons coming in to occupy it. What I had seen as a town on wheels actually was several towns—separate clusters of wagons and folks, each group an entity within the broader scale of the staging grounds. There was a thirty-eight wagon party forming up to head out beyond the Neosho valley to claim patented land for farming. Another party, sixteen wagons strong and expecting more, aimed to try its hand at Fort Dodge where there was a small community of soddies now, and room for more with a small army detachment in place to keep the Indians friendly. The freight wagons, heading out on the wide trail, were bound for Santa Fe by way of Bent's Fort. Elsewhere there was a cluster of big overlanders, some aiming for the North Platte, others looking beyond to Oregon.

Most of the wagonmasters and scouts knew one another, and they passed the word from group to group—folks wanting news of other folks, folks wanting to trade what they had for what they needed, suggestions and advice from this group to that. But the groups were separate, each a law unto itself, each getting ready to go someplace where that law would be the thing they lived by.

Wagons rolled back and forth from the river bluffs and the crossing, carrying supplies from the outfitters of Westport, taking tackle in to be mended, bringing out stock dealers and hostlers to make their deals. And people came out from Westport to join the various parties . . . those like the Tuckers and their friends who had arrived by river separately from their wagons and goods.

There were people everywhere, bustling around and all anxious to be on the move. Nobody kept track of them, except party by party. There was no reason. They were all just passing through. A pair of riders, dour dark-coated men on tall horses, glanced at us as we walked toward Talbot's wagon. They reined in and the first one asked, "Whose party is this?"

"Tucker party," Solomon said. "Bound for Denver City. Who are you looking for?"

"Nobody," he said. "Just looking."

As they turned away the blacksmith said, "What was that all about?"

Solomon shrugged elegant shoulders. "Like they said, they're just looking."

"Can't say I blame them," I said. "A sight like these

grounds is worth seeing." I looked again at the head of trail, where the string of freight wagons was lumbering along toward the rise where the trail curved away out of sight. They would go a mile or so, maybe a mile and a half, before they were swallowed by the hills. Then they would go another day or more before their trail separated itself from the head of trails to angle southwestward where it would eventually run along the Arkansas River—through the flint hills that I had heard about but never seen, and on up toward the great plains which I had heard about and dreamed about. Somewhere out there, a long ways off, they would see the mountains rising ahead of them and their trail would separate again. They would go southward toward Santa Fe while another trace headed for Pueblo and the new town on Cherry Creek, Denver City.

I was so enthralled with it all, hobbling across the compound there on my crutch, that I bumped into somebody without seeing him. I almost fell, and twisted to get my balance on the crutch, then the crutch was knocked aside and I went to one knee.

Anson Griggs and Solomon Talbot, a few steps ahead, turned and hurried back. Off to one side someone disappeared around the tailgate of a wagon.

Anson helped me up. "What happened?" he wondered. "Who was that?"

"I don't know. I didn't see him. I just bumped right into him. I wasn't watching where I was going."

Solomon was looking where the man had gone. "Didn't stop to say aye, no or maybe, did he?"

"Must have been in a hurry."

"I'd say he sure as hell was," Anson rasped. He pointed at my crutch, an inch below the arm-bar.

I lifted it to look. The wood was deeply scored there, a fresh cut that bit into it and left a half-inch peel of solid wood split off.

It was a cut made by a heavy knife with a strong arm

269

behind it.

Solomon took one look at the cut in the crutch and his eyes went wide. Then with a wild yell he wrenched a jackhandle from the sideboard of the nearest wagon and took off, the way the man had gone. I started after him, stumbled and yelled at him, but he was already gone. Some distance away, a woman screamed. Anson Griggs started to run, but I caught his sleeve. "Go get Judd Rawlings," I said.

Three wagons away was the perimeter of another circle, a party being assembled by a Methodist preacher to settle land on the Smoky Hill River. It was slow going for me. At least it seemed so. The crutch was a hindrance, but without it I fell. I veered around wagons and tents, squeezed between the wheels of a pair of overlanders parked hub to hub, ducked through somebody's holding corral and heard shouts and commotion just ahead. I didn't remember hauling out the Dragoon, but it was in my hand.

There was a crowd of people, and I pushed through, then stopped. At its center, in a clear space, Solomon Talbot stood over the body of a dark-coated man. Solomon was brandishing his jackhandle, dancing around the fallen one and shouting things I couldn't understand. He looked like a banty rooster cavorting around a fallen chickenhawk. Just beyond him the crowd parted and a pair of mounted men came through—the same pair we had seen before. I pointed the Dragoon and ran toward them. They looked at one another, exchanged shrugs, then carefully put their guns away and stepped down. One of them shouldered Solomon aside, warily, watching the stick he was swinging. The other knelt by the fallen man and turned him over.

"I got him!" Solomon trilled. "By Heaven, I got him!"

The man on the ground was Bo Singer. His Arkansas knife lay in the dust beside him.

"He tried to kill my wheelwright!" Solomon was so excited his voice was a chirp. "But I got him!"

I had reached them, and dodged a careless swing of Solomon's jackhandle. I took it away from him.

"This is Bo Singer," one of the strangers told the other. "Let's get him out of here."

Singer was coming around, beginning to moan and fret at the bump on his head. Casually, the two stood and lifted him between them.

"What are you doing?" I was still holding my Dragoon. "You can't have him. I want to . . ."

"It's all right, Zack." I tried to turn, at the voice beside me, then clung to my crutch when my leg buckled.

"I do wish you'd stop getting shot," Uncle Earl fussed, helping me get upright again. "You make it difficult for me to look out for you sometimes."

"That's Bo Singer," I told him. "Where in hell have you been, anyway?"

"I know who he is, Zack. It's all right. These men are with me."

XXVII

Like I've said, anybody who knows Earl Donovan knows that it just isn't any use trying to get information out of him unless he happens to want to tell it. I even tried sitting on his head one time back yonder when we were growing up, but I never did find out how my good sheep-skin coat came to be Harley Pope's saddle blanket. All sitting on Uncle Earl's head accomplished was to make his eyes cross.

On the other hand, once Uncle Earl decides to tell you about something, he'll talk 'til the cows come in.

I never found out where those men took Bo Singer, but I found out who they were. They worked for Bailey Kingston. Some of the others with them worked officially for Kaygee Freight, but those two and a few more like them worked directly for the old man. And right now they were taking orders from Uncle Earl.

It was late evening and I had finished the new spindle mounts on one of Solomon Talbot's wagons, when Uncle Earl showed up again and said he had decided there were some things I ought to know.

We went and sat by Judd Rawlings' fire, with several others there listening in, and Uncle Earl began to explain some things. He explained for a minute or two, and then I came unglued.

"Why didn't you tell me that before?" I asked his face, which was pulled up an inch from mine because I had hold of his lapels. "Damn it all, Uncle Earl, ever since I left New Albany people have been trailing me and shooting at me and trying to do mayhem on me! I've been shanghaied, blown up, drowned, shot at, crippled, chased most of the way across Missouri . . . all because you never told me what was going on so maybe I could have done something about it! Why didn't you tell me?"

"Now, Zack, don't get upset," he grinned. "I figured what you didn't know wouldn't hurt you."

If there isn't something in the Good Book to condone the ceremonial stoning of uncles, there ought to be.

Sure enough, Uncle Earl was on a treasure hunt. But what he was after wasn't the treasure itself, so much as the reward he had contracted with Bailey Kingston for — a reward for the treasure safely returned and for "appropriate means" to deal with the culprit who took it.

The culprit was Bailey Kingston's son, Frank.

And the treasure was the missing bullion from that Kaygee gold shipment that had disappeared.

"So tell us the rest of it!" I demanded. "Tell us all of it, Uncle Earl."

Judd Rawlings put a hand on my shoulder. "He'll tell it better if you turn loose of his throat, Zack. He's turning purple."

The gist of it was, old Frank had got tired of being the old man's maintained public nuisance around New Albany. He had decided to go into competition with Bailey. Somehow he had got Milt Downey to get his brother Tim to waylay a gold shipment coming from the western mines, and hide it. Then, probably, he got rid of Milt Downey. Then he had discovered, a little bit late, that the Downeys had cooked up a few ideas of their own, one of which was to put the gold someplace other than where he told them

273

to.

"All this is over a shipment of government gold?" I just couldn't make it all fit, somehow.

"Bonded carrier gold," Judd Rawlings suggested. Uncle Earl nodded sagely.

"Bonded carrier, that's the key to it," Caleb Tucker said. "A man in the position of Mr. Kingston—Bailey Kingston, that is—has ways of dealing with people who steal shipments. Security people, detectives, you know."

"Aside from plain highway robbery," Rawlings said, "there isn't much of major value that gets stolen in transit. The rewards aren't worth the risk. I'd guess Frank Kingston didn't just go after the gold."

"No," Uncle Earl expanded, "he went for the bond. Kaygee's bond. Frank decided to go into business for himself, by putting old Bailey out of business."

"Like father, like son," I mused.

"Like son, like father," Uncle Earl corrected. "You've noticed how it gets when you cross Frank Kingston."

"I've noticed that, yes."

"Frank's a wooly lamb compared to old Bailey. And the thing that aggravates the old man most is that it's his own son who did that to him. That's how I got in on this good deal, Zack. How *we* got in. I intend to share with you, you know."

"Sure you do. What you mean, how you got in. How?"

"Bailey Kingston is no longer reasonable. That's the time to cut a deal, Zack. When the worthy client is no longer reasonable."

Solomon Talbot edged close to me. "Did you say he's your uncle?"

"Yes. I said that. He is."

"Is he always like this?"

"Sometimes he gets treacherous."

"What deal, exactly, did you make with Bailey Kingston?" Caleb Tucker gazed at Uncle Earl.

"Just what I said. I told him what had happened, and I promised to get his gold back for him, in such a manner that the entire blame for the incident would rest on Frank personally."

"So Kaygee Freight can keep its contract."

"Yes. With the war and all, that contract is worth a very large fortune."

It was my turn. "What war?"

"The next one," Uncle Earl said.

"It won't be long," Solomon Talbot added. "Those South Carolinians are behaving abominably in the Congress. All they need now is an issue."

Now and again I've had the feeling that everybody but me knows what is going on. Usually that feeling comes after I failed to pay attention.

At any rate, the whole mess sort of boiled down to various people's plans. Somehow Uncle Earl had let Frank Kingston figure out that he had been double-dealt by the Downeys, so Frank just naturally had to find out where that gold was. He'd stolen it. It was his. I could see how Frank might think that way.

Then there was my plan, that Uncle Earl had sort of encouraged after the wagonworks folded—to head on west and see the yonders, like I had always wanted to do. Then there was our shop crew's plan to complete Mr. Tucker's wagons and get them to him one way or another, which led to Uncle Earl's plan to sort of lead Frank Kingston down to the wagonyard that day when I'd be sure to be there, so maybe something would come up and I'd keep Frank busy long enough for Uncle Earl to make off with Tim Downey's letters.

I had him by the lapels again, my nose an inch from his. "It was your fault that he shot Lady Blue?"

"Now, Zack," he wheezed, "you know I wouldn't have had a thing like that happen. I can't think of everything. All I did was count on you being in his way and keeping him busy. Shoot, I didn't think you'd take his horse, either."

"He's turning purple again, Zack," Judd Rawlings pointed out.

Uncle Earl backed off and caught his breath. "You were supposed to go by keelboat, Zack. So you would be around to take care of those boxes until I caught up."

"Why the hell didn't you tell me?" I went at him again, but Solomon Talbot got in the way. "And here I thought *I* had a family tradition," the merchant said.

Plans within plans, and Earl Donovan—my Uncle Earl—pulling everybody's strings. It was just like old times back yonder . . . except that back yonder it got so that folks knew about Uncle Earl. They got used to him. These folks hadn't had that honor.

"This is all fascinating," Caleb Tucker said after a while. "Outside of politics, I've heard nothing like it. But what does it have to do with our train, Judd?"

"It has a lot to do with it," Rawlings said. "You see, Mr. Frost and Mr. Donovan and several others are members of our party. Subscribing members."

"He stole my money to do that," I assured Rawlings. "I had no intention of . . ."

"My fault," Will Posey spoke up. "I didn't know . . ."

Caleb Tucker raised a hand. "I see. This is serious business, Judd. What do you suggest?"

"I don't see any choice, Caleb. We can't include people in our party who have become targets for scoundrels. It makes the train a target. I'm afraid . . ."

Uncle Earl came to his feet, staring at Rawlings with that odd, thoughtful look of his that I'd seen before . . . like when he had leaned down to look at that yayhoo out in the woods after he had shot him, or the day back yonder when he decided he'd have to kill the gambler Claude Ledet. He wasn't grinning any more. "The point is," he said slowly, "Frank Kingston won't be tagging this

276

train any more. He has Tim Downey's letters now, so he won't waste time with a slow-poke bunch of wagons. He'll be going after that gold as fast as he can, to get a jump on the Kaygee security men."

"He has the letters?" I squinted at him, still marveling after all the years at the way a body could change so much and so fast, just by the way he stood or the way his eyes turned.

"He has them. So he thinks he knows now where the gold is."

"He *thinks* he knows?"

"He knows where Tim Downey's letter says it is. So he won't be bothering you folks any more. That's why I came back, to tell you that. I know my nephew has his heart set on going west, so if he decides he wants to travel with you all I don't want you having second thoughts about it. That's all."

Nobody else there could have caught it. Nobody else there had been raised up in the Knob Hills with Earl Donovan for an uncle. But when he said, 'that's all,' my hackles went up. With Uncle Earl, 'that's all' never meant anything but 'that's all you need to know.'

But he usually didn't lie. If he said Frank Kingston wouldn't be after me any more, then I believed it. There was something else to it . . .

The bounty! "Uncle Earl, all you told these folks is that *Frank Kingston* won't be baying at my heels. You didn't say anybody else won't be. Why, just today, Bo Singer was . . ."

"Bo Singer won't be around any more, either. But I'm not forgetting about the bounty, Zack. For that reason, if these folks decide you can travel with them, then Mr. Jones and Mr. Johnson will go along, too."

"Who?"

"You met them earlier. Mr. Jones and Mr. Johnson. They . . . ah . . . relieved you folks of Bo Singer today.

They are credentialed guards, Mr. Tucker. The very best. I am empowered to offer their services, and I'm doing it. It will make amends for any inconvenience I might have caused any of you."

"How about yourself, then?" Rawlings asked. "The group listed with our party is Frost-Donovan. Do you intend to travel with us?"

"No." The grin came again, that old slantwise grin that was like a lantern lighted abruptly in the dark. "No, I still have things to do. As I told you, I have a contract with Mr. Bailey Kingston. I intend to complete it."

My hackles were still tingling. I wished there were some way I could explain to all of them about my Uncle Earl. Then their hackles could tingle, too. But it's not easy to explain about Uncle Earl.

The rest of them all looked at one another.

"Well," he said, "that *was* the question, wasn't it?"

Rawlings nodded. "That was it."

"So far as I'm concerned," Solomon Talbot said, "I would be grateful to have Mr. Frost accompany our party."

"All right with me," Anson shrugged. "If he'll show me how to temper bore bolts thread-on."

Rawlings glanced at Will Posey, and Posey looked toward Julius Altman. Altman stood off in the shadows, away from the main body of men. "Not my say," he said. "We're add-ons. But I favor a body that's willin' to help folks now and again. Y'all could do worse."

That itch was crawling up my scalp again, the same itch that got there whenever Uncle Earl was up to something and I didn't know what it was.

"You did say a wheelwright would be handy to have along, Judd," Tucker said quietly.

Things were getting out of hand. "Mr. Tucker," I said, "I don't think things are as they seem here. Why don't I just take my money and . . ."

A hard elbow poked me in the ribs. "Zack, shut up,"

Uncle Earl whispered. "You don't know what's good for you."

"That's the whole point," I growled at him. "I know what's good for me, I just don't know what's . . ."

"Hush. Let the gentlemen handle things."

"It would take a vote of the entire party to disqualify you, Zack," Judd Rawlings said. "From what I'm hearing here, I don't think they'd do that."

"But you don't know the whole story, Captain."

"Oh?" He raised a brow. "What is the rest of it, then?"

"I don't know. I just know there's more."

"How do you know that?"

"Because I know Earl Donovan. He's my uncle."

It was as though he didn't hear me. "Zack, there are proven procedures for the organization and governing of wagon expeditions. They're proven because they work. You have paid your money to be a member of this party . . ."

"I didn't pay it. Uncle Earl did."

". . . and you have agreed to the obligations of membership . . ."

"That was for the transit train."

". . . which obligations extend to the conclusion of the expedition. You have pledged appropriate equipment and personnel, to wit one freight wagon, one surrey, five able-bodied men and one woman, livestock in the amount of . . ."

"One of those able-bodied men—to wit my Uncle Earl—has already backed out!"

"Mr. Jones and Mr. Johnson are my replacements," Uncle Earl said, smiling his best fox-in-the-henhouse smile.

". . . and in general have obligated yourself to serve as a member of the Tucker party until relieved by decision of the company." Judd Rawlings had never stopped talking. "You don't have any option, Mr. Frost. If the party allows you to go, you must. If not, of course, you can't."

"Don't you want to go west, Zack?" Uncle Earl asked.

"Well, sure I do. I always . . ."

"Do you have something against us?" Solomon Talbot demanded.

"You can have the use of my forge as need be," Anson offered.

I hadn't even noticed Uncle Earl's sidekicks, the brothers grim, returning. But now there was one of them on each side of me—tall, dour men with flat eyes and hardrock features. The one at my right tipped his head to whisper, conversationally, "Don't aggravate us, Mr. Frost. Go with the train."

The itch had taken root in my scalp. Whatever hand Uncle Earl was playing now, there was big money on the table. "I haven't made up my mind," I told them all. "Be nice, though, if just once somebody would ask instead of telling."

I saw the humor in Caleb Tucker's eyes, and he opened his mouth to ask me politely if I would consider staying with his company. But Judd Rawlings interrupted. "No reason for that. It's decided. If the party wants you, you have to go."

It had gone just exactly the way Uncle Earl had intended for it to go. I was stuck there—short of lighting a shuck and gaining a reputation as a turncoat. I was part of the Tucker wagon party, whether I liked it or not.

The problem was, I hadn't ever decided whether I wanted to do that or not. I had never had a chance to say, "Fellers, count me in," or "Fellers, count me out."

The other problem was, I knew that whatever Uncle Earl was planning, whatever came of it would be worse than what had come before. Maybe even Uncle Earl didn't know that. But I knew it. It was just like old times.

I have the same number of hands as the Lord gave most folks. Two. On me, they serve different purposes. The right one uses tools, the left one holds things still so tools can be used on them. When I left that gathering Uncle Earl went right along with me because my left hand was on his neck and he didn't have any choice at all about it.

We got off a ways, out in the shadows, and I turned him around. "Uncle Earl, I know you aren't going to tell me what you're up to. But I want to know one thing. If Frank Kingston has Tim Downey's letters, how did he get them?"

"I rode out on your trail back there and left them lying on the ground. Then I watched until he backtracked and saw him find them."

"In that case, I want to know one more thing. If Frank Kingston has those letters, and is high-tailing west to find the gold, how can you be so sure that you're going to find it before he does?"

"Zack, the letters don't say where the gold is, I told you that before."

"Then how come he thinks they do? He can read."

"Oh, Zack, for Heaven's sake!" He worked his neck out of my grip and rubbed it with his hand. "You don't think Tim Downey was going to just write that out and send it to New Albany, do you? One of the letters does say a place, but that isn't really where he hid that shipment."

"How do you know?"

"Because there was a map with the letters and Frank doesn't have that."

"Do you?"

"It's in a safe place."

"Where . . . ?"

"It's safe. That's all."

The way my scalp was itching, you'd have thought I had lice.

XXVIII

So whatever his reason, Uncle Earl had decided that I was going to travel west with the Tucker party. And Uncle Earl being Uncle Earl, he had left me no real choices in the matter.

Of course I never *had* to do what Uncle Earl decided I was going to do. Had I been a mind to, I could just have dug in my heels and said no. I could have gone over into Westport and maybe set up a wheel shop if I could borrow the money, or got a job in a wagonyard or something. I had thought about it. Where the trains made up to travel, there would always be work in season for a man with a craft. Then again, I could have saddled the roan and done just what I had been wanting to do all along—just set the morning sun on my back and put the miles behind me and devil take the hindmost.

I *could* have done either of those things. There would have been prices to pay, but I could have.

The price for staying on at Westport? Well, I'd have lost any chance to ever recover my money that Uncle Earl stole and paid to the wagon party. And maybe I'd have had to thump Mr. Jones and Mr. Johnson—I had a notion that Uncle Earl had told them to make sure I went along—and from the looks of those two that might have been a sight more difficult than thumping Buster Stuckey. And, of course, I would have been branded a bad risk for contracts. That might have taken a few years to live down.

The price for just heading west on my own was that I would continue being a bountied and hunted man, and on my own without a crowd to support me. And I wouldn't ever have a chance again to look at Mindy Tucker's blue eyes and see if they really did look like Yolanda's. And I would be a bad risk for contracts, anyway.

But I *could* have.

It's a funny thing . . . the only critter I ever knew that could out-think my Uncle Earl was a balking mule named Sweetpea. Uncle Earl won Sweetpea in a dice game down by the river when we were younger. He brought him home and decided to use him for a buggy mule. But Sweetpea didn't care for halters and he couldn't stand traces. And when something didn't suit Sweetpea he balked. And when he balked there wasn't anybody or anything that was going to get him to move.

Well, Sweetpea hadn't ever met the like of Uncle Earl. The first time he hooked up that mule and it balked, Uncle Earl went and got an armload of split stovewood and built a fire under it. A nice, crackling fire, right there amongst its legs, directly under its belly.

"Now that mule will move," he said.

I guess Uncle Earl hadn't ever met the like of Sweetpea, either. Sweetpea moved, all right. He moved precisely eight and one-half feet. Then he balked again.

That buggy burned right down to its axles, and Sweetpea stood there, looking back at it and smirking as only a mule can smirk.

I learned something from that. The way around Uncle Earl is to just simply balk. Whatever he has arranged for a body to do, if a body doesn't want to do it, and just plain doesn't do it no matter what kind of fire he builds, then Uncle Earl is at a loss.

283

I could have balked. The trouble was, despite having my back up over him running my life for me, I did sort of want to go along. But it was a thing I could damn well make up my own mind about, without Uncle Earl pulling my strings for me. I was of a mind to twist his tail for him, but by the time I came to that he was off at the supply camp, three miles away, along with most of his detectives and marshals. Only Mr. Jones and Mr. Johnson had stayed behind, and the situation between them and me had turned pretty bleak.

I had sat out by Solomon Talbot's lead wagon for a time, drinking coffee with him and Anson Griggs and trying to simmer down a mite—I really hadn't got my fill of strangling Uncle Earl right then, and every time I thought about him and his fancy steps that kept landing on other people's feet, I got mad all over again. I guess I wasn't very good company, because about the time Anson's wife hollered him home Solomon suggested that I go and turn in too, and maybe I'd feel better tomorrow.

I had been bunking in the company wagon that Percy Smith drove, since that was where they put me when they picked me up out on the trail. But when I went there, toting a lantern, there was a dark form sitting on the off front wheel. Narrow, feral eyes glinted in the light. Mr. Jones.

"You better go sleep somewhere else," he said. "We claimed that bunk in there."

That didn't even deserve an answer, so I ignored him and climbed in. Sure enough, Mr. Johnson was snoring in my bunk. I had had all I could take for one night. I set the lantern down, hauled the soogans off him and grabbed his arm as it came up, toting a pistol. He hadn't even got his eyes open, but he had drawn his gun and was cocking it. I slapped it away from him, hoisted him and threw him out the tailgate. He flipped past Mr. Jones, just coming around the corner, and in an instant there was a gun in Mr. Jones'

284

hand, too. Mercy, but those two were sudden with those guns! But I was right there, up on the high bed, and I kicked the gun away and leaned low to fetch a good swat upside the head of Mr. Jones. He staggered back, fell over Mr. Johnson, and my leg gave way and I pitched out and fell on both of them.

It winded all three of us. But being on top, I stayed in charge. I got upright somehow, hauled them up and bounced them together a couple of times the way us kids used to bounce one another in free-for-alls back in the Knob Hills. Generally that sort of treatment would settle folks down and show them the error of their ways. Mainly, though, those two were tough big men, and I didn't want them to get their balance back until I'd had my say.

I shoved them away, then picked up Mr. Jones' gun and tossed it up into the wagon with the other one. "Now *you* go sleep somewhere else," I told them. "I'm sleeping here."

By the time I had crawled back into the wagon they were up and brushing themselves off, glaring at me. Mr. Jones pointed an ominous finger. "You'll settle with us for this, Frost."

"You'll take your orders from me," I told them both. "You heard what my Uncle Earl said. You're in my group. That means you answer to me while you're on this train."

"Your Uncle Earl!" Mr. Johnson growled. "We don't answer to that weasel."

"You answer to *somebody*, and that somebody wants you with these wagons. That means you'll answer to *me* starting now."

I kept their guns until I was good and ready to give them back, the next day. But the hard eyes of them said I hadn't heard the last of it. By then I had other things to think about, though. Captain Rawlings' chief scout, Tory, rode in a little after sunrise and reported that the transit train would be in by noon. I saddled the roan and went out to meet them.

Three miles out I saw them in the distance, coming around a bend. I angled up a hillside for a better look.

Riders paced them, front, rear and flank, and among them I could make out George Bullard and Cassius Altman. Some of the others were Judd Rawlings' crew. General Jackson led the train, high and handsome, with General Ames right behind. Morning sun dappled their white canvas and glinted on brown superstructure and bright yellow running gear. Curly Joe's sporting house had never been so well saluted. And Carl Froehner's venture had never produced a wagon finer than those. I knew.

The transit overlander came next, big teams stepping high as Mahlon Krause worked the reins. Then the two Conestogas, like giant boats on wheels, Thomas Madden walking alongside his to drive a six-up team, Paul Conway riding his lazy board on the second, driving from there.

The Honeycutts' prairie schooner looked small, following the great Conestogas. But then, most anything looks small compared to a Conestoga.

At the distance, I almost didn't recognize the Lawrence surrey. It looked sturdier now, more sure-footed, and canvas curtaining draped from its headbars. But there was no mistaking its driver. She sat straight and prim, sure small hands guiding one horse while another followed along behind. She raised her head, scanning the countryside, then white teeth flashed in a pixie face pulled tight by bunned hair. She waved. She had seen me. She turned, beckoned, and then pointed toward me and I recognized the flank rider on the far side. What fool, I wondered, had put Ezra on a horse and given him a gun to carry? Only the Lord knew what kind of mischief that could lead to.

Waylon Gibbs followed with his wagon, then the weathered, sturdy little Altman wagon, and finally Todd Conway with his supply freighter.

"Sight to behold, ain't they?" Julius Altman had followed me out and come up alongside. "What are you doin', countin' noses?"

"Just wanted to take a look," I said.

"Yeah. Same as me. I knew all along they was all right, but I still like to see for myself."

Below, the tended stock came around the curve and the entire transit party was in sight. More people had spotted us now, and they waved.

"Mite of a scuffle last night," Julius drawled. "Everything come out all right?"

"Nothing much. I was just establishing bunk rights."

"What I figgered," he said. "Probably ought to keep an eye on them two, Zack. They may be all right, like your uncle says. But they look to me like bad 'uns."

"They're on our side," I reminded him.

"Reckon so." He paused, then added, "On the right side, but they're still the wrong kind."

I agreed with that. "Uncle Earl makes strange friends, now and again."

Down on the trail, Waylon Gibbs had pulled his wagon out of line and started up the slope toward us. One of Captain Rawlings' flank guards galloped ahead, hauled rein in front of his team and brought him up short. Voices didn't carry that far, but I could see the man waving his rifle around, gesturing with it. They argued for a moment, then Waylon switched up his team and turned, back into his place in the line of march.

"Fresh off a keelboat," I told Julius.

When they passed below us we rode down to join them. Abe Miles waved from the seat of General Jackson. "I guess they were right about you being alive, Zack. You sure don't look dead to me."

"You've kind of adopted that lead position, haven't you, Abe? Don't count on it after Westport, though. There's some high-class wagons yonder."

He looked like he was going to say something, then changed his mind and shrugged. "General Jackson will

287

stand up to anybody's rig, Zack. We built her that way."

Julius Altman rode on back to check on his family, and I watched General Jackson pass and waved at Benny Strother on General Ames. He grinned and drew up alongside where I could pace him. From his high seat he glanced down at me, then took a longer look. "Right fancy wardrobe there, Zack. Things must be good at Westport. What's that thing you're carrying?"

"It's a crutch. I've got a hole in my leg. Comes of being shot at. Is everybody all right?"

"Fit as fiddles. How does the town look to you? Good prospects?"

"I haven't looked at it. I've been busy. But I guess it's all right. Prospects for what?"

"For a business. Isn't that what . . . oh. You weren't there. Well, Abe and I got to talking. We'll get paid off for delivering these as soon as we get to Westport and sign them over. We're thinking we'll set up a wagonyard there, if things look right. Thought you might throw in with us, too."

So that was it. I had been so busy, and thinking so much about the train going west, I hadn't thought at all about what anybody else might do from here. I guess I had just assumed that Abe and Benny would go on with the train, just the way I had . . . and right then I knew that I had decided. I wasn't interested in Westport. I never had been, except as a milestone. The yonders were still out there. They weren't at Westport, they just started there. Somewhere back along the way, even while I was telling myself— and everybody else, I guess—that I wanted to see what kind of opportunities the staging towns might offer . . . even then I guess I knew that I wouldn't stop there. I wanted to see those yonders. I wanted to see the shining mountains. Even if I had to do it Uncle Earl's way.

"I won't be staying, Benny," I told him. "When Mr. Tucker's train makes up, I'll be with it. You might talk to

Waylon and George, though. They're craftsmen. They'd be good hands for you."

Then he looked at me the way Abe had, like he meant to say something and decided not to. Instead he just grinned again, and turned his attention to his driving. But as I started to wheel away he turned back. "Zack, do you recollect back there when we were building these wagons, after they'd closed Froehner's down?"

"Sure I do. Why?"

"Do you remember when we painted them?"

"Yeah."

"Did we check the lazy boards afterward?"

"Probably. I guess so. Why?"

"Oh, nothing. Except the lazy board on General Jackson up there is stuck shut. It won't pull out."

"Painted shut?" I couldn't believe it. Not a one of us was German.

"No, not painted. Just stuck. Oh, well, it doesn't matter anyway. Drive seats are a lot handier."

Along the line I got friendly waves and good words from the Madden tribe and the Conways—though I noticed that Mahlon Krause was leaning around the transit wagon's cover, glaring at me suspiciously when I passed that one. I rode alongside the prairie schooner for a minute to shake hands with Buck Honeycutt and grin at the babies, and Betsy leaned down to grasp my hand. "We were so worried, Zack," she said. "Those awful men—I'm glad you made it safely."

I waited for the surrey to come up, and tipped my hat. "Good day, Miss Lawrence. I hope you've had a pleasant journey."

"Most pleasant, Mr. Frost," she said. "Not to mention eventful. Have your wounds been tended? You look gaunt. Have you been eating well and getting your rest? They said you had been shot again, and I see you are lame. In my opinion, Mr. Frost, it was an exceedingly stupid thing you did back there. Don't you agree?"

"What?"

"I said . . ."

"I heard what you said, Miss Lawrence. I just don't know which part of it you are asking me to agree with."

"You could have been killed, you know."

"Well, it wasn't for lack of them trying that I wasn't. But what do you expect I'd have done? Just sat there and watched those outlaws overrun the wagons?"

"It's the principle of it that worries me, Mr. Frost. We are going to have to talk about that. I have some definite ideas on how we should go about modifying . . ."

"Miss Lawrence . . ."

". . . your behavior in situations of that . . ."

"Miss Lawrence . . ."

". . . nature, although I must admit to being tired of such situations ever . . ."

"Priscilla!"

". . . what?"

"Will you hush? I only said 'good day,' for heaven's sake. I wanted to look at the surrey."

"At the . . . oh, yes. Mr. Miles and Mr. Strother fixed it. They said you suggested it . . ."

"Will Posey suggested it."

"Be that as it may, I have some misgivings about it."

"It got here, didn't it?"

"Yes, but they said it is a Mormon surrey now. I am not at all sure I approve."

"Miss Lawrence . . ."

"Oh, mercy, are we back to that? A moment ago you called me Priscilla. You may call me Priscilla, Mr. Frost. Please do."

"Yes, mam. Priscilla, who put Ezra on a horse and gave him a gun?"

"Why, Mr. Donovan did. When he came back with those awful men. I was bandaging Ezra's shoulder—he'd had a minor accident during the shooting . . ."

"Yes, I heard. A sword cut."

". . . and Mr. Donovan said it was time for Ezra to grow up, so he saddled a horse for him and told him to ride it, and gave him a gun and told him to wear it, and urged him strongly to stop preaching and start listening. From this moment on, he said. Or else."

"Or else, what?"

"I'm not really sure. Ezra didn't want to talk about it. But Mr. Donovan explained that he had practically raised you, and he pointed out that if you could benefit from his advice, anyone could. It's really remarkable. Ezra has been behaving quite responsibly since then."

That would be worth seeing. I wheeled around the tail of the surrey and rode out to flank. Ezra was plodding along there, on one of the owlhoot horses, a big gun at his hip. When I approached he lowered his head, not meeting my eyes.

"Ezra," I said, "that's no way for a man to act. Look at me!"

He raised his face and glared.

"That's a whole lot better. If a man goes armed like a man, then he ought to look the world in the eye. What did my Uncle Earl say to you?"

He hesitated, swallowing so that his adam's apple bobbled. "He said I was to grow up. Right now."

"What else?"

"He said he had things for you to do, and he didn't want you bothered, so if I made trouble for you anymore he was going to nail me to a honey tree."

"What else?"

"He said for me to give up preaching. He said the Lord isn't there for my pleasure, and neither is anybody else."

It was a real shame that Uncle Earl never could practice what he preached. What did that mean, *he had things for me to do?* I went back to the surrey. "What else did my Uncle

Earl say to you, Priscilla?"

"That we would all be going west with a wagon party, all the way to the Rocky Mountains, and that I should keep an eye on you. He said I should concentrate on showing you the errors of your ways."

All the way back there, he had said that? Lordy, he didn't even know if I was alive then . . . did he? Or maybe it just never crossed his mind that anything would ever be any way except just how he planned it. *Nothing happens to Zack. Zack doesn't get hurt.*

Waylon Gibbs had been waving at me from the next wagon back, trying to get my attention. I dropped back.

"Your Uncle Earl gave me a message for you," he said.

Gave Waylon a message for me? "When?"

"What?"

"When did he give you a message?"

"Back yonder, the day them Democrats jumped us. The one with the bandaged face, and them."

Uncle Earl had come on ahead, though. I had just been with him a few hours ago. My scalp itched again. "What was the message, Waylon?"

"He said on the way to Denver City for you to keep a special sharp eye on that General Jackson wagon. He said it's important."

The itch in my scalp was worse than all the head lice there ever were. I reined the roan about and put heels to it, heading back to the Westport staging grounds.

I could have taken my time. Uncle Earl had been gone for hours, off along the great trail westward, him and all of his toughs except Mr. Jones and Mr. Johnson.

"Your uncle couldn't wait around any more, Zack," Solomon Talbot said. "Told me to tell you he'd see you along about Denver City."

XXIX

In all, there were forty-seven wagons making up the
Caleb Tucker party when it set out from Westport Stage
on the Grand Territorial Route. Forty-four various overlanders, freighters and high-sides, plus two spring wagons
and a surrey. One hundred and sixty three people on the
way to Cherry Creek, Colorado Territory, with their
housewares and goods, their livestock and supplies, their
ambitions and skills and dreams, headed for the shining
mountains. Solomon Talbot estimated that we would about
double the census of Denver City the day we rolled in.

I had been right about the Froehnervagens not having
the lead when the trek began. Judd Rawlings was wagonmaster, and he organized the march like a military campaign. Every piece of rolling stock had its assigned place,
and he put Conestogas fore and aft and in key positions
where they could be pulled out to roll on the flanks of the
train. Visibility and stability, he explained to the assembled party our last evening at Westport. The big rigs could
be seen from miles away, and would warn other traffic off,
thereby preserving our grass for graze. Also, being as big
as they were — thirty-five hundred pounds of plain wagon,
not counting payload — the Conestogas were less likely to
be hauled astray by bolting teams.

Will Posey said privately that there was another reason. The breadth of the timbers in the Conestogas made them hard to shoot through. Captain Rawlings wasn't a man to take chances.

So the lead wagon was Solomon Talbot's second wagon, with a hired driver.

But General Jackson was second in line, with Caleb Tucker himself at the reins, traveling with his wife Elaine and his daughter, Mindy. Except that most of the time, Mindy chose to ride with Solomon Talbot so they could talk and make plans.

I should explain about that. Through all those times—first at Cairo and then across Missouri—when I had dreamed of Mindy Tucker's blue eyes, nobody had ever mentioned to me that Caleb Tucker's daughter was betrothed to a merchant named Solomon Talbot who would be making the trek to Denver City. Some things happen to come up in conversation, some don't. That one was a don't.

But at second inspection, her eyes didn't look that much like Yolanda's, anyway. They certainly were eyes, though.

General Ames followed right along behind General Jackson, loaded now with the stock in trade of the Tucker ventures and handled by the two Tucker boys, Tom and Samuel. Right from the outset, Uncle Earl's toughs—Mr. Jones and Mr. Johnson—set themselves to flank the Froehnervagens, big dour men on tough saddlestock, men with their hands never far from their guns and their eyes never far from those brown and yellow wagons. Especially General Jackson. Nothing I could say would budge them from there, and Captain Rawlings just shrugged and assumed they were his front flankers.

Keep an eye on the General Jackson wagon, Uncle Earl's message for me had said. And those two he had left behind were doing just that.

The first day out, Captain Rawlings and his crew were

on the move constantly, up and down the line, keeping ranks closed and drovers aflank, looking at teams and checking harness. And they drilled the drivers — and everybody else — on the proper conduct of a line of march for a wagon train. We made eleven miles that day, then spent another hour drilling on bed-down procedures.

With forty-seven vehicles, the pattern was to break out in two arcs — one to the right and one to the left, the next to the right and the next to the left, circle out and back, closing the arcs into a circular compound. As they closed up, each wagon pulled in close behind the one ahead and its teams were turned inward. When it was done right, which it was the third time they tried it, the big wagons formed a complete circle of high sides and canvas tops with all the teams inside and just a small opening left at the rear for herding in — if conditions called for it — of the animals on drove. This opening was then closed with rope, and the circle became a corral. Generally, though, the stock would be put out with tenders and guards, and the circle inside the wagons was campsite for the travelers.

The surrey and pair of spring wagons were not part of the circle. They lacked structure to serve as barricade or stock fence. They were simply driven inside and placed near the rear where their harnessing and tending would not interrupt the handling of draft stock on the big wagons.

"A real hand with teams," Rawlings told us, "can get a six-up in harness and be at the reins in two minutes, even in the dark."

I saw Mahlon Krause do that. Not in the dark, but in less than two minutes by Solomon Talbot's German watch. Early on, no one else could come near to it.

And when we finally closed our circle and began unhitching teams, I saw the sense of some of the placements of wagons in the line. What had seemed a random, arbitrary assignment of positions wasn't random at all. There were natural clusters of wagons in the company—family groups with more than one vehicle, bachelor freighters, stores and supply wagons—and when the line broke up and reassembled as a circle all of these just came together in groups. It was one of many little details that said Caleb Tucker had chosen his wagonmaster carefully. Judd Rawlings and his crew had guided trains before. They knew how it was done.

My "family group" included Waylon and George's wagon, the surrey and assorted draft stock. Thinking about it, I got mad at Uncle Earl all over again. Just the idea of a "family group," for a man who had set out to see the west alone and unburdened. And the *family!* Miss Priss with her bun and her irritating manner. Waylon Gibbs and George Bullard . . . a tillerman and a poler, both fresh off the keelboat. Mr. Jones and Mr. Johnson . . .

And Ezra.

Uncle Earl owed me another turning of purple.

There was no common cookery now, as there had been with the transit train. There were just too many of us. So cookfires came alight where the various groups were. The Altmans and the Honeycutts shared a fire with us, and Priscilla supervised the cooking.

I wasn't sure at that point what else Priscilla was good for—though I recalled having some notions the time her bun was down—but there wasn't any question about one thing. She could cook. With the Altmans and the Honeycutts joining in, there were eighteen mouths to feed at our fire. With Lib Altman and Betsy Honeycutt helping out, Priscilla came up with a pot of stew and dumplings that would have done anybody proud.

The table was Waylon's tailgate laid across the raised poles of the surrey. Using chairs, bales and boxes, and with the surrey's drop-board as one place, we pulled eleven seats to the table. One for each man. The babies—Lib Altman's Horatio and Hannibal and Betsy's Penny and

296

Anna—had places in the surrey and the three women scurried around getting everybody served.

We got a couple of things settled there that evening.

"If you all intend to eat at this table," I told Mr. Jones and Mr. Johnson, "You'll take off your hats."

Mr. Jones glared at me. "Why should we?"

"Well, for one reason, if you don't I might shoot you."

"You and who else?"

"Me," Julius Altman said.

"And me," Marcus added.

"And me," Cassius and Brutus chimed in together.

They took off their hats. So did Ezra, who hadn't thought about it until then, I guess.

While Lib Altman tended to the babies, Priscilla and Betsy filled our plates. Spoons were digging in when Priscilla said, "Mr. Frost, would you say grace, please?"

"Be happy to," I said. "Put down the hardware and bow your heads, gentlemen."

Mr. Jones and Mr. Johnson both had their mouths full, and went right on eating.

"You heard me," I said.

Musket hammers clicked and the two's eyes widened as muzzles prodded their bellies under the table. Waylon and George grinned. "Y'all heard him," Waylon said.

With everybody being properly pious I bowed my head and asked, "Lord, bless this food to the nourishment of our bodies and this company to the enrichment of our souls. And bless the invention of powder and balls, for by these means may we adjust the attitudes of those that need it." Buck Honeycutt snorted and Betsy hissed at him. "Amen."

"I don't know how long I'm gonna put up with this," Mr. Jones growled. But Mr. Johnson was stuffing his face with stew, so he didn't say anything.

I didn't have the bunk in Percy Smith's wagon any more. All the crew wagons were loaded with trail supplies and freight, and when it came to sleeping arrangements it was every man for himself. But I had a good bedroll and a groundcloth, and as long as it didn't rain I had no problems. I decided as long as I had no problems, I should do no less for the rest of the men in my "family."

The Altmans had only one wagon, and four men. I had noticed in staging camp that when it came up a drizzle the extra three spread their rolls under the wagon. So I told my group, "From now on, Miss Priscilla sleeps in the wagon." George and Waylon's eyes lit up. "But you two don't," I added. "You sleep out, just like Ezra and me, and Mr. Jones and Mr. Johnson. If it rains, we'll sleep under the wagon."

"Not us," Mr. Jones said. "If we sleep under a wagon it's going to be that one yonder." He pointed across the circle at the Tucker wagon.

There was something about him . . . seemed like he couldn't open his mouth without aggravating me. But I had no reasonable objection. Let them sleep wherever they wanted to. I changed the subject. "Waylon, why don't you and George spell off on the driving. One can drive and one ride flank, then turn about . . ."

"I can't ride any horse," Waylon erupted. "I tried it once. Horses don't like me, least not on top of 'em. I'll drive."

"Fine with me," George agreed. "Teamsterin' is against my nature. It's like bein' tillerman. I don't know how an' I don't want to learn. I'll ride."

"You want somebody spelled on drivin'," Waylon said, "Why not spell her?" He pointed at Priscilla, over by the cookfire. "She ain't told you, but a couple times her hands has got so sore she had to wrap 'em in linen."

"Well, she should have said something about it."

"Not to you, she won't." He squinted at me and his big monkey face went as severe as a schoolmarm on a scold. "She's got it in her head that you don't much want her goin' along with you, so she ain't about to give you cause

298

to turn her back."

George nodded soberly. "Waylon's right about that, Zack. Maybe you ain't noticed, but that woman's got her eye on you an' she's dead set to go where you go."

"George is right about that, too," Waylon said. "We talked about talkin' to you about it before now, but you wasn't around."

I had lost the drift, so I turned away, sipping hot coffee from a tin mug. Mr. Jones and Mr. Johnson had wandered off, now that supper was over. The Altman's and the Honeycutts were at their wagons, bedding babies and having family talk. Now Ezra grunted something and went to look at the riding stock.

But the keelboaters were still there, still frowning at me. "All right," I said. "I'll get Ezra to drive the surrey."

"Ezra can't drive worth squat," Waylon shook his head. "You got to do it."

"Me?" I scalded my throat with coffee, then put it down.

"It's the gentlemanly thing to do," George said. "Be a kindness, too. Make the missy feel like she's wanted here."

"I never said she was wanted," I told them. "It wasn't my idea for her to be here. It was hers."

Waylon shrugged. "You got a thick head, Zack."

"Zack," George put a rough hand on my arm, glancing around at Priscilla by the fire, then pinning me with his eyes. "She's got nowhere else to go."

I looked across at her, fussing around the fire, scraping pans and the like. Her severe dark dress and that silly tight bun gave the impression of a person who knew exactly what she wanted and how to get it, and would brook no interference. But abruptly I remembered—back there on the river when she fell in and got mud all over her, when I saw her with her hair down and wearing just her shift and she made me look the other way . . . the thing that had struck me then, for just a second, along with a few other fool notions, was that she didn't look the same then at all. Without her bun, her face was just her face. And it was a frightened, determined, vulnerable face, a little lost and not quite sure where to turn.

Well, I never was the suddenest yayhoo around when it came to how folks felt about things. Sometimes it took me a while, and I guess sometimes I never did catch on. But I felt pretty low right then. It took a displaced keelboat poler to tell me what I already knew so that I'd realize it. It didn't matter at all whether Priscilla Lawrence was a nuisance, or whether I'd have been better off if she'd taken her brother and just gone away.

What mattered was that she didn't have anyplace else to go.

Waylon's face unscrewed itself and he grinned. "Yeah. You see how it is. She's with you, Zack. She counts on you."

Anson Griggs came over from across the circle. "One of those freighters that joined up yesterday has got a loose tire, Zack. I told 'em you'd tend to it first graze-stop tomorrow. That all right?"

Then Priscilla was back, pouring the rest of the coffee for anybody who wanted it, and Ezra meandered by crowing about what a fine horse Mr. Donovan had picked out for him and wanting to know if he had occasion to shoot his gun at Indians or anything would I show him how to load it up again. And Buck Honeycutt wanted me to check the wedges in his repaired wheel, and Caleb Tucker came around to say that I didn't need to worry about the stuck lazy board on General Jackson—the Tuckers had adopted the names Abe and Benny gave their rigs—because he wouldn't need it anyway. He'd drive from the seat, and Elaine was using the lazy board for a shelf for her salt and seasonings inside the wagonbed.

Then I had tools to tend and the roan to look to, and first thing I knew it was late and the whole camp was asleep except for me and the wagonguards. So I didn't talk

300

with the boatmen any more about Priscilla. But I thought about it a good bit.

The evening back yonder in the Knob Hills when Pa brought home an unweaned cougar cub for Ma to nipple-feed, Ma was just a mite upset with him. I recollect her standing in front of him, hands on her hips in fighting stance, and wondering, "But why did you bring it home, Jedediah? There isn't any earthly use for a cougar cub except to grow up and raid the henhouse and become a threat to life and limb. So why did you bring it home?"

"Because it was there," he said. "It needs help, Mary."

"Every stray young thing there is needs help!" Ma was on a tear right then, and a wondrous sight to behold. "You can't take them all in."

"Nor can I pass it by, Mary. It would have starved. It's one of God's creatures, after all."

"Picking up strays," she said. "You're always picking up strays."

I guess Pa got a might testy, because he said, "One stray I picked up is your baby brother Earl. Don't forget that . . ."

"Well, he isn't a cougar cub!"

"No, but he's no more earthly use than one, but I wouldn't let *him* starve, either."

That put her off for a while, but later on, when that cub was full of warm goat's milk and she was holding it on her lap and rubbing its ears, she said, "Well, I guess we can make do one more time, Jedediah. But mercy, I do not understand how you fall into the stewardship of things like this."

He puffed on his pipe and thought about that for a while, then he smiled at her. "I'm just awful lucky, I guess."

What came of that cougar is another story, but they still talk about it back yonder in the Knob Hills . . . how it was Mary Frost's kitty cat that ran the thievin' Elsworth clan out of Pinot Cove and made Bad Jack McGill see the error of his ways.

But I guess I take after Pa in some ways besides size. When it comes to picking up strays, I'm just about luckier than I can tolerate.

But, like he said, the thing about a stray is that it's there, and it needs help.

The second morning on the westward trail I saddled the roan like always, but he got no sport from me that morning. I led him over and tied him on behind the reinforced surrey, then I harnessed its team — both animals — and climbed aboard to take the reins. Priscilla looked at me like I'd gone off on a yodelberry spree.

I tipped my hat, leaned out and offered her my hand. "Well, what are you waiting for?" I asked. "We haven't got all day."

It was four-five miles later that she asked, "Mr. Frost, why are you driving my surrey?"

I kept a good, honest, straight-ahead look on my face and lied to her just bigger than Baltimore. "Because I need to test out the reinforcements on the running gear. I may need to test them pretty regular for a while."

"Oh," she said. But a little later I glanced at her and she had a little, satisfied smile on her face that almost pulled her bun loose. Just like a cougar cub full of warm goat's milk and getting its ears scratched.

XXX

For three days the trail wound through peaked hills where the tall grass grew on slopes between the brushy tops and the wooded valleys. It was a test of wheels. For miles and hours every wagon in the train would roll along, canted sharply to the right. Then for as many miles and hours, making a reverse bend around a long rise, they would be canted to the left. Spokes squeaked and strained in their felloe sockets, fighting against the implacable weight on their hubs. And between each span of cantation was either a rough ridge to cross or a gully to hump through. I took my rest in the saddle or at the reins of Priscilla's surrey, and glad of it. For during the rests, when stock was rotated and let to graze, I worked on the maintenance of wheels.

There were one hundred and eighty eight wheels in the Caleb Tucker party. By the time we passed the bend at Council Grove I was on a first-name basis with fifty-four of them and keeping a weary and wary eye on the rest.

After the fifth day the land began to rise and the forests to diminish. It was not abrupt, just a little more uphill than downhill each day, and sometimes the nearest tree of any kind would be a half mile away. The land itself was changing, too. The grass was shorter, and the soil was littered with shards of broken rock. We were coming into the flint hills, Will Posey said. Somewhere along there the pattern of guards was changed, flankers riding further out, the far outriders making from ridge top to ridge top to see what they could of the lands around.

Tory was seldom seen. He rode out each morning to scout trail ahead, and sometimes returned well after dark. Will Posey took the trail lead then, riding tall and wary far out ahead of the train, staying just in sight of the lead wagon. And every man of us who could be spared shared turns at guard. At night, the wagons were circled tightly with their tongues inward, and some nights the stock was brought in for corraling. Those were the days when Tory or Will, or a ridge rider, had seen a distant smoke or a fresh Indian crossing.

We had seen Indians during our first few days. They came and went, and always watched us. Twice we had seen whole villages off in the distance. But they were trade parties, drawn to the gathering places of the white man where the wagon trains were staged. By the time we came into the flint hills, Indian sign was call for a closing up of the march and a doubling of guards.

I was riding left flank with morning sun on my shoulders when Cassius Altman appeared at the top of a rise a few hundred yards out. He waved at me and I turned and rode out to meet him.

"Thought you might want to see this," he said, and turned his mount away. I followed, over the ridge and a short way down the other side. The wind was southerly, and I smelled the stench before he reined up. He pointed.

"Man decides to ride this country alone, he takes his chances," he said.

The body half-hidden by rocks had been stripped of coat, boots and anything else of value. Then the summer sun had done its work. Nobody would have recognized him.

"Found this," Cassius said. He held a piece of an arrow, maybe two feet of shaft with the fletching intact but the point gone. Half the length of it was stained dark brown, and Cassius held it at arm's length. "It was in him. Maybe some more, too, but I didn't wait to look."

We left the fallen man where he was. That evening when Tory and Will came in, Judd Rawlings showed them the arrow.

"Pawnee," Tory said. "Might have been a Pawnee or an Osage that used it, maybe even a Wichita. But it's a Pawnee arrow."

Cassius had circled the scene, and had showed me what he saw. Three ponies. Two had chased the man, like coyotes after a rabbit, while the third had waited in that clump of rocks. "They might've dogged him for an hour," he said, "but he wasn't goin' anyplace. They knew the land. He didn't. They just run him in circles 'til he found a place to hole up, then one was waitin' there."

"Would a man travel without a gun?" I wondered.

"Maybe without gun enough," Tory said. He glanced at the Dragoon at my belt. "Not many of those out here yet. Maybe he only had one shot. Maybe he missed. They wouldn't have given him a chance to reload."

I wish nobody had told the women what he had found. But then, nobody has ever yet figured a way to keep a thing from women. They knew, and it was a more subdued party from that point on. Where the hills hid distances, children were kept in the wagons and the teams hauled closer, each lead team almost nosing the gate of the next wagon.

In camp that night Priscilla was tight-lipped and silent. When I asked her what was bothering her, she said, "In my opinion you could have taken time to give that poor man a Christian burial."

"We couldn't do that," I told her. "Cassius did the right thing waving me over, so that two of us saw what he found. But we couldn't call off more men than that—not with Indian sign plain in front of our noses." I wrinkled my nose the way Cassius had done. The smell of sun-cooked death stays in the nostrils for a long time. "Couldn't stay back, either, not with the wagons moving."

"Well, you should have done something!"

"I did, Priscilla. While Cassius circled for track, I got down and bowed my head and prayed for his soul."

Cassius Altman had been listening, standing by his wagon a few feet away. "You did?" He seemed to mull that over. "Funny thing. I done that too, before I came and got you."

She seemed to feel a little better about it, then, and turned away to get supper. But Mr. Jones had come up behind us and heard what was said.

"The man was a damn fool," he allowed to anybody who wanted to listen. "Travelin' alone out here, no better armed than to let three bucks take him, he deserved nothin' better."

Priscilla whirled on him, furious. "You just hold your tongue, sir! Who's to say who deserves what? Just because a man wants to travel alone . . . why, he probably was just like Mr. Frost here . . . probably just wanted to see where the sun went down without being burdened by people he hardly knew . . . people tagging after him like . . . like . . . well . . ."

Mr. Jones glanced at her, then looked down a cynical nose at me—he was nigh tall enough to do it, too. "All that proves is one fool's like another."

"That is uncalled for!" Priscilla advanced on him, maybe not even aware of the skillet in her hand.

But he saw it, and his hand went up, balled into a fist. I was about to cure him of sucking eggs, but Ezra came from somewhere and was right there with a cocked revolver in both hands, reaching to point its muzzle right at Mr. Jones' nose. "Behave yourself!" his thin voice cracked on the high notes. "This is a house of God!"

I really don't know what happened then. It happened too fast to think about. Somehow I got between them and took Ezra's pistol away from him and somehow it didn't go off and shoot any of us, and somehow Mr. Jones found himself surrounded by tall, skinny Altman brothers with levelled rifles.

"Mister, you better apologize," Julius said. His voice sounded like rattlesnakes singing.

"There's no need for . . ." I started.

"I don't apologize for what I say," Mr. Jones rasped.

"Not for sayin'," Julius nudged him with a rifletip. "For raisin' your hand to a lady. We don't tolerate that."

By then I had Ezra's gun in one hand and Priscilla's skillet in the other, and I was busy fending off irate Lawrences.

Mr. Jones fumed for a minute, then turned away. "I apologize," he muttered. "For that." He stalked off into the dusk.

"I don't like that man," Priscilla announced.

"Can I have my gun back?" Ezra looked at me, owl-eyed. "I'll be careful."

"You ought to watch that'n," Julius told me. "He's got mean ways about him."

"I don't know," I said. "Maybe we all ought to exercise a little charity in our judgments."

They all looked at me.

"I mean, it must be a real burden for a man to set himself up as chief horse's ass among the multitude, then find out he's going it alone."

Priscilla squinted. "Alone? What . . ."

"Look there," I pointed to where the chuck box rested on the ground a short distance away, up near the rear wheel of Percy Smith's wagon. Mr. Johnson sat there. Penny and Anna Honeycutt were on his lap, one on each knee. Little Hannibal Altman perched on one of his shoulders, and

Horatio Altman squatted in front of him listening intently.

In a moment of silence, his voice came clear. ". . . so ol' Bre'r Turtle, he told ol' Bre'r Fox, Well, sir, was it me, I believe I'd shoot the scutter on sight an' save the questions for later . . ."

Priscilla looked up at me with eyes that sparkled in a face that might have laughed—maybe—if there'd been enough slack in her bun to allow it.

"Set up the table," she said. "Supper's about ready."

By then we had passed the cutoffs of the other trails, the Great Trail out of Westport dwindling down to one trace, the Santa Fe Trail.

The flint hills stretched out ahead of us, always climbing just slightly, and now the only trees were along watercourses. The main one, and the one the trace followed, was the Arkansas River. But all along there we stayed off from it a few miles. Other rivers came in from the west and north, angling to meet it, and the best fords were upstream. Some days we made twenty miles or more. Some days we were lucky to make seven or eight. But we kept rolling, those big wagons bright with each morning's sun and casting long shadows behind them the last miles of each day.

Mr. Jones kept right on spoiling for trouble, but I didn't see him much. He and Mr. Johnson stuck to those Froehnervagens like ticks on a potlicker, always riding flank on General Ames when we were on the move, so that they never lost sight of General Jackson. At night they slept near them, and I think they took turns sleeping.

At one nooning Caleb Tucker came and asked me about that, and I shrugged and told him I didn't know. "Something to do with my Uncle Earl," I said. "You know as much about it as I do."

"I believe they make Elaine nervous sometimes," he said. "You don't think their interest is in us in some way, do you? Or in our goods?"

"I don't think so. I think Uncle Earl told them to watch your wagon, and that's just what they're doing. And knowing Uncle Earl, I'd bet those two don't know why, either."

Nothing came of it, but it was a puzzle.

Fifteen days out I got rid of my crutch. I gave it to Horatio and Hannibal to play with.

And I guess on that day I realized that I was seeing the yonders.

"Three-four more days," Will Posey said, "we'll be half way to Denver City."

"Halfway from where?"

"From Westport. Where the Cimarron trail cuts off, that's the halfway point. Captain Rawlings charted it one time. Six hundred miles and a bit from Westport to Cherry Creek crossing. The Cimarron cutoff is square in the middle. We'll be comin' into the high plains by then. You never seen that, did you?"

"I've never seen any of this."

"Well, if you think this here is some spread-out country, wait 'til you see that. Feller really never knows how much country there can be 'til he's seen the great plains. That's what I call scenery."

"I thought the plains were flat."

"Sure enough is," he nodded. "Flat. Flat-out flat to the naked eyeball and so big you can look in any direction and not ever see a thing at all except more of it. That's where a man goes does he want to look at the scenery, Zack. 'Cause there ain't anything there to get in the way."

We were riding together out past the point of the wagon train, Will holding lead to watch for Tory's traces, me taking my turn at lead escort. It was a thing Captain Rawlings had insisted on since we entered the flint hills. There was always a second man out on point with his lead scout. An escort. If a signal came from the long rider, who might be several miles ahead, the scout could hold the point while the escort relayed the message back to the train.

The only law past Westport was the law of the land, and the price of safety for an immigrant train was caution. Judd Rawlings was a cautious man.

Will prattled on sometimes. His job was a lonely one, I figured. It didn't allow the freedom of the long rider, to scout as he saw fit and leave sign where needed. Neither did it offer the comfort of companionship, as the guards with the train had. So, from time to time, Will Posey liked to just bust loose and talk for a spell. Like a teakettle with a whistle valve, sometimes he just liked to hear his voice. I didn't mind. I listened for a while, then just thought my own thoughts.

A few more days and we would have come three hundred miles from the staging ground at Westport. I had wanted to see the yonders, out there where the sun went when it banked down toward the rising forests beyond the Knob Hills. Many's the time as a tad I had climbed to the top of a breakaway ridge just so I could look west and imagine what those places must be like. Had I ever thought about what there might be three hundred miles beyond Westport? Maybe a thousand miles from our old home place back yonder? Well, here it was, and generally I was too busy to more than glance at it. Now I took a good look.

Though we had been climbing steadily since the train began, still the sky above us seemed to have climbed faster. Back in the Knob Hills, the sky was just there—blue or gray or fleecy with scudding clouds, overcast or sunny or near and dark and strewn with stars—a sky familiar and close and comfortable. But here it was beginning to change as we moved west. It was more distant. Higher and wider and more remote than back yonder, this was a sky fit for the sun to ride in. The weather had been fair for us most of the way, but there were storms out there in the distance, and a man could watch them walk across the earth, dragging curtains of gray rain behind them as they went. Back yonder, clouds had been just clouds. But out here they were banked thunderheads reaching for the sun . . . or mare's-tail wisps that meandered lazy trails bigger than the world a man could see beneath them.

The thing out here was distance. There was a Lord's plenty of that, anywhere a body took a notion to look.

And just ahead was the high plains. According to Will, flint hills country looked small and cramped by comparison.

Will had run down again, and we rode in silence for a time just looking at the broad land. Then Will hauled rein and circled, looking at the ground. He pointed. "Tory's sign."

I wouldn't have seen it without his point. A little row of stones and a tuft of grass tied with a stalk, like a little haystack.

"Indians," Will said. "Off yonder, to the north. A big bunch. Tory's gone to look. You best get back yonder and tell Captain Rawlings, Zack. I'll hold point 'til you get back."

I saw nothing out there, but Tory had seen something. I wheeled the roan and headed back at a brisk run, letting him have his head. The lead wagon was just in sight, coming over the top of one of those rolling hills. Others showed, one by one, behind it.

Judd Rawlings and Julius Altman came out to meet me. I told them what we had seen and what Will said. Rawlings squinted into the distance, then nodded. "Indians, but not a war party. Maybe a village. Julius, go back and tell Bill to take close lead, and tighten the line but keep moving. Women and children in the wagons. Nobody out on foot. Send a couple of men out to me . . . I'll be on that rise over there. Zack, you go on back and hold the position with Will. We'll bring the wagons up to there, then see what we've got."

I headed back across the hills, looking for Will. It was maybe two miles and I should have been able to see him, but I didn't. When I looked back, though, I could see the wagons pulling into close order and flank guards fanning out. Rawlings was off to the north and moving, his rifle across his arm.

Nearing the place of the sign, I still saw no sign of Will Posey, and that was odd. The sign, where I'd left him, was right out on the rising prairie, plain as day. And he had said he'd wait there. But I remembered that there was a little gully just to the south, meandering past. Maybe Will had ridden down there to look around. Maybe he'd seen something. I trotted the roan up the rise. The sign was there, Tory's message of stones and grass. And a little trace went off from it toward the gully—just a shadow of bent-over grasses where a rider had passed. Will must have seen something down there and gone for a look.

Less than two miles back now, the wagons were coming on. I circled and waved my hat, letting them know where to aim for. Then I wheeled and headed for the gully. I was Will's escort. I was supposed to stay with him.

The gully was wide here, a bend with short drop-off sides and step-down slopes below, falling toward a brush-choked bottom.

At the rim I cupped my hands and called, but only the wind answered. It was clear where Will had ridden down the slope. His trail was obvious, angling a little to the left. I urged the roan down the drop-off and followed. The track curved away, around a shoulder of eroded clay, and it narrowed to a two-foot shelf with slopes below. There were boot tracks. Will had dismounted and led his horse. I did the same. I was beyond the claybank when I saw Will. He sprawled head-down on the falling slope, not moving. Dark blood stained his shirt. I was reaching for the Dragoon when a voice behind and above me growled, "Don't fool around, Frost. Just stand still."

Brush ahead pushed open and a man came out, grinning at me with a grin I had seen before. "Big Zack Frost, as I live and breathe," Waverly said. "You sure don't look so big now, knobber."

Gravel fell, and there were boot-thuds on the trail behind me. I turned. Frank Kingston's bruiser, Hantz. He held a rifle before him, pointed at me, past the roan.

"We can do this hard or easy, Frost," Waverly said. "I reckon Bo Singer missed, but we don't miss. Where's the gold, Frost? You know where it is. You tell us now."

I shook my head. "I might if I knew, but I haven't the vaguest notion. I thought all you fellas went to Denver City to get it."

"We did," he smirked. "But it wasn't where Frank figgered it would be. So he's headin' back to find out where it really is. But Hantz and me, we decided to do this ourselves. We come on ahead. Tell you what, Frost, you just tell us easy where that strongbox is, and maybe we'll forget about collectin' the bounty on you."

XXXI

I had seen the man called Waverly a time or two, back at New Albany. A known killer, folks said. A *duelist*. I had wondered what that meant, until Uncle Earl told me one time, "That means at least one of the men he murdered had a gun in his hand at the time. Could be, I guess. He's quick with a fancy gun, and not one to miss."

The gun he held now, drooped casually but still pointed my way, was a different breed of handgun than the Dragoon in my holster. His was longer, sleeker-looking, and even at a glance I could see that a gunsmith had spent some time with it. It fit his hand as though it had grown there. I suppose it was the same one he used to carry around in the streets of New Albany, but I hadn't paid note to it before. I did now, because there wasn't any question about it . . . he meant to kill me with it, one way or another.

"I told you before, and I told your boss," I reasoned. "I don't know anything about any letters and I . . ."

"He got the letters." He smiled again, a thin, cruel smile. "But they were fake. We been all the way to Denver City, and then found out that strongbox wasn't where they said. But you had the letters . . ."

"I never even saw them."

314

"You had them, so you know where that bullion really is. Do you want to tell us now, while you still can?"

"I don't know a thing about it."

He shrugged and raised the gun. Then he paused. "Hantz, haven't had much exercise lately. Come on up here. Tell me if this feller is really as big as he looks."

Hantz was crowding the roan's rump on the narrow trail, pointing his rifle past it. He lowered the rifle and raised a hand to swat the horse, and I remembered the first time I took a bath in the cold Ohio River. I still held the reins, so I reached back, pushed under the horse's chin and forced the bit down against his jaws, just as Hantz slapped him on the rump. The roan came unglued. He hunched his back, lowered his head and I heard the thud as both rear hooves took Hantz in midsection. I didn't wait to hear him fall. I dived off the little trail, lit on my shoulders on the slope below and rolled.

Gunshots racketed in the gully and gouts of earth erupted around me. Gravel stung my cheek. Something tugged at my sleeve, then I was in brush, still rolling, flipping over and sliding away. Somewhere a bull voice was shouting . . . or screaming, I couldn't tell which.

I slithered through brush, veering this way and that. A bullet cut branches above my head and showered me with splinters. I stopped moving, lay dead still for a moment until I heard sounds on the slope, then I heaved up and sprinted a few yards to dive into new cover. How many shots had he fired? It seemed like a hundred, but I thought it was five. If I was right, he had one left. I wanted him to use it, to waste it like the others. Waverly was a gunslick. I could barely shoot. Unless he emptied his revolver I had no chance.

Was it five shots? Echoes in the gully were confusing. It could have been only four. No, it had to be five. It *must* be five. I eased a few feet beneath a spreading thornbush, then raised up on the other side of it. In that instant he was off balance, coming down the slope, looking at where I had been. I raised and fired, pointing carefully, and saw earth erupt at the ledge of the gully beyond him. I had missed him by a yard. Uncle Earl was right about one thing. I should have taken the time to learn to shoot better.

I flattened myself in the brush and rolled away, then raised and fired again. That time he was looking right at me, but still he didn't fire. My shot clipped brush off to one side of him and he grinned. He raised his pistol and I dived into the last sprig of cover above the sandy wash at the bottom of the gully. There was no shot. I lay still, listening, and heard his movement through brush not far away. But he didn't seem to be coming toward me. Across the wash was more cover. If I could get there I could start the game over again. I eased to the little ledge above the wash. Open sand stretched ahead of me, several yards of it. I would ease down there, try to slip across . . . it was instinct, I suppose, or maybe it was from wondering why he hadn't come toward me—I didn't slip into the wash. I hit it running, all out, full tilt, and the shot that he leveled at me from six yards away tugged at my coat and gouged my belt.

Six shots! I skidded to a stop, turned and he was standing there just yards away, still pointing his gun.

"You're empty, Waverly!" I shouted. I raised the Dragoon and emptied it at him as fast as I could fire. The second or third shot flattened him, dead through the heart. He still had a surprised look on his face when he fell.

I sat down right there and shook for a minute, then I reloaded the Dragoon. Somewhere above, Hantz was still hollering.

With fresh loads set, I walked to Waverly and knelt beside him. He was as dead as he would ever be, and I took the revolver from his hand and started to pocket it, then glanced at its cylinder. It was cocked, and the cap under its hammer was fresh. He had still had one shot left, after all. He just hadn't been counting, either.

I slipped back up that slope like a heathen Indian on stalk, but it didn't matter. Hantz wasn't going anywhere. He lay on the slope, head-down, right alongside the body of Will Posey. His shouts had subsided to moans, and only his arms were moving. His back was broken. Even now his lungs were starting to fill. He wouldn't last long enough for the wagons and the doctor to arrive.

I'd have done something for him if I could, but there was nothing to be done. When I knelt by him he glared at me and tried to speak. I bent to listen.

"Frank's comin'," he whispered. "We missed but he won't. He'll bring you . . . down, Frost. Frank will . . ."

I hadn't been watching his hands. Suddenly they were around my neck, crushing, and he grinned as he pressed. And died.

The thumbs I wrenched back, to get those big hands off my windpipe, were a dead man's thumbs. When I dropped his hands, his arms fell limp. And when I moved aside his grinning face went on grinning at the place where I had been.

If Will Posey had seen the man who killed him, it was only for an instant. I found his plains rifle and it was still loaded. Waverly had never given him a chance. One shot, dead center. Then they had waited for me.

Down in the bottoms I found their horses, and Will's. One by one I loaded dead men onto their saddles and led their horses up to the prairie to ground-rein them beside Tory's sign. When I finally led my roan up there, with all the extra guns hanging from the saddle, the wagons were coming up the rise.

Bill Lovell was in charge, and he circled them there. Late in the day Rawlings and his group returned. The Indians they had seen were a village of Kiowa, on the move and posing no real threat to us. They were looking for buffalo, not white men's rolling lodges.

We buried Will Posey with the honors due a good man. Then as a courtesy, we buried Waverly and Hantz. But few could bring themselves to do honor to the men who had killed Will. They were just buried.

It had the effect on the wagon party that death always has on communities of people. The men worried and the women cooked. One of their own had fallen—abruptly and brutally. The cookfires weren't so many that evening. They gathered together for their cooking and Priscilla was busy tending three fires and a dutch oven while she supervised half a dozen others. Those women came up with everything from stew to fresh bread to dried-apple pie. People drew together and ate together and talked about Will Posey.

And I kept remembering what the Kingston men had said.

"Frank's headin' back," Waverly had told me.

"Frank's comin'," Hantz' voice had whispered. "He'll bring you down, Frost."

And I remembered that old halfbreed mastiff back in the Knob Hills. I knew why he went out after that bear. He went because he had to.

I found Ezra and took him aside. "You have a horse and a gun now, Ezra. Do you want to go back to the way you were before?"

"No, sir." His gaze wavered for a moment, then held my eye—just the way I'd told him. He straightened his shoulders. "No, sir, I don't. Not ever."

"Duty goes with a horse and a gun, Ezra. Your duty is to your sister. You look out for her. Listen to good men and act like them, and be one of them. And don't let harm come to your sister because if it does, when I come back you'll answer to me."

"Yes, sir," was all he said, but his gaze didn't waver.

I found Priscilla sitting in the unhitched surrey—just

sitting there, as though she were waiting for me.

"I have to leave for a while," I told her. "You know why, don't you?"

She nodded. "In my opinion, Mr. Frost . . ."

"Zack."

"In my opinion, Zack, the men here would help you . . . in your fight. We all would. You have friends here."

"And if I let the fight come to me here, what might happen to the babies?" She didn't respond to that. "Priscilla, will you keep my tools for me while I'm gone? I'll need them when we get to Denver City. There will be work there for a wagonwright."

"Don't get hurt again . . . Zack."

"Don't be ridiculous. I never . . ."

"Your uncle told me. Nothing ever happens to you, he said. No harm comes to our Zack Frost. Just please be careful, Zack. People can die of no harm done, you know."

She brought out a sack of provisions. I don't know when she had packed them, but I guess she knew I would be going.

I saddled the roan and hung Will Posey's rifle from its saddlehorn. I put Waverly's fine-tuned revolver in my holster and dropped the Dragoon into my coat pocket. Then I went to the crew wagon, where Judd Rawlings had gathered his scouts.

"I'm leaving for a while," I told him. "Frank Kingston is my problem, not yours."

"You think you can lead them away, Zack?" he tipped his head, appraising me. "By yourself?"

"It's my choice to try."

He didn't like it much, but he didn't like the alternative, either—that Frank Kingston and a bunch of toughs were out there somewhere, waiting for his train, waiting to do whatever Frank decided to do, no matter who it hurt. He just shrugged and shook my hand. "Do you know where you're going?"

"I'm going after bear."

Two days later I saw the high plains. They were everything Will Posey had said. They were more. Broad lands, abundant with short grass, vistas that climbed away into distances the eye refused to comprehend, and no feature anywhere except the textures of wind on the grass, the huge bowl of sky overhead . . . sometimes a trace of horizon, but more often none. It was as though the Lord had created a world just that far—out there a ways—then at the end of the sixth day had just shrugged and said, "All right, that's enough variety," and had pointed creation west and gone off and left it working.

A day or two into the high plains I knew why all the stories that came back east, from those who had come this way, all told of the high plains but never really described them. They really didn't want to talk about them very much. The plains were vast, empty . . . and lonely.

I was doing what I had meant to do. I was traveling west across the lands where the evening sun went. And I was doing it alone. On the high plains, of all places on God's good earth, no man should be alone.

I wondered where Uncle Earl was.

I stayed close to the trail, but mostly off it. Anyone watching would be watching the trail, where the traffic was. With a good horse under me, not traveling hard but traveling steady, I guessed I was covering forty miles a day though there was no change in scenery to say so. And I saw traffic eventually—far in the distance, a little line of dots. A few hours later I was close enough to make them out. It was freight wagons, maybe the same party that had left the staging ground at Westport while I was there.

I followed them for several hours, coming up on them at two miles to their one, but staying off the trail. I wanted to find Frank Kingston. But I wanted it my way. I wanted to find him, not him find me.

Maybe I was thinking that the freight wagons might draw in anyone coming this way. Certainly they would attract attention of anyone who saw them. There was nothing else out here to see except a whole lot of out here. So I followed, but stayed low in the rolls of the prairie.

But after a while there was a spot on the distant land, and the wagons reached it before I could make it out. They were a mile ahead and going on when I rode down to see what it was.

It was a pile of stone—slabs of grayish sandstone stacked five feet high, where the trail branched. The wagons were on the south route. We had come to the Cimarron cutoff. They were on their way to Santa Fe, but my trail here angled northward, toward Pueblo.

I looked back at the rock cairn several times. The awful loneliness of the vast land settled in with the miles that stack of rocks receded behind me. Ahead the land climbed steadily, slowly, seeming to go on forever . . . flat, but only to the eye. The flatness was an illusion, a trick of distance and the sameness of the grass. Hidden by illusion were the rolls and swells, the crests and bottoms. There were places on those plains that could hide an army.

For days I had watched rainstorms, mostly to the north and west. They had been a blessing to a man concentrating on staying out of sight. I didn't have to cross the trail or stay near the river to find water. It was in the creeks and gullys. The same rains that had greened the land ahead provided water where I needed it to be.

In a hollow shielded by cottonwood growth I left the roan to graze while I scouted ahead. At the top of a rise I bellied down to study the climbing trail in the distance. The Pueblo trace showed no sign of traffic this early in the season, or none that I had seen, but its route was dimly visible even from two miles away. Hooves and wheels of past seasons had left their mark upon the earth.

I rested, thinking my own thoughts and watching the prairie birds dance in the distances, the clouds out there where sometimes there was a horizon, the patterns of wind in the endless grass. Then there was movement, and I fixed on it. Off to my right, not more than half a mile, horsemen appeared. By twos and threes they seemed to grow there, coming from some hidden bottom, coming over a rise. Indians. Bright daubs of color glistened in the sun. Feathers hung from crests of raven hair bound up to flow above them, wild as the wind. Twenty I counted, then three more. No porting village, this was a party of hunters or warriors, all mounted and carrying lances and bows.

They passed below me, going toward the trail. As they neared it they spread and circled, reading the ground beneath them. Then they crossed and went on, diminishing in distance. Ahead of them was the river, and above — upstream — another stream meandering toward it. Pale tops of greening cottonwoods marked its course.

The Indians angled to the right, heading upstream.

From there I stayed well north of the trail, just near enough for an occasional, careful glimpse of it.

The sun was low when I saw riders on the trail, a large group coming east.

It could have been anyone. But I knew, somehow, even at the distance. I had found Frank Kingston.

XXXII

Once back yonder, when we were still tads, Uncle Earl had a run-in with a wild kid from Big Lick and got the best of him fair and square, but the kid took offense about it and two days later there was a whole tribe of them from Big Lick going from place to place, stealing chickens and looking for Uncle Earl. They intended to catch him and break his bones.

The thing was, we knew the country around there better than they did, so I followed along and Uncle Earl went looking for them. I didn't do much about them, but he did. When we spotted the gang he worked up fairly close behind them and beaned a pair of them with rocks. I never saw anybody could chunk a rock like Uncle Earl. Well, that brought the rest of them out on a tear, hot on his heels. I hung back and watched them chase by, then shinned up a tree where I could watch the rest. Uncle Earl led them down the Potter Creek path, then doubled back so they lost him.

They split up to search, and when they were all pretty well separated Uncle Earl let one bunch of four see him and off they went. He headed straight for the O'Dell barn, where we had locked Mr. O'Dell's bull in before we started. He went in through the front with them right behind him, and a minute later Uncle Earl came out the back, slammed the door and bolted it, then ran back around front and closed that door and dropped the beam.

There was mayhem done in that barn that day, but Uncle Earl didn't wait around. He had another bunch of Big Lickers spotted up on Clay Ridge, so he went after them and led them down to the old sump that we called Black Bog because a body that got into it had a dickens of a time getting out. He and I knew where the dry path was, but they didn't.

Three more of them he left penned up in Sheriff Coulter's henhouse, and another one in Miller Todney's smokehouse. That only left one, a big red-haired brawler named Pud. Uncle Earl found Pud and popped him with a rock, then took off running with Pud right behind. He led him right back to where we had started, and I climbed down from the tree to see what would happen.

I should have stayed where I was. Uncle Earl ran right up to me, then turned around and popped Pud with another rock. Pud howled, picked up a rock of his own and hurled it, and Uncle Earl ducked.

That rock got me right in the breadbasket.

But later, after I had stomped Pud and sent him home, Uncle Earl said, "Zack, let this be a lesson to you. Divide and conquer. Works every time."

"You might have divided," I pointed out, "but it seems like when it came to conquering Pud, it was me that did it."

"And don't ever think I don't appreciate it, Zack," he nodded. "I couldn't have done that better myself."

I learned things from my Uncle Earl when we were growing up. Going up against long odds single-handed wasn't one of them. I'd never known him to do that. But as they came closer and I counted them, I just couldn't see much choice. Frank Kingston had to be stopped here and now . . . or at least led away from the wagon train. He wouldn't stop at anything to have his way, and people would get hurt.

Counting him, there were fourteen armed men out there.

There was a map someplace, saying where a bonded strongbox was hidden. He wanted that map. And he wanted me dead. I didn't know where the map was, of course . . . and then, suddenly, I did know. Uncle Earl up there in the bed of General Jackson, going through his boxes. And then the boxes later being in General Ames. And General Jackson's lazy board was stuck. Wedged shut, most likely. So it couldn't be opened and the map be found. And then two hoodlums — Mr. Jones and Mr. Johnson — riding guard on General Jackson . . . I wondered what they would have done if any of us had decided to fix that lazy board.

Frank thought I had it. Maybe I could lead them away. But if they got me, and I didn't have the map, they would still head for the train. Or if I got away, they would go there anyway just to be sure. Bounty hunters don't change their minds, and Frank Kingston wouldn't change his.

At its closest point the swell I was following was within a thousand yards of the trail. When Kingston and his bunch were close enough that I could see their faces, I put heels to the roan and crested out and headed across, right in front of them.

A bullet cut turf in front of me as I hit the trail, and two more sang right behind me as I crossed it, and I heard Frank's bull voice shouting orders at them. The shooting stopped, but as I headed the roan racer down the incline toward the distant river I heard hoofbeats behind, a swelling thunder, spreading out and coming on.

Glancing back, I held the roan in just a little, just holding pace ahead of them. But it wasn't much of a restraint. There were some good horses back there, and the men on them could ride.

A quarter-mile, and the river's flat valley spread before me. I took the final crest at a run and clung for my life as the roan slipped and dusted down the slope beyond. Then I eased him left, downstream, and let him have his head. Somewhere close behind I heard a scream and the sound of a horse falling. But it didn't slow the rest of them. They were so close behind me that I could hear their horses breathing. I let the roan out all the way.

A half-mile of shelving valley passed beneath our feet, and the river curved away ahead. I hoped I wasn't wrong. I could only guess, but my guesswork had one chance to prove itself. Ahead there was a bend in the high bank, curving away out of sight. It looked like one I had seen earlier, but I had seen it from above, out on the plains. Then I saw furtive movement atop it, and I figured the Good Lord had given me all the clue I was going to get. I drew the fancy revolver from my holster — the precisioned gun that Waverly the duelist had carried — and turned and emptied it at the pursuing pack, timing and placing my shots, but not wasting time about it. I saw two of them go down, and maybe another.

Gunfire answered me, bullets whipping back as I ducked low and the roan took the bend belly-down, powerful legs driving . . .

. . . Right into the middle of an Indian camp. Some of them were just getting to their feet, but others were more ready. A lance thudded into my saddle, twisting away to drag the ground alongside the roan's rear hooves.

Then I was through them, and I didn't even look around at the chaos behind me. Those warriors were mad as hornets, and Kingston's bunch ran right into them.

I kept going, watching for the shelving slope I had seen. When I saw it I heaved left and we went up and over and hightailed it for the trail and the open prairies beyond.

When I hauled up, finally, the roan was heaving and foamed with sweat. And I noticed how dark it had become. I hadn't noticed the sun going down, but a heavy dusk lay on the land.

I got down and led the roan another mile, westward, then found a secluded place in a little wash where he could rest . . . and I could too.

I thought again about Uncle Earl leading that bunch of Big Lickers into the O'Dell barn. He had known perfectly well that barn was full of angry breed bull, and I'd had my doubts about that being a right civil thing to do. But then, Uncle Earl never was just like other folks. He had his own ways of doing things.

I slept and the roan rested. Come dawn, we might be real busy again. I didn't sleep well, though. In the chase I'd had a clear look at Frank Kingston's face — what was left of it. Never in my life I had seen such rage — such insane rage — in a pair of eyes. And one of those eyes stared out of a face. The other looked like a bright marble in a mold of scar tissue — burn scars that covered half his face.

Somehow I expected to see . . . well, something, at first light. Something more than the endless prairie all around me, that I had been seeing now for days. Somewhere within ten or twelve miles of me were hardcases and painted Indians, men with weapons and horses, looking for one another . . . looking for me. Somewhere there were the bodies of men, sprawled in the greening wilderness.

But there was nothing to see with the dawn. Only the prairie, that went on and on. The prairie that looked so featureless and flat, yet could hide armies within its rolling folds. I ate a handful of the dried provisions Priscilla had packed, then I saddled the roan and moved out. With light they would be out circling, looking for tracks. They? Maybe the Indians, maybe Kingston's men. Maybe some of both. Whoever was left, they would be looking.

I went another mile left, crossed a dry wash, then doubled back and followed it south, riding along its verge where runoff had exposed sandstone. Not easy to track on stone, I imagined. Some men had died back there, of that I was sure. But not all. Probably not even very many.

On the high plains, a hundred square miles is small terrain. Cozy, in its fashion. And within a hundred square miles, this part of the rising plain was crowded. I saw the first ones at mid-morning, a pair of riders far off, skylined momentarily on a rise. Others saw them, too. A half-dozen painted warriors came from a draw just ahead of me — A few more minutes and I would have ridden right into them — and thundered away toward that rise.

There was a dead man in the draw where they had been. One of Kingston's men, he must have gotten away in all the shooting. But not far enough away. They had found him. Hours ago. He had taken a long time to die.

With high noon the buzzards began to appear, one circling far to the east, three more nearer, spiralling downward, a few at two points off to the south. Was it over? I wondered. I found a sheltered place finally, just a little cutback wash at the rim of the river's flat valley, and I waited there as the sun settled toward the west. I waited, and watched the river.

I wouldn't have seen the Indians, except that they rode close to where buzzards were and I saw the birds rising ahead of them. A mile from where I hid, downstream, I saw them — a file of warriors, crossing the river, going away. I counted nineteen or twenty in all, and several extra horses. I couldn't tell how many.

An hour later I saw them again, tiny dots in the sunset, far away to the south, going away. I slept where I was, and with dawn I began a search of the prairies, starting at the river where I had led Kingston's men.

I found nine bodies, all white men. If the Indians had

dead, they had taken them. Most of the bodies were muti-
lated, some unrecognizable. I searched all day, and found
no more. Nine dead, out of fourteen. That left five. Was
Frank Kingston still alive? I couldn't be sure.

Another morning dawned and I saddled up and rode a
wide circle, starting at the bend in the river. I held beyond
the places where the dead men lay, studying the ground.
There had to be some sign of where the rest had gone. It
was past noon when I found sign, shod hoofprints and
droppings, a faint trace angling westward, more than two
riders. I wished I had the craft of Will Posey then. My
eyes were fit for setting spokes, not for the following of
spoor. I found it and lost it within a mile.

At a place where the land dipped and rolled in long
swells like ripples on a pond, I rode to the top of a rise
and stood in my stirrups to scan the distances to the west.
Far out there, almost at the discernible horizon, there was
a change in the land. The colors were lighter, and seemed
to ripple. Will Posey had said we'd see sand hills before we
saw the mountains. How far away were they, those men
who wanted me dead? And didn't I want them dead now,
too? I wanted them stopped, once and for all. It amounted
to the same thing.

I saw no trace of them. Finally I eased the reins to turn
back, and something burned my shoulder. I raised my
arm and saw blood there, then heard the sound of a
gunshot, hard and flat on the prairie wind. And I saw the
shooter. He was behind me, a man on foot, at least five
hundred yards away. He held a revolving cylinder rifle,
and even as I spotted him I saw smoke as he fired again.
His bullet tugged at my hatbrim, and when the sound
reached me he was already working his action for another
shot.

I lifted Will Posey's big old Plains rifle from its thong,
raised it, sighted and fired. It kicked like a roan horse and
its voice was sudden thunder. Out there on the next rise

the man raised his head to stare at me. Then he toppled backward and lay still.

My arm throbbed and I felt a lump there. Maybe his rifle was undercharged. Maybe it just wasn't enough rifle for the distance. His spent ball had lodged just below the skin. I got my coat and shirt off, then used my knife to cut it out. And passed out a couple of times in the process. I should have saved my woozies for when I cauterized the wound with a dab of gunpowder. I could have used them then.

The man still lay out there, where he had fallen. Eventually I went to him, leading the roan. Will Posey's rifle had done its work. The man had been dead when he fell. But I knew him. He was one of those who had been with Frank Kingston back yonder. One of the hill men. He had no horse, but somehow he had evaded the Indians and gone on. Then he had seen me. Bounty hunters have one thing on their minds, and they don't change.

I reloaded both rifles and hung them on my saddle. Again I was leaving death behind me, and the endless prairie wind whispered mournful lines that I'd heard somewhere back yonder, a long time ago:

> *Where have the young men gone? they cry.*
> *Young ladies, do not mind them,*
> *For they have gone a'Westering*
> *And only God can find them.*

The dead man lay there, behind me, and the land didn't care. The great plains went on and on, winds playing hopscotch with its endless grasses, and there was a loneliness about it that tore at the soul.

I had gone after bear, just like that old breed mastiff back in the Knob Hills. And I had played Uncle Earl's game for him. Divide and conquer. But I hadn't got my bear, and I hadn't won the game.

When you see Frank Kingston's face, the bounty tracer said—back there in Cairo—when you see his face you'll know.

I had seen his face, and I knew. Frank Kingston was out there somewhere, with half of his face ruined by blacksmith's coals. He had lost me for now, but he wouldn't stop. By now he knew I wouldn't catch him on these vast plains, and he knew as well that he wouldn't find me. So he would do the other thing he could. Somewhere up ahead, somehow, he would make a try for the train.

The map he wanted was in the lazy board of General Jackson. He might not know that—I couldn't be sure—but he knew it was with the train and he would go for it. I'd missed the bear. Now the bear would lie in wait for a lot of decent people.

A few miles from the trail I saw a rider in the distance, and I checked the load in the plains rifle and went on. When I saw him again he was closer, and he waved his hat. It was Tory, riding far scout for the train.

We camped under the rim of the river's valley, and I told him what I could. He just looked at me and kept shaking his head. But when I came to the part about the gold map, that I believed was hidden in the Froehnervagen, he went still and thoughtful.

"Then I reckon they know it's there by now," he said, finally. "Your man Jones . . ."

"He isn't mine."

"*That* man Jones, then . . . he's gone. Rode out in the night, three days back. Headed west. Now I reckon we know what that means."

I nodded. We knew. Jones had counted his cards and decided to play a better hand. If he wasn't with Frank Kingston by now, he would be soon.

"What about Mr. Johnson?"

"He stayed. The past few days he's took to shavin' his whiskers, and he's been callin' on one of the Conway sisters each evenin'."

With morning light we headed east along the trail, to meet the wagons. In the far distance northwest, buzzards were circling. Tory squinted at them. "Another one?"

"Another one," I said.

"I'll say this for you, Zack. When you go lookin' for bear you're pure hell on skunks."

XXXIII

There were four left, I thought. If Mr. Jones had found them and joined them . . . had he maybe been with them all along? . . . that made five. Unless there were more someplace else, which didn't seem likely. Frank could pick up all the shooters he wanted, where there were men to draw his pay. But not out here.

At first night camp after I rejoined the train, after I got Priscilla to stop stuffing me full of antelope stew and tutting about the scar on my shoulder, we had a council and went 'round and 'round about it all. The upshot was that from here on it didn't make any difference if I was with the train, because if Frank decided to try for the map he would go after the train whether I was here or not. And the more guns the better, if he did.

One thing we did, though — it was my notion, but Caleb Tucker and Judd Rawlings both approved it. We emptied everything out of Waylon Gibbs' rebuilt freighter. When it was empty and cleaned, we emptied everything out of General Jackson and put all the Tuckers' travel gear into the freighter. Then I spent an hour springing the lazy board. Uncle Earl had wedged it, and driven the wedges beyond the rim of its frame where they wouldn't show. It was a good thing Abe and Benny hadn't tried their hammer trick on it back at Westport. They would either have busted a hammer or demolished the wagon's sideboard.

The map was there, a folded oilcloth sketch with some lines and markings on it that I couldn't make head nor tail of. "It's a vector chart," Caleb Tucker said. "It isn't any good unless you know where it begins. Maybe that was what was in those letters your uncle talked about."

I put it away and replaced the lazy board, then we repacked the Froehnervagen with Waylon and George's goods and as much of Caleb's left-over stores as there was room for. The rest went into several other wagons in the party. For the duration, we traded wagons. It was a precaution. If anything *did* happen, better we be the target than the Tuckers.

Mr. Johnson had watched the procedure gloomily. When it was done he went to Captain Rawlings. "I just want you all to know that I didn't have anything to do with Jones leaving," he said. "I ain't much, I guess, but I ain't a damn turncoat. I'd be obliged for a chance to prove it, but that's up to you."

Rawlings looked at me. "He's your man," he said.

"He isn't *my* . . ."

"He's here as a member of your group."

"Then let him stay," I said. "If he's lying, I'll tend to him myself." To Mr. Johnson I said, "You just keep on doing what my Uncle Earl set you to do. You ride guard on that wagon. The same one. I helped build that wagon and it's worth your hide if it's damaged."

It was a quiet and wide-eyed wagon community that rolled through my "bloody sixty thousand" two days later. Word had gone around about what Tory had seen out there, and I guess they all expected to see the road littered with dead men. Truth was, there wasn't anything to see. A hundred square miles of high plains—or sixty thousand acres, as Tory said it—can hide an awful lot of death. Still, they could imagine.

"You should hear what they're saying," Priscilla told me as I drove the surrey. "Zack, by the time these people are done, they'll be saying you left a hundred dead men out here."

"It was ten," I reminded her. "And the Indians got most of them."

"Well, that isn't the way it's starting to sound. Mercy, I can't think what these children's children are going to hear about all this. Do you know what I heard the Reverend Moore—of all people—say? He was making a rhyme. He said, 'Zachary Frost went riding out to set the wage of sin . . . and all the outlaws bit the dust before he came back in.' In my opinion, Zack . . ."

"Priscilla . . ."

"In my opinion, that's what legends are made of."

"Exaggeration?"

"Misguidance."

"Priscilla, please hush. I don't care to talk about that."

"Of course not."

It was that same day when Priscilla took another burden off my shoulders. "I realize that we—Ezra and I—have been a worry to you," she said as we ate our evening meal. "But I want you to know that when we reach Denver City we shall no longer trouble you."

"Oh?" I almost choked, it was so abrupt.

"I was talking with Mr. Tucker. He says there should be a market for a cookery at Denver City. He wanted my thoughts on it. We have decided—well, *I* have—to open a business. Good, Christian cookery, wholesome meals for a reasonable price. No spirits, of course, and no profanity on premises. Ezra can help me, and Mr. Tucker will provide the . . . ah . . . working capital."

"Priscilla . . ."

"So you see, we shall be provided for. Very nicely, I expect. And Mr. Gibbs and Mr. Bullard have plans . . ."

"We're thinkin' we'll go in with Anson Griggs," Waylon

said. "Barrels and troughs, stablery, maybe even bring in a sawmill. Lots of money in sawmills."

It kind of hit me then, that they were all setting me free. Just like I had always wanted. No responsibilities, no burdens . . .

Julius Altman leaned over to whisper, "Man's got to be careful what he wishes for, Zack. He might get it."

Eleven more days we crawled across featureless prairie, distances behind and climbing distances ahead, with horizons so far away that sometimes they were out of sight. On the eleventh day it rained—a steady, soaking rain that lasted into the evening. Wagon wheels rutted the running soil and spokes tightened into their felloes until the great train moved silent as a ghost in the gray shroud of the rain. We made no more than twelve miles that day, and slept that night exhausted. But with morning the clouds were gone, and there were mountains on the horizon. New sun hit them away out there and they shone, diamonds in the morning light. The shining mountains. A sight to see.

We angled northerly from there, with the mountains growing day by day on our left. Somewhere west was the settlement of Pueblo, Rawlings said, but we held to the trail and passed it. We were in foothills now, with many a ridge and canyon to be crossed. Westward they were higher and deeper, ranging toward the big mountains.

At a clear, flatbed stream which Tory called Sandy Bottom, we laid over for a day to do repairs and graze our stock. We took turns bathing and doing wash—men first, the bachelors among us carrying armloads of garments, and later the women and children. I greased hubs and bound a few loose spokes, and I had the roan out in longside pasture combing him down when I glanced toward the stream. A dozen of the younger women were sitting on a rock shelf over there, most of them in their shifts, soaking in clean sunshine and brushing out their hair. It was a sight to make a man wonder why he had ever had the notion of being alone. And when they came back to the circle a little later, I hardly recognized Priscilla. Her bun was gone, and instead of her old dark garb she wore a dress of lime green. Dark hair flowed behind her as she walked, and all I could do was stand off and goggle at her.

All those long miles of our acquaintance, when she had been a desperate waif needing a protector—and she knew it, right enough—she had been Miss Priss of the pursed lips and stretched cheeks. Only now, when her goal was in sight and her future secure, did she come out of her shell and let a man see why he should have been panting eager to be of service to her back then when she needed him. Pa was right. He who tries to understand women shall learn in good time that women are not to be understood.

From Sandy Bottom the wagons rolled on, high and proud, and I rode out to a ridge to watch them. Forty-seven vehicles, lined out and homing on Cherry Creek and the little settlement they called Denver City.

And a city it would be, when this party arrived. Merchants and craftsmen, storekeepers and traders—a town on wheels, still averaging twelve miles a day even in the foot-hills. Creeping capitalism was headed for Denver City, whether Denver City was ready for it or not.

Four days up from Sandy Bottom I rolled out of my soogans in frosty dawn and Uncle Earl was there, sitting on a tacklebox, drinking coffee from a mug. When he saw I was awake he poured some for me.

"I've been talking to Tory," he said. "Sounds to me like you solved your problems back there."

"I could have used some help, Uncle Earl."

"Doesn't sound like you needed any. Besides, I was busy."

"Busy doing what? Where are all your thugs? Beg pardon . . . your marshals and detectives?"

"Why, they're a long way from here, Zack. Some of them are in jail over at Pueblo, but most of them are on

337

their way back east. Some of them are prisoners, in the custody of others. Like I said, I've been busy."

"Sounds like it. Are you going to tell me about it, or not?"

Oh, he told me about it, all right. It took the better part of an hour.

Seems as though his contract with Bailey Kingston wasn't the only contract Uncle Earl had. First and foremost, he had an agreement with the bonding company back in Philadelphia that held the bond on Kaygee Freight.

"Old Bailey's been stealing those folks blind for years," he said. "Now and again he'd send out a fake shipment, and arrange for it to just disappear. Then the bonding company would have to make good on it, and Bailey squirreled away the bullion. They never could make anything stick, so I said I'd help them out . . . for a price."

And he had done that. First he had got in with the Downeys, and figured out when a fake shipment might be coming along. Then he'd got in with Bailey Kingston and let on that Frank Kingston was stealing from him, and made his deal with Bailey. Then he'd got me crossways of Frank Kingston and manipulated the whole thing from there.

"I probably can't collect from Bailey Kingston on that," he said, sadly, "because Bailey Kingston will be in prison by the time I can get back there. The bonding company has all the evidence it needs to put him away for a few lifetimes. Too bad, though. I did what I told him I'd do. They have proof that Frank Kingston engineered the robbery of the latest shipment, which is what Bailey wanted them to think. It's too bad, Zack. A fellow who can bag two birds with one stone ought to be able to collect for both of them."

I have to admit, I was impressed. I always knew Uncle Earl could play four hands at a five-chair table and deal from the middle of the deck to boot, but this piece of work really took the taw. Right at the moment, I couldn't even keep up a good mad where he was concerned.

Others had gathered around to listen, and Julius Altman muttered to me, "If I had an uncle like that I'd put him in a tote sack with a hundred pounds of rock and throw him in the river."

"You damn near got your nephew killed," Rawlings rasped. "What kind of dealin's is that?"

Uncle Earl just grinned, that disarming, lopsided grin he always had. "I wouldn't jeopardize Zack," he said. "I told his folks I'd look out for him. But Zack takes care of himself. Nothing bad happens to him. See, here he is, in the best of health and enjoying a pleasant journey to the west."

There was some grumbling, but he grinned again and stood. "I'll be rejoining the party now," he told Rawlings. "I'll go the rest of the way to Denver City with you, so you can rest easy on that score."

He wandered away, toward where Waylon and George were hitching a team to General Jackson. He stopped when he saw them, and glanced back, puzzled. Then he shrugged and went on, to saddle his gray horse.

"Move 'em out," Judd Rawlings said. "Come Sunday we'll put down at Denver City, and from that point on I don't give a hang what sort of flim-flam y'all do to one another."

High mountains stood west of us, and trail's end was ahead. But my scalp kept on itching, and I talked to Rawlings and Tory about not letting their guard down. Whatever Uncle Earl had done to set the law on Frank Kingston, I still didn't know where Frank was and I wouldn't feel right until I knew. But we rolled along, and the bright days crept behind us, and it was good to be out here where the world was of a size to match the sunshine that fell upon it.

It was not uncommon now to see other people from time to time. Twice we passed Concord stages going the other way, and once a party of miners going cross-trail, looking for diggings on Sunbird Mesa. We stood wide of the trail to pass a nine-wagon party going south, and exchanged visits with them. They had separated from a big train up north somewhere, decided to go their own way, and were making for the Rabbit Ears Pass region to the south.

Tory and his scouts worked closer in now, seldom out of sight of the lead wagon. In the evening of the fourth day from Sandy Bottom, Snell Boyd reported on seeing riders in the hills to the west, moving north parallel to our route.

Since the encounter out on the plains, Judd Rawlings had insisted on a tight circle at every camp, and we always kept guards. But now I called my party together after supper, starting with Uncle Earl.

"I think Frank Kingston is still out there," I said. "Maybe he doesn't know about the fake shipment . . . or maybe he isn't after the map at all. But I don't feel just right about things."

"He'd have to move at night," Uncle Earl said. "How would he get in?"

"Say it was you, then. How would *you* do it?"

"I don't know. I'd have to think on it."

"They could crawl under the wagons," Ezra offered. "That's what I'd do."

"And be caught afoot in a circle of guns," Waylon shook his head. "No, they'd have to ride in somehow."

"Not with these wagons tongue-in and tight," Uncle Earl said. "Not at night."

"Then you don't believe he'll come for us," I said.

"No, I don't. Not in a million years."

"Waylon?"

340

"Don't see how. No, I'd say they wouldn't even try."

"George?"

"I'll go with that," he shrugged. "It's over, Zack. They ain't comin'."

"In my opinion . . ." Priscilla started to speak.

"Julius?"

"Man's a fool to reckon what another'n will do, but I reckon they're beat. They won't come."

"No real reason to," Uncle Earl said. "Not any more."

"In my opinion . . ."

"We're darn near to Denver City," Buck Honeycutt allowed. "They wouldn't come now, I guess."

Priscilla was squirming. "It seems to me . . ."

"I reckon that's it, then," Julius said. "We don't expect there'll be trouble . . ."

"I would."

I turned around. Mr. Johnson shrugged at me. "Was it me, I would."

"You would what?"

"I'd try one more time. But then, what do I know?"

"You're barking at shadows, Zack," Uncle Earl assured me. "Let's all get some rest. You'll feel better about things tomorrow."

"Honestly!" Priscilla grumped, and stalked off to find her bunk.

They came that night. Long after midnight, when false dawn was in the sky and one or two breakfast fires were burning, they came. It was easy. The wagons were never a full circle. There was always a gap, where the stock was corraled. Our group had always been next to the gap, and trading wagons hadn't changed that.

They came with guns blazing and all hell broke loose.

XXIV

The man most likely wrong is the one who is surest that he's right. I can remember Uncle Earl saying that, a long time ago. Probably right after he had skinned somebody out of something and was gloating about it.

I have always wished that Uncle Earl would practice what he preached.

I came awake to chaos—shouts, gunshots and the thudding of many hooves. I rolled out from under General Jackson and a bullet gouged the dirt a foot from my ear. I rolled back and another whanged against frame strapping above me. Women were screaming, men were shouting and the corraled stock was running in all directions. They had come in through there, driving the stock ahead of them. I scooted back beneath an axle and came out the end, next to the tongue. At first they were only dark forms, men on horses circling the inner ring of the wagons, dodging stock, firing at random to drive people into cover. But they homed in then, aiming for General Jackson and I saw them coming. Three, then another and another. I had a revolver in each hand, Waverly's in my right, where it would do some good, the Dragoon in my left because that was the only other hand I had.

Dark shapes, looming close — then vagrant wind caught the embers of a rekindled cookfire and there was light. I saw them and they saw me, and the voice that came from one of them was Frank Kingston's voice. "There he is! That one! Kill him!" Splinters from the wagon tongue stung me as I dodged aside into shadows, and two more shots lanced out at where I had been.

"Kill him!" Kingston roared. "Then get this wagon hauled around!"

I wasn't where I had been any more. I pivoted and ran the length of the wagon, leaped the tongue of the surrey just behind it and came out among them from that side, firing. The first to swing toward me was to my left, so I let fly with the Dragoon. The masked man was levelling his gun, but when I fired his horse reared and went wild. He clung as it spiralled and pitched. With Waverly's gun I fired at the next one over, nearest the wagon, and he fired back. I was spinning and dodging, and his shot went wild. He fired again and my foot went numb, as though a horse had stepped on it.

"Get him, damn you!" Kingston yelled. I spun toward the voice and thumbed two shots at it. He swerved his mount and turned, trying to get a sight on me.

From somewhere I heard Uncle Earl's voice. "Zack, won't you ever learn to shoot?"

His gun barked twice and a man went over backward, off his horse. He fired again and another grabbed his arm and howled. But Kingston had come full around then, and he levelled and fired in a single motion. I heard a thump just above me, and somebody sprawled out of the wagon's tail, right in front of me. It was Uncle Earl.

I remember roaring or growling or something . . . no words, just a blind anger . . . and trying to get a shot off at Frank Kingston. But another rider crossed between us and I took him instead. He pitched forward and rolled from his saddle under the dancing hooves of his own

343

horse. His mask fell away and for an instant I saw his face. It was Mr. Jones.

Other guns were talking then. Julius Altman's long rifle spoke its piece from somewhere and the rider with the injured arm went down. A musket boomed and another's hat sailed away in the darkness as he returned fire. The firelight blazed, full on that one, and suddenly there were men afoot on both sides of him. Mr. Johnson fired twice and I think Ezra emptied his gun. The rider twitched and writhed as bullets swatted at him, then he just sort of crumpled and fell.

All that I saw in the time it takes to wink an eye. Then Frank Kingston was coming at me, his gun ablaze, charging to bring me down. His bandanna was gone and his burned face was hideous in the dancing firelight. I felt a bullet strike, and another somewhere, and I was emptying both guns at him as he came. If I hit anything I couldn't tell it then. He was right on top of me, his horse rearing and pawing. And Uncle Earl lay there at my feet, not moving.

Something bright spun through the glare and swatted his horse across the nose. A curved sword . . . a damned curved sword, thrown like a stick!

The horse quartered away and I went for him. Frank Kingston was a burly man, but I pulled him out of that saddle as though he were a straw doll. As he fell I turned him, locked my legs around him and flipped over backward. He went over me, screaming, and hit the ground. His scream cut off, echoes of no sound at all. When I rolled away from him he toppled sideways and lay still. His neck was broken.

For a while there was only the stamping of animals and the whisper of morning breeze in tall canvas tops. Then voices, and people came. And more people.

* * *

There came a day that felt like summer does in the high country, and I was up and walking around, seeing what there was to see of Denver City—an ugly, cheerful, bustling little settlement where people did business from wagon-beds while their buildings were going up around them.

It had taken me a while to get to that point. A man can take a wound or two, now and then, and if they don't kill him he can recover in a few days. But if he takes more wounds than that and they don't kill him, it can take weeks to get better.

Captain Rawlings and his crew had gone. There was time enough to bring another train west before the snows. Caleb Tucker's new building had its roof in place and workmen were putting up the walls. It would be half a block long and would house three businesses, a doctor's office and a barber shop. Caleb Tucker was already counting his rent.

Solomon Talbot was doing business from his wagon, outfitting miners and townsmen with the best in ready-to-wear, while Mindy Talbot kept his books and tended his inventory. Solomon had met his match, I realized. He'd settle for twice what a thing was worth, but not Mindy. Not if it would bring half again that.

Hammers rang on anvils at the end of the street. Anson Griggs' smithy didn't have a building yet, but a tent gave shelter for Anson and Waylon as they worked, and for George Bullard as he hobbled about on my old crutch, supervising.

Priscilla's cookery was doing a landoffice business, already housed in the first shack Caleb Tucker had run up. And I had just begun a campaign that I realized might take a while. This time I was going to do it my way. This time I was going to go to her, and we would talk about all kinds of things, then maybe we would go for a walk now and then—sort of get acquainted all over again. Start from scratch, on equal terms . . . like that. Both of us knew that I didn't want a homeless waif to protect, and she didn't want some kind of Biblical nonentity to follow after and nurture in his ways.

Things change, sometimes, and if a body gives them half a chance, they might change for the better.

I walked around until I felt a little weak-kneed, then I sat on the split-rail porch in front of the slap-up hotel building that Percy Smith was still trying to get paint for.

I was sitting there just enjoying the sunshine when a shadow fell across me and I looked up. Uncle Earl was just looping the reins of his gray horse at the rail. With his bad arm he was awkward about it, but he managed. He looked fit and trim in a gray riding coat that didn't have a speck of dust on it.

"Morning, Zack," he said. "Getting out a little these days, I see."

"Little more each day," I said. "How are things at Pueblo?"

"Seedy," he grinned. "But I got my money. Bank draft came through." He handed me a wad of bills. "Here's what I owe you, I think."

I counted it carefully. When you deal with Uncle Earl, you should always count carefully. "It's all here. Everything I'm out from the trip."

I waited, just curious whether he intended to share the profits over expenses, but that was all the money he brought out, so I just sat back and enjoyed the sun.

But after a few minutes, he was still there.

"You want something, Uncle Earl?"

"Well . . . just a matter of curiosity, is all. I stopped by and talked to Caleb Tucker, and had a look at that lead wagon of his. Notice the lazy board works just fine."

"I fixed it for him."

"So he said. Ah . . . I was just wondering, though, Zack, you recall that map that was in there? What did you do with it?"

346

I thought about it for a minute. "Put it in my saddle-bag. Why?"

"Oh, nothing. It's just a . . . well, sort of a sentimental thing, you know. I believe that was the sweetest deal I ever pulled off, Zack. Be nice to have a memento of it."

"Do you want that old map, Uncle Earl?"

"Do you still have it?"

"Seems like I do. 'Course it's useless, the way things turned out."

"Absolutely worthless," he agreed.

"But you'd like to have it."

"For sentimental reasons."

"Sure. I understand. What's it worth to you, Uncle Earl?"

"Now, Zack, is that any way to . . . ?"

I just looked at him. "Make me an offer."

"Ten dollars."

"A hundred."

"That's ridiculous. Maybe twenty-five?"

"Seventy-five."

He shelled out fifty dollars and I handed him the oil-cloth chart. I'd been carrying it with me for a week, figuring he might show up and want it. He looked it over, nodded and put it away in his coat. Then he took up his reins, balanced himself and swung aboard his gray horse.

"You going somewhere?" I asked.

"I sure am, Zack. I think with this, I can find out where the Downeys hid that gold. No claims on it now. That's all been settled back east. So it's finders keepers now."

"You said there wasn't any gold, Uncle Earl."

"Now, Zack," his old sideways grin flashed in the sun. "I didn't say that. You think back. What I said was that old Bailey Kingston had been stealing the bond company blind for years, sending out false shipments that disappeared and they had to pay for. Never once did I say *that* shipment was false. You got to learn to listen, Zack. And while

347

you're at it, I surely do wish you'd learn to shoot."

Going down the street that led out of town, he looked trim and handsome, just like he always did.

Some day, though, as sure as my name is Zachary Scott Frost, *somebody* is going to break my Uncle Earl of sucking eggs.

POWELL'S ARMY
BY TERENCE DUNCAN

#1: UNCHAINED LIGHTNING (1994, $2.50)

Thundering out of the past, a trio of deadly enforcers dispenses its own brand of frontier justice throughout the untamed American West! Two men and one woman, they are the U.S. Army's most lethal secret weapon—they are POWELL'S ARMY!

#2: APACHE RAIDERS (2073, $2.50)

The disappearance of seventeen Apache maidens brings tribal unrest to the violent breaking point. To prevent an explosion of bloodshed, Powell's Army races through a nightmare world south of the border—and into the deadly clutches of a vicious band of Mexican flesh merchants!

#3: MUSTANG WARRIORS (2171, $2.50)

Someone is selling cavalry guns and horses to the Comanche—and that spells trouble for the bluecoats' campaign against Chief Quanah Parker's bloodthirsty Kwahadi warriors. But Powell's Army are no strangers to trouble. When the showdown comes, they'll be ready—and someone is going to die!

#4: ROBBERS ROOST (2285, $2.50)

After hijacking an army payroll wagon and killing the troopers riding guard, Three-Fingered Jack and his gang high-tail it into Virginia City to spend their ill-gotten gains. But Powell's Army plans to apprehend the murderous hardcases before the local vigilantes do—to make sure that Jack and his slimy band stretch hemp the legal way!

Available wherever paperbacks are sold, or order direct from the Publisher. Send cover price plus 50¢ per copy for mailing and handling to Zebra Books, Dept. 2559, 475 Park Avenue South, New York, N.Y. 10016. Residents of New York, New Jersey and Pennsylvania must include sales tax. DO NOT SEND CASH.

J.J. MARRIC MYSTERIES

time passes quickly . . . As *DAY* blends with *NIGHT* and *WEEK* flies into *MONTH*, Gideon must fit together the pieces of death and destruction before time runs out!

GIDEON'S DAY (2721, $3.95)
They mysterious death of a young police detective is only the beginning of a bizarre series of events which end in the fatal knifing of a seven-year-old girl. But for commander George gideon of New Scotland Yard, it is all in a day's work!

GIDEON'S MONTH (2766, $3.95)
A smudged page on his calendar, Gideon's month is blackened by brazen and bizarre offenses ranging from mischief to murder. Gideon must put a halt to the sinister events which involve the corruption of children and a homicidal housekeeper, before the city drowns in blood!

GIDEON'S NIGHT (2734, $3.50)
When an unusually virulent pair of psychopaths leaves behind a trail of pain, grief, and blood, Gideon once again is on the move. This time the terror all at once comes to a head and he must stop the deadly duel that is victimizing young women and children—in only one night!

GIDEON'S WEEK (2722, $3.95)
When battered wife Ruby Benson set up her killer husband for capture by the cops, she never considered the possibility of his escape. Now Commander George Gideon of Scotland Yard must save Ruby from the vengeance of her sadistic spouse . . . or die trying!

Available wherever paperbacks are sold, or order direct from the Publisher. Send cover price plus 50¢ per copy for mailing and handling to Zebra Books, Dept. 2559, 475 Park Avenue South, New York, N.Y. 10016. Residents of New York, New Jersey and Pennsylvania must include sales tax. DO NOT SEND CASH.